WHEN AMERICA IS IN PERIL,
AMERICA'S TOP GUNS MUST ANSWER THE CALL . . .

Dreamland

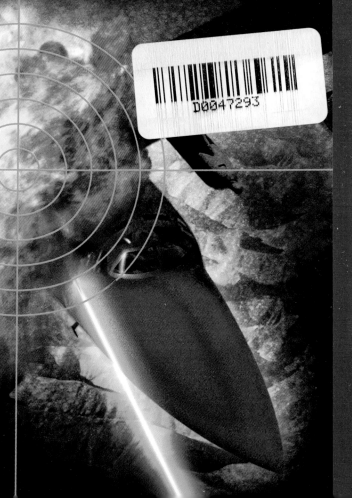

D0047293

THE MASTERS OF
DREAMLAND

Lieutenant Colonel Tecumseh "Dog" Bastian: A former ace fighter pilot, he's *Dreamland*'s "top dog," a brilliant strategist and a bad man to cross.

Captain Breanna Bastian Stockard: Her father's daughter in nearly every way—this hard-as-nails test pilot is bravely coping with a personal tragedy that would crush a weaker spirit.

Major Jeffrey "Zen" Stockard: "Dog's" son-in-law, crippled for life in a horrific test-range crash, he now mans *Dreamland*'s Flighthawk program, while wrestling inner demons that could destroy a lesser man.

Captain Danny Freah: Commander of the covert "Whiplash" Special Forces ground action team, no one at *Dreamland* is more courageous, rebellious and unorthodox—which makes him "Dog" Bastian's most valuable officer.

Major Nancy Cheshire: The Megafortress project's capable and driven senior officer, she is constantly having to prove she can lead in the "Dog-eat-everybody" man's world of *Dreamland*.

Major Mack "Knife" Smith: An iron-nerve Top Gun who would fly through hell to become *Dreamland*'s chief. Bitter, egotistical, and impossible, he's nonetheless the man you want on your wing in hostile skies.

(more . . .)

Also in the Dreamland Series

Titles by Dale Brown

DALE BROWN'S

Dreamland
RAZOR'S EDGE

DALE BROWN and JIM DeFELICE

AVON BOOKS
An Imprint of HarperCollinsPublishers

AVON BOOKS
An Imprint of HarperCollins*Publishers*
10 East 53rd Street
New York, New York 10022-5299

Copyright © 2003 by Air Battle Force, Inc.
Excerpt from *Air Battle Force* copyright © 2003 by Air Battle Force, Inc.
ISBN: 0-06-009439-7
www.avonbooks.com

First Avon Books paperback printing: January 2003

Avon Trademark Reg. U.S. Pat. Off. and in Other Countries, Marca Registrada, Hecho en U.S.A.
HarperCollins® is a registered trademark of HarperCollins Publishers Inc.

Printed in the U.S.A.

10 9 8 7 6 5 4 3 2 1

DALE BROWN'S

Dreamland
RAZOR'S EDGE

I

"Chee-Ya!"

_____

TORBIN DOLK POSITIONED HIS SIZE THIRTEEN BOOT ATOP the engine fairing for the F-4G Phantom Wild Weasel, then carefully levered himself from the boarding ladder to the aircraft, easing his weight onto the ancient metal like a kid testing lake ice after an early thaw. The metal had been designed to withstand pressures far greater than the bulky electronic warfare officer's weight, but he always climbed up gingerly. He wasn't so much afraid of breaking the plane as he was of somehow offending it, for if anything mechanical could be said to have a personality or even a soul, it was *Glory B*.

The broad-shouldered Phantom was one of the last of her kind still on active duty in the Air Force, and in fact she had escaped orders to report as a target sled two weeks ago only because of some last minute paperwork snafu with the plane designated to take her place patrolling northern Iraq. She waited on the ramp in front of the hangar with her chin up proudly, no doubt recalling the first flight of her kind nearly forty years before. The F4H-1 that took off that bright May day in 1958 was a very different aircraft than *Glory B*—cocky where she was dignified, fidgety where she was staid. The F4H-1 was also a *Navy* asset, a fact *Glory B* with her USAF markings glossed over in her musings. The Phantom, for all its imperfections, surely qualified as one of the service's most successful airframes, a versatile jet that notched more hours in the sky than the sun.

Torbin touched the glass of the raised canopy, patting it gently for good luck. Then he put his hands on his hips and looked down at the tarmac, where his pilot was proceeding with his walkaround. Captain Dolk had flown with Major Richard "Richie" Fitzmorris for nearly a month; during that time, Fitzmorris's preflight rituals had nearly doubled in length and rigor. Pretty soon he'd be counting brush strokes on the nose art.

"Yo, Richie, we flying today?" yelled Torbin.

Fitzmorris, who probably couldn't hear him, waved. The crew chief, standing a few feet behind the pilot, smirked, then ducked forward as Fitzmorris pointed at something below the right wing.

Torbin lowered himself on his haunches atop the plane. His gaze drifted across the large airfield toward the F-16s they were to accompany, then to a pair of large C-5A transports and a fleet of trucks taking gear away. Torbin's mind drifted. His brother-in-law had recently offered to go partners in his construction business back home, and he was giving it serious thought. His career in the Air Force seemed to have come to a dead end, though that was largely his own fault. He'd come back to the Weasels two years ago even though he knew they were doomed to extinction. Life at the Pentagon had become boring beyond belief, and he'd wanted to go where the action was. Once the Phantom bit the dust, his options would be severely limited.

"So we going or what?" said Fitzmorris, who'd managed to sneak up on him.

The major's voice surprised him so much, Torbin didn't have a comeback. He dropped into the cockpit sheepishly, and hadn't even finished snugging his restraints when the pilot and ground crew began negotiating for power. The start cart on the tarmac revved up its turbine; a few moments later the Phantom's right engine cranked to life, its growl mimicking a tiger protecting his food. *Glory B*'s left engine kicked in and the plane shuddered against her brakes, Fitzmorris pushing power to about fourteen percent. Fuel flow nudged 500 pounds per minute. The indicators swung up green—good to go, boys, good to go.

Glory B rocked expectantly as her two passengers worked through their checklists, making sure they were ready. Finally she loped forward, winking at the end-of-runway crew as she paused to have her missiles armed; she was so anxious, she almost refused to hold short when the pilot had to stop and run through another of his interminable checklists. Finally cleared, she roared into the sky after the F-16s, a proud mare chasing down her foals.

Roughly an hour and a half later *Glory B* held her wings stiff as she bucked through turbulence deep in enemy territory. The area below belonged to Iraqi Kurds, who were currently engaged in a low-intensity, multidimensional war against not only Saddam Hussein's army, but themselves. Infighting between the various Kurdish factions had helped Saddam consolidate power in the northern mountains above the Euphrates. Though ostensibly forbidden to use force there by the decrees that ended the Gulf War, he was currently backing "his" Kurds against the others with light tanks and ground troops. The F-16s were on the lookout for helicopters; the Iraqis occasionally used them to attack villages sympathetic to the guerrillas.

"You awake back there?" Fitzmorris asked.

"Can't you hear me snoring, stick boy?"

"Just don't play with the steering wheel," answered the pilot. It was an old joke—the G model of the Phantom featured a stick and flight controls in the rear cockpit.

"*Glory B*, this is Falcon leader," the F-16 commander broke in. "We have some movement on the highway in box able-able-two. We're going to take a look."

"Roger that," replied the pilot.

Fitzmorris adjusted his course to take them farther east, following the fighters. As they swung south, their AWACS gave them an update—nothing hostile in the sky.

Thirty seconds later an SA-2 icon blossomed in the right corner of the Plan Position Indicator at the center of Torbin's dash. In the quarter second it took his fingers to respond, his brain plotted the flicker of light against the mission brief. Then he began doing several things simultaneously, cursoring the target and transmitting data to one of the AGM-88 HARM missiles beneath his wings. Two small gun-dish icons flashed on the left side of the threat screen, their legends showing they were about five miles closer than the SA-2 but well beyond their firing range. Smart enough to sort and prioritize the threats, the APR-47 concentrated on the long-range missile. Torbin, who could override the system, agreed.

"Got a Two," he told Fitzmorris. They were about thirty miles away.

His gear flashed—an SA-8 had come up. It was flicking on and off, but his gear got a decent read anyway, marking it just beyond the SA-2 site, out of range for the admittedly nasty missile.

He'd take it after the SA-2. They were almost in position to fire.

The SA-2's radar went off, but it was too late—Torbin had the location tattooed on his HARM's forehead. But just then one of the Falcon pilots broke in. "I'm spiked! An SA-8!"

No you're not, thought Torbin; don't overreact. The radar had just flicked off. There was a launch, but it was the SA-2—which now seemed to be running without guidance.

"Torbin!" said Fitzmorris. "Shit, twenty-five-mile scope. Shit."

"Right turn," Torbin said. "Relax. The F-16's okay. The only thing that can get him is the two, and its radar just went off. He'll beat it."

"Yeah."

"All right, we have an SA-8 south. There are SA-9s well south," said Torbin. His threat scope was suddenly very crowded. "Not players."

"Shit."

"Out of range. We'll take my two, then the eight."

Balls of black, red, gray, and white flak rose in the distance. More indications lit the screen, more radars.

Torbin had never seen so many contacts before. Radars were switching on and off throughout a wide swath of territory. The Iraqis were trying something new. The APR-47 hung with them all like a trooper, though the sheer number of contacts was pushing it toward its design limits.

"Torbin!"

"Fifteen miles. Start your turn in three," Torbin told the pilot.

"The SA-8." Fitzmorris's voice was a loud hiss, pointing out another threat that had popped onto the screen.

"You fly the plane." An SA-9 battery fired one of its short-range missiles well off to the west. Torbin concentrated on the SA-2, had a good read. "Target dotted! Handoff. Ready light!"

"Shoot him, for chrissakes!"

"Away, we're away," said Torbin, handing off the SA-8

to a second HARM missile and firing almost instantaneously. The two radar seekers thundered away, accelerating past Mach 3 as they rushed toward their targets.

"Rolling right!" said Fitzmorris, jinking to avoid the enemy radars.

"Triple A," warned Torbin, who could see a large patch of black roiling over the canopy glass as they tucked around.

"Shit." Fitzmorris's voice seemed calmer now.

"We're clean," said Torbin. He craned his head around as Fitzmorris spun to a safe distance. A white puff of smoke appeared on the ground off the left wing.

Bagged somebody. Meanwhile, the other Iraqi radars had flickered out. Their jinking cost him a shot at any of the smaller SA-9 batteries; they were too far north now to fire.

"Falcon Flight, what's your status?" Fitzmorris asked the F-16s as they regrouped.

"Where the hell were you guys?" the Falcon leader snapped. "*Two*'s down."

"*Two*'s down?" said Torbin.

"You have a parachute?" asked Fitzmorris.

"Negative. Fucking negative. He's down."

"What hit him?" Torbin heard the words coming out of his mouth, powerless to stop them.

"What the hell do you mean?" the F-16 pilot answered. "You're the damn Weasel. You should have nailed those motherfuckers, or at least warned us. Shit, nobody told us jack."

"I nailed the SA-2. Shit."

"Go to hell," said the F-16 commander.

Torbin pushed back in his seat, staring at the now empty threat screen. He listened to the traffic between the AWACS and the F-16s as they pinned down a search area and vectored a combat air patrol toward it. The short-legged F-16s would have to go home very soon; other airplanes were being scrambled from Incirlik to help in the search but it would be some time before they arrived. The Phantom, with its three "bags," or drop tanks of extra fuel, had the search to itself.

"They launched at least three missiles," said Fitzmorris over the interphone.

"The missiles that launched were well out of range," said Torbin. "They were SA-9s. No way they hit the F-16. No way."

"Tell that to the pilot."

The Nevada desert
0832

THE WHIPLASH ACTION TEAM MADE IT OUT OF THE BUILD-ing with only minor injuries—Kevin Bison was dragging a leg and Lee "Nurse" Liu had been grazed in the arm. Two of the three men they'd rescued from the terrorist kidnappers were in good enough condition to run, or at least trot, as they made their way down the hillside. Perse "Powder" Talcom had the other on his back.

Captain Danny Freah, who headed the Special Forces squad, caught a breath as he reached the stone wall where Freddy "Egg" Reagan was holding down their rear flank.

"Action over the hill, Captain," Egg told him, gesturing with his Squad Automatic Weapon. The SAW was a 5.56mm light machine gun that could lay down a devastating blanket of lead. It happened to be one of the few weapons the team carried that hadn't been tinkered with by the scientists and weapons experts at Dreamland, where Whiplash was based. Some things just couldn't be improved on—yet.

Danny flipped the visor on his helmet down and clicked into the target mode, which put a red-dot aiming cursor on the screen. The bulky visor looked like a welder's shield and shifted the helmet's center of gravity forward. The initial awkwardness was worth getting used to, since it offered four different viewing modes—unenhanced, infrared, starlight, and radioactive detection. The bulletproof carbon-boron helmet it was attached to provided not only GPS and secure discrete-burst, short-distance communications with the rest of the team, but linked into a combat system in Danny's bulletproof vest that allowed him to communicate with the Dreamland Command Center—aka Dream Command—via purpose-launched tactical satellites. Once connected, Freah had virtually unlimited resources available at a whisper.

He didn't need them here. What he needed was to reach the waiting MH-53J beyond the hill.

"Listen up," he told the squad. "Powder and I go over the hill, make sure it's clear. Egg, you got our butts."

"Yo," answered Egg.

"Sound off," said Danny, more to give his guys a last breather than to make sure they were with him. As the team checked in alphabetically, the captain examined his MP-5, which was connected to the helmet's targeting gear via a thin wire that plugged in at the rear. It had a fresh clip; he slipped a second into the Velcro straps at his wrist, not wanting to waste precious microseconds retrieving it under fire.

"Let's go, Powder," Danny said, hopping the wall and moving up the slope. A few feet from the peak he threw himself down shoulder first, raising his gun as he rolled just to the crown of the hill. He peered over with his visor at ten times magnification, quickly scanning to check the terrain.

The Air Force Special Forces helicopter sat on the level

flat twenty yards from the foot of the sharp cliff, exactly where they had left it.

The six-man crew was there as well.

Except they were all dead.

"Shit," whispered Powder, popping up behind him.

"All right, relax," said Danny. The enemy was nowhere in sight but undoubtedly hadn't gone far. He pointed to a small rock outcropping on the right. "They'll be hiding there, waiting for us to hit the helicopter," he told Powder. "There's probably two or three guys circling around to ambush us once they pin us down."

Powder glanced toward the rear. Danny wasn't worried—Egg could hold his own. "What are we doin', Cap?"

"We play along. You make like you're going to the Pave Low, I'll jog that way and nail them. Try not to get killed before I waste them."

"Shit," cursed Powder. He continued grumbling as Danny dropped down to flank the spot.

"Whiplash, hold your positions," whispered Danny as he ran. "Helo crew has been neutralized. Egg—we think there're probably two or three guys trying to flank us."

Egg acknowledged for the others.

As Danny ducked down near the end of the ravine, he lost contact with the rest of the team; unless hooked to the satellites, the com system was line-of-sight.

Even if he hadn't used all of his grenades earlier, he wouldn't have now, because he didn't want to risk damaging the helicopter. But that meant getting close and personal to flush them out.

He knew they'd have a guard at the crevice, watching the flank. Drop him, and the rest would be easy pickings.

Danny took out his short, four-inch survival knife, in his opinion better suited for this kind of work than the longer models. He turned it over in his hand as he scouted the situation.

He could crawl to within ten yards of the spot from behind the rocks. But then he'd have to run over open terrain. He positioned his gun against his left hip, then began working his way forward. As he jumped to his feet he realized that even if he got to the crevice without being seen, he'd never be able to pirouette his arm up quickly enough to take the guard without firing. He ran anyway, all his momentum committed to the plan.

There was no guard.

He flopped back against the rocks, winded, temporarily confused. Had he miscalculated? Or was his enemy overconfident?

Overconfident.

Hopefully.

They were maybe twenty yards from him, fifteen, up along the crevice, waiting for the Whiplash team to come running down the hill toward the helo. Danny stowed his knife, shifted his gun, then tried to contact Powder. The sergeant didn't answer. He raised his head, trying again.

"Powder—now," he hissed.

Nothing.

Danny sidled along the jagged crevice. The sharp cuts made it impossible to see—maybe their guard was posted farther up.

Once they started firing at Powder, he could run up and nail them.

"Powder!"

Nothing.

Maybe they were *in* the helo.

"Chee-ya!" shouted Powder from the other end of the slope. He fired a burst from his gun.

Two men rose from behind the rocks five feet from Danny. Completely intent on Powder, they trained their guns and waited for an easy shot. Danny held his fire as well, sidestepping to see if anyone else was there.

"Chee-ya!" Powder shouted again, throwing himself down.

One of the enemy soldiers began firing. Danny pressed the trigger, greasing the two men, then a third who bounced out from the rocks to their right as the first fell. Danny emptied the clip on a fourth, caught stunned behind the others.

"Bang! Bang! Bang!" said Freah, pushing up his helmet. "You're all dead."

"They cheated!" shouted the Pave Low pilot, from his dead-man squat down by the helicopter. "They're wearing Whiplash gear, the fucks."

"Hey, you cheats!" yelled Powder, running over. "No fair!"

"Hey, you're dead," said one of the "enemy" gunners. "I got you."

"Bullshit—check the computer. Read it and weep, my friend."

"Egg, Pretty Boy, up. Four dead Delta troopers in those rocks beyond the helo," said Danny. "Watch out for stragglers."

"There's no stragglers," said the helo pilot. "They're fucking cheaters."

"Hey, you can't talk to him," said one of the men Danny had mock-killed. It was the leader of the Delta team, Major Harmon Peiler, who was indeed wearing Whiplash black camos. "Come on, Freah. You know the rules."

Danny laughed at the Delta commander, then climbed up out of the crevice. He walked behind the position, checking to make sure there weren't any more D boys in the rocks.

Counterfeit clothes. Not bad.

"We may be dead, but you lost this one, Danny boy," said Peiler. "You can't get out. Advantage Delta. You're buyin' tonight."

"Saddle up in the chopper," Danny told his team.

"You can't get out," said Peiler.

"Why not? My aircraft is still here."

"Your pilot's dead."

"*That* pilot's dead," said Danny, pointing.

"Yeah—you're going to freakin' fly it yourself?"

"Egg, you're up," shouted Danny. The sergeant waved, then climbed into the helicopter.

"What the freakin' hell are you doin'?" Peiler demanded.

"Egg's gonna fly us out," said Danny as his sergeant settled into the cockpit.

"Like hell! Shit."

Danny shrugged.

"Bullshit he can fly," said Peiler.

"Well, you better hope so, because you're going to be sitting in the back."

"Hey, uh, Captain, I don't know," said the pilot.

"Relax. Egg used to fly Apaches. Ain't that right, Egg?"

Egg, listening on his smart helmet com set, corrected him. "Uh, Captain, that was Cobras. Kind of a different thing."

"Yeah, just give them the thumbs-up."

Egg leaned out the cockpit window and did so. Peiler cursed.

Staff Sergeant Frederick K. "Egg" Reagan had, in fact, flown on the Army gunship, though as a gunner, not a pilot. Nonetheless, the experience had encouraged him to obtain a helicopter pilot's license, and he was indeed checked out on the MH-53J. Everyone on the Whiplash action team had a specialty; his was handling heavy equipment. Had there been an M1A1, he would have been equally at home.

The rotor started skipping around as the engine coughed and died.

"I don't know about this," said Peiler.

"Well, you can come or you can walk," said Danny.

"It's ten miles to the safe zone."

Danny shrugged.

"Dead men, up and into the helicopter," said Peiler as the twin turbos caught.

"Uh, Captain," said the Pave Low pilot, pulling Danny aside. "If we crash, they're going to take this out of my pay for the next hundred years."

"You should've thought about that before you got suckered by these bozos," Danny told him. "They don't even have carbon-boron vests, for chrissakes."

**Over Iraq
1930**

ARMS CRAMPING, NECK STIFF, LEGS NUMB, ELECTRONIC warfare officer Torbin Dolk pushed back against the ejection seat, a piece of furniture that would never be confused for an easy chair.

"How you holding out?" his pilot asked.

"Yeah," said Torbin.

"Excuse me?" Fitzmorris asked.

"Fine. I'm fine." He adjusted the volume on the radio, which was tuned to the emergency Guard band the downed flier should have been using. Standard procedure called for the pilot to broadcast at certain times, but the searchers monitored the radio constantly, hoping to hear something.

Fifty-five antennas protruded from various parts of the Phantom. Not one was of any particular use at the moment. The Iraqi radar operators hadn't juiced up their sets since the shoot-down.

Bastards were probably all out at a monster party, celebrating, Torbin thought.

That or looking for the pilot.

"We're going to have to go back," said Fitzmorris.

"Yeah," said Torbin. There were now four other planes scouring the peaks, waiting for any signal from the downed airman; they wouldn't be leaving their comrade alone.

Still, Torbin didn't want to go.

"*Glory B*, we're wondering what your fuel situation is," said the AWACS controller.

"Yeah, mom, we're close to bingo," answered Fitzmorris. The pilot was fudging big-time—bingo left about twenty minutes of reserve in the tanks. They were past it by nineteen minutes.

"*Falcon Two, Falcon Two*, you up? Jack, you hear me?" said Torbin, keying into the Guard band.

Silence.

"*Falcon Two, Falcon Two*. Jesus man, where the hell are you?"

"We're going home," said the pilot over the interphone circuit.

Brussels
2145

MACK SMITH HAD JUST ABOUT GOTTEN TO THE DOOR OF his hotel room when the phone rang. Ordinarily he would have blown it off and gone on to dinner, but he'd given his room number to a French aerospace consultant just before leaving NATO headquarters this afternoon. The memory of her smile and lusciously shaped breasts—mostly her breasts—grabbed him and pulled him back into the room.

"Bonjour," he said, exhausting his French.

"Major Smith, this is Jed Barclay."

"Jed?"

"Uh, listen, Major, sorry to bother you but, uh, I need kind of a favor."

Smith sat down on the bed. Barclay, though probably too young to shave, was a high-level aide at the National Security Council.

"Where are you, Jed?"

Barclay didn't answer. "Listen, I need you to, uh, get a hold of General Elliott for me."

"What? Why?"

"I need you to get General Elliott over to a secure phone and call me, okay? He'll know the drill."

Brad Elliott, a former three-star general, was in Brussels briefing some of the NATO brass on the recent problems with Iran. Technically retired, Elliott had headed the Air Force's High Technology Aerospace Weapons Center—Dreamland—for several years. He was now somehow involved with the ultrasecret Intelligence Support Agency, which coordinated black operations with the CIA and elements of the military. Mack wasn't exactly sure what the involvement was—his own clearance didn't extend that high. Except that he'd seen the general this afternoon—briefly—he wouldn't even have known he was in Brussels.

"Why me?" asked Mack.

"This has to be done discreetly," said Jed.

"Well, I'm your guy," said Smith, "but I'm not really sure where the hell he is."

"Uh, this is an open line," said Jed. "I need you to get him."

"Yeah, all right, kid. Relax. I'll do it."

"As soon as possible, Major."

"Gee, really?" Smith hung up the phone. He'd come to

Europe on very temporary duty a few days before, assigned to deliver a seminar on differentiating between missile and other damage for visiting VIPs and crash experts next week. He'd hoped he might be able to use the assignment to troll for an interesting berth—though nominally still assigned to Dreamland, he was actually looking for a new command.

Elliott and ISA might be just the ticket. Smith went downstairs and then across the street to a pay phone, where he dialed the European Command liaison office temporarily hosting him.

"Hell-o?" answered a somewhat high-pitched feminine voice.

Patti, the English girl. Good teeth, skinny legs. He'd been working on her before meeting the aerospace consultant.

"Hey, Patti, this is Mack Smith. How were those chocolates?"

"Oh, Major Smith—very good."

He flashed on a picture of her sucking them down. Those legs wouldn't stay skinny for very long.

"Listen, I'm really an airhead today—I was supposed to see General Elliott for drinks but I totally forgot where."

"Brad Elliott? But I thought he was having a late dinner with General Stumford."

Stumford. Second in command of JSSOC, the Joint Services Special Operations Command. Army guy. Thick neck, small ears. Here for some sort of consultation. Probably more ISA stuff.

"Yeah, I'm supposed to meet them—where was it, exactly?"

The restaurant happened to be only two blocks away, on one of the three streets in the city that Mack had memorized. As he walked over he wracked his brain for a way of getting General Elliott alone. Either the walk was too short or the chilly evening air froze his brain; not a single idea occurred to him before he opened the door.

Mack ignored the long string of foreign words the maitre d' spewed at him as he walked into the dining room. Elliott and Stumford were sitting at a table at the far end of the room, watching as a sommelier opened a bottle of wine for them.

"Hey, General Elliott," said Mack, walking forward.

"Mack? I didn't know you liked French food."

"Well, I don't, actually." Mack glanced around, then over at Stumford, whose frown would have stopped an M1A1 in its tracks. "I, uh, I have a message for you, General. Phone call you need to make. Uh, personal, but uh, important. You're supposed to call right away."

Mack hesitated. Elliott wasn't married, so he couldn't tell him to call his wife.

"Your mom," said Smith, lowering his voice to a near whisper. He glanced at Stumford and nodded seriously before turning back to Elliott. "It's, well, it's—you probably ought to call right now. If you want, I can let you use my phone over at, uh, the temporary office they gave me. No charge."

Elliott gave him a quizzical look. "Okay," he said finally, pulling his napkin from his lap. "Bill, I'm sorry."

Stumford nodded. Mack swung away, feeling reasonably proud of himself for pulling it off until Elliott grabbed his shoulder in the front room.

"You're a good pilot, Major, but you're going to have to work on your lying."

"Why?"

"Bill Stumford was at my mother's funeral."

MACK TOOK ELLIOTT TO HIS OWN OFFICE TO USE THE SE-cure phone, managing to get him down the hall without meeting anyone besides the security people. If Elliott had any clue what was up, he didn't betray it, nor did his face show any emotion when he was finally connected with Barclay. "Go ahead, Jed," was all he said, and he didn't so much as grunt in acknowledgment as Barclay filled him in on what was up. He listened without comment for nearly five minutes, then stood up from the chair with the phone still at his ear.

"I'm on my way," he said before returning the phone to its cradle. Elliott looked up at him so sharply that Mack almost didn't ask what was up.

Almost.

"So?" he asked, looking for a way to start his pitch for help finding a new command.

"So what, Major?"

"Well, I was just wondering if . . . well, I—" It had been quite some time since Brad Elliott's eyes had bored through his skull, but the effect now was immediate. "You think you could drop me off back at my hotel, sir?"

"You're coming with me, Major."

"Really? Great," said Mack. "Fantastic. This is back channel stuff right? That's why Jed called me instead of going through official channels."

"You're sharp as ever, Major."

"You know, I'd like to broaden my horizons a bit," added Mack, deciding to make his play. "I could do a lot with ISA and, you know me, I want to be where the action is. The projects at Dreamland are drying up, and the only thing I've been able to find in the real world is a D.O. slot in a squadron at Incirlik. Armpit of the world. Jeez, I don't want to go there."

Elliott ignored him, starting out of the office so quickly that Mack had to run down the hallway to catch up. "Girls all wear veils, if you know what I mean."

Elliott harrumphed as they left the building, heading for his car.

"If you can help me come up with something—"

"I can ask around," said Elliott finally, unlocking the car.

"Thanks, General, I truly appreciate it."

"Hmmm."

"So where we going?" Mack asked as they wheeled out of their parking spot. "D.C.?"

"Incirlik," said Elliott. "There'll be a jet at the airport."

**Aboard *Raven*, over Dreamland Range 2
1600**

MAJOR JEFF "ZEN" STOCKARD SWEPT HIS EYES AROUND the readings projected on the instrument screen, confirming the computer's declaration that all systems were in the green. The Flighthawks' Comprehensive Command and Control computer, known as C^3, had never been wrong yet, but that didn't mean Zen was going to give it a bye.

"Major?"

"Keep your shirt on, Curly."

Captain Kevin Fentress fidgeted at the nickname but said nothing. A reference to the short, well-furled locks on Fentress's head, it was Zen's latest attempt at giving the newbie Flighthawk pilot a decent handle.

"Handoff in thirty seconds," said Zen. "Begin the procedure."

"Right." Fentress blew a hard breath, trying to relax. He was sitting only a few feet from Zen at the left-hand console in the Flighthawk control bay of *Bear One*, an EB-52 Megafortress outfitted to support test flights of the small, unmanned fighters, officially designated U/MF-3s. Taking over the robot wasn't as simple as reaching over and grabbing the stick. Fentress's fingers stumbled through the long panel sequence twice before he could give the voice command to transfer control to his console. The procedure included two different code words—a third, if Zen didn't consent within five seconds—as well as retina scan by the gear in Fentress's control helmet. By the time it was completed, the Flighthawk had traveled several miles beyond their planned turnaround and was nearing the end of the test range.

"Let's go, Fentress. You're behind the plane."

"Yes, sir."

"Tighter," Zen told his pupil as he began the turn. "You're not flying a Predator. Use the plane."

Fentress gave more throttle, still obviously out of sorts; he had to back off to get the robot's nose onto the right heading. Zen knew how hard it could be to get a precise feel for the robot. It was as much a struggle of the imagination as anything physical. But Fentress had been practicing this for several days—he ought to know it cold.

Zen took another quick glance at the U/MF-3's instrument readings, then looked at the sitrep map in the lower left video screen. The map presented a synthesized "bird's-eye view" of the area around *Bear One*, showing not only the unmanned robot, but its planned flight path and the location of the target drone, which in this case was an ancient Phantom F-4 flown completely by computer. Today's exercise was simple: As the Phantom flew a racetrack oval around Dreamland's Test Range 2, Fentress would approach it from the rear and launch a simulated cannon attack. It ought to be easy.

Except that Fentress overhandled the robot, his inputs shifting it left and right and up and down so much that the computer twice gave him warnings that the plane was dangerously close to pitching toward the dirt. Zen shook his head but let the computer do the scolding—the safety parameters were set so that C^3 would take over if Curly did anything truly horrible.

Which he nearly did as he angled to catch the Phantom drone, swinging wide then overaccelerating and sailing over the plane without managing to get a firing cue from the computer.

"Try again," said Zen as patiently as he could manage.

"Sorry."

"Try again."

Fentress did even worse the second time, violating the test parameters by flying into the next range, which fortunately was unoccupied. Zen grabbed control of the plane ten seconds after he crossed the line, overriding the usual command sequence with a push-button safety switch on his control board.

"Jesus, what's going on?" said Fentress, at first unaware that he didn't have control.

"You went into Range 3B," said Zen. "I have it."

Zen slid his speed back and ducked the Flighthawk's wing, gliding toward the designated airspace like an eagle checking the crags for a new aerie. He'd grown so used to flying the Flighthawk with his control helmet that handling it with the screens felt a little like backseat driving. He pushed the Flighthawk into a rough trail on the drone, setting his speed precisely to the drone's at 280 knots. All Fentress had to do now was nudge the slider on his throttle bar, located on the underside of the all-control stick, and wait for the "hit me" sign from the computer.

"All yours, Curly," he said, punching his hot switch again to give control back.

His student hunkered down in his seat, pushing forward against the restraints as he concentrated. Zen watched the targeting screen count down as Fentress closed on the drone in a rear-quarter attack. The pilot pressed the trigger the second C^3 cued him to fire.

And he'd been doing so well.

"I told you, the computer is almost always optimistic from the rear," Zen told Fentress as the bullets trailed downward toward the empty desert. Oblivious, the Phantom began its turn, taking it outside the target cone. "Count three before you fire."

Firing the cannon—an M61 from an F-16 modified to fit the robot plane—killed some of the U/MF's momentum, and Fentress struggled to get back into position. Finally he dropped his speed to the point where Zen worried the Phantom would lap him. Gradually, Fentress pulled himself toward the F-4's tail. After nearly a half hour of nudging, he finally got the fire cue, waited this time, and then fired—only to see his target tuck its wing and disappear.

Not completely. It zipped up behind him as the Flighthawk's RWR blared and nailed him from the back.

"Bang, bang, you're dead," said Zen, who had overridden the controls.

"That's not fair," said Fentress.

"Damn straight. Let's try the whole deal again. Try and close a little faster, okay? We have to land while it's still daylight."

Megafortress Project Office
Megafortress Bunker, Dreamland
1745

CAPTAIN BREANNA "RAP" STOCKARD FOLDED HER FINGERS into tight fists behind her back, controlling her anger as she waited for Major Nancy Cheshire to answer her question.

"I'm not saying you're not fit for duty," said Cheshire. "What I'm saying is, you have to follow regulations like everyone else."

"I've had my physical exam already," said Breanna. "I'm completely healed. What? You think I can't fly? I'm rusty?"

"You have to follow procedures like everyone else on this base," insisted Cheshire. "That means ten hours as copilot, and then a reevaluation."

"And I can't take *Galatica*."

"*Galatica* is not cleared beyond the stage three static tests," said Cheshire.

"Sure it is."

"No, Breanna, the repairs covered more than forty percent of the airframe, and that's not even counting what they've added. Rules are rules—that plane has a long way to go. They haven't even painted the nose, and the radar hasn't been replaced. Don't worry—I'll take good care of it."

"The rules are bullshit," said Breanna, pushing her fingers together. "That's my plane."

"The planes don't belong to anyone, Breanna."

"You're only being a bitch to me because I'm a woman. If it were Chris or Jerry, you'd cut them some slack."

Breanna caught her breath, realizing what she'd said. Major Cheshire didn't react at all, which made Breanna feel even worse.

"You have a flight at 0500," said Cheshire. "I would expect you might want to get some sleep."

"Yes, ma'am." Cheshire started to turn away. Breanna caught her sleeve. "I'm sorry, Nancy. I didn't mean that. I didn't."

Cheshire nodded almost imperceptibly, then turned and walked from the simulator walkway.

Breanna hadn't flown since crash-landing a Megafortress

several weeks before. Her actions had won her an Air Force Cross—and a stay in the hospital for multiple injuries. But she'd just blown away the standard Megafortress simulations, proving she was fit to return to full duty.

In time, Breanna thought, to take *Galatica* up tomorrow for its first flight test after being repaired. She'd even be willing to take second seat if it meant flying her plane again.

Not that the planes belonged to anyone, exactly.

"Problem there, Captain?"

Breanna jerked around to find Clyde "Greasy Hands" Parsons standing with a canvas tool bag a few feet from the ramp.

"No, I'm fine."

"Ah, don't let 'er get your goat, Captain. She's always going around like she just stuck her butt in a power socket." Parsons put his bag down and pulled a small tobacco tin from his pocket. He continued to speak as he wadded a tobacco plug into the side of his mouth. "She's always looking to give someone a hard time's all."

"She's doing her job, Chief," said Breanna sharply.

Had she said that to any other chief master sergeant in the Air Force, the chief master sergeant would have snapped erect and walked on, undoubtedly cursing her under his breath. But Parsons and Breanna had been through a great deal together, and in fact the gray-haired chief liked to claim he'd been in the delivery room and pulled Breanna out from her mother's womb.

An exaggeration, though not by much.

"You're taking it all a bit hard, Bree," said Greasy Hands gently. "Truth is, a lot of guys banged up like you were would take six months getting back, maybe more."

"I wasn't banged up."

Banged up was what happened to her husband, a year

and a half ago. That accident had cost him his legs—but not his career.

"You're as stubborn as your old man. A real bee whacker," said Greasy Hands, not without admiration. He started chewing his tobacco very deliberately.

"That's a disgusting habit," Breanna told him.

"Pretty much its main attraction."

Breanna laughed as a small bit of tobacco juice dribbled from his mouth.

"You'll have a good flight tomorrow in *Fort Two*," he said. "Garcia's going along for the ride."

"Oh no, not the Dylan freak!"

More tobacco squirted from Parsons's mouth as he smirked. Garcia was one of Parsons's best technical people, a whiz at both electrical and mechanical systems; supposedly he had once reassembled two turbofans blindfolded. But the staff sergeant was also an insufferable Dylan freak who saw fit to quote the master at every turn.

"Your dad wants everyone on the base to fly at least once a month. Garcia's up," said Parsons. "I told him not to touch nothin' or you'd whack his fingers."

"You did that on purpose," Breanna told him. "You know I can't stand Dylan."

"Me? Never."

Aboard *Raven*, over Dreamland Range 2
1620

IF THE MACHO WORLD OF FIGHTER JOCKS WAS EVER COMpared to a high school football team, Kevin Fentress would be the water boy. Maybe not even that. The short, skinny kid was also painfully shy, and hadn't been the type to join teams or clubs in high school. In fact, most of his classmates would have been surprised to find he had gone to an Army recruiter one warm day toward the end of his junior year. Intelligent and very good with math, Fentress was hoping for a way to fund a college education. The recruiter spoke to him for a half hour before Fentress finally volunteered that his true wish was to fly aircraft. After a slight hesitation—and undoubtedly observing that the would-be recruit weighed less than an Alice pack—the soldier dutifully directed the young man to an Air Force sergeant down the hall. Fentress surprised the skeptical recruiter by blowing away not one, but three different aptitude tests. He eventually found his way into an ROTC program with high hopes of becoming a pilot.

He hadn't, though, for a variety of reasons both complicated and uncomplicated. His tangled path through engineering and into robotics made sense if one kept in mind two things: the original aptitude scores, and the fact that in his whole history with the Air Force, Fentress had never expressed his personal wishes or desires to any superior officer. He had never questioned any order, let alone assignment, no matter how trivial. That alone meant he would never be a fighter jock—pilots seemed to have been bred to view orders not given under fire as optional requests.

Which did not mean that Fentress didn't have personal wishes or desires. At the moment his dearest wish was to show his boss, Major Zen Stockard, that his selection as a pilot on the U/MF program—and the only pilot in the program besides Stockard—wasn't a huge mistake.

"One last thing, Curly," Zen said to him. "You have to always, always, always stay in the proper test range." He clicked off the video replay of the test mission.

"Yes, sir."

"You're not flying a Global Hawk or a Predator," added Zen, mentioning two other projects Fentress had worked on. "This is real stuff."

"Yes, sir. I know. I'm sorry, sir."

"Sorry doesn't cut it."

"Yes, sir. I know. I'm sorry."

Fentress tried to bite the words back. Major Stockard embodied everything he'd once dreamed of becoming—he was a bona fide member of the Right Stuff gang, an F-15 jock who'd shot down an Iraqi jet during the Gulf War. Testing the Flighthawks, he'd survived a hellacious accident that had cost him the use of his legs. Though confined to a wheelchair, he had won his way back to active duty. Not only did he head the Flighthawk program, but he had seen action over Somalia and Brazil.

"We try again tomorrow," added Zen, his voice still harsh.

"Yes, sir. I'll do better. I promise. I can do better."

"I suggest you hit the simulator."

"I will. The whole night," said Fentress.

"Not the whole fucking night, Curly. Get some sleep."

"Yes, sir," said Fentress. "I will."

The major wheeled himself away, shaking his head.

**Dreamland
1800**

"SOME OF THE D BOYS WERE PRAYING, I SWEAR TO GOD." Danny laughed so hard he nearly dropped the phone. His wife Jemma made a little coughing sound in acknowledgment. He knew from experience that it meant she wanted to change the subject, but he was having too good a time to stop.

"You shoulda seen Russ, the helo pilot, when we landed. White as a ghost. And he's blacker than me," added Danny. He stretched back on his plush but very worn gold chair so his head touched the bookcase. "And Peiler. Shit."

"Peiler is which?"

"Major running the Delta Force squad we just finished the exercises with. Smug son of a bitch is going home with his tail between his legs. Top dogs, huh? We whomped 'em!"

"I can't keep track of all these names," said Jemma. Her tone was absent, distant—further away than the nearly three thousand miles between them.

"So what'd you do today?" asked Danny, finally taking her hints.

"As a matter of fact, I had lunch with James Stephens." Her voice changed dramatically; suddenly she was all perky and enthusiastic. "You remember him? He worked for Al D'Amato and George Pataki."

Big-time New York state politicians—D'Amato a senator and Pataki the governor. Jemma was a black studies professor at NYU and heavily involved in politics; she was always dropping names of big shots.

"They're Republicans," she added. "Conservative Republicans."

"And?"

"Jim Stephens is a good man to know," she said. "He believes African-Americans need to be more involved. And it's a good time. A time when things can be done."

"Yeah? So when are you running?" Danny asked, reaching for his drink on the table—lime-flavored seltzer.

"Not me. You," she said sharply. "War hero. Conservative. Man of color."

"Who says?" said Danny.

"You're conservative."

"Who says I'm a war hero?" He didn't necessarily consider himself conservative, either. Nor liberal, for that matter.

Hell, he wasn't even comfortable with "man of color."

"Come on, Daniel. Give yourself some credit. You would be an excellent congressman. From there, who knows?"

Danny rolled his eyes but said nothing. They'd had conversations along this line two or three times before. At some point he thought he might want to work for or in the government somehow; a lot of service guys ended up there. But as far as politics was concerned, he didn't think he could manage the bullshitting.

"I want you to talk to him," said Jemma. "I gave him your phone number."

"What?"

"The general line, routed through Edwards," said Jemma quickly. "Don't worry. I was vague on your assignment, as per instructions."

"Jem, I really don't want—"

"You can't stay in the Air Force forever, Danny. You have to think about your future."

"Right now?"

"Yes, now—you have to think about us."

"I do think about us," he said, and had an impulse to throw down the phone, grab a flight to New York, race to the small apartment she rented near campus, and throw himself on top of her.

Not that that would solve anything. It'd feel good, though.

"You have responsibilities," she said, back in her professor's voice. "Responsibilities to our people."

Jemma really did believe in cultural and societal responsibility, but generally when she started talking about it, she was skirting some issue between them.

"I miss you a lot," he told her.

"Me too," she said. "I saw little Robert today."

"How are they?" Danny tried not to let the wince get into his voice. Little Robert was the cuter-than-hell two-year-old son of a friend of theirs who lived near Jemma. His father had served with Danny in the Air Force, leaving to take a job in the city as an investigator for the SEC.

"They're great. He called me Auntie," she said. "I like it."

"You feeling those urges, Jem?"

"What? For a kid? No way. No way."

They talked for a while more. When Jemma brought up Stephens again, he agreed to at least talk to him.

"Don't go back on your word," she said. "I'll know."

"All right, baby, I won't." As he hung up the phone, the urge to go to her was so strong that he got up and decided to hit the gym before dinner.

Melcross, Nevada (outside Las Vegas)
1900

THE RESTAURANT ADVERTISED ITSELF AS HANDICAPPED AC-cessible, but like most places, the advertisement fell far short of the reality. The first barrier was a two-inch rise at the curb from the parking lot—not a great deal, certainly, and not the biggest bump Zen Stockard had even faced that day, but it was an annoying precursor of what lay ahead. The front entrance sat behind three very high and shallow steps; Zen had to wait outside as his wife went in to ask that the side door be unlocked. That was at the end of a tight ramp, and Jeff had to maneuver through the door and into the narrow hall with a series of pirouette reversals that would have been difficult for a ballerina, let alone a man in a wheelchair. Getting into the dining room involved passing through the kitchen; Zen was almost smacked in the face by a waitress carrying a tray full of fancy spaghetti. On a different day, he might have laughed it off with a joke about not wanting his calamari in his lap, but tonight he was in a foul mood and just barely managed not to complain when the kitchen door smacked up against his rear wheel as he passed onto the thick carpet of the eating area.

It was no wonder many disabled people thought A.B.'s—the abbreviation stood for "able bodied" and was not necessarily benign—had it in for them. It wasn't a matter of being different; that was something you could accept, or at least view as a necessary condition. It was more the smiley stares that accompanied the bumps and turns, the "look at all I've done for you and you're still bitchin' at me?" attitudes.

"We'd like a better table," said Zen as the maitre d' showed them to a small, dim spot at the back, basically hiding them from the rest of the clientele.

"Jeff—"

"How about that one," Zen said, pointing toward the front of the room.

It was a challenge, and the maitre d' knew it. But give the man credit—despite his frown, he led them there.

"You really want to sit up here?" Breanna asked. "It's going to be right in a draft."

"I like drafts," said Zen.

"And I thought I was in a bad mood."

"I'm just hungry." He took the menu.

"Wine?" Breanna asked.

"Beer."

"I doubt they have anything you like," she said, glancing around the fancy Italian restaurant.

Her prediction proved incorrect, as there were several

relatively good brews on tap, including the Anchor Steam that Zen opted for. But even that failed to lift his mood.

"Happy anniversary," said Breanna, holding up her glass—a reserve Chianti from Antinori that she pronounced "perfect."

"Anniversary of our first date," said Zen, clicking the glass gently. "If it was really a date."

"A date is a date is a date. Boy, you are in a bad mood," said his wife. She took a long sip from her glass. "I should have ordered a whole bottle."

"Hmmph."

"Fentress did bad today, huh?"

"He's lucky I don't wash him out."

"Oh, come on, I saw him fly yesterday. He wasn't that bad."

Zen took up his menu, trying to decide between the gnocchi with pesto or one of the ten thousand spaghetti choices.

"You said yourself there'd be a transition," said Breanna.

"I was optimistic."

"Jeff—sooner or later, there are going to be other pilots in the program."

"You think I'm giving him a hard time on purpose?"

Breanna gave him one of her most severe frowns—her cheeks shot inward and her brow furrowed down—before pretending to study the menu.

Zen didn't consider Fentress a bad sort, really; he was smarter than hell, with an engineering degree and several published papers on complicated computer compressions that Jennifer Gleason said were quite good. But he also had a certain lapdog quality to him, an I'll-do-anything-you-want thing that irked Zen.

Plus he'd screwed up on the flight today.

So had he, Zen knew, on his first few flights.

Still, the kid—he *was* a kid, not even twenty-five yet—pissed him off.

Fentress wanted his job. He'd said something like that the first day they met, during one of the bullshit orientation "talks," actually an informal job interview.

Still, he had gone ahead and selected Fentress for the program anyway. What the hell was he thinking?

That Curly was better than one of the jocks who wanted his job.

Less threatening?

Bullshit.

"You havin' fish?" Zen asked his wife.

"With Chianti? No," said Bree.

The waiter approached. *"Buona sera,"* he said, using Italian to say good evening.

It was the sort of thing Breanna ate up. *"Buona sera,"* she replied lightly. *"Per piacere, un po' d'acqua fresco,"* she said, asking for water, then added in Italian that he could bring it later, after they ordered.

The waiter treated her like a long lost cousin. They began debating the merits of several dishes. Zen watched sourly. He loved Bree—truly he did—but she could act like such a jerk sometimes. He wouldn't have been surprised to see her get up and start dancing with the buffoon.

Finally the waiter turned toward him. *"E signor?"*

"Yeah, spaghetti," said Jeff.

"Just spaghetti?" asked the waiter.

"Yuppers."

The man took the menu and retreated quickly.

"You know, you used to be fun," said Breanna.

She meant it as a joke, but there was something serious behind it.

"When I walked, right?" he snapped.

"Jeff—baby, that's not what I meant. Jeffrey. Jeff." She reached her hand across the table and gently touched his face. "Are you okay?"

"I'm all right," he said.

"Jeff."

She rubbed her forefinger lightly against his cheek. He tried to will away the anger and resentment, realizing that, of all people, she shouldn't bear the brunt of it. He remembered her face on the stretcher a few weeks ago when they'd come back from Brazil. She'd crash-landed the plane after saving them from an altimeter bomb.

He'd said a prayer then, probably the first he'd uttered since his own crash.

"Don't let her be crippled," he'd prayed. "It would be better for her if she died."

He'd meant it.

"Jeff?"

"I'm sorry, Bree," he said. "Bad day. I'm just—just a tough day. You going to give me some of your veal?"

"I ordered braised lamb in a port reduction sauce with sorrels and shaved truffles."

"Yeah, that's what I meant," he said.

Incirlik Air Base, Turkey
27 May
0413

THE HOUR OF SLEEP TORBIN CAUGHT AFTER THE LENGTHY mission debrief had served only to increase his restlessness. He came back to the base and wandered back and forth between his ready room and the hangar area, alternately checking on his aircraft and plans for a morning mission. The downed pilot hadn't been found yet, but they now had a fix on the wreckage of his plane. Two planes were orbiting the area and a full-blown search package would launch a half hour before first light. Torbin planned to be in it, even if he had to fly *Glory B* himself.

The debriefers had grilled him pretty hard about the Iraqi missile sites. Their questions were nothing compared to the single one he'd asked himself over and over since the Falcon had been hit:

How the *hell* had he missed the missile?

The answer was that he hadn't. The Iraqis had fired a bunch of missiles from long range without guidance, and somehow, some way, they had gotten the F-16.

Nailed it. Clipped the sucker. Waxed his fanny.

But there was no way, no way in the world, that it had been one of the missiles he'd had on his gear. Not possible.

The APR-47 threat detection radar was an extremely capable piece of equipment—old, perhaps, but still a notch ahead of anything Iraq possessed. Assuming it was in operating order—and the technicians who swarmed over it after they landed assured him it was—the APR-47 could not have missed any Iraqi radar, certainly not one operating long enough or close enough to successfully target the plane.

Nor could he, Torbin thought.

Somehow the bastards had claimed the plane with a one in a million blind shot. Though he wasn't even sure how they could have managed *that*.

Torbin folded his arms against his chest as he walked toward *Glory B*'s hangar. Possibly, the F-16 pilot had screwed up. Possibly. Still, he was pissed—he wanted to pound those bastards into the sand with his bare fists.

A Humvee barreled toward him as he turned the corner toward the maintenance area; he frowned at it viciously, as if that might make it miss him, then stepped off the macadam as the truck veered to a stop.

"Captain Dolk?" asked the driver, who was wearing civilian clothes.

"Yeah?"

"Hop in."

"Who the hell are you?"

"My name's Smith," said the driver. "Come on."

"Hey, no offense, but I've got a mission to prep."

"Just get in," said the driver.

A figure leaned forward from the rear. "Relax, Captain," the man told him. "My name is Brad Elliott. General Elliott. I'd like to speak to you for just a second. We'll give you a lift to wherever it is you're going."

"I have a mission, sir," said Torbin.

"We won't interfere with that."

Torbin shrugged, then stepped around the vehicle to get in the other side. Elliott opened the door for him. He too was wearing civilian clothes.

"I gave a full briefing when I landed, sir," said Torbin.

"Yes, we've seen the preliminary report and spoken to Colonel Hashek," said Elliott. "I'd like to hear what happened in your own words."

Torbin sighed. This figured to be a big fucking deal, even if they got the pilot back—no one had been shot down over Iraq since the Gulf War.

"A lot of flicks on and off," said the general, summarizing the incident after Torbin finished. "And then a barrage of missiles."

"Pretty much," said Torbin. "Everything was out of range, except for that SA-2 site that I nailed. And maybe the SA-8. We hit both. The tapes bear me out."

Elliott nodded. The driver had turned around at some point during the story; Torbin looked now into his face. Even in the darkness he could see the frown.

"I have a job to do this morning, sir," said Torbin.

"Understood," said Elliott. "One more thing—did you see the missile that hit the F-16?"

"No, sir. We weren't that close to the fighters and, uh, my eyes would have been on the scope at that point, sir."

"I wasn't implying they weren't," said the general mildly. "Can you think of anything else?"

"No, sir."

"That's fine," said the general. "Thank you, son."

"Yes, sir."

Torbin got out of the vehicle. Before he closed the door, the general leaned toward him across the seat.

"Don't worry about what happened yesterday," Elliott told him. "Just do your best this morning."

"Yes, sir," said Torbin. "That's what I figure."

He closed the door, stood back and saluted as the Hummer sped off.

"WHAT DO YOU THINK, MACK?" ASKED GENERAL ELLIOTT as Major Smith geared the Hummer toward the command buildings.

"He blew it big-time and doesn't want to admit it," said Mack. When Elliott didn't answer, he added, "That's only my opinion."

"Understood."

"Maybe there was a gear screw-up," said Mack. "Or maybe the Viper flew into flak and the other guys on the flight just got his altitude wrong. Things get tangled. It could even have been a shoulder-launched SA-14," he added, though he thought all of those possibilities were fairly remote. "Just got lucky."

"Possible."

"Say, General, I want to be on the mission. Hook me up with one of the F-16s. I'll find him. I promise."

"We have our own job to do, Major."

"No offense, General, but you can snag an airman to do your driving. Hell, I'm a better pilot than any of these guys. You know it, sir."

"Mack, you haven't changed one bit."

"Thank you."

"I didn't mean that as a compliment."

Mack steered the Hummer into a parking spot near the small, squat building headquartering the squadron in charge of the operations. Elliott jumped out, breezing by the air policemen and striding into the building. Mack followed along as Elliott headed back to Colonel Hashek's office. By the time Mack caught up, Hashek was already laying out the game plan for the morning search and rescue mission.

"I have a pair of MH-53 Pave Lows at this forward area here," he said, jabbing at a large topo map showing southeastern Turkey and northwestern Iraq. "They'll wait at this old airstrip in the mountains. From there they can jump into Iraqi territory in two minutes, maybe less. I'm going to bring in a Combat Talon and fly it back and forth over the wreckage—if that radio comes up, he'll hear it."

"He'll also be a sitting duck," said Elliott. The Combat Talon was a specially modified MC-130E Hercules, a four-engine aircraft designed to fly over hostile territory. Despite its many improvements, it was unarmed, relatively slow, and would be exceedingly vulnerable, especially during the day.

"I need ears," said Hashek. "And that old Herk has to be very close. Now the plane you came in—"

"It's not my plane, so it's not my call," said Elliott. "But frankly, it's not worth the risk"

Mack had been thinking along the same lines as the colonel, and was nearly as surprised as Hashek at Elliott's response. Granted, the converted 707 carried a wide range of highly sensitive electronic spy equipment, most of which wouldn't be much help in locating the pilot. But the damn thing could pick up all manner of radio communications a hundred miles out. Not worth the risk?

Mack looked at Elliott. Was this the same general who'd defied Washington and half the Air Force to get DreamStar back? The general who'd personally flown a suicide mission to Russia to prevent World War III?

The General Brad Elliott?

He looked tired, face white, pockmarked with age and fatigue, maybe even fear.

"I want to fly one of the F-16s," Mack told Hashek. "I want to be in on this."

Hashek turned toward him. "Thanks, Major, but we're full up."

"No offense to your guys, but I can fly circles around them. I can."

"Sorry," said Hashek. Two other men entered the office, both in flight suits. The colonel nodded at them. "I'm sorry, General, I have some business to attend to."

"I want to be on the mission," insisted Mack. "I don't really feel like twiddling my thumbs back here. Hey, Colonel." Mack caught Hashek's arm as the colonel started to leave with the other men. "Give me a break, huh? Anything. I'll go on the Herk even."

"Mack, you will be in the middle of things," said Elliott. "I want you on a Pave Low."

"A Pave Low?"

Mack let go of Hashek's arm. The colonel looked at him like he was an ant before stalking out, his pilots in tow.

"I've never flown an MH-53, General," said Mack, who in all honesty had never even sat in the front seat of a helicopter. "But I'll figure it out. Hell, I can fly anything."

"I don't want you to fly it," said Elliott. "I'm assuming they didn't send you to Brussels to give that seminar on missile damage just because they wanted to get rid of you."

"Um, well, no," said Mack, not quite sure what the point of the general's sarcasm was.

"There should be a Huey waiting to take you to the helicopters. Find a camera and anything else you need, then get there."

Over Iraq
0701

TORBIN HUNKERED OVER THE RADAR DISPLAY IN THE BACK-seat of the Phantom, every cell in his body sensitive to its flicker. Traditional Weasel missions contained a fairly short stay over hostile territory, generally organized around a ten-minute spiral to low altitude as the pitter tracked radars and then launched missiles against well-briefed targets. Today's mission was far more open-ended and demanding, even compared to the freelancing gigs they'd been doing for the past few weeks. Overflying the area where *Falcon Two* had gone down, they would fire on anything that turned on during the hunt. They'd stay in the air for as long as it took to find the pilot and drag him back to safety. That meant three or more hours of staring at the small tube in front of him.

Four Iraqi SAM sites had been targeted for attack in strikes set to be made at the moment *Glory B* crossed the border. In theory, those attacks would remove the major threats the searchers faced. But reality had a way of differing from the nice crisp lines and lists of call numbers drawn on maps. Those attacks might simply stir the hornets' nest.

"We're on track," said Fitzmorris. "Zero-three to Box able-able-two."

"Zero-three," acknowledged Torbin. They'd been like that the whole flight, nothing but business.

Fitzmorris obviously thought he'd fucked up somehow. Probably because he was a pilot—they stuck together.

"Scope clean," Torbin said as they reached the grid area where the Falcon had gone down. The blue-gold tint of dawn would shade the mountains a beautiful purple, but he kept his eyes on his radar screen.

The other planes in the flight checked in, the Herky bird driver nonchalantly trading jibes with one of the F-16s escorting him. The transport plane was a spec ops version equipped for deep penetration of enemy lines, but that usually occurred at night and at low altitude. He was now at roughly twenty thousand feet, above flak but an easy target for a SAM.

Not today. Not with Torbin on the job, he thought. He blew a wad of air into his mask, then pushed his neck down, trying to work out a kink. He tracked through his instruments quickly, then glanced to his right console, double-checking his key settings out of habit. His eyes strayed briefly to the small toggle beyond the telephone-style keypad. Long ago the thin thumb had safed—or unsafed—nuclear stores.

We ought to just fry the sons of bitches and be done with it once and for all, he thought.

He jerked his eyes back to his job, pushing his face down toward the blank radar scope.

"What?" asked Fitzmorris.

"Scope's clean."

"Copy that."

The static-laced silence returned. Torbin pushed himself up against his restraints. Inevitably his attention began to drift; inevitably he thought of the construction job that waited if he quit the Air Force.

Or if they forced him out as a scapegoat.

It's what he got for wanting to be where the action was. Should have stayed in the Pentagon, or used his stinking engineering degree at NASA like they suggested.

Screw that. And screw getting out. He didn't want to build houses.

"*Falcon Two* to any allied aircraft."

The transmission sounded like a snippet of dialogue from a TV in another room.

"*Glory B* to *Falcon Two*," said Torbin. "*Falcon Two*? I'm reading you, boy. Acknowledge."

As Torbin clicked off, the frequency overran with six or seven other voices, all trying to make contact with their downed comrade.

"Radio silence! Radio silence!" shouted Fitzmorris. "*Falcon Two*, identify yourself."

"Captain Terry McRae," came the answer. "I'm sure glad to hear you guys."

"We're glad to hear you," said Torbin. "Give us a flare."

"Slow down—we have to go through authentication first," said Fitzmorris.

"Copy that," said McRae from the ground. "But let's move, okay? I am freezing my butt off down here."

Torbin knew no Iraqi would have said that, but Fitzmorris dutifully checked with the AWACS controller and began relaying personal questions designed to make sure McRae really was McRae.

"I can see you and your smoky tailpipe, *Glory B*," the pilot told them as they finished. "And by the way, you guys must have missed an SA-2 or something yesterday. Smoked the shit out of me. I never saw the damn thing."

"We're sorry for that," said Fitzmorris.

"Why do you think it was an SA-2 if you didn't see it?" asked Torbin, his voice sharper than he wanted.

"What else could it have been?"

Torbin bit his lip to keep from answering. The pilot had enough to worry about for the time being.

Over Iraq
0750

MACK SMITH TRIED TO STEADY HIMSELF ON THE SEAT across from the minigun station as the big Pave Low whipped through a pass in the mountains, rushing toward the spot where the pilot had been sighted. The big helicopter tucked sharply left, the tip of its rotors about ten feet from a sheer wall as it hunkered through a pass. The low altitude tactics made it nearly impossible for an enemy radar to detect them, but at this point Mack would have traded a little safety for a smoother ride. It was one thing to jink and jive when you had the stick yourself, and quite another to be gripping the bottom of a metal ledge in the back of a flying pickup truck.

He'd managed to get out of his jeans and sport coat and into a borrowed flight suit. The boots were a little small and his shoulders felt cramped across the back, but at least he looked like he actually belonged here. The crewmen had given him a helmet connected to the com system via a long umbilical cord.

"We're zero five from the crash site," yelled the copilot. "We're holding back as reserve until we're sure they've got the pilot. Then we'll move in and put you down. Smoky'll go out with you. How long do you need?"

"I don't know," said Mack. "Half hour? I have to take some pictures. See what I see. Kick the tires, check the lights."

The copilot didn't laugh. "Ten minutes, max. The Iraqis are all over the place down there."

Over Iraq
0805

TORBIN TOOK HIS EYES OFF HIS RADAR SCREEN MOMENTAR-
ily as the Phantom tucked southward. The helicopter that
had been tabbed for the pickup was now talking directly
to the downed pilot, who had managed to climb about a
third of the way up a crag about a mile from a dirt road.
This was serious mountain country, but it wasn't entirely
uninhabited—a hamlet big enough to host a mosque sat
about a mile and a half to the south, and Torbin saw, or at
least thought he saw, the blurred shadows of some other
buildings closer to the east.

Torbin turned his head back toward the radar when
something in the sky caught his eye. A red light sparkled
in the distance.

McRae's flare.

Hot damn.

"Lookin' good," said the Pave Low pilot over the circuit. "Hang tight. We'll be on you in thirty seconds."

"Yeah, I'm doing my nails," said the pilot.

Torbin studied his scope. There had been a few brief,
long distance flickers, nothing long enough to actually
grab on to.

How could they even think he'd screw up? Saddam had
nothing up here that could catch even an unescorted F-16.
All he had up here was shit. The SA-2's Fan Song radar?
Crap. The low PRF was surprisingly good at picking up
stealth aircraft, though it hadn't been designed for that.
But it was easily jammed. The SA-3? Arguably better, or
at least more variable, supported by Spoon Rest and a
Side Net, or Squat Eye with a Flat Face and Thin Skin.

Garbage nonetheless. Tiny little wavy lines straight out
of the sixties, competing with *I Love Lucy* and even *Father Knows Best*. The systems had been compromised

years ago. Junk from the days when tubes ruled the world and transistors came one to a chip. SA-6s, Rolands, SA-8s—better, admittedly, but still outclassed, outmatched by the ECMs the Falcons carried.

Even if he had screwed up big-time—and he had *not*—Torbin knew that the Falcon pilot should have had his jamming pod ready. He could have gone to his chaff, juked, jived—

The radar scope flared.

"I have a Three up," Torbin told his pilot. One of the antennas on the Weasel frame had pulled the tight rap of a radar signal from the air. It held it there for him, waiting for him to catch up. He didn't bother with the usual back and forth with the pilot, just went for it. The RIO's fingers flew, cursoring the enemy, pushing the data to the missile, firing, nailing the son of a bitch.

"Away. Have another radar. Hold on, hold on—it's a Two. Out of range. SA-2. I'm on it. I'll nail it."

"Torbin!"

"Dotted. I need you to turn, damn it! Get into him."

"Fire at the bastard."

"Two miles—I need two miles. Get us closer!"

The enemy missile site was at the edge of the HARM missile's range; they needed to draw closer to guarantee a hit.

No time. He fired.

Glory B jinked a second after the AGM-88 left her wing, taking evasive action.

Traveling at over 3.1 times the speed of sound, it took the antiradiation missiles nearly fifty seconds to reach their targets. Those were not the longest seconds of Torbin's life, but they did take an eternity to pass. Finally, the warhead of the first missile detonated into several thousand shards of tungsten alloy, perforating the puny walls of the SA-3's control van as well as a radar dish and all four of the missiles standing in the paired launchers. Five seconds later a massive fireball erupted in the northern launch area of Iraqi Army Air Defense "Victorious Glory" Battalion Two, a piece of the HARM warhead igniting the liquid fuel stage of a Guideline missile that had been poised for launch.

**In Iraq
0811**

MACK HUGGED THE HELICOPTER'S SIDE AS HE MADE HIS way to the rear ramp. A Ma Deuce .50 caliber machine gun sat in the middle of the opening, its long belt draped across the right side of the bay. The helo whipped around as it neared the wreckage, exposing its stinger to the crumpled metal on the side of the hill. The gunner angled the gun around as the helicopter spiraled; Mack nearly fell against the wall as the aircraft whipped practically onto its side before heading toward a small, relatively flat depression just below the slope.

A fat hand grabbed him by the shoulder. It was one of the pararescuers, "Smoky." He'd traded his flight helmet for a soft campaign hat and had a Special Tactics Squadron 203—an M-16 with a grenade launcher attached—in his right hand.

"You ready, Major?" he shouted.

"Kick ass," shouted Smith.

Smoky snorted. The helicopter jerked hard and the sergeant fell against Mack, the gun landing in his ribs. As Mack pushed him off, a volcano seemed to erupt just beyond the tail opening. Mack thought the gunner must be firing, then realized it was only the cloud of dust churned up by the rotors. He grabbed hold of something on the helicopter wall and threw himself toward the opening, following Smoky onto the ramp and then down to the ground, ducking instinctively and racing through the hail of dirt and rocks. Air rushed behind him as if a hole had just been blown in the side of the earth. In the next second he threw himself onto the slope, starting up hand over hand toward the wrecked F-16.

The dust had settled somewhat by the time he reached the wreckage. The Viper had slapped into the hillside almost nose first; most of the fuselage in front of the cockpit had disintegrated. The next six or seven feet of the plane had been crunched into about three-quarters of its original size; long ribbons of metal protruded from the twisted mass, as if they were the spines of a porcupine. The jagged left wing sat down the slope, about twenty or thirty yards away. The rear tail fin was crumpled but more or less intact. The right wing was missing, sheered near the pylon fixing in a shallow diagonal away from the body of the plane. Some of the fuel system piping was visible; it seemed clean.

Mack reached for the tail fin. As his fingers neared the surface he hesitated, as if fearing it would be hot.

"What we lookin' for?" asked Smoky, catching up behind him. The PJ had a microphone and headset so he could talk with the helicopter. He also humped a pack.

"Shrapnel holes, black streaks from a fire, basically a big hole or tear that can't be explained by the impact," said Mack. Actually, the list went on and on—nearly twenty minutes during one of Mack's lectures, not counting time flirting with any pretty girls in the audience.

He pulled out the small 35mm camera and began taking pictures, walking along the side of the downed aircraft. The missing wing was undoubtedly the key, though the break looked remarkably clean for a missile hit.

Possibly torn off in flight after being weakened by a

fire, though the fact that the fuel piping hadn't burned meant . . .

Meant what?

"Missile?" Smoky asked.

"Yeah," said Mack. "Probably took off the wing, exploded the fuel tank in the wing."

"Wow."

There had definitely been an explosion—there were shrapnel holes all over the place. But no fire?

Too wide a spread for a missile, actually, unless the explosion had been right under the wing or maybe in it, smashed it to smithereens so that this jag and that one, and that one and all the others, were from the wing sharding off.

"This thing catch fire?"

"No." Mack shrugged. "Sometimes you get a fire, sometimes you don't. This looks like a pretty direct hit with a really good-sized warhead."

He remembered a crash he'd seen where there hadn't been a fire—the accident that had claimed Jeff Stockard's legs. Funny that he remembered that and not his own shoot-down a few months ago.

"Wow, look at these holes," said Smoky, pointing to the belly of the plane. "Flak?"

Mack bent down to take a look. "Too varied. Probably from the explosion. Besides, see how this folded down there? This damage here was from the impact. Metal came away. See the bolt on that panel? Gave way." He stepped back and took a picture.

Two small warheads maybe? Happened to hit just right and snapped the wing clean off?

He'd want odds on that.

"A missile probably got the wing and exploded it. That big an explosion, though—I don't know. Pilot got out."

He went to study the cockpit, which had been munched by the impact into the mountain. Still—no fire.

Mack walked back to the right wing root. The wing had almost certainly been sheered off before impact.

He'd need to see it.

Some parts of the root were white, as if the metal had been on fire and just disintegrated into powder. But there clearly had been no fire. Mack bent over an internal spar; the bolts were loose.

Sympathetic vibrations after the explosion, he thought, shock wave knocks the metal loose.

He took some pictures.

What the hell missile hit them? An SA-2?

That clean, it had to be something smaller. Three little shoulder-fired missiles?

Three heat-seekers all nailing the wing? Very strange.

Crashes were strange by definition. Mack stood back and took pictures, changed his film, took more pictures. The engineers could tell a lot by looking at the way the metal had been bent; those guys were the real experts. He was just a moonlighting pilot who'd happened to command a crash investigation during the Gulf War. He moved in for close-ups, then bent his head under the fuselage. The metal was scraped and not exactly smooth. Some panels and spars seemed to have buckled, probably on impact. He saw a few more loose bolts and popped rivets, but nothing here contradicted his theory that the damage emanated from the right side of the plane.

Nice to find that right wing, he thought. Real nice.

He backed off the plane onto the top of the slope, taking more pictures as he walked upward.

Stockard had managed to eject after a collision with a robot plane he was piloting from an F-15E Eagle. He'd been way low when he went out, and his chute never had a chance to fully deploy—though it was never clear to Mack whether he'd been injured going out or landing. His plane had been a mangled collection of thick silver

string strewn over the desert test area where they were
flying at the time. Mack could close his eyes and still see
Zen's body lying in a heap against the flat dirt, the lines to
his parachute still attached. The canopy had furled awkwardly, as if trying to pull him to his feet.

What if a stream of flak had shot through the metal, exploded the wing tank, sliced the wing right off, he asked
himself.

Not to be totally ruled out—except for the shrapnel
over the rest of the plane's body. The wing definitely
seemed to have exploded.

Had to be a missile, had to have ignited the wing tank.
Except that it clearly hadn't.

Mack took some more photos, then stopped to change
the roll. As he closed the back of the camera, Smoky
came running across the rocks.

"We got problems, Major!" shouted the PJ. "Company
coming."

Before Mack could answer, the ground shook and he
fell backward against the hillside, the roar of an exploding tank shell blaring in his ears.

Over Iraq
0815

As the Pave Low lifted off with the injured pilot,
Torbin and Fitzmorris saddled up to go home with the
rest of the escorts. The Wild Weasel ducked her wing
gently to starboard, steaming gracefully into a turn. Her
turbines chewed on the carcasses of a thousand dead di-
nosaurs; the slipstream melted into a swirl of blue-white
vapor. Torbin jerked his bulky frame forward, still mind-
ing his gear but more relaxed now, redeemed by the hits
on the missile control radars.

Let them try and say he fucked up now, he thought. He had two fresh scalps to prove he hadn't.

Screw building houses. Honorable profession, oh yes, but just not what he wanted to do right now, even if his brother-in-law's cousin Shellie was pretty good-looking.

Find some sort of job doing something worthwhile. Crew on a stinking AWACS if it came to that.

Torbin pushed his legs against the side consoles, stretching some of the cramps out of them. He rolled his shoulders from side to side, still watching the threat scope. They had a long haul home, made all the longer by the fact that the Pave Low they were accompanying would be lucky to top 175 knots.

A jumble of happy voices filled the radio as the escorts checked in with the AWACS. Then the pilot in the second Pave Low called for radio silence.

"*Flag Two* has vehicles on the roadway," said the strained voice over the loud cluck of helicopter blades in the background. "I'm looking at two BMPs, a tank maybe."

"*Snake One* acknowledges," answered the leader of the F-16 flight.

Torbin did a quick check of his gear as his pilot rejiggered their plans—they'd dog south to provide cover for the F-16s wheeling to attack the vehicles.

"How you doing back there?" Fitzmorris asked as they came to the new course bearing.

"Not a problem." Torbin shrugged. "Scope's clean."

In Iraq
0821

THEY WERE NAKED ON THE SIDE OF THE HILL, EXPOSED TO the tank firing from the dirt road two hundred yards away.

Mack spotted a large group of boulders on his right and began sliding toward it. Smoky had the same idea, but not nearly as much balance—he flopped past Mack, just out of his grasp as another shell hit the hillside, this one so close that Mack smelled the powder in the dirt that flew against his helmet. He tumbled after the sergeant, rolling over three or four times before landing on his belly and sliding another four or five feet. He pulled himself up against the rocks, twisting his head back to get his bearings. Smoky's leg lay nearby, off at an odd angle.

Severed?

It began to writhe, and Mack felt his stomach falling backward into a vacuum.

The dirt beyond the leg moved. "Jesus, this hurts like hell," groaned Smoky, unfolding himself from the ground.

Mack stumbled over, took his arm and dragged him behind the rocks. Another volley resounded against the hillside. Mack heard the MH-53 hovering in the distance, then something else.

"Duck!" he yelled.

If the bomb whistled in—and undoubtedly it did—he never heard it. What he did hear was the muffled crack of a pair of five-hundred-pound iron bombs bracketing the turret of a T-62 Iraqi main battle tank. A chain of explosions followed as a second F-16 loosed a pair of cluster bombs on the other vehicles. The bombs hit slightly to the south of their aim point, the pilot's mark thrown off slightly by the gusting wind and the vagaries of trying to hit a moving object while diving at five or six hundred miles an hour from fifteen thousand feet. Nonetheless, the loud rumble of a secondary explosion followed the rapid-fire popcorn of the bomblets going off.

The earth shuddered and Mack found himself lying flat on his back, eyes cupped with grit. He flailed his elbows, struggling to get upright like a frog tossed on his back. When he finally got to his feet, he realized he'd pulled Smoky up with him.

"I'm all right, I'm all right," said the PJ.

"We got to get ourselves out of here," said Mack. "Where's the helicopter?"

"He cleared back to let the fighters in," said Smoky, who'd lost his headset somewhere. "He won't leave us, I guarantee."

"Where the fuck is he?"

"He'll be back." The sergeant put some weight on his right leg, grimaced, then fell against the rock.

"All right, come on," said Mack, though he wasn't exactly sure where they were going.

"You don't have to carry me," said the sergeant.

"I ain't fuckin' carrying you," snapped Mack. "Just lean on me. We'll go back to the flat where they dropped us. Shit—what are you doing?"

As Smoky swung his 203 up from his side, Mack ducked back, sure that the sergeant had lost his mind and was about to waste him.

Two quick bursts later something fell from the hillside above the airplane behind them.

A dead Iraqi soldier.

"Come on!" yelled Mack.

"Smoke!"

"What?"

As the sergeant reached below his vest, Mack took hold of his other arm and looped it around his neck. He pulled Smoky down around the rocks as the ground erupted behind them—bullets from two more soldiers coming across the hill.

"Smoke!" The sergeant's voice had gone hoarse. He had a small canister in his hand.

A smoke grenade. Good idea.

Mack leaned against the sergeant to prop him up as he flicked his arm, tossing rather than throwing the grenade. Soot began spewing from the canister, which landed only a few yards away.

"Down the hill," hissed Smoky.

"No shit," said Mack, helping him through the rocks.

A freight train roared overhead, its wheels pounding the loose ties of a trestle bridge with a steady, quick beat. Mack slid but kept both of them upright as the Pave Low threw a stream of lead on the Iraqi soldiers who had tried to ambush them. The gunfire—besides the .50 caliber and the minigun, one of the crewmen was unloading a 203— seemed to sheer off the hilltop. Mack stumbled through a thick haze of pulverized rock, his mouth thick with dirt. He spun around and landed in a heap on the ramp, the sergeant rolling on top of him.

An angel or a pararescuer—same difference—grabbed him in the next instant. They were aboard the helicopter and airborne before his lungs began working again.

Over Iraq
0832

"SNAKES ARE CLEAR. ALL VEHICLES SMOKED. BOYS ARE aboard and headed home."

"*Glory B* copies," said Fitzmorris.

"En route to the Grand Hotel," said the pilot in *Flag Two*. "Kick ass."

"You kicked butt down there," said *Snake One*.

"Y'all didn't do too poor yourself."

All right guys, quit with the attaboys and get on home, Torbin thought.

"Fuel's getting a little tight," said Fitzmorris.

"I can get out and push if you want," Torbin told him.

"I was thinking maybe you'd just pop your canopy and flap your arms a bit," said the pilot.

Torbin laughed. Good to hear Fitzmorris making jokes again, even if they were lame. He scanned his gear; no threats, no nothing. Two of the F-15s flying escort radioed for an update. The planes had blown south in the direction of the nearest large Iraqi air base when things got tight, just in case Saddam decided to reinforce his troops farther north.

Fitzmorris filled them in.

"Blue skies ahead," said one of the F-15 pilots. He had a bit of a Missouri twang in his voice, and Torbin decided to ask where he was from.

"Kansas City," answered the pilot. "How 'bout yourself?"

"Jefferson City," said Torbin. "Well, almost. My dad had a farm 'bout ten miles south of Moreau River."

"Maybe you know my cousin, sells tractors out near St. Thomas, or in St. Thomas, one of those little burbs down there."

"What is this, old home week?" asked Fitzmorris.

"Where you from, cowboy?"

"Pittsburgh, P.A.," answered the pilot.

"Hey, my wing mate's from Philadelphia, aren't you, Gunner?"

Torbin didn't hear the reply—six or seven Iraqi radars had just flashed on simultaneously to the south. Two missiles were launched almost at the same instant.

"Shit!" was the only warning he could give before the pilot from Kansas City overran the transmission with a curse.

After that there was nothing but static.

II

Gone

**Dreamland
27 May 1997
0453**

LIEUTENANT COLONEL TECUMSEH "DOG" BASTIAN LENGTH-ened his stride as he jogged onto the long stretch of macadam that paralleled the razor-wire fence on the southeastern perimeter of the Dreamland "residential" area. This was inevitably his favorite part of the morning run, not least because the three-quarter-mile straightaway led to the last turn and the trot home. A boneyard of old aircraft lay to the right; the shadows seemed not so much ghosts as spirits urging him onward. In truth, he saw only shadows of shadows, since the skeletons were too far away in the dark to be made out. But even thinking of the old-timers disintegrating into the desert somehow comforted him. The bare skeletons reminded him that the admonition of "dust to dust" meant not only that conceit was ill-advised, but that everyone had a purpose and a role, and the reward of rest was guaranteed no matter how trivial your job in life, or how short you fell from your goal.

Not that Dog Bastian was a man who fell short of his goals. Indeed, his record since arriving at Dreamland the year before was one of astounding achievement.

And one conspicuous incident of direct insubordination—
which had averted the destruction of San Francisco and
Las Vegas.

A lot had changed since Dog had arrived at Dreamland. The base, then on the verge of being excised, was
now charged not merely with developing weapons, but of
using them in extreme situations. A new President had
taken office, and with him there had been a new cabinet
and a fairly thorough reshuffling of the civilian and military defense hierarchies. Dog's patron—the NSC director
herself—had lost her post. But he had remained and even
thrived.

Temporarily, at least. Two months before, Dog had
been placed "under review" by the three-star general who
was his immediate and at the moment only military superior. Precisely what "under review" meant remained un-
clear. Lieutenant General Harold Magnus had made no
move to discipline him for disobeying orders against flying, and it was obvious he wouldn't—given the circumstances, it would have been ridiculous. In the interim, a
new defense secretary had taken over, along with a chief
of staff from the Navy. "Under review" might apply to
Dreamland's status in the defense structure, which admittedly was hazy. While part of the Air Force, the base was
not included under any of the normal commands. Its personnel were predominately Air Force, but they included
many civilians, and a smattering of men and women from
the Army and Navy as well. In developing weapons,
Dreamland was in all practical effect a contractor—not
just for the Air Force, but for the Army, Navy, CIA, NSA,
and in one case, NASA. Its covert "action team"—aka
Whiplash—consisted of a ground force commanded by
Danny Freah and any other assets assigned to a mission
by Dog himself. Once a Whiplash order was initiated by

the President, Dog was answerable only to him or his designated deputy.

He knew that eventually all of this would change. Dreamland and Whiplash were too important to be commanded by a puny lieutenant colonel. The latest rumors posited that Whiplash would be expanded to full squadron size and then placed under the Special Operations Command (USSOC). A two-star would take over the base, which would remain a hybrid command. While such a split was antithetical to the concept that had established Whiplash, as well as the reason Dog had been sent here in the first place, it had a certain Washington logic to it that made the rumor seem fairly authentic.

Yet it didn't bother Dog. As a matter of fact, he no longer thought about his career in the Air Force. He even considered—albeit lightly and without focus—what sort of job he might take if he returned to civilian life. Nothing about the future bothered him these days, especially while he was jogging.

The reason waited a few yards ahead, stretching in the chilly morning air.

"Hey, sleepyhead," said Dog as he approached.

"I had a late night," said Jennifer Gleason. She paused in her warm-up routine long enough to accept a light peck on the lips, then fell into a slow trot alongside him. "I had to help Ray on some last minute coding for *Galatica*. The navigation section in the autopilot programs developed some nasty bugs when the spoof lines were imposed and the GPS signal was blocked. Major Cheshire's supposed to fly it this morning, and we didn't want her landing in Canada."

"Spoof lines?"

"Well, the ECM coding in the three-factor section doesn't interface with the GPS at all, but for some bizarre reason there was this variable table that was affected. It had to do with the allocation of memory—"

"I think we're venturing into need-to-know territory," said Dog, picking up his pace. "And I don't need to know."

"Too technical for you, Colonel?"

"Nah."

Jennifer tapped at him teasingly. He caught her hand, then folded it into his, her long, slim fingers twining around thumb and pinkie. They ran like that for a few yards, Dog luxuriating in the soft echo of her footsteps next to him.

"I get off here," he said as they approached the narrow road that led to his quarters.

"You're not running with me?"

"Hey, I've done my time." Dog slowed to a trot and then a walk. Jennifer let go of his hand, but also slowed, trotting backward to talk a few more moments before saying good-bye.

"Come on, you can do another circuit."

"Can't. Chief Gibbs probably has the papers three feet high on my desk already," said Dog. "Maybe we can meet for dinner?"

"How about lunch?"

"Can't do lunch. How about off base for dinner?"

"Are you sure Gibbs will let you off base?"

"Ax works for me, not the other way around."

"Have you checked the organizational chart?"

"No way. He drew it up," Dog said, laughing.

Chief Master Sergeant Terrence "Ax" Gibbs was the colonel's right-hand man; the chief tended to the p's and q's of the job and at times acted as a substitute mother hen. Ax came from a long line of top-dog sergeants, a chief's chief who could organize a hurricane into a Sunday picnic.

"The question is, can you get away?" said Dog. "You're the worst workaholic on this base, and that's saying something."

Jennifer jogged forward. Her long hair framed a beautiful round face, and even in rumpled sweats her body pulled him toward her.

"I will meet you at the Dolphin port at 1800 hours," she said a few inches from his face. "Be there or be square."

Dog laughed, then leaned in to kiss her. As their lips touched, he caught the flash of a blue security light in the distance.

"Now you've done it," said Jennifer. "Chief Gibbs heard you talking about him."

"I have no doubt," said Dog. He turned toward the approaching truck, one of the black GMC SUVs used by the base's elite security force. The Jimmy whipped so close before halting that Dog took two steps off the pavement, nudging Jennifer out of the way as well.

"Colonel, got a message for you," said the driver. Lieutenant William Ferro, the security duty officer, was out of breath, as if he'd run instead of driven. "You have to, you have a secure call."

"Relax, Billy," Dog told him. "Gleason, I'll see you at 1800."

"You got it," Jennifer told him, whirling and breaking into a smooth stride.

"Whiplash," said Ferro as Dog got into the truck. "I didn't know if I should say that, in front of the, uh, scientist, sir."

"That scientist has seen more combat than you have," said Dog, who might have added that her clearance was also considerably higher. "But you did okay. When in doubt, don't."

"Yes, sir." The lieutenant stepped on the gas and whipped the truck into a 180, shooting toward Taj, the main building at the base. Dog's office and a secure communications bunker known as Dreamland Command were located in the basement.

The colonel ran his hands over his face as they drove, mopping the perspiration. His shirt had a wide, wet V at the chest. He'd change once he knew what was up.

"Do me a favor, Billy," he said as the lieutenant screeched to a stop in front of the building. "Roust Captain Freah and ask him to meet me up in my office as soon as he can make it."

"Yes, sir."

"And Billy—slow down a bit, all right? This thing's a truck, not a tank. You'll get hurt if you hit something."

THE DOORS TO DREAMLAND'S SECURE COMMAND CENTER snapped open with a pneumatic hiss. As Dog stalked across the threshold, the automatic lighting system snapped on. He went to the bank of video consoles on the left, hunkering over the keyboard as he pecked in his password. The screen's blue tint flashed brown; a three-option menu appeared, corresponding to the communication and coded protocols. Dog nudged the F3 key, then retyped both his password and the Whiplash activation code. Then he opened a small drawer beneath the desk and took out a headset.

"Configuration Dog One," he told the computer that controlled the communications suite. "Allow pending connection."

The screen popped into a live video from the situation room at the Pentagon. Lieutenant General Magnus, in his shirtsleeves, was conferring with an aide at the side.

"General," said Dog.

Magnus turned toward him with his familiar scowl. "Tecumseh. Sorry to wake you."

"I wasn't sleeping, General. I'd just finished my run."

"We're having some problems in Iraq," said Magnus. "Very bad problems. You'll be hearing news reports soon. We're getting ready for a press conference upstairs. The executive summary is this—Saddam has shot down three of our planes."

"What?"

"We recovered one of the pilots and had a quick look at the wreckage. We weren't able to get a full team out there but we have some of the photos. One of your men happened to be in Europe and was routed out there by coincidence. Mack Smith. He looked at the wreckage."

Dog nodded. Mack wasn't a true expert on plane damage—though of course he thought he was. Still, he knew enough to give a lecture on it to terrorism experts and had commanded an investigation in the past.

"What did Mack say?"

"I don't have the report yet, or the photos," said Magnus. "This is still developing. Two of the planes are still missing. They're definitely down."

Dog felt a surge of anger as the news sank in. He'd flown missions over Iraq, commanded guys in both Southern Watch and Operation Comfort. If there were men down, there was a good chance he knew them.

Iraq should have been taken care of six years ago, steamrolled when they had a chance.

"Retaliatory strikes are under way," continued Magnus. "We're stepping up reconnaissance. We have satellite coverage, but we've pulled our U-2s until we're sure they'll still be okay. We need one if not two Elint aircraft there, and we believe the RC-135s might be vulnerable, at least if they stray close enough to hear what's going on in Baghdad. It's a precaution, of course, but until we know precisely what happened, we'd prefer to—"

"I can have a pair of Megafortresses in the air this afternoon," said Dog.

"Two?"

"I believe we can have two," said Dog, thinking of *Raven* and *Quicksilver*.

"Two would be optimum. We'll want a black base, not Incirlik."

"Okay," said Dog, realizing that was going to be considerably more difficult than merely sending the Megafortresses.

"You're not being chopped to CentCom on this, Tecumseh," said Magnus. "You're supplying them with information and support, but you remain an independent entity. This is a Whiplash operation. You understand?"

"Yes, sir, absolutely."

"If you can find the radar and the missile sites, take them out," added Magnus, making the implications of the order explicit. "Don't bother going through Florida and pussyfooting with the political bullshit. Full orders will follow. Jed Barclay is going to bird-dog you on this, for the President. I'm only tangentially involved." Magnus turned away from the screen briefly, nodded to someone behind him, then turned back. "Your orders should arrive no later than 1400."

"The planes will be en route by then, General."

"Very good."

The screen went blank.

Dreamland
0603

"WHERE YOU GOIN', MY BLUE-PAINTED PAIN IN THE YOU-know-what?" twanged Staff Sergeant Louis Garcia, half singing, half cursing at the errant wires in the hard-point assembly he was trying to adjust. Breanna rolled her eyes and took a sip of her Diet Coke, painfully aware that anything she said would not only further delay their takeoff but elicit a riff of bad Dylan puns from the man on the portable scaffold.

"How's it looking?" asked Merce Alou, keeping his voice down.

Breanna shrugged. "Something about the wire harnesses fouling up the hydraulic fit," she told Major Alou, *Quicksilver*'s pilot.

"New antennas in the nose okay?" asked Alou, nodding toward the gray and silvery front section of the plane. Thanks to updates in their electronic intelligence, or Elint, gear, both *Raven* and *Quicksilver* had new blunt, almost triangular, noses. The faceted proboscis not only accommodated the latest array of sensors, but would also facilitate a false-echo electronic countermeasure system still being developed and scheduled for installation next fall. The new nose was not yet coated with its radar-deflecting Teflon paint, which took several applications and could ground it for some time.

"Checked and rechecked," said Breanna. "Least of our problems."

Alou grunted noncommittally. He'd done much of the work shaking down the new gear in *Raven*, his usual mount, and he seemed to be remembering those teething problems.

"We only have a clear satellite window for another hour and a half," he said finally. "We'll have to scrub if we're not ready to fire the Hydros in forty-five minutes. I'm not sure we can even preflight by then."

Breanna took another sip of her soda. Russian satellites crisscrossed overhead on a predictable schedule. The Megafortress was no longer considered top secret—both *Jane's* and *Airpower Journal* had written articles on the aircraft in the past few months. Many of the details were wrong, but that was undoubtedly the idea of whomever

had leaked them. *Newsweek* had published a grainy photo
following the so-called Nerve Center affair, and *Time* had
run not one, but two artists' sketches.

The Hydros they were to launch from the bulky hard-
point, however, were very secret. From the distance, they
looked like sleek red tubes with a slightly swelled rear. In
fact, they could easily be confused for water or gas pipes,
were it not for their aerodynamic noses and tiny fins at
the back. But the thin, titanium-ceramic bodies held a
pair of gossamer copper-carbon wings and a large tube of
hydrogen. After the Hydros were dropped, the wings
were inflated either by remote control, timer, or preset altimeter. The foot-long stubs allowed the tubes to glide
back down to earth. While still in its early stages, the Hydros were expected to form the basis of next-generation
disposable sensor devices or even bomb kits. And the implications of the technology—airfoils on demand, as one
of the scientists put it—were far-reaching.

"Knock-knock-knockin' on heaven's door," said Garcia. He stood back triumphantly.

"That mean we're ready?" Alou asked.

"One more cup of coffee 'fore we go," sang Garcia, apparently meaning yes.

"Can we mount the Hydros?" asked one of the scientists who stood in front of the knot of ordies and the Hydro.

"Just don't go mistakin' heaven for that home across
the road."

"One more song lyric and you're going to heaven,"
said Breanna, "and it won't be in an airplane either."

Thirty minutes and at least a half-dozen song allusions
later, Breanna and Alou had the Megafortress on the taxi-
way. A black SUV Jimmy sat ahead at the turn into runway one. They trundled toward it then braked; they had to
wait for *Galatica* to land.

"Holding at Heaven's Gate," said Alou.

The controller acknowledged. *Galatica* was on final approach.

Breanna curled her arms in front of her chest, undecided about whether to watch "her" plane land or not. She looked up at the last moment, just in time to see the plane drop into view. Her undercarriage and tail had been severely damaged in the crash landing, but there was no way to tell now; she descended toward the dry lake bed like a dark angel with her wings spread, her Teflon-coated surface smooth and sleek black.

"I'll be with you as soon as I can," Bree muttered to the aircraft.

"Don't worry, I'm still saying my prayer too," said Alou.

Breanna felt her face flush, embarrassed that she had spoken out loud.

"Okay," said Alou. He held up his thumb, then gave a wave in front of the window to the crewman at the security truck. They removed their brakes and stepped to the line, toeing along the back apron of the runway for a moment before giving *Quicksilver* the gas. Breanna scanned the glass wall of instruments in front of her; all systems were green as they skipped lightly into the air.

Breanna's disappointment at not being the first to take *Galatica* disappeared as soon as her stomach felt the impact of the two g's or so that *Quicksilver* pulled getting off the runway. She'd missed that rush of adrenaline these past few weeks. The maneuvers in the simulator had touched eight negative g's, a fairly hard shove—yet they hadn't felt as sharp, as nice, as warm as this.

"Preparing to clean gear," she told Alou.

"Proceed."

"Computer—raise landing gear," she said.

"Raise landing gear," repeated the automated flight assistant. They worked through their flight plan, bringing the Megafortress to ten thousand feet over the northernmost test area. They reached it about ten minutes ahead of schedule and had to wait for the recovery team to get ready on the ground.

"I didn't know you were religious," said Alou as they began a wide orbit around the range. "I saw you pray before takeoff. That happen after the crash?"

Bree grunted, not caring to get into a discussion. She hadn't actually been praying.

"God had to be watching out for you that day," said Alou. "Peter, you ready back there?"

Peter Hall, the engineer in charge of the Hydro test, replied that he was. Breanna concentrated on her instruments. She hadn't thought about what role, if any, a higher power had played in her survival. She rarely if ever thought about God at all. Not that she was an atheist; she and Zen had been married in a church, and after his accident she had often found herself praying. For him, though. Not for herself. And probably more out of habit than any firm conviction.

Lying on the stretcher, waiting for the ambulance to take her to the hospital, she'd thought at first she'd lost her legs. She hadn't prayed then.

"How's our altitude?" Alou asked.

"Ten thousand feet precisely," she said. "Clear skies. We're set."

"*Quicksilver* is ready when you are, Hydro Team," said the pilot.

They hit their mark and turned the aircraft over to the computer for the launch. The handles grasping the long pipe snapped open as the plane nosed upward in an alpha maneuver, a shallow dive and recovery that transferred launch momentum to the Hydro. The missile's nose angled toward the earth at precisely fifty-three degrees once loosened; the angle increased slightly as it fell. The pilots watched the flight with the aid of cameras in *Quicksilver* and the nose of the Hydro; it wobbled unsteadily as it continued to pick up speed.

"Gonna be a problem when the wings deploy," said Peter. "Deployment in five, four . . ."

Breanna watched the screen as the tube seemed to burst apart. The screen showing the feed from the Hydro's nose whipped into a frenzy.

"Just a spin," said Peter. "It can deal with that."

"Coming to our turn," said Alou, who'd retaken control of *Quicksilver* from the computer.

By the time they came out of their bank, the onboard controller for Hydro had managed to recover from the spin and turned the craft toward its designated landing area. Breanna and the others watched on their monitors as it skidded into a rough landing about two hundred yards beyond its target line—not great, but not horrible either, especially since they weren't particularly worried about accuracy. The Hydro's nose camera showed the recovery crew's vehicle kicking up dust as it approached.

"Want to take the wheel?" Alou asked.

"Oh, sure, let me drive now that all the fun stuff is done." Breanna laughed, but then pulled back on the stick abruptly and hit the slider for maximum power, pushing the big plane into a sharp climb.

"Ladies and gentlemen, our pilot is now Captain Breanna 'Rap' Stockard," said Alou over the interphone in his best tour guide voice. "Fasten your seat belts, please. Remember to keep hands and body fluids inside the car at all times. Things are likely to be hairy. The all-time record for climb to eighty thousand feet is in jeopardy."

Breanna had in fact started to level off. But a remark

from Garcia about working on a farm—another obscure reference to a Dylan song—did encourage her to add a quick invert to the flight plan.

Dreamland
0845

DOG MET MAJOR CHESHIRE AS SHE CAME DOWN *GALAtica*'s access ramp in the Megafortress bunker.

"Better than new," Cheshire told him. "I think the tweaks on the engines add ten knots to the top speed—we'll break the sound barrier in level flight yet."

"Major, come here a second," he said as another crewman started down the ladder. They walked a few yards away, where he could tell her about the Whiplash order.

"We'll need the two Elint planes, *Raven* and *Quicksilver*," he said after giving her a brief overview of the situation. "Assuming *Quicksilver* can go."

"She's fine. The new nose hasn't been coated because we didn't want to take her out of service during the Hydro tests, but she can fly fine. The increase in the radar profile won't make much of a difference."

Dog nodded. He had already considered that, but wanted to make sure Major Cheshire agreed. The increase in the radar profile compared to a standard Megafortress had been calculated at roughly thirty-five percent, which was still a considerable improvement over a standard B-52. Given that unstealthy planes flew over Iraq all the time, it would not be much of a handicap.

"Major Alou and I will be ready to fly as soon as the planes are serviced," said Cheshire.

"You're not going," said Dog. "Sending you will disrupt too many things. We still need to select a team for the Unmanned Bomber Project, and the congressional inspection of the new Megafortresses is set for Tuesday. I need you here."

Cheshire's face turned to stone. "With respect, sir, I believe I should be on the mission. I have the most experience of the Megafortress pilots."

"You're also project officer for both the Megafortresses and the XB-5 Unmanned Bomber."

"I'm giving the XB-5 up."

"We're going to need someone on duty in the secure center twenty-four hours a day," said Dog. "You may have to sit in for me there, and help with some of my other duties as well. I want you to take charge of drawing up the deployment plans. I would imagine Major Alou should head the mission. Choose another crew. Danny's already on his way over."

Though still unhappy, Cheshire was too good a soldier and knew Bastian too well to argue further. Her sentiments could only be read in the crispness of her "Yes, sir" before she left to change.

Over Dreamland Test Range C
0930

THEY HAD JUST COME BACK LEVEL WHEN THE CONTROLLER hailed them.

"*Quicksilver*, we have a message for Major Alou and Captain Stockard," said the controller. "You're needed back at base, stat. Priority Whiplash."

Alou clicked the mike to answer but Breanna cut him off. "Acknowledged," she said. "We're inbound."

"I have it," said Alou.

"Sorry," said Breanna. She concentrated on turning the big plane onto a new course for the runway as Alou cleared the security protocols to allow a coded communication with Major Cheshire. The direct link was available on their com sets only.

"We have a deployment situation," Major Cheshire told them as soon as the line snapped on.

"I'm ready," Breanna said.

"We both are," added Alou.

"It's a Rivet mission over Iraq," said Cheshire. "Rivet" was shorthand; it referred to Rivet Joint, top-secret Elint missions they had both flown in RC-135s. Two Megafortresses, *Raven* and *Quicksilver*, had been equipped to undertake similar missions, though under considerably more dangerous circumstances.

"Not a problem," said Alou.

"Major, I'd like to speak to Captain Stockard alone. Would you clear off the circuit?"

"Yes, ma'am," said Alou, who voided his connection with a verbal command. Bree felt her cheeks flashing red, embarrassed.

"Breanna, do you think you can handle a mission?"

Damn sure, she wanted to say. Let's go kick some butt. But instead she answered, "Yes, ma'am. Not a problem."

"I want you to be honest with me."

"I try to be. I was out of line the other day."

"That's forgotten. I want you to be honest with me."

"Piece of cake, Major," said Bree lightly. Then she asked about her plane.

"Engineers and ground crew did a great job," said Cheshire. "I want you to pilot *Quicksilver*," she added, changing the subject. "Do you want Chris with you?"

Chris Ferris was *Galatica*'s—Breanna's—copilot. He'd flown with her on every important mission she'd had at Dreamland.

"Yes. When are we taking off?" Bree asked.

"As soon as possible."

"You ready?"

"I'm not going," said Cheshire. Her words were so flat her disappointment was obvious. "Colonel Bastian wants me here to help monitor things from the command center. Major Alou will lead the mission in *Raven*."

Alou?

Of course Alou. He ranked her, even though she had more combat hours in the Megafortress than anyone, Cheshire included.

Why did that bother her? Because she'd shown him the ropes on his first few orientation flights in the Megafortress? That was three months ago.

"The deployment may last awhile," Cheshire told her. "Meet me in my office in the hangar bunker as soon as you land. Both of you."

Incirlik, Turkey
2100

IF IT WEREN'T FOR THE WIND OR THE STICKINESS OF THE black vinyl cushions against his face or the thousand thoughts rushing through his head, Mack Smith might have caught a quick nap on the couch in the lounge while waiting for General Elliott. Instead he spent nearly three hours sliding back and forth on the thoroughly uncomfortable chair, kicking against the rail and wedging his head in the crack at the back. When he finally drifted off, the lights flicked on.

"Sorry, General," he said, rolling upward. But instead of Elliott he saw a tall man in chinos and white shirt.

"Garrison. CIA," said the man. He frowned, as if Mack were sleeping on his time. Or maybe his couch.

"Smith. USAF," said Mack, annoyed.

"I'd like to speak to you about what you saw at the crash site."

"Yeah, you and the rest of the world," said Mack. "But I'm not talking to anybody except General Elliott."

"General Elliott is busy," said Garrison.

Mack got up slowly, his body kinked from the couch. At six feet, he was tall for a fighter pilot, but Garrison had at least six inches on him. The spook's hair was so white and thick it looked like a carpet.

"I've already been debriefed. Twice," said Mack.

"Sometimes details have a way of slipping away."

"Don't you have some insurrection to start?" said Mack. He started toward the door, deciding he was hungry.

"Major." The CIA agent grabbed his sleeve.

Mack spun and stuck his finger in Garrison's chest. "These aren't my clothes, Jack. Don't rip them."

Garrison let go so sharply—maybe it was a spook technique, Mack thought—that he nearly fell backward.

"You're a real jerk, you know that?" Mack said.

"That's what they say about you."

Shaking his head, Mack turned toward the door, where he nearly knocked into General Elliott.

"General—"

"Mack, I see you've met Agent Garrison."

"We were just getting introduced," said Garrison.

"Real personable spy," said Mack.

"I'd like to hear you describe the wreckage," Elliott told him. "Agent Garrison should listen too."

Mack frowned, then began recounting what had happened.

"We don't need a blow-by-blow of your courageous encounter with the Iraqi army," said Garrison caustically when Mack began to describe what had happened when the tanks came.

"I just wanted to show that we didn't have enough time for leisurely inspections," Mack said.

"Burn marks?" asked Garrison.

"No," said Mack.

"The edges of the metal where it sheered off—powdery white?"

Mack shrugged. "Look at the pictures."

"They're blurry as hell. You need photography lessons."

"See how good you are at taking pictures when a tank's firing at you."

"Mack, did you see any trace of the missing wing?" asked the general.

"No," said Mack. "I didn't see it in the area, and when all hell broke loose, we had too much else to worry about. How's the PJ?"

"He's fine. They're a tough breed," said Elliott.

"This is inconclusive at best," said Garrison. "I'd still like to get in there."

"Not possible," said Elliott.

The frown Garrison had been wearing since waking Mack deepened. He stared at the general for nearly a minute, then walked from the room.

"What the hell's up his ass, sir?" Mack asked, adding the "sir" belatedly.

"Mr. Garrison and his agency are going to have to defend some rather rash predictions they made," said Elliott. "I expect that accounts for a small portion of his hostility."

"What's going on, General? Do the Iraqis have a new missile?"

"I'm not entirely sure," said Elliott.

"How did they target those planes? The SA-2 radars? Impossible," said Mack. "The F-16, sure, okay. The Weasel operator let it slip through and the Iraqis got seriously lucky. But two Eagles? And what got them? I have a hard time believing they could get nailed by flying telephone poles."

Elliott said nothing.

"How did they do it?" asked Mack.

"How do you think they did it?" asked Elliott.

Mack had flown over Iraq during the Gulf War and nailed a MiG-29 in air-to-air combat. He'd had several encounters with SA-2s, including one where he had seen a missile sail within five or six hundred feet of his canopy. But he couldn't imagine how a pair of Eagle pilots could get shot down in the same engagement, especially with a Weasel flying shotgun; it just shouldn't, wouldn't, couldn't happen.

"Honestly, I don't know what hit the F-16 I saw," he told Elliott. "Maybe it was a new kind of missile, something like the Russian SA-4 with a proximity fuse and shrapnel, or maybe just a fluke whack that got the wing, shattering it without exploding or at least without a fire. But I don't know, operating in a bizarre radar band the jammers didn't see? And that not even the AWACS could track? I really don't think it's possible."

"Neither do I," said the general.

**Dreamland
1002**

DANNY LOOKED AT THE CALLER ID SCREEN, TRYING TO puzzle out the number. It had a New York City area code but wasn't Jemma's apartment or school. It might be Jimmy Ferro, or even Blaze, his buddy from the bad days in Bosnia.

Then again, it probably wasn't.

He grabbed it just before it would have rolled over into the answering system.

"Danny Freah."

"Daniel, hello. Jim Stephens."

Danny couldn't place him.

"I used to be Al D'Amato," said Stephens. It was obviously meant as a joke, but the name still didn't register for Danny. "I worked for the senator. I was his alter ego. I was talking with your wife Jemma the other day and I told her I'd call."

Oh yeah—the politico. "Hi," said Danny.

"Listen, I'd like to sit down some time and talk about your future."

"My future?"

"I like to think of myself as something of a scout. I have a lot of friends, a lot of people who are interested in giving other people the right kind of start."

In his junior year of high school Danny had been briefly—very briefly—recruited by two colleges, which offered athletic scholarships for his football skills. That was his first introduction to the wonderful world of unadulterated bullshit. He fought off the flashback.

"I don't need a start," he told Stephens.

"No, you've actually got it all started already. Headed in the right direction, definitely. Can I talk frankly? There aren't many people like you in government right now. Straight-shooters. Honest. Military background."

"That's a plus?"

"I checked with some friends in Washington. You have quite an impressive record, Captain."

"Uh-huh."

"Long-term, you could make important contributions to your country, very important contributions. There aren't many of us in important jobs right now," he added. "And the Republican party is wide open. Believe me, Captain, you have a real future. An important future. The country needs a wide base of people in government. Congress. There are too many lawyers and milquetoasts there now. We have a duty to straighten it out."

Stephens sounded sincere; he probably *was* sincere,

Danny thought. And the duty card, if not the race card, did resonate with him.

But he wasn't quitting the Air Force, certainly not to become a politico.

Could he stay in here forever? Away from Jemma?

It was important, and it was thrilling, but it was dangerous, very dangerous. And it made it very difficult to raise kids.

Which he did want.

"A job in D.C. helping a committee make the right choices for the military, hop from that into an election inside a year," Stephens continued. "Fast-track to Congress if we pick the right district. From there, who knows? The sky's the limit."

"Yeah," said Danny finally. "You know what? You got me at a bad time."

"Oh, not a problem, Captain. Not a problem at all. We should talk in person sometime. Have lunch. No pressure or anything like that—this is a thing you'd want to think about for a long time. Talk with Jemma about, of course."

"Yeah. Well, listen, I have your number here. I'll give you a call soon."

Stephens hesitated ever so slightly, but remained upbeat. "Great. Think about it, Captain."

"I will," said Danny, hanging up.

Dreamland
1357

COLONEL BASTIAN SAT BACK FROM HIS DESK AS GIBBS barged into the office.

"Your meeting, sir," said Ax. "Everyone's down in the torture chamber wondering where you are. But you didn't sign my papers."

"I'll get them later, Ax."

A frown flew across the chief master sergeant's face. "Let's take them in the elevator," offered Ax. "You can sign them on the fly and be done."

"I have to read them."

"Ah, these aren't reading ones. I didn't read half of them myself."

Dog pushed his chair back and rose, shaking his head. But instead of picking up one of the three piles of forms and files on Bastian's desk, the chief put up his hand.

"Colonel, a word." Gibbs's voice suddenly became uncharacteristically officious. "I have the identity of the F-15 pilots. Back channel, of course."

Bastian nodded.

"Both on temporary assignment with the 10th. Major Stephen Domber." Ax paused to let Bastian run the name against his mental file of friends and comrades without finding a match. "Wing Commander Colonel Anthony Priestman. They call him—"

"Hammer," said Bastian.

"Yes, sir," said Ax. "Looks like DIA."

Bastian walked quickly out of the office suite, nodding at the secretaries outside but not pausing to say anything. Ax followed him out. Inside the elevator car, the chief held up papers, pointing to where they should be initialed. Bastian gave each only a cursory glance before signing off.

Dreamland
1412

THE SECOND ZEN TOOK A SIP OF THE SODA, HE KNEW IT was a big mistake. The ice cold soda hit the filling in the back of his mouth like a Maverick missile unbuttoning a

T-72 main battle tank. Trying to stifle his yelp of pain, he ended up coughing instead, sending a spray of soda over the video display at the console in Dreamland's secure center. Fortunately, Major Cheshire had just begun her presentation, clicking a large map of northern Iraq onto the screen at the front of the room. She swung the combination remote-control laser pointer around, flashing its arrow at the upper-right-hand corner of the screen.

"The first aircraft went down in this vicinity," said Major Cheshire. "The pilot was recovered approximately here. The F-15s were struck while they were following this route. Barrage-launched SAMs, at least some of which were unguided at launch, are thought to have taken them out. The missile bases on the next screen have been struck." A political map with a half-dozen radar dishes covered by explosions appeared. "You'll have to forgive the graphics. Our friend Jed at the NSC prepared them for, uh, for some VIPs," she added tactfully. "I won't run through the entire radar sets or the missiles, but SA-2s, some Threes, and a Roland launcher were struck this afternoon, their time. Iraq is ten hours ahead," she added, "which makes it an hour after Turkey."

"It's midnight in Baghdad," said Danny Freah dryly. "In more ways than one."

Zen had flown over Iraq in the war and knew exactly how dangerous it could be. The fact that there was still some doubt about what had shot down the fighters bothered him, as well as the others, even though that sort of thing sometimes took days to figure out. Obviously the Iraqis had some sort of new strategy or missile, or maybe both. The Flighthawks would be close to immune, but there had been no time to complete the complicated painting of *Quicksilver*'s nose necessary to help deflect radar. While the plane would still be comparatively stealthy, he knew that Bree would be in that much more danger.

So would he, of course, flying the U/MFs in their belly. But he ordinarily didn't think of himself as even aboard it—he was in the Flighthawks. Besides, he didn't worry about himself.

"There will be an additional round of strikes in the morning. CentCom is ramping up," said Cheshire. "An operation to recover the two Eagle pilots is ongoing. There was no word at last report."

"The prospects aren't very good," said Danny.

"This operation may continue for quite a while," continued Cheshire. "Iraq has ordered UN weapons' inspectors out of the country, and the President is considering a wide range of options. In the meantime, we've been asked to deploy two Elint-capable Megafortresses to provide CentCom with round-the-clock real-time surveillance of the Iraqi radio net, command communications, and other electronic transmission data. Two specialists familiar with Rivet Joint missions have been detailed to join us in-country; we're hoping to get two more. Jennifer Gleason and Kurt Ming will accompany us to help facilitate their familiarization with the gear, which of course they're not up to speed on. Let me cut to the chase," she said, pressing the small clicker in her hand.

A large map of southeastern Turkey appeared on the screen.

"To the extent possible, we'd like to preserve operational secrecy regarding our deployment. Additionally, from a strategic intelligence perspective, the Elint-capable model of the Megafortress remains highly classified. As such, we'd like to find another base to operate from besides Incirlik. Danny Freah and I, along with Colonel Shepherd from the Material Transport Command, have come up with a solution involving a small, disused airstrip twenty miles from the Iraqi border."

Cheshire clicked her remote again. An arrow appeared

in the right-hand corner of the map—extremely close to a wide line showing the Iraq-Turkey border.

"There's a village nearby, connected by a donkey road through the hills. It's called Al Derhagdad. We'll designate it 'High Top,' unless someone comes up with something better."

Zen and some of the others snickered when Cheshire said "donkey road," but she wasn't making a joke.

"We're close to the border, but the terrain is almost impassable except by foot," said Cheshire.

"Or donkey," said Danny—he wasn't joking either.

"Security will be provided by a Whiplash team, to be supplemented by a detachment of Marines from the 24th MEU(SOC) available for reinforcement. We're still hanging on the Marine timetable. They may come with us, they may not; we're still working that out."

"For the uninitiated," said Bastian, "which included myself until a half hour ago, MEU stands for Marine Expeditionary Unit, and SOC means they're special operations capable. The 24th has been in the area before; they kicked Saddam out during Operation Provide Comfort. They're our kind of guys," added the colonel, "even if they are Marines."

Everyone laughed except Cheshire, who remained stone-faced as she flipped through a series of satellite photos of the airstrip and surrounding terrain. Zen nudged the keyboard at his console, getting a close-up of the last photo in her sequence.

"Nancy, is this scale right?" he asked. "Six hundred feet?"

"The strip is presently six hundred feet," she said.

"I can't even land the Flighthawks there," said Zen.

"We're going to make it longer," she said. "This area here is flat and wide enough, with the exception of this ridge here. The ridge only stands about eighteen inches high; if we get rid of it, we think we can get it to fifteen hundred. Danny has worked out a plan. Incirlik is our backup, but for security reasons we prefer not to fly the Megafortresses out of there."

Zen glanced toward Breanna as Cheshire continued. She'd obviously gone over this earlier, but even so, her lips were pressed tightly together.

"Taking off should be no problem. We can use the Flighthawks and/or the short-field assist packs. Since we'll have access to the tankers out of Incirlik, we can keep our takeoff weight to a bare minimum fuelwise. And of course we'll have braking parachutes. They'll work," added Cheshire, apparently seeing some skepticism in the pilots' faces. Though the chutes had been used in B-52s, they were not exactly standard equipment on the Megafortress.

"So how do we get rid of that ridge?" said Zen, ignoring his receding toothache. "And even if you do that, I see maybe seven hundred feet you can lay mesh over, but what about that hill at the end there?"

"We have something special planned." There was a note of triumph in Cheshire's voice. She pressed her remote and the satellite photo morphed into a live feed from one of the Dreamland weapons development labs. A small, white-haired woman frowned in the middle of the screen.

"Dr. Klondike."

"That would be *Mrs.* Klondike," said the weapons scientist testily.

"Hi, Annie," said Danny.

The old woman squinted at a monitor in the lab. "Captain."

"Dr. Klondike," said Cheshire, "if you could explain—"

"That would be *Mrs.* Klondike."

"Mrs. Klondike, if you could explain about the special application JSOW—"

"Yes. In fact, the configuration of the Joint Standoff Weapons was tried last year and found to be wanting, so we redesigned the delivery vehicle around a standard AGM-86 ALCM frame. But the key was—"

"What *Mrs.* Klondike is talking about," said Major Cheshire, losing her patience, "is a controlled explosion to blast the rock into bits. They create a field of explosive powder by exploding very small weapons, focusing the blast in such a way that they can control the shape of the force. I'm told it's similar to the principle of an air-fuel bomb."

"That is *most* inaccurate," said Klondike on the screen.

"We'll move a bulldozer in, lay the steel mesh, and land the planes," continued Cheshire.

"As Jeff pointed out, most of the runway is already there," said Danny, looking at Zen. "Annie's bombs will take care of the rest. She knows her stuff."

"Thank you, Captain."

"We'll run the 'dozer over it before we pop down the mesh," said Danny. "Once we're established, we ought to be able to expand a bit more. Some Pave Lows used the site yesterday or earlier this morning, and the Turks landed helos and light aircraft there in the eighties. I honestly don't anticipate too much of a problem."

"You don't have to try landing a Megafortress on a postage stamp," said Ferris.

"How long's this going to take?" asked Major Alou. "Two days? Three?"

"Two hours," said Danny. "Maybe four."

"Two hours?" Alou laughed. "Right."

"The area will have to be examined before the explosion," said Mrs. Klondike testily. "And then the detonation points calibrated and adjusted prior to the launch of the weapons. The captain is, as always, optimistic concerning the timetable."

"Nah. I have faith in you, Annie."

"It's not the weapon I'm referring to."

"You're getting a bulldozer in there?" asked Zen.

"That part's easy," said Danny. "C-17 slows down and we kick it out the back."

"Who works it?"

"My equipment guy, Egg Reagan."

"Oh, the Pave Low pilot," Zen said, laughing. He'd heard two different versions of the Whiplash team member's stint as a helicopter pilot the other day. One claimed that he'd almost put the bird into the side of Glass Mountain; the other claimed that he did.

"Don't worry," said Danny. "You'll be pulling operations there twenty-four hours from now. We may use two 'dozers, just to be sure."

"Even if we take off in thirty minutes," said Chris, "it'll take twelve, fifteen hours to get there."

"Fourteen," said Breanna. "With refueling. We can push it a little faster. *Raven* will launch the tactical sats to maintain communication with Dreamland Command. *Quicksilver* will take the Flighthawks and the AGMs."

"I have a question, Colonel," said Zen, trying to ignore the stab of pain from his tooth as he spoke. "Why the hell is Saddam shooting at us now? What's his game plan? Beat up on the Kurds?"

Bastian had been involved in the planning for the air war during the Gulf conflict and had spent considerable time not only in Saudi Arabia but behind the scenes in D.C. That didn't make him an expert on Saddam Hussein—in Zen's opinion the dictator was certifiably insane—but if anyone on the base would have a good handle on the conflict there, it was the colonel.

Dog got up and walked toward the front. He began

slowly, deliberately, but as he came down the steps to the center of the semicircular room, his movements sped up. An ominous majesty seemed to descend over him even before he spoke.

"I don't know why the Iraqis are trying to provoke us. As far as I'm concerned, it's irrelevant." He was standing erect as he spoke, yet somehow seemed to draw himself even taller and straighter before continuing. "Getting to the Gulf is not going to be a picnic, and neither are the missions. But we've just lost three planes, and unofficially it doesn't look good for two of the men. That toll may increase by the time you get there. This is precisely the sort of job we were created to handle. We're going to do it, and do it well. Questions?"

Dreamland
1522

AN HOUR AFTER COLONEL BASTIAN'S SPEECH, HIS DAUGH-ter sat in the pilot's seat of *Quicksilver*, going through her final preflight checks.

"Check, check, double-check, green, green, green, chartreuse, green," sang Chris Ferris, her copilot.

"Chartreuse?" asked Breanna.

"Did you know that chartreuse is green?"

"Well, *duh*."

"I never knew that. Honest to God. I thought it was pink or something. Red."

"Any more colors on your chart today?"

"Negative. Ready to take off, Captain. Good to have you back."

"Good to be back, Chris." Breanna hunched her shoulders forward against her seat restraints, unlocking her muscles. She remembered Merce Alou's preflight prayer.

What the hell, she thought. Then she laughed, realizing it wasn't exactly righteous to be using the word hell in connection to prayer, even in her mind.

Then she prayed.

Lord, help us today, she thought, then turned to Ferris. "Ready, Captain?"

"And willing."

"Major Stockard, are you ready?"

"I'm ready for you anytime, baby," said Zen, who was sitting downstairs in the U/MF control bay.

"A little decorum, Major," snapped Breanna. She checked with each of her passengers in turn, making sure that they were all snugged and ready to go. Behind Breanna and Ferris on *Quicksilver*'s stretched flight deck were the two specialists who would handle the electronics sniffing gear, Master Sergeant Kelly O'Brien and, on loan from an Army SOF unit, Sergeant First Class Sereph Habib.

An Arab language specialist, Habib had been at nearby Edwards Air Force base for a joint services exercise and still seemed dazed at how quickly he had been shanghaied. He answered, "Present, ma'am," when Breanna asked if he was ready to go.

The upstairs or back bay of *Quicksilver*—the domain of the defensive weapons operators in a standard B-52—ordinarily contained two additional Elint stations, as well as space for the collection computers that processed and stored the gathered intelligence. The secondary control panels for the gear had been removed to save space, as had some of the black boxes. In their place sat a collection of spare parts, two medium tents, sleeping bags, and enough MREs to ruin appetites for a week. In between the supplies were Jeff Hiu, one of the electronics wizards responsible for *Quicksilver*'s "Deep Drink" ALR-98 intercept receiver suite, and Staff Sergeant Louis Garcia, who'd brought along a Walkman and a sizable portion of his Bob Dylan collection.

No change of clothes, though.

Sitting next to Zen downstairs in what would have been the radar navigator/bombardier's post on a standard B-52 was Captain Michael Fentress, Zen's apprentice and gofer on the mission. Zen had included him in the mission reluctantly—after being ordered to do so by Colonel Bastian.

"For those of you who aren't regular passengers, *Quicksilver* is not quite an airliner," Bree told them. "Please keep your restraints on until we reach altitude. We have a long flight, and a bit of weather along the way, but we should be well over it. I'll wake you up when we're getting close to Turkey. Any questions?"

"Where's the bathroom on this thing?" asked Habib.

There were a few snickers.

"Chris, can you help the sergeant out once we're under way?"

"You got it."

"Can you cross your legs until then, Sergeant?"

"Guess I'll have to."

Quicksilver's four single-podded power plants were a special set of Pratt & Whitneys, highly modified from the engines originally developed for the F-22 Raptor. This latest variation on engine configuration for the Megafortress traded off a bit of speed for greatly increased range, but the thrusters could definitely get the plane off the ground in a hurry. Cleared by Dream Tower, Breanna pushed the slider to maximum takeoff power, released the brakes, and pointed *Quicksilver*'s new and still unpainted nose toward the wild blue. The plane lifted off smoothly, her wings drooping ever so slightly because of the weight of the Flighthawks strapped below. Breanna felt a brief flutter of apprehension as the indicated airspeed dropped a few seconds off the runway, but the problem was momentary, maybe even just an indicator glitch.

"We're green, we're green," said Chris quickly.

"Clean the gear," said Breanna.

The plane began picking up speed as the massive wheels slid up into their bays.

"Looking good, crew," she said as they climbed through five thousand feet. "Just thirteen hours and fifty-nine minutes to go."

Over the Pacific
1672

AMONG DREAMLAND'S LESS GLAMOROUS PROJECTS WAS designing a replacement for the venerable C-130 Hercules transport, a capable and highly versatile aircraft that came in an almost endless series of flavors. The Hercules was such a successful aircraft, in fact, that the wizards at Dreamland could not hope to fully top her—though even Herky bird partisans might claim they had come close with the MC-17B/W, which was taking Danny Freah and his six-man Whiplash advance team to Turkey. Based on the short-field capable C-17, the MC-17B/W had been thoroughly refashioned. Besides the dark black paint job, the most noticeable difference between the Whiplash mutation and the standard Globemaster III was the multiconfigurable wingtips that made up about a third of the outer wing, just inside the winglets. The leading and trailing edges had double trapezoid panels that generally operated as standard leading and trailing edge slats, functioning much as the C-17's considerably smaller ones did. But the slats also had narrow hinge stakes, allowing them to be set as miniature wings; when set, they looked a little like small biplane sections at the end of each wing. The effect increased the aircraft's ability to land on short airfields, even with a full load. Where the standard C-17 could deliver 150 troops or 81,000 pounds of cargo to an airstrip of 625 yards—an incredible achievement in itself— the MC-17B could land the same load in half the distance. The stock P&W PW2040s with their 41,700 pounds of thrust could get a fully loaded C-17 into the sky at 1,200 feet; the Whiplash version needed a hair under eight hundred, though that involved a bit of prayer and a stiff wind. And the notoriously turbulent airsteam that made certain parachuting deliveries difficult—especially those involving troops—had been tamed by the Dreamland experts.

To the seven men in the cargo area of the big plane, however, the major difference between the Dreamland mover and all others came down to eight regulation-size cots, one large-screen TV, and one oversize poker table, all squeezed into a self-contained, motorized trailer that had been designed to fit in the rear bay. Not only did it fit, but it left room for two large, skid-mounted bulldozers, which were to be air-dropped in a low-and-slow insertion at the temporary base.

Which they had never practiced from the aircraft.

Danny Freah was not worried about the drop; the mission specialists aboard the MC-17B/W had more than twenty-five years of experience between them, the pilot and copilot had been flying together for years, and, at least in theory, he thought the Whip Loader ought to be at least as good at delivering "packages" as the standard model. Nor was he concerned about Annie Klondike's special-order AGM-86s; the diminutive weapons scientist had demonstrated her far-ranging talents often in the past. Freah wasn't even bothered by the fact that "his" MV-22 Osprey, which was too large to fit in the MC-17, wouldn't be arriving in theater until a day, or maybe even more, after he arrived. After all, they weren't expected to go anywhere.

Freah's worries had to do with intelligence, or rather, the lack of it. His entire store of information on the area they were flying into amounted to a single paragraph, which itself could be summarized in one word: mountainous. The area to the south was populated by Kurds, and it had been surveyed by American forces during Operation Provide Comfort in 1991. But things had changed dramatically there in the past five or six years. Some of the Kurds the Americans had helped in their rebellion against Saddam Hussein were now allied with the dictator. Others were involved in an all-out war with the Turks. And the CIA backgrounder he had on his notebook computer said that the Iranians were funding two other Kurd groups, trying to foment revolution, or at least give their old enemy Saddam Hussein headaches.

The Iranians weren't likely to be friendly. The Iraqis definitely were enemies. The Kurds might or might not be, depending on their mood. The Turks, ostensibly allies, were arguably the most deadly of all.

He had six men to hold the base with. The Marines wouldn't be available for at least forty-eight hours.

"Read 'em and weep," said Sergeant Kevin Bison at the poker table just beyond the cot where Danny was reading. "Ladies over jacks. Full house."

"Nice, but not as good as four eights," said Sergeant Lee Liu.

Bison threw down his cards. "You musta had that up your sleeve, Nurse."

Liu laughed. He'd gotten the nickname "Nurse" because of his paramedic training, though in fact all of the Whiplash team members could pull duty as medics.

"Down your pants, more likely, Bison," said Powder.

"Screw you," snapped Bison.

"All right, boys, think about getting some sleep," said Freah, snapping his laptop closed. "We have a long day ahead of us. We're jumping in six hours."

"Hey, Cap, can I ride the 'dozer down?" said Powder. The others laughed, but he wasn't necessarily kidding.

"Tell you what, Powder," answered Freah. "I hear anything out of you or anybody else that doesn't sound like a snore, I'll strap you to the blade and push you out myself."

Dreamland
1810

COLONEL BASTIAN GLANCED AT HIS WATCH AND JUMPED from his desk—he was supposed to meet Jennifer at the Dolphin dock ten minutes ago.

Then he remembered she'd deployed as part of the technical team supporting the Megafortresses. She was in Alou's plane to monitor the launch of their tactical satellites—one to ensure wide-band instant communications between the team and Dream Control, the other a small optical satellite officially known as a KH-12/Z sub-orbital surveillance platform, and more generally as the KH-12-mini. Propelled by solid-fuel boosters, the sats would be launched from *Raven* over the Atlantic. Their low orbits and small size meant they'd only "live" for a few weeks before burning up in the atmosphere, but that was perfectly suited for the mission.

Dog sat back down in his seat slowly. He was done with Chief Gibbs's paperwork for the day, but he had a pile of reports to look at on the right side of his desk. At the very top was one dealing with ANTARES, or Artificial Neural Transfer and Response System, the once-promising experiment to use human brain impulses to control aircraft.

To say that the experiment had failed was incorrect, or at least imprecise. What it had done was make its subject into a paranoid schizophrenic who'd actively participated in a plot to destroy an American city with a nuclear device. Intercepted before he could reach his target, he'd tried to strike Dreamland itself.

If it were up to Dog, the ANTARES equipment and all of the records would be ground into little pieces. But it wasn't up to him. His job was only to make a recommendation to the NSC. He picked up the report, written by Martha Geraldo, who had headed the program, and began reading.

> The potential of the human mind is awesome and incredible. We have seen its darkest side as a result of the ANTARES experiments and the so-called Nerve Center affair. In the future, artificial neuron connections may allow for the control of an entire squadron or wing of aircraft. At present, however, we clearly do not understand enough about the human brain to continue in the vein we have undertaken.

Dog realized that even though it sounded negative, Geraldo was gearing up to make an argument to continue the program, albeit in a drastically changed fashion. Maybe she was right—maybe a great deal of good could come from it. But he just wasn't in the mood to read an argument in favor of a project that had cost one of his best people and nearly killed his daughter. He tossed the report down on his to-be-read-later pile on the floor. It was already nearly a foot high.

He knew that Tony Priestman, aka Hammer, would have told him to deal with it right away. That was his main philosophy as a flight leader—attack.

Maybe that's what got him shot down over Iraq, Dog thought.

He had been a freshly minted hotshot jock when he met Hammer. Then a captain, Hammer wasn't all that much older than he was, and nowhere near as good a pilot. However, he did have five years more experience—five years that included a short but eventful stint over Vietnam at the very end of the war. Dog served as his wingman in an F-15 squadron, one of the first to fly what was then a hot new aircraft.

Hammer hadn't been particularly kind at first. In fact, he'd never been particularly kind. It took Dog two days to get over the first dressing down—the new F-15 pilot had failed to keep his separation during their flight and had landed a bit fast. It was petty criticism. For weeks afterward, anger mixed with the fear of really screwing up every time he prepped a flight, though they melted once he was in the air—he was, after all, a good pilot, and he knew it.

Gradually, Dog came to realize that Hammer's harassment was a reaction of his own fears. Hammer was much harder on himself, something Dog learned when he sat in on a briefing for the wing commander following a training exercise. Later that same night they found themselves left at a bar together after the rest of their group drifted away. Dog told Hammer he thought he'd done pretty well, certainly better than Hammer seemed to think when he'd told the boss.

Instead of answering, Hammer flicked a cigarette out of the pack in front of him on the bar. He stared at it a moment, then took a silver Zippo lighter from his pocket.

"This lighter belonged to one of my commanders," he said after a drag on the cigarette. "Left it to me when he went home."

Dog expected a story would follow about the lighter or the commander, but instead Hammer slid the Zippo into his pocket and took another puff of the cigarette. Then he sipped his seltzer—he didn't drink, at least not that Dog ever saw. After a few minutes, he went on.

"I got a MiG one afternoon. It was pretty funny, in a way. I should have been nailed myself. They had this tactic—this is end days in the war, remember; I'm just about the last guy out." Hammer sounded almost rueful about the war ending. "Anyway, we go in, drop our sticks la-di-da, and just as we're turning home—well, no, we had recovered and we were still in the process of getting bearings. I'm a little bit back of my lead and we're about to saddle up when this MiG appears. MiG-21. Anyway, they have this tactic where basically what they would do was run one guy out as a decoy, suck you in. They get you to follow, or at least pay attention for a moment—they can turn like all hell, I mean, it's like trying to follow a motorcycle with a tractor trailer. I'm in a Phantom, of course."

"Right," said Dog.

"So anyway, like an idiot—and I mean a true idiot—I bite. My Sidewinder growled on the guy—I'm that close. It happens bing-bang-boom. My lead's here, the MiG comes up out of the bushes there, I'm here."

Hammer gestured in the smoky air of the bar, trying to conjure the remarkable fluidity of a three-dimensional dogfight with his hands. Dog could see it, or imagined he could—the glittering knife of the enemy plane cutting up out of the ground clutter, the tight cockpit of the Phantom, the Sidewinder screaming at him to fire.

"So he starts to turn—I slipped outside the firing envelope." Hammer's hands started to mimic not the flight of the planes but his action on the stick. "So I start to bite because I want the shot and then I realize—and maybe it was actually my backseater or even somebody else in the flight yelling at me, I don't really remember—anyway, I suddenly realized there was going to be another one of these suckers coming at my butt. Because that's what they did. You're here, you start to follow, they get you flat-footed. So instead of following, I flick down—yeah, as incredible as that seems, I roll and duck, and I'm not kidding, I look up and I'm six hundred yards from the second MiG's nose. Nose on nose. He winks—big balls of red and black pop out in front of me. It's not slow motion. It's more like I'm looking at a painting. Everything's stopped. Those flashes are—you ever see that Van Gogh painting of stars at night? 'Starry Night' or something? That's what it is, and it's the middle of the day. And I mean, he's right here, I could have flown right into him. Popped the canopy and shook hands. But I didn't use the gun. It happened so fast, I couldn't."

Even if his weapon were charged and he was ready to fire, the likelihood of scoring a heads-on shot under the circumstances Hammer described were slim. But he suspended his story, blowing a deep puff of smoke into the air from his cigarette to underline his failure.

"So, I turn," he continued finally. He turned his head to the left, as if watching the MiG pass. "He goes that way. I'm—slats, flaps, I would have thrown out an anchor, if I could have, to turn and get on his tail. I would have put the engines into reverse. Rewind."

A long pull on the cigarette took it down to the filter. Hammer put it in the ashtray thoughtfully and picked up the pack for another.

"So I come out of the turn and the first MiG is right there, three-quarters of a mile. Sidewinder growls again. Bing. Launch. And just about then the second MiG splashed my flight leader."

That was the end of the story, and though Dog waited

for details—such as what happened to the two men in the Phantom that went down—Hammer didn't offer them. After a few minutes of silence, he added a postscript: "Never underestimate the importance of luck." Then he left the bar, without lighting the second cigarette.

Hammer's criticism didn't seem quite so harsh after that. In spite of it, Dog and he became reasonably decent friends. Dog was in his wedding party and had been invited to Hammer's son's christening, though he was in Germany at the time and couldn't attend. The boy, whom he'd met several times, would be four or five now.

Hammer and his wife had waited to have kids, largely because he thought what he did for a living carried a hefty risk for a young family. He'd wanted to wait until he was close to retiring. Then he'd enjoy the kid and be safe—safe for him and the wife.

"Penny for your thoughts," said Ax, materializing in front of his desk. "I knocked, Colonel—sorry."

"It's okay, Chief."

"Secure line for you. It's back channel." Ax pointed to the phone.

Dog hesitated, suspecting the call was from someone in the Pentagon looking for inside information he didn't have.

"You're going to want to take it, Colonel," said Ax, who'd retreated to the doorway. "It's Brad Elliott. He's in Turkey."

Dog nodded, then reached for the phone as deliberately as Hammer had sipped his soda that night.

"Hello, General," said Dog.

"Colonel, I have some information I'd like to give you, so that you have a full understanding of the situation over here," said Elliott.

Dog had only spoken to him once or twice; never had

Elliott introduced small talk into the conversation. Which was just fine with him.

"It's unofficial, of course," added Elliott.

"Yes, sir, General."

"I'm not in the Air Force and I'm not your superior," said Elliott. "I don't believe the planes that went down were hit by missiles, contrary to what the analysts are saying."

"I'm not sure I follow," said Dog.

"Tecumseh, how much do you know about Razor?"

In any given week, ten or twelve of the pieces of paper that came across his desk dealt with Razor, the favored nickname for the S-500 mobile deuterium chemical laser system. Ground-based, it was being developed as an anti-aircraft weapon and had an accurate range of roughly three hundred miles. Aside from some niggling problems in the cooling system and some glitches in the targeting computer and radar, the system was ready for production. Indeed, Dreamland was slated to receive some of the first production units for its own air defense system any day now.

"I know a little about it," said Dog.

"My suspicion is that the planes were taken out by a clone. It would account for the fact that the radars weren't on long enough for a missile to acquire the target. The damage is consistent with a Razorlike weapon."

"Everything I've heard points to missiles."

"Everything you've heard is driven by CIA estimates and conventional thinking," said Elliott. "The problem is, no one believes Saddam has a laser, so naturally they're looking for something else."

Deuterium lasers were cutting-edge weapons, and it was difficult to believe a third world country like Iraq could develop them or even support them. Then again, few people had believed Iraq had a nuclear weapons program until the Gulf War and subsequent inspections.

"If this were the Iranians or the Chinese," continued Elliott, "everyone would connect the dots. Let me let you talk to someone who was there."

Before Dog could say anything, Mack Smith came on the line.

"Hey, Colonel, how's the weather back there?"

"Mack?"

"Hi, Colonel. I bet you're wondering why I'm not in Brussels. General Elliott borrowed me. He's on some sort of task force thing, investigating a shoot-down, and since that's my area of expertise, I hopped right to it."

Dog rolled his eyes. Elliott obviously said something to Mack, and Mack's voice became somewhat more businesslike.

"So what do you want to know, sir?" asked Mack. "I'll give you the whole layout. I saw it. Wing came off clean. Has to be a laser. Iraqis must have stolen it."

"Did you take pictures, Mack?"

"Yes, sir. Being processed now. CIA has its head up its ass, but what else is new, right?"

Elliott took back the phone. "You know Major Smith," he said, in a tone one might use when referring to a wayward child.

"Yes," said Dog. "I'd like to get some of my people on this."

"I agree," said Elliott. "Dr. Jansen—"

"Jansen's no longer here, I'm afraid," said Dog. Jansen had headed the Razor development team at Dreamland. "I'll have to check with Dr. Rubeo to get the people together. If we could look at the damage ourselves—"

"Wreckage was blown up in the tangle Mack got involved in," said Elliott. "Some of the people from Livermore who worked on high-energy weapons have been analyzing it for the CIA."

"And they don't think it was a laser?"

"They hem and they haw. The NSA has been picking up information about new radars, and the Iraqis have been working on adapting the SA-2," added Elliott.

"What's CentCom's opinion?"

"Their intelligence people are split. There were a lot of missiles in the air, and at one point the AWACS does seem to pick up a contact near the F-16. On this other shootdown, the AWACS had moved off station and the F-15s were temporarily out of range. Heads are rolling on that." Elliott's voice had a certain snap to it, the quick understatement a commander used to indicate someone down the line had screwed up royally. "Their view is that it's irrelevant to their planning—they have to proceed no matter what the threat. Saddam can't get away with this."

Dog agreed that CentCom had to press its attacks, but a weapon like Razor changed the tactical situation a great deal. Razor had considerably more range and accuracy than conventional antiaircraft weapons, and defeating it was much more difficult. Most SAMs would be neutralized by jamming their radar. In Razor's case, however, that was problematic. The jammer itself was essentially a target beacon, alerting a sophisticated detection system to the plane's location, giving it all the coordinates needed to fire; once the weapon was fired the electronic countermeasures were beside the point—the ray worked essentially instantaneously. On the other hand, waiting to turn the ECMs on until the laser's targeting radar became active was nearly as dangerous. In theory, though not yet in practice, Razor could work on a single return—by the time the radar was detected, it had fired. Other detection systems, including infrared and microwave located far from the laser itself, could also be used to give the weapon targeting data, making it even more difficult to defeat.

But he knew there was no way Saddam could manage the sophistication needed to develop such a complicated weapon, let alone field it. He couldn't even build a secure phone system.

"Is ISA involved?" asked Dog.

"No. We're up to our ears with China and the rest of the Middle East right now. This is CentCom's show. Things are ramping up quickly here, Colonel," said Elliott. "I wanted you to know what you might be up against. The Megafortresses would be prime targets."

Dog leaned back in the chair. The seat, the desk, everything in the office had once belonged to Brad Elliott. He'd built this place, fashioned it into a high-tech center comparable to the fabled Lockheed Skunk Works, maybe even Los Alamos, if you adjusted for the difference in budgets and the times.

Then he'd been kicked out, sacrificed because of politics. No, not entirely, Dog amended. Elliott did bear some responsibility for the so-called Day of the Cheetah spy scandal, if only because he was sitting at this desk when it happened.

He'd landed on his feet with ISA, and yet . . .

"I appreciate the information, General," Dog told him. "I'm going to take it under advisement."

"I don't want our people, your people, getting surprised," said Elliott.

"That's not going to happen," said Dog, sharper than he intended.

Elliott said nothing. It occurred to Dog that the retired general had probably had a hand in getting the Whiplash order issued—in fact, it may have been the reason he'd been sent to investigate in the first place.

"Thank you, General," Dog told him. "I appreciate the heads-up."

"You're welcome."

The line went dead. Dog keyed his phone. "Ax, get Rubeo over here. I need to talk to him."

"Dr. Ray is on his way," said Ax. "How 'bout lunch?"

"How'd you know I wanted to talk to him?"

"Musta been a coincidence," said the chief master sergeant. "Ham or roast beef?"

"Neither," said Dog.

"Yeah, I know you want a BLT. I was just testing you."

Dog was tempted to call Ax's bluff by saying he'd have something completely different, but before he could, there was a knock on the door and an airman entered with a tray.

"Ax," said Dog, still on the phone, "if—"

"Light on the mayo, easy on the burn," said the chief, sounding a little like a short-order cook. "Anything else, Colonel?"

**Incirlik
28 May 1997
0700**

TORBIN DRESSED QUICKLY AND THEN HEADED OVER TO THE squadron ready room, skipping breakfast. Though he'd managed nearly six hours of sleep, his body felt as if he'd spent the time driving a jackhammer into several yards of reinforced concrete. He walked with his head slightly bent, nodding as others passed without actually looking at them. He'd gotten a few steps into the building when a lieutenant called his name and told him that General Harding wanted to talk to him.

Harding was in charge of the wing *Glory B* was assigned to. Torbin didn't know where his office was and had to ask for directions.

"General, I'm Captain Dolk," said Torbin when he finally arrived. He stood in the doorway of the office, one hand on the doorjamb.

"Come in, Captain. Close the door, please."

The general began talking before Torbin sat. The first few words blurred together—rough out there, all hell breaking loose, a difficult job. "The Phantom is an old airframe," continued the general. "I used to fly them myself, back in the Stone Age."

"Yes, sir," said Torbin.

"Things have changed tremendously. Hell, we're using AWACS, standoff weapons, GPS—we're even going to have a pair of Megafortresses helping out. The Wild Weasel mission belongs to an earlier era."

He thinks I fucked up, Torbin realized.

"These days, we can jam radars with ease. Locate 'em, knock 'em out before they turn on. That's the way to go. Much safer than waiting for them to turn on. I have a pair of Spark Varks and a Compass Call en route."

"General, we can still do the job."

Harding drew himself up in the chair and held his round face slightly to the side. His cheeks, ruddy to begin with, grew redder. "There's no mission for you today, son. You're to stand by until further notice."

Torbin waited for the general to continue—to ball him out, to say he screwed up, to call him an idiot. But he didn't.

"I didn't screw up, sir," said Torbin finally. "I didn't. My pilot didn't and I didn't."

Harding stared at him. He didn't frown, but he sure didn't smile. He just stared.

"I'll do anything I can," said Torbin finally. "Anything. The radars that came on, the missiles—they were too late and too far to hit those F-15s."

"I appreciate your sentiments," said Harding.

Torbin felt the urge to smash something, kick the door or punch the wall. He wanted to rage: *No way I screwed up! No stinking way!*

But he took control of himself, nodded to the general, then walked slowly from the office.

Aboard *Quicksilver*, over southeastern Turkey 1300

ZEN FELT A SUDDEN SHOCK OF DISPLACEMENT AS THE Flighthawk slipped away from the Megafortress, launching herself as the mothership rose on the stiff wind's eddy. No matter how many times he did this, it still took a moment to adjust to the difference between what his body felt and what his eyes and brain told him it should feel.

And then he was in the Flighthawk, seeing and feeling the plane through his control helmet and joystick. He fingered the speed slider and nudged toward the rift in the peaks where the scratch strip sat.

"Systems in the green," said Fentress, monitoring the flight from his station next to Zen.

"Thanks." Zen pushed the Flighthawk downward against the violent and shifting winds. A thick layer of clouds sat between the Flighthawk and the airstrip, but the synthesized view in his screen showed every indentation in the rocks and even gave a fairly accurate rendering of the brownish-gray concrete that formed the landing area. It looked to be in much better shape than they'd expected.

Still, even if Danny's plan worked, the strip was going to be on the narrow side. Zen slid the Flighthawk into a bank, gliding five thousand feet above the shallow ridge that formed the main obstacle to lengthening the runway.

"I'm going to get under the clouds so we can get the

precise measurements," he told Breanna over the inter-phone.

"Go for it."

"Looks narrow down there, Bree," he added.

"Thanks for the vote of confidence."

Zen slipped under the clouds and manually selected the video feed for his main display. Mountaintops spread out on the horizon, giants sleeping beneath green and brown mottled blankets.

"Bree could slide pickles into an olive jar," said Chris Ferris, the copilot.

"Watch your language," joked Breanna.

"I didn't say you couldn't handle it," Zen said. "I said it would be tight."

"I thought you slept on the way over," said Breanna.

"I did. Why?"

"You sound a little testy."

"Airspeed dropping," said Fentress.

"No shit," snapped Zen, turning his full attention back to his plane. Indicated airspeed had nudged below 300 knots. He backed his power off even more, letting it slide through 250. The small-winged U/MF became in-creasingly unstable as its speed dropped, but Zen needed the slow speed so they could get a good read on the target area. "Computer, begin dimension survey as programmed."

"Computer," acknowledged the Flighthawk's C^3 flight system. "Dimension survey initiated."

"Captain Fentress, give the feed to the flight deck," said Zen.

"Aye aye, sir," said Fentress, apparently trying to joke—a new development that Zen had to leave unre-marked, as the Flighthawk hit a gnarly gust of wind. He ramped up thrust but was nudged off course and had to start the whole run over again.

"If we had more altitude, I could get a better angle for Captain Freah," said Fentress, who was giving Freah the feed so he could plot his jump after the missiles did their work. "Save some time."

"Curly, let me fly my plane, okay? We'll do it like we rehearsed."

"Yes, sir," said Fentress.

They were silent until he reached the end of the runway area and began recovering.

"We've got it up here, Jeff," said Breanna. "Glitch downloading the targeting data to the missiles. Take us a minute."

"Flighthawk commander acknowledges."

"Getting awful formal," said his wife.

"Just doing my job, *Quicksilver* leader."

Breanna didn't answer. Chris Ferris marked the location on the Megafortress's automated targeting system, then opened the bomb bay doors. The two hand-built missiles whose noses looked like spherical clusters glued together sat on a massive rotating bomb rack in the rear of the plane. Ferris gave a countdown to launch, handing the process to the computer at five seconds. A sharp metallic *trrrrshhhhh* sounded over the interphone circuit as the first missile launched; 3.2 seconds later the second tore away.

"Ground wire loose somewhere," said Louis Garcia, who was sitting in the rear bay. "Going to have to fix that when we get down."

"Three seconds to target," said Ferris. "Two, one—"

Over southeastern Turkey
1310

WHEN THE BACK DOOR OF THE MC-17 OPENED, THE TEMperature inside the hold dropped dramatically. The cold bit at Captain Danny Freah's skin despite the layers of thermals and special drop suit he wore. But at least it meant they'd be getting to work soon—the worst part of any operation was the wait.

Danny moved his hand up to the visor of his combat helmet, clicking the control to increase the resolution on the feed he was receiving from Zen's U/MF. A fair amount of smoke lingered from the explosion, but the weapons seemed to have done their job perfectly.

"We're up next," said the transport pilot. The communications and video were piped in through a hardwire; the MC-17B/W did not yet have an internal wireless connection. "Should be good to go in zero-one minutes."

"Show's under way," Danny told the others in his team.

"Look alive, look alive," said Hernandez, the team jumpmaster. Though he'd already checked everyone's equipment twice in the past five minutes, he began one last inspection.

"First pass is for the 'dozers," Danny said, though the reminder wasn't necessary.

"Sure I can't ride one down?" asked Powder.

"Next jump," said Danny.

"He just wants to make sure he gets his turn driving," said Egg Reagan. "Trying to bump me."

"I ain't bumpin' you. It's Nursey who shouldn't be at the wheel. You ever ride in a Humvee with him?"

"I'm not the one who lost his license," answered Nurse.

"Who lost their license?" asked Danny.

"Just a rumor," said Powder.

"We're cleared," said the MC-17B/W pilot. "Dust is settling. Okay, boys, look good."

One of the loadmasters near the tail ramp waved a fist in the air, then pushed a button on the thick remote control panel in his hand. The bulldozer closest to the doorway jerked forward on its skid; lights flashed above the opening. In the meantime, the MC-17 slowed dramatically, its jet engines whining and shuddering. Danny tightened his grip on the rail behind him as the plane turned herself into an elevator, gliding down ten stories in the space of a few half seconds. The two bulldozers lurched forward on their automated launch ramp. They slowed as they cleared the door, seeming to stop in midair before bobbing outward, one after another.

Danny turned his gaze back to the top half of his visor and its feed from the Flighthawk. A lot of dust, nothing else. Then a large black rock furled into view, followed by another. As the U/MF flew past, smoke and dust started to clear and Danny saw the drogue chutes chuttering off to the right, the 'dozers sitting on the ground.

"Fuel's up," said the loadmaster. Two more crates made their way toward the door. These were perfectly square. Four barrels of diesel fuel for the 'dozers, along with some hand pumps and additional equipment, were contained inside custom-made cylinders packed into the spidery interior lattice of the special shock-absorbing crates. Following the fuel were two more skids with jackhammers and assorted gear. After they were out, the MC-17 began climbing to give them a little more room for their jump.

"Wind's a bitch out there, boys," said Hernandez. "Be sharp."

"As a pin," said Powder.

Danny took a breath as the yellow light came on above the door, indicating that they were almost ready. He took his place in the second line, still holding the rail as they waited for Hernandez's signal. The seven men on the team went out practically together, two teams abreast holding hands.

A "normal" rig for a recreational parachuter always includes a special altimeter device to deploy an emergency parachute once the jumper passes a preset altitude in case the main chute fails. A device that worked on essentially the same principles in the Whiplash jumpers' gear deployed their MC-5 ram-air parachutes based on a preprogrammed glide course. Sending GPS data as well as altimeter readings to their combat helmets, the "smart rigs" turned the Whiplash team members into miniature airplanes. They steered the boxy, rectangular chutes through the swirling winds, their bodies lurching as counterweights as they fought through the difficult fall. All seven men came down within ten yards of each other—a tight squeeze between the equipment and the work area, though if this had been an exercise at Dreamland or the Military Free Fall Simulator at Fort Bragg, Danny would have made them repack and jump again.

Stowing his chute quickly, the captain cleared his rucksack off the work area and recalibrated his smart helmet's com set, waiting while it searched for the tactical communications satellite deployed by *Raven*. That took only about five seconds, but by then the others were already pumping fuel into the 'dozers, which seemed to have come down okay. Danny walked over to the pile of rubble created by the AGM-86s.

There were rocks all over the place. Annie had promised a fairly even pile.

But the ridge itself was gone, and the pockmarks from the explosion seemed a few inches deep at most. They'd have it flattened and meshed in no time.

"All right, get the 'dozers, let's go," yelled Danny. "The rest of you guys, get the equipment squared away and then get ready for the mesh. Should be here in thirty minutes."

"You sure we can get it all down, Cap?" asked Bison. "Timetable's tight."

"Bison, if you had a problem, you should have spoken up before," said Danny.

"No sir, not a problem."

"He's just trying to slow things down because he's got the latest time in the pool," said Powder.

"What pool?"

"We bet on how long it would take," admitted Bison sheepishly.

"You guys get to work before I make you take out hammers and pound these boulders into dust," Danny told them.

Liu fired up his bulldozer first, moving it off the thick planks of its landing crate. The sergeant had claimed that he had worked two summers with a construction firm; as improbable as that seemed—Liu stood perhaps five-six and weighed 120 soaking wet—he had demonstrated at Dreamland that he knew how to work the 'dozer, slamming the levers around like an expert. He pushed ahead now, angling the rocks straight off a shallow cliff at the right side of the strip.

Egg had trouble getting his 'dozer started.

"Hey, use it or lose it," shouted Powder from the ground as Egg fumbled with the ignition.

"What's the story?" shouted Danny.

"Something's screwed up with the engine," said Egg. He pulled off his glasses, cleaning them on his shirt, then pushed back his cap on his bald head as he studied the machine. He looked more than a little like an owl in cammies.

"Pull out the doohickey," said Powder.

"Shut up," snapped Egg. He leaned over the front of the 'dozer, looking in the direction of the engine.

"Loose wire or something?" Danny asked.

"You got to pull the doohickey out. It's basically a Volkswagen with a big ol' blade on it," said Powder.

"What the hell is he talking about?" Danny asked Egg, who by now was strung over the front of the machine.

"Got me, Cap."

"Can I try?" Powder asked.

Danny was about to order him to help square away the rest of the gear when Egg jumped down. "You want to try it? Go ahead, fucker. Be a wise guy."

"Captain—if I get it going, can I drive it?"

"Go ahead," insisted Egg before Danny could say anything. "Come on, know-it-all. Let's see you start it up. This is a diesel. It's not a Volkswagen. It's a bull-fucking-dozer."

"Bull-fucking-dozer," laughed Powder, clambering into the seat.

"He'll never get it going," Egg told Danny. "No way he's going to. I think the—"

The rumble of the second 'dozer coming to life drowned out the rest of what the team's heavy equipment expert had to say.

Aboard *Quicksilver*, over southeastern Turkey
1413

ZEN EASED THE FLIGHTHAWK BACK BEHIND THE MEGA-fortress then gave the verbal command, "Trail One," telling the computer to put the plane into a preprogrammed escort course behind the mothership. They had refueled just before approaching the target area; assuming things went well on the ground, they'd have nothing to do for the next two hours. A pair of MH-60 Pave Hawk helicopters were en route out of Incirlik, escorting Chinooks carrying runway mesh. O'Brien and Habib, meanwhile, had finished testing the combat configuration on *Quicksilver*'s Deep Drink sensor suite and were scanning Iraq for signs of trouble.

The Deep Drink gear, which was carried by *Raven* as

well as *Quicksilver*, could be divided into two broad categories. The first was a set of radar receivers and jammers. A passive-detection system swept six bands and was capable of finding radars five hundred miles away, depending on their strength and profile. A high-powered detector could analyze A-J radar bands simultaneously, delivering real-team target data directly to GPS-based munitions or to B-1 and B-2 bombers equipped to receive it. And there was a combination repeater-transponder-noise jammer that worked like the ALQ-199 ECM unit.

Deep Drink's second set of capabilities were based around a wide net of wires and dishes embedded in the Megafortress's skeleton, turning the plane into a giant radio antenna, a combat version of an E-3 Elint gatherer. A dozen intercepts could be processed at once, with *Quicksilver*'s onboard computer able to handle one channel of 64-byte coding on the fly. The Deep Drink gear included what its designers called "hooks" to allow the data to be transmitted via a broadband satellite network back to an NSA or military analysis center, but neither the satellite nor the transmission system had made it off the drawing boards yet.

Additionally, *Quicksilver* carried IR detectors designed to monitor missile launches. With a little bit of fine tuning they could pick up the flare of a shoulder-launched SA-3 from a hundred miles away. The gear was stowed in the bay normally used for Stinger antiair mines on other EB-52s, including *Raven*.

O'Brien took the radar detection duties, while Habib began making and plotting intercepts. Zen, meanwhile, clicked his own radio through American frequencies, listening in as a pair of patrol planes cruised south of them, just over the Iraqi border. F-16 jocks, they mixed irreverent banter with terse instructions and acknowledgments, flying a simple "racetrack" or extended oval the length of their patrol zone. An AWACS control aircraft flew about a hundred miles to the northwest of *Quicksilver*, scanning for radars in the area as well as watching for enemy aircraft. Zen hailed them all, asking how things were going.

"Quieter than my mom's bedroom," said one of the Eagle jocks. "Where are you from, *Flighthawk One*?"

"Edwards," answered Zen. It was SOP to mention the large base just south of Dreamland rather than Dreamland itself.

"Meant where'd you grow up, homeboy," answered the pilot. "I'm guessing Virginia."

"Spent a lot of time there," said Zen.

"You northerners are all alike," said the other pilot, who had a deep Georgia twang.

"Who you calling a northerner?" countered the other pilot.

"What are you flying there, Flighthawk?" asked the Georgian. "And what's your location?"

"I'm in Turkey, and you wouldn't believe me if I told you," said Zen.

The pilot's undoubtedly sarcastic response was overrun by the AWACS controller.

"Gold Flight, break ninety!" he yelled.

Before either plane could acknowledge or the controller could explain further, O'Brien cut over the interphone. "SA-2 radar active in box alpha-alpha-six. Refining calibration."

They'd divided Iraq into squares or boxes for easy reference; AA-6 referred to a northeastern portion about 150 miles from *Quicksilver*—and maybe seventy from the F-16s. But the next thing Zen heard was the shrill anguish of the AWACS controller, screaming over the open mike.

"Oh my God, they're gone. Oh God, they're gone."

III

High Top

———

**Whiplash Forward Operating Area "High Top," Turkey
28 May 1997
1640**

DANNY FREAH KNELT DOWN BEHIND THE THEODOLITE, TRY-
ing to make sure the ridge beyond the runway was low
enough for the Megafortresses to land. If he was reading
the device's screen right—and while it was extremely
simple, that was not guaranteed—there was about three
meters of clearance, well within parameters. They were
running close to an hour behind schedule but at least they
had the mesh down. They'd run into some troubles with
the helicopters that had delivered it, but they'd probably
set a world's record getting the rough strip ready.

To Danny, it looked like a hell of a lot of space. According to the surveying instruments, new and old sections together stretched exactly 1,642.7 feet. Not counting
the slight bump—more like a six-inch ramp—between
new and old sections, and a stubborn group of pockmarks and bumps about forty yards from the northern end, it was as flat and level as any runway in the
States.

There was a ton of work to do yet—widen the turnaround, finish out the parking section, set up a command
area and better perimeter posts, augment the lights,

maybe even add cable and a swimming pool. But it was time to land the planes.

"Hey, Cap, ready to rock," said Clark, one of a pair of combat air control or CCT specialists who'd come in with the helicopters. "Landing lights, strobes, cloth panels—we could put a 747 in here if you want. Get kinda squished at the far end, but it would land pretty."

Danny nodded, following the controller across the parking area toward a set of sandbags where Clark and Sergeant Velis had set up a radio to talk the airplanes in. Clark grabbed a pair of chemical light sticks and a portable radio, then trotted toward the end of the runway. He would direct the first plane in to the parking area.

"Hey, Cap! Thanks for letting me work the 'dozer," shouted Powder as Danny sat on one of the sandbag piles, the only available seating. "What I'm *talkin'* about!"

"I'm surprised you gave it up," Danny told him.

"Only until the planes land, Cap. Most fun I had with my pants on ever."

"Yeah, well, keep them on," said Danny, reaching into his pocket for a candy bar, which was all the dinner he'd have tonight.

Aboard *Quicksilver*, over southeastern Turkey 1730

"*QUICKSILVER* READS YOU FINE, HIGH TOP GROUND," BREE told the controller as she orbited the freshly meshed field. "I have a visual on the field. Looks real pretty."

"Ground acknowledges," said the controller, all business. "Dreamland Hawk?"

"Dreamland *Hawk One* reads you fine, High Top ground," said Zen. Unlike their usual procedure at Dreamland, here the Flighthawk would remain airborne until the other planes were down, providing additional protection in case of an attack. While that was unlikely—two flights of fighters were patrolling the sky above and to the south—the apparent loss of two more F-16s over Iraq provided a potent reminder that nothing could be taken for granted.

CentCom had reacted to the loss of the two planes by ordering more retaliatory raids. But they were caught in a catch-22—more raids exposed more planes to danger. Everyone was on edge, and even the Megafortresses had been challenged by fighter patrols as they flew into south Turkey.

The ground controller turned his attention back to Major Alou and *Raven,* which was up first in the landing queue. They ran through a quick exchange of vitals about the airstrip, wind, and weather conditions, along with the basic instructions on where the controller wanted him to put the plane once they landed. The exchange was somewhat pro forma, as the Megafortress could compute her own data and adjust accordingly, but the routine itself was comforting. The well-trained CCT on the other end of the radio did his job with the high precision a pilot could appreciate; it boded well if things got complicated down the line.

"Raven on final approach," said Chris as their sister plane pushed in.

Quicksilver was about a mile away and roughly parallel to the runway, opposite *Raven* as it settled down. Zen had brought *Hawk One* into a chase pattern behind and above *Raven* to feed Alou additional video view if he needed it. Breanna had the feed displayed on her console; she watched as Alou came in a bit high to avoid the rocks at the approach end, then flopped down onto the mesh grid, chutes deployed, thrusters in reverse. Dust spewed as the plane shuddered onto the ground. *Raven* began drifting to the left about ten yards after her wheels hit; Alou held it for the next twenty then seemed to overcorrect. In the last fifty yards the plane moved sharply back to the left, jerked right, then disappeared beneath a massive cloud of dust and smoke.

"Shit," said Breanna.

The video veered into the countryside as Zen brought the Flighthawk around quickly. Breanna jerked her attention back to the sky in front of her. The radar plot showed one of the Pave Hawks crossing ahead.

"Hold pattern, all aircraft," said the controller sharply.

"We're all right," said Major Alou. "We're okay."

The Flighthawk video showed the dust clearing. The Megafortress had come off the far edge of the runway, clipping its wing against some of the rocks. The ground people were running toward it as *Hawk One* passed overhead.

"*Raven*, please hold your pattern," said the CCT.

"*Raven.*"

"Going to have to recalculate our fuel," said Chris Ferris.

Breanna grunted in acknowledgment as she widened their orbit, waiting for the people on the ground to sort things out. Two of *Raven*'s sixteen tires had blown and the wing had been lightly damaged, but otherwise the plane was fine. No one aboard had been hurt, assuming the pilot's bruised ego didn't count.

"My fault," Alou told Breanna as the Megafortress was rigged to one of the bulldozers so it could be towed off the runway. "The wind kicked up crazy and pulled the drogue chutes. The computer didn't know how to compensate and I had to fight it. Then the wind kicked out again and I lost the runway. That tooth to the east between the hillsides—it's like a blowpipe."

Breanna could imagine. Crosswinds were always a

complication for any airplane when landing or taking off. The Megafortress's main asset was also its greatest weakness—it was an immense and heavy airframe. Sharp gusts of wind on landing could make a pilot's life difficult even on the best runway.

"I say we dump the chutes," said Chris.

"I don't know if we can stop in time without them," said Breanna.

"Chop 'em at the tooth."

They worked the numbers—they'd run off the end of the runway, maybe even the mountain.

"What if we drop the other Flighthawk?"

The lighter load would lessen the plane's momentum as it landed, making it easier to stop. Still, the computer calculated they'd need another fifty yards without the chutes.

"Burn off more fuel. Dump it even," said Chris, working the calculations. The most optimistic—which had them running out of fuel during the final approach—left them ten yards too long.

"We can all eject," joked Breanna.

"Still leaves us ten pounds too heavy," answered Chris.

"I think we're better off just losing the computer," said Breanna. "We'll figure the chutes will pull us and compensate."

"I don't know, Bree. If they couldn't handle the crosswind with the computer's help—"

"The computer routines weren't set up with the chutes," said Breanna. She'd made up her mind. "We can cut it lower too, so we don't put quite as much strain on the tires. I think they lost them on the touchdown. That hurt their steering."

"I don't know, Bree."

"I do. I've landed in forty knot winds in an old B-52. It'll be easier than that." She clicked her com setting to talk to Zen. "Jeff, we want to lighten our load. Can you launch *Hawk Two*?"

"What's the game plan?"

Breanna explained quickly.

"I don't know, Bree."

"What don't you know?"

"You guys are going to land on that postage stamp without any help from the computer?"

She'd expected Chris to object—though highly skilled, her copilot was by nature extremely cautious. But Zen was ordinarily the opposite, and routinely chafed against the computerized autopilot systems that helped him fly the U/MFs—even though he'd helped develop the damn things. If anyone should be in favor of turning off the training wheels, it should be him.

"I can do it with my eyes closed," she said.

"Your call, Captain," said her husband.

"Thank you, Major," she said. "Tell me when you're ready to fuel *Hawk Two*. I'd like to top off *One* as well."

"Hawk leader acknowledges."

ZEN CHECKED THE SITREP ON HIS VIEWER, WAITING FOR *Quicksilver* to finish its climb to 26,000 feet. Before he started working with the Megafortress fleet, he'd had a typical fighter jock's attitude toward big planes and their pilots: basically they were airborne trucks, slow and easy to control. But the airborne launches and refuels had taught him to appreciate exactly how difficult a large air-craft could be to control. Its vast weight and wing sur-faces, complicated flight systems, and powerful engines made for a complicated minuet. The dancers at the helm had their hands full, even with the sophisticated flight computers that helped control the Megafortress. Landing the big jet on the smooth surface in the shadow of Glass

Mountain was one thing, landing on this mountaintop metal-covered sand trap quite another.

And Breanna hadn't fully recovered from her injuries either.

"Want me to fuel and prep *Two* for launch?" asked Fentress.

"I got it," said Zen, louder than he'd intended. He worked quickly through the checklist, jumping momentarily into the cockpit of *Hawk One*, then handing it back over to the computer in its orbit around the airstrip. Fueled and powered, *Hawk Two* purred beneath the EB-52's wing, eager to launch.

"Can I take it?" Fentress asked.

"Sorry," said Zen, immediately telling Breanna they were set to launch because he didn't care to debate with his sidekick.

"READY?" BREANNA ASKED CHRIS AFTER THE GROUND controller gave them the all-clear.

"Ready as I'll ever be."

"Engines are yours," she said. "Like we chalked it up."

"Gotcha, coach," said Ferris.

They brought the big plane out of her last leg on the approach pattern, lining up with the runway. They were at an off angle, their nose about fifteen degrees away from a straight-on run. Several simulations on the Megafortress control computer showed this would give them the best handle on the swirling winds.

"Four's too hot," Breanna said. She had the power-graph in the configurable HUD, its green bars overshadowing the rocks as they approached.

"Backing off four, five percent. Seven percent."

"Five thousand feet," said Breanna, reading the altitude against the runway, not sea level—which would have added nearly seven thousand feet to the total. "On course."

"Crosswind!" warned Chris. *Quicksilver* moaned as he said that, the plane lurching slightly to their left as a gust of wind caught them.

"I have it," she said. "Gear."

"Gear," confirmed Chris. The plane shook slightly, her airspeed quickly dropping below 150 knots against the stiff head wind as the landing gear doors opened. Their momentum bled away; within seconds they were no more than three knots over their stall speed, with a goodly distance to go.

"Hold our power," said Breanna.

"Gear set and locked," said Chris. "Okay okay okay."

"Systems," prompted Breanna.

"Green, we're in the green, we're in the green. Jesus— too low, Bree, we're going to clip the rocks."

Breanna resisted the impulse to break off the approach and instead held back on her stick ever so slightly longer than she had intended. They did cut the lip of the ridge close, but they cleared it.

"Chutes!" said Breanna and Chris together. They'd timed the deployment down to the millisecond, trying to balance the different effects and maximize the drag without ending up too far off course. The jet wobbled slightly but held herself in the air, the extended trailing edges on the wings adjusted by a series of small actuators that responded in micrometer increments to the pilot's input.

"Reverse thrust! Reverse!" Breanna shouted.

The swirling gusts suddenly changed direction and died. The Megafortress's tail threatened to whip out from behind her and the plane rolled faster than she'd wanted, its speed jumping nearly fifty knots, if the speedo were to be believed. Breanna's fingers compressed around the stick, her soft touch suddenly gone, her biceps cramping.

An alarm sounded in the cockpit, and Chris shouted another warning.

Then she did something she'd never done before when landing a Megafortress: She closed her eyes. The plane's wings seemed to hulk over her shoulders, extensions of her body. Her stomach felt for the runway, her legs dragging the brakes. She fought the muscle knots in her hand and back, pushing the plane as gently as she could, willing it along the path as she'd planned, compensating for the wind, feeling her way dead onto the middle of the runway.

God, she thought. The word filled her head, the only conscious idea. Every other part of her belonged to the plane.

"Holding, holding, oh yeah, oh yeah," Chris was saying. "Fifty knots. Thirty. Oh mama! Stopping! We're stopping! This is pretty, Captain!"

Someone behind her started to cheer. Breanna opened her eyes, looking out the windshield of the jet for the ground controller who was supposed to meet them and steer them to their parking slot.

High Top
1800

DANNY FREAH WAITED AS THE HATCHWAY BENEATH THE Megafortress hissed and began to lower. He jumped onto the steps as soon as they touched the ground. Hopping aboard, he popped up into the Flighthawk control deck, where Zen was busy bringing the U/MFs in for their landings. The major's new sidekick, Captain Fentress, looked around with a surprised expression, but Zen remained oblivious, hunkered over his controls. Danny waved at Fentress, then clambered up the access ramp to the flight deck, where the crew was just stowing their gear.

"Nice landing, Bree," said Danny. "Welcome to the No-Tell Motel."

"Glad to be here," she said.

"Colonel Bastian wants to conference," he told her. "I was hoping I could sit in *Quicksilver* with you guys when we take it. We don't have the headquarters trailer down yet, and our only radio is the SatCom."

"Not a problem," she said, stepping back as he climbed into the ship. Breanna caught his arm as he reached the deck. "We appreciate your getting that strip together so fast. Thanks."

It was the first thank-you he'd heard all day, and it felt incredibly good. "Thanks."

"Now that I've brown-nosed you," added Breanna, "can I drive one of those bulldozers?"

Dreamland Secure Command Center
1012

DOG PACED BACK AND FORTH ACROSS THE FRONT OF THE situation room like an anxious father-to-be waiting word from the delivery ward.

He should have found a way to go himself. Nobody had ordered him not to this time—so why hadn't he even thought of it?

Because he was superfluous. Because his job was here. Because Major Alou and Breanna were much better Megafortress pilots than he was.

Bree, at least. Alou was still a little new. But the arguments that had kept Cheshire here went triple for him.

Except that he wanted to be out there, in the mix.

Why had he sent Jennifer? Because she knew the computer systems better than anyone in the world, including her boss, Ray Rubeo, who was sitting at one of the nearby consoles. Not only had she helped develop half of the avionics in the Megafortress and Flighthawks, but she could probably figure out the rest with her eyes closed.

If he was worried about Jennifer, why wasn't he worried about his own daughter, Breanna? She was taking much more risk, flying the plane into combat.

Because Breanna had never seemed vulnerable?

Vulnerable wasn't the right word.

Rubeo sighed loudly, leaning back in his chair. He'd brought a book to read as well as a pile of technical folders, and seemed to flit back and forth between them as if reading them all simultaneously.

Losing two more F-16s—it still had not been confirmed that the planes had been shot down, though everyone assumed they were—had sent CentCom as well as Washington into a frenzy. It didn't help that no one knew what had shot down the planes. The latest CIA theory was that the Iraqis had managed to acquire modified versions of the Russian Straight Flush radar, a low PFR radar that had been modified not only to frequency skip but to resist jamming. The theory held that they were able to use the radars in conjunction with older but also undoubtedly modified Fan Gong F radars, all of which were turned on for extremely short periods of time in a predetermined pattern. Data from these extremely brief bursts were then used to launch several missiles.

The theory did explain some things, such as the many brief radar indications and the barrage missile launchings. But as Rubeo pointed out, it did not account for the uncanny accuracy of the missiles, most especially since some of them didn't have their own terminal guidance and those that did should have been defeated or at least confused by ECMs.

Perhaps the guidance systems had been altered. Perhaps the barrage firings increased the relatively poor odds of a single missile finding its target. Perhaps the Iraqis were just lucky.

"And perhaps Pooh Bear is God," Rubeo said.

But a laser also seemed farfetched. If the Iraqis had it, why didn't they use it on everything in the air?

Whatever it was, the Dreamland team had to find it—and neutralize it.

"Really, Colonel, when are we going to get on with this?" asked Rubeo. "We are wasting time that even at government rates is not inexpensive." Rubeo frowned and fingered his stubby gold earring. He was brilliant—half the gear in the room had been designed by him or one of the people who worked for him—but Dog thought that sometimes he pushed the eccentric scientist a bit too far.

"What are you reading there, Doc?" asked Dog, trying to change the subject.

"Commentary on Plato. Wrong-headed, but diverting."

"High Top Base to Dreamland Command." Major Alou's voice boomed over the speaker system. "Colonel, do we have a connection?"

Dog turned toward the screen at the front of the room, even though he knew there would be no video; they were using the Megafortresses to communicate. The Whiplash portable command center, with its full suite of com gear, hadn't even been delivered from the MC-17 yet. "Go ahead, Major."

"You wanted to speak to us?"

"I have information that may be relevant. We're going to try to get Jed Barclay on the line to sit in on this." He nodded at the lieutenant handling the communications, who punched in the commands to connect the NSC secure line. A signal indicated that the line—which had been open just two minutes before—was now unavailable.

"Hi, Daddy," said Breanna lightly. She sounded like a kid calling from college.

"Captain."

"Weather's fine, if you like windchills approaching fifty below," she told him.

"She's exaggerating," said Alou. "Windchill only makes it feel like thirty below."

"Colonel, High Top came through on Channel B, the uncoded backup," said the lieutenant at the com board. "I can only invoke eight-byte encryption."

"Well switch it to the secure channel," said Rubeo, whose tone suggested he considered the lieutenant about as intelligent as an earthworm.

"I've tried, sir. I don't know whether it's the satellite or something on their end."

"Oh, just peachy," said Rubeo, getting up from his console and walking toward the lieutenant.

It was unlikely that the Iraqis could intercept the communications signal, let alone break it. The Russians, on the other hand, were capable of doing both.

"I'm told we're not secure," said Dog.

"That is *not* correct," said Rubeo. "And from a tactical point of view—"

"Excuse me, Doc, I'm talking here." Dog gave the scientist a drop-dead frown. He couldn't tell them about the laser; doing so would risk tipping the Russians off about Razor. "I have a matter that I want you briefed on. I'll find a way of getting the information to you. In the meantime, we have to fix our communications glitch."

"I'm working on it," said the lieutenant.

"How long to fix this?" Dog asked.

"Sorry, sir. I'm not sure."

Dog looked at Rubeo. The scientist shrugged. "Hours. Days."

"Better not be days." Another thought occurred to him—was the glitch deliberate?

The idea obviously hit Rubeo at the same time.

"We haven't been compromised," said the scientist. "These are the difficulties inherent in new systems. Believe me, Colonel, it is perfectly safe to proceed."

Rubeo was undoubtedly correct—and yet Dog couldn't take that chance. Security at Dreamland had been blown disastrously once before.

Under General Elliott, as it happened.

"What's up, Colonel?" asked Zen.

"I'm going to send you a visitor, I think," said Dog, improvising. "He has a theory I want you to hear about."

"We're not going to tell them anything?" said Rubeo. "We've wasted all this time—"

"The line isn't secure," said Dog.

"Colonel, please, let me explain a bit about the encryption system we're using as backup," said Rubeo. "Once we invoke the key, even though—"

"Dr. Ray is rehearsing his vaudeville act," said Dog. "I'm sorry. I can't explain."

"At least give them perspective," added Rubeo. "General Elliott's assessment of technology has *always* been overly optimistic."

"General Elliott?" asked Zen.

"I'm sorry, guys," said Dog. He walked over to the lieutenant's console and killed Rubeo's input line. "I'll get the information to you."

"Okay," said Alou.

"Dream Control out," said Dog.

"Wait!"

Jennifer's voice pulled his head back toward the screen. Still blank, of course.

"How are you, Doc?" he asked.

"I'm kick-ass fine, Colonel. Yourself?"

Dog wrapped his arms around each other in front of his chest. "I'm doing well. Was something up?"

"Just to say hi."

"Yes." He tightened his arms, squeezing them as if wringing a towel. "Dream Command out."

A slight pop sounded over the circuit as the feed died, the sort of noise a staticky AM radio might make when the lights were switched on in a distant part of the house.

"The odds, Colonel, of the transmission being intercepted and decoded would surely be measured in range of ten to the negative one hundredth power," said Rubeo.

"I can't take any chance on that if we're discussing Razor," said Dog.

"We weren't going to talk about Razor," said Rubeo. "Please, Colonel, give me some credit."

"If I didn't, I'd have you in front of a firing squad."

"If you want to question my adherence to security protocols, Colonel, I welcome a formal inquiry."

"Relax, Doc. Fix this coding thing."

"I doubt it's more than a switch in the wrong position," said Rubeo.

"Communication pending, sir," said the lieutenant. "NSC."

"Secure?" asked Dog.

"Yes, sir."

"It's only the important communications that get screwed up," said Rubeo.

"Connect," said Dog.

The screen at the front flashed with color. Dog turned toward it as Jed Barclay appeared in the NSC secure room. His eyes were red and drooping, his hair disheveled even worse than normal. Uncharacteristically, he was wearing a suit that seemed to have been recently pressed, or at least dry cleaned.

"I'm ready," said Jed. "Sorry for the delay."

"That's all right, Jed," Dog told him. "We ran into some technical problems and we're going to have to take another approach anyway. What's the latest?"

"Someone might suggest Major Smith sign up for some camera lessons. His photos were kind of blurry and the analysts all say inconclusive. The two F-15 shoot-downs clinch it for me, but the CIA's still holding out."

"Naturally," said Rubeo.

"Meantime, we're reassessing targets," continued Barclay. "CentCom wants ground action to help the Kurds. Your orders still stand."

All of this could have been prevented, Dog thought, if we'd simply nailed Saddam when we had the chance. Calling off a war simply because a hundred hours had passed—what a wheelbarrow of bullshit.

"Uh, Colonel, I have someplace to get to," added Jed. "The director himself will contact you if there's any change or new developments while I'm, uh, in transit."

"Just one more thing," said Dog. "Where is Brad Elliott right now, and can you get me through to him?"

"Uh, that's two things," said Jed.

Incirlik
2100

MACK SMITH HAD BEGUN THE DAY WITH HIGH HOPES OF finding a slot with one of the squadrons flying south. He'd begun at the top—the F-15C guys flying combat air patrol—and worked his way down. The message was always the same: no room at the inn.

Which was bullshit. Here was, without doubt, the best stinking fighter pilot in the stinking Gulf, the hottest stick on the patch—bona fide, with scalps on the belt to prove it, for chrissakes—and he couldn't even get a gig pushing A-10s across the lines.

Actually, there were no Warthogs in Turkey, and Mack

wasn't sure he could fly them if there were. But he would have jumped at the chance. Hell, he'd have taken the copilot's seat in a Piper Cub if it meant getting into the action.

But nada. Stinking nada. Without exception, the idiot wing and squadron and section commanders, even the stinking D.O.'s and the intel guys and the maintenance people, for cryin' out loud—every stinking anybody with any sort of authority had it in for him.

Probably they were scared he'd hog all the glory.

Jerks.

Elliott was sequestered in some hotel somewhere with the CIA jerks. Mack ended up wandering around the base, looking for something, anything, to do. He finally found himself staring at CNN in an Army psyops office that was being shared with USAFSOC. The SOC guys were out, the psyops people were off planning their head-shrinking stuff, and Mack was left alone to view a succession of correspondents in Saudi Arabia talk about a situation they knew absolutely nothing about. Reports of bomb strikes were attributed to reliable sources speaking on condition of anonymity. None of what they said was wrong—they just didn't know what was going on.

But they were a lot better than the talking heads. One civilian expert talked about how "potent" the high-altitude SA-3 missile was and how it was likely the reason the F-16 had been shot down. In Mack's opinion, the SA-3 was a fairly decent little weapon in its day, and no piece of explosive that could move through the air at three times the speed of sound could be taken for granted. But it was a medium-altitude missile, designed more to stopgap the vulnerabilities of the SA-2, and at least arguably more effective at 1,500 feet than at 35,000. And hell—the Israelis had befuddled the damn things in the 1973 Yom Kippur War. You couldn't ignore the stinkers, but there were a lot more gnarly problems over Iraq, that was for damn sure.

Like SA-2s? Talk about a weapon system that had been thoroughly compromised. So how had it nailed three F-16s and two F-15s?

No way. General Elliott had to be correct. It had to be a Razor, or a close proximity.

How would he fly against it? he wondered.

He'd taken a few turns as a sitting duck against Razor during its development; he could go on that. Clouds decreased the laser's efficiency, so that was the first thing to look for. It didn't operate in bad weather.

There was some sort of latency thing; it had to warm up between bursts. So you sent out decoys, got it to target the ghost, then nailed the sucker while it recharged or recalibrated or *whatever* the hell it was lasers did.

Mack got up off the couch as CNN went to a commercial and walked down the hallway in the direction of the squadron commander's suite. He got about halfway there before an airman caught up to him from behind.

"Captain Smith—"

"That's *Major* Smith, kid," Mack told the airman, who stood about five-four and was thinner than a cherry tree.

"Sorry, sir," said the airman, so flustered he proceeded to salute. "Sir, General Elliott, uh, retired General Elliott, he's looking for you. He's in Colonel Witslow's office, back this way."

Everybody on the damn base has it in for me, Mack thought as he stomped through the hallway. He found Elliott buttoning a parka in Witslow's office.

"Ah, there you are Mack. Grab some flight gear, we're going for a ride."

"No shit, General, great," said Mack, relieved that he finally had something to do. "Where to?"

"To the mountains. The official name is Al Derhagdad,

but they're calling it High Top. You'll see some old friends."

"We taking a helicopter?"

"There are none available till morning, and I'd like to get out there right now."

"Hell, let's grab our own plane," said Mack, instantly fired up. If they borrowed an F-15E Strike Eagle, he'd be able to wangle into one of the mission packages for sure.

"My thought exactly," said Elliott. "There's an OV-10 Bronco with our name on it out on the tarmac."

"A Bronco?"

The Bronco was an ancient ground support aircraft once used by the Air Force and Marines. Diving with a tailwind, it might break 300 knots.

Might.

"You've flown one, haven't you?" added Elliott.

"Uh, sure," said Mack. He wasn't lying, exactly—the Marines had had a few in the Gulf, and he'd hopped aboard one for a familiarization flight just before the start of the ground war. He'd gloved the stick for perhaps five minutes.

"If you're rusty, we can find someone else," offered the general.

"No, sir, I can handle it," said Mack quickly. He could fly anything. "Marines still using them for covert insertions?"

"Actually, this aircraft belongs to Thailand and was en route to an air show in Cairo, where it was going to be sold. The Thais seem to think they might get a better offer from an unnamed American company that I happen to be slightly affiliated with." Elliott didn't even hint at a smile. "We're going to take it for a test drive."

High Top
2205

DANNY FREAH SQUATTED BEHIND THE ROCK AS BISON GOT ready to ignite the charge. It had started to rain ten minutes before; the wind whipped the drops against the side of his face like pellets of dirt.

"Ready!" shouted Bison. "Clear the area!"

"Bison, only you and I are out here," Danny told the demolitions man.

"Yes, sir. Clear the range!"

"Clear."

Bison pushed the button on his remote detonator. The ground shook slightly, and dust spun up from the cliffside just out of range of the halogen spots. Danny got up and walked toward the ridge obstructing the end of the runway; the charges had loosened more stone, but most of the stubborn mountain had refused to yield.

"This is a bitch fuck," said Bison, cupping a cigarette in his hands to light it. "We're gonna have to blow it again."

"Let's check it first. We got a few feet off," said Danny.

"Inches maybe."

Bison's estimate was probably nearer the mark, Danny realized. The runway wasn't going to get much longer without considerable effort, nor were they going to be able to knock down the approach. But at least the loose rocks would give his guys more to do. Guard duty was already starting to wear thin, and they hadn't been on the ground twelve hours yet. He'd have to find them something real to do once they got bored playing with the bulldozers.

A half-dozen medium-size tents had been set up, along with two large ones that were supposed to serve as mess and an auxiliary headquarters. The Whiplash Mobile Command Headquarters—the trailer—had been brought in on the MC-17 and was now fully operational, except for the link to Dreamland. The problem was in the satellite system, which was brand new. The scientists back home had it isolated and hoped to have it fully operational soon.

The Megafortresses were parked only a few feet away—*Raven* with its wingtip half apart. To Danny's mind, it wasn't the most secure setup; the planes were out in the open and bunched together, very vulnerable to a mortar attack. On the other hand, it would take an extremely dedicated fanatic to approach the base. His men had established an IR and ground radar picket around the slopes; a chipmunk couldn't get within three hundred yards without them knowing about it. And even though it twisted every which way, they had the rock-strewn dirt road covered for a good half mile in both directions.

It was more a path than a road. A donkey—or a goat— would scrape its flanks on some of the curves.

Danny itched to get in on the action south, maybe hop down and look for the pilots. If the Marines ever got here, they might be able to do that.

"Can I fire up the 'dozer and clear the rocks away?" asked Bison.

"Yeah, go ahead—wait a second. Maybe I'll take a shot at that."

"Privileges of rank, huh?"

"I want to see what all the fuss is about," said Danny. But as he took a step toward the 'dozer he heard the drone of a propeller in the distance.

**Over southeastern Turkey
2230**

MACK JAMMED THE THROTTLES FOR PROBABLY THE EIGHT hundredth time since taking off, looking for the Bronco to give him even two more knots. He told himself it was a damn good thing it was dark; if it had been daytime, he'd be able to see how slow he was going and really get frustrated. The gauge pegged 260 nautical miles per hour, but Mack doubted he was going half that fast. The altimeter showed 18,000 feet, and that he almost could believe—he had cleared a peak a short while ago by what looked like a good three inches.

Though a propeller plane, the Bronco wanted to be taken seriously. You had to wear a speed suit and strap yourself in, just like in a pointy-nose, go-fast jet. And it did respond—you could stick where you wanted it to go, by God; the sucker moved its nose and tail with good, solid jerks.

But it wasn't an F-22 or an F-15 or even an F-16. And the damn cabin was colder than hell. General Elliott, sitting in the seat behind him, had given up his campaign to cheer him up; more than likely he'd passed out from hypothermia.

Somewhere ahead was the scratch base they were heading to, High Top. Two Megafortresses had managed to land on a strip that probably wasn't even long enough for this plane. Typical Whiplash/Dreamland stunt, he thought. Probably patting themselves on the back.

He couldn't get away from them, try as he might. Zen would be there, with his gorgeous wife. Merce Alou. Danny Freah.

Odds were Jennifer Gleason would be too. Now there was a brain worth digging into. Though to be honest, Bree was more his style.

Mack checked the INS against his paper map. He'd long ago learned to rely on GPS readings that showed his location on three-dimensional maps accurate to half a centimeter. This—hell, this was just about dead reckoning, same sort of navigating Christopher Columbus used when he thought he'd discovered China.

God, was he going soft?

Bullshit on that. Mack knew right where he was. And he could fly anything—any friggin' thing—any time, anywhere. This old workhorse was proof of it.

Slower than horseshit, though. God. Taxi would've been faster. Donkey cart.

So where the hell were these jokers? He knew he ought to be in their face by now.

Mack hit the UHF radio, trying to get the controller at High Top. Nothing came back.

The wind whipped up. His forward airspeed stepped lower, dropping below 250 knots.

"How we doing, Major?" asked Elliott from the back.

"Pluggin' along, sir."

"Handsome aircraft, isn't it?"

Handsome?

"Uh, yes, sir."

"A lot of grunts owe their lives to OV-10s," said the general, renewing his pep-talk bid. "Impressive little airplane in its day."

"Yes, sir."

"Eight-eight Delta Zeus, this is High Top base," said a low but clear voice on the Bronco's UHF channel. "Hey there, *Wild Bronco,* we have you at ten miles. You're looking good."

Wild Bronco?

"Delta Zeus acknowledges." Mack did a quick check of the INS—stinker was right on the mark.

"Getting close, General," Mack told his passenger.

"Very good, Mack. You made good time. We may turn you into a bird dog yet."

"Yes, sir."

The ground controller ran down the runway's vital statistics, emphasizing not only its relatively short run but the obstruction at the approach. The lights flicked on, and Mack was somewhat surprised—he'd expected a simple box and one, a very basic pattern often employed at scratch bases. But the CCTs had enough lights out to make a 747 pilot comfortable; they'd even managed a warning strobe on the ridge near the start of the runway.

"Looks like LAX down there," said Mack.

"Uh, sir, we can do without the insults."

"I was kidding," said Mack.

"So was I. Wind has been a bitch. I'll give you readings all along. There's a notch in the hills that seems to amplify it about fifty yards from the leading edge of the runway; we've measured it at sixty there."

Sixty. Holy shit.

"We're looking at only thirty knots at the moment," added the controller, "but God only knows if that'll hold. At least it stopped raining, huh, Major?"

"Delta Zeus."

"That's—hold on—thirty-two knots, gusting, uh, gusting to forty-five. Thirty knots."

"Thirty knots, Delta Zeus," acknowledged Mack. The high-winged Bronco would be buffeted by any wind, but 30 knots—let alone 45 or 60—would make things somewhat hairy on the narrow and short runway. He'd have to push his right wing down, stick and rudder himself into what amounted to an angled skid across the tarmac.

Check that, metal grid.

He came at the runway well off to the east, no flaps, expecting the winds to push him in line as they tried to tear his wing over. Mack wasn't disappointed. As he fought the stick and left rudder, the plane touched down almost perfectly on the center line of the runway. That was about the only thing that was perfect—he went reverse pedals, reverse engines, reverse prayers, then jammed the brakes so bad they burned, and still nearly fell off the edge of the runway. Fortunately, the wind finally died and he turned around to follow a crewman waving him toward a parking area at the extreme northeastern end of the field. He bumped over a dirt and rubble ramp, the plane jittering a bit as he found a spot next to one of the Megafortresses. The big black plane loomed in the darkness beyond a hand-portable spotlight, a puma ready to strike.

General Elliott had his canopy open and was clambering out the side of the plane before the props stopped spinning. Mack waited for the crewman who'd flagged him in to help chock the wheels and secure the aircraft, then made his way toward some nearby tents.

"Here's Mack," boomed General Elliott as Mack entered the large tin can that served as Whiplash's temporary headquarters.

"The whole gang's here, huh?" said Mack, glancing around and nodding to Merce Alou, Breanna Stockard, Jeff, and Chris Ferris. Jennifer Gleason's beautiful body was tucked into a loose sweater—Mack turned a 150-watt smile on her before waving to everyone else.

"Okay, so here's my theory," said Elliott, already well into his business here. He told them about how the planes could only have been shot down by a long-range laser, possibly guided by the SA-2 and other radars. "Mack looked at one of the planes," added the general.

"So?" There was an edge in Jeff Stockard's voice as he nudged his wheelchair forward from the corner where he'd been sitting. Same old Zen—he probably still blamed him for the accident that cost him his legs.

"Like the general said, only thing that could have nailed that plane was the laser," Mack told him. "Exploded the wing, sliced it right off."

"So why isn't CentCom telling us this?" said Alou.

"CentCom doesn't completely buy the theory," said Elliott. "They don't think Saddam has a laser. And neither the satellites nor any of the sensor aircraft have picked it up."

"If it's as potent as Razor," said Zen, "it'll have at least a three hundred mile radius. It could be well south of the shoot-downs."

"Absolutely," said Elliott.

Zen pulled the map of Iraq off the table into his lap and began plotting the shoot-downs. He drew a rough semicircle about three hundred miles south of them. The swath included Baghdad as well as more northern cities like Kirkuk and Al Mawsil.

"If they set things up right, they could theoretically feed coordinates from any of the radars they have to direct the laser into the vicinity of the aircraft," said Elliott. "Then they could turn on a fire-director radar quickly, and fire as soon as they locked, which could be within seconds."

"They wouldn't need radar to get the general location," said Mack. "A standard air traffic job in Kirkuk would give them enough of a lead. They could even use an IR sensor to lock on the target."

"They could use the laser itself to find the target," said Jennifer. "We used a similar technique when we were studying optical solutions for the C^3 communications systems. They might also be able to overcome targeting limitations by shooting through a calculated grid after they get a contact. Say they have a target down to a certainty of three hundred meters, following a certain vector. You fill the box with as many pulses as you can cycle. You could increase the number of shots by trading off some—"

"However they're doing it, the laser has to be located and destroyed," said Zen.

"I don't know," said Alou. "If CentCom doesn't think it's possible—"

"The Iraqis nearly built a nuclear bomb. This would be child's play compared to that," said Bree.

"Not exactly," said Elliott. "But still doable."

"Hey, the hell with CentCom. They're relying on the CIA," said Mack. "They have an arrogant attitude that's blinding them to reality."

Zen laughed.

"What?" said Mack.

"Jennifer, how do we detect the laser?" asked Zen.

"Can we detect the deuterium?" asked Mack.

The computer scientist shrugged. "Not my area. Deuterium is hydrogen with a neutron in its nucleus. I doubt it would be easy to detect. We'd have better luck looking for the energy discharge. It would be in the IR spectrum, intense but extremely brief. A sensor looking for a missile launch might be able to detect it theoretically, but the computer code would probably kick it out because it was so brief."

"There are no launch detection satellites configured for Iraq," said Elliott. "What do we have that we can use?"

"Our gear on *Quicksilver*? Hmmm." The scientist twirled her hair around her finger as she worked out the problem. "*Quicksilver*'s IR launch detector is fairly sensitive, though I'm not sure about the range or the spectrum. C^3 takes selective data from it, so obviously the software can be screened—I have to think about it. I might be able to work it. I have to talk to Ray Rubeo."

"Secure connection with Dreamland is still pending," said Alou. "Lieutenant Post told me it'll be at least an hour more."

"Where's Garcia?" asked Breanna. "He might know something about the sensors."

"He went with Hall to look after Mack's airplane," said Alou.

"Not just any airplane. An OV-10D Bronco," said a loud voice from outside. "Talk about your house down the road."

Mack turned as a short, somewhat squat technical type breezed into the trailer, shoulders bouncing as if he were listening to a Walkman. Garcia snapped to attention as he caught sight of Brad Elliott.

"General!"

"How are you, son?"

"Fine, sir. Thank you for remembering me, sir."

"Oh, I remember you quite well," said Elliott. "You spent twenty minutes in my office one afternoon explaining why *Blood on the Tracks* is mankind's greatest artistic achievement."

"It is, sir. Thank you, sir."

The others cracked up. Mack wondered how they could all be so damn cheerful. Even with the heaters going full blast, it had to be under thirty degrees in there.

"That Bronco out there is in great shape," said Garcia. "Pretty plane. I cut my teeth on those suckers."

"What do you know about the launch sensor in *Quicksilver*?" Alou asked.

Garcia shrugged. "Spanish leather. Why? Need to be calibrated?"

"You think you could alter it to pick up a laser flash?"

"Light's a flashin'?" The techie turned back toward Elliott. "That's actually the Who, sir. It just came to me."

"I thought so. What about the sensor?"

"Have to study it a bit. You know, I can get at least twenty percent more power out of those Garret engines on the Broncos. See, they put better—"

"Let's concentrate on the launch sensor for now," said Alou. "Dr. Gleason will help you. Everybody else, try and get some sleep. We're supposed to be off the pavement at 0530, and word is the Whiplash boys brought a very limited supply of coffee."

High Top
2350

POWDER TOOK ANOTHER SIP OF WATER AND RUBBED HIS eyes. Five small television screens were arrayed in front of him, showing the infrared scans from the devices Whiplash had arrayed on the slopes. The Dreamland-designed units could pick up a dead mouse at three-quarters of a mile; Powder suspected that with a little tweaking they could see mosquitoes. By contrast, a "stock" AN/PAS-7 thermal viewer would have trouble seeing a cold Jeep at that distance. A small computer the size of a briefcase monitored the images for any sudden change, a kind of computerized watchdog.

The gear made it too easy, Powder thought. He stared at it and stared at it, and he felt himself nodding off.

"Hey," said Liu, sneaking up behind him.

"My M-4's loaded, Nurse," he growled.

"Falling asleep, huh?"

"I hate guard duty."

"Yeah."

"General Elliott just landed with Major Smith."

"No shit. The old dog himself?"

"Yup."

"We oughta go say hello. Think he'll remember us?"

"Might be better he didn't," suggested Liu.

"Nah. I wasn't driving that truck."

"You were in the truck."

"True." Powder paused to reflect. "Wasn't that much damage to his car."

"Insurance companies declare year-old cars total losses all the time," said Nurse. "Even if they've just been scratched."

"It's a tax thing," said Powder.

A low beep sounded from the audio alert. The two men turned to the IR screens. A shadow had stumbled into the far corner of the second screen, near the far bend on the dirt trail southwest of base.

"Uh-oh." Powder picked up his M-4/W, a short-barreled version of Colt's M-16 with a 204 grenade launcher and a special laser sight that could transmit target data directly to his smart helmet, displaying it on the visor. "Get the guys."

While Liu trotted over to alert the others, Powder watched the figures scoping the hill. There were two native types, bundled in bulky clothes that concealed their weapons.

"Scouts," Powder told Liu when he returned out of breath. He'd put on his smart helmet and Velcroed his bulletproof vest. "Probably saw the lights and came to check it out. Nobody on the screens and the radar's clear."

"Okay." Liu pointed to one of the ground-radar screens, which covered part but not all of the western approach. "Send somebody to cover me," he said, starting down the slope.

Powder slipped on his combat helmet and adjusted his throat mike, listening to Liu's deep breaths while staring at the IR screen.

"What's up?" asked Bison, coming on a dead run.

"Sshhh!" Powder motioned him to the gear. "Number two. Cover us."

"Powder! Yo—"

Bison obviously didn't want to be left out of the party, but that was tough nuggies as far as Powder was concerned. He trotted to the north side of the hill, opposite from the angle Liu was taking. He had a little trouble with the rocks, climbing across a sheer cliff for about fifteen feet and losing his sense of direction momentarily. But the starlight mode of the smart helmet projected a compass heading at the bottom right-hand corner, along with GPS readings; he got himself straightened out and then began picking his way down toward the trail. He had the path in sight and his M-4 ready when Liu hissed that their subjects had stopped.

"You're about fifty yards above them," said Bison, watching from the sentry post. "It's just two. They may be setting up weapons."

"If it's a fucking mortar, we better hit 'em quick," said Powder. He loaded a grenade into his launcher but moved his finger back to the rifle trigger. "Go for it, Nurse!" He jumped forward, balancing himself with his gun and yelling a war hoop. He nearly tripped as his feet hit the rutted but clear path. Liu shouted something and Powder saw a blur of images in his visor screen, everything blurring. He pointed the nose of his gun upward, crosshairs bouncing as he ran.

He saw three figures, Liu to the right—marked by a fluorescent "good guy" triangle transmitted by the smart helmet—and two to the left, one lurching toward him.

"Get down! Get down!" yelled Powder, sliding to his knee to steady his aim, cursing himself that he'd left his buddy vulnerable, cursing himself for getting Nurse killed.

"Wait! Wait!" yelled Liu. "Hold your fire! Hold your fire!"

The figure closest to Liu slid backward then collapsed to the ground. Liu dropped down beside him.

Her. It was a woman.

A pregnant woman.

"What the hell's going on?" demanded Bison.

"Yo—Nurse, Powder. We got you covered!" shouted

Hernandez. His voice was so loud Powder thought his eardrums would break.

"She's pregnant, real pregnant," said Liu. "Somebody get me a medical kit! Fast. Real, real fast."

Powder put his weapon on safety as he walked forward. A thin, worried-looking man stood to the side of Liu and the woman, gesticulating wildly. He held his hands out at Powder and started talking a mile a minute.

"Yeah, listen, I don't speak what you speak, but I'm on the same wavelength," Powder told him. "My man Liu's gonna help. He's the best." He pushed his visor up. Even in the darkness the poor husband looked scared shitless. "Hey, this is a natural thing, right?" he said to the man. "Happens every day."

The woman on the ground moaned loudly.

"Where the hell is that medical kit!" yelled Powder. "Hernandez! Bison! Come on! Get on the ball here!"

Hernandez came down the path in a dead run. "What's the story?"

"Pregnant lady. See if Liu needs help while I check the road."

"No way. You help Liu, I'll check the road." Bison raced down the hill before Powder could stop him.

"Wimp," he said.

"Wimp yourself," said Liu over the com set.

"How we doing, Nurse?" asked Powder, walking over to his partner.

The answer came from the woman on the ground, who screamed louder than an air raid siren. Liu reached down and cleared her feet apart, exposing everything to the air. Nurse had his armored vest, helmet, and other gear off, his sleeves rolled. His hands moved gently across the woman's stomach. As Nurse put his ear down toward her belly, the woman screamed again.

"Jesus," said Powder. "Can we move her?"

"Too late for that," said Nurse. "Come here and hold her legs."

"What?"

"Now!"

Powder took a tentative step forward, but as he started to crouch down, the woman screamed again—and this time even louder.

"Shit! Shit! Shit!" yelled Powder, jumping back.

"Shut the hell up, Powder," said Captain Freah, walking down the hill. "Nurse, you got a handle on this?"

"Baby's turned around, Captain. This isn't going to be easy."

"What are you saying?"

"Breech birth. Kid's backward. Supposed to come head first."

"You sure?"

Nurse didn't answer. "I need that medical kit, ASAP. And towels."

"Should we boil water or something?" asked Powder.

"You did take medical training, right?" asked Liu. "You *are* a certified paramedic, right?"

"Man, I do *not* remember anything on birth. No birth. Nope. Not once."

"How close is she?" asked Captain Freah.

"If the kid wasn't turned around, I'd say she'd be ready any second," said Liu. "The contractions are two minutes apart. Here's the thing—"

The woman screamed again. Her husband dug his nails into Powder's arm. The sergeant tried to reassure him, though it was hard to tell if this had any effect.

"Go ahead," Danny told Liu.

"Captain, this is what they invented C-sections for."

"What do you mean? You have to cut her open?"

"No way, not here, not me. That'll kill her for sure."

"Call for evac?"

"No time. This kid is coming out now, butt first, or they're both dying. It's a squirmy little SOB; gotta be a boy. It's tiny, so maybe he'll slide out if she's strong enough to push. I need to keep the kid warm, very warm, so it doesn't breathe inside the mother until it's out. Shit—I've only heard about this, I've never seen it done."

"If we don't do anything, she'll die anyway," said Freah. His voice was calm, almost cold. He took off his vest and then pulled off his shirt and gave it to Liu. "Get some of the chemical hand warmers down here, blankets, everything we got to generate heat," he said into his com set.

Within ten minutes the Whiplash team had a small tent erected around the woman. A portable kerosene heater had been hauled down from one of the tents above; sweat flowed freely. As the woman's screams grew more desperate, Freah suggested they give the woman morphine, but Liu said that would affect the baby. Besides, he needed her conscious to help push.

All of a sudden, Powder realized the woman had stopped screaming. He looked down at her; she had closed her eyes.

"Liu! Did she die?"

"Transition," said Liu, who was stripped to the waist. He had his hands over a soft shirt and blanket between the woman's legs. "Her body's taking a rest before the real work. What I'm thinking is, when she's ready to push, we stand her up."

"Stand her up?" asked Freah.

"Yeah. Gravity'll help."

The woman moaned.

"Already?" Liu said, looking at her. He doubted if she understood a word of English, but she nodded anyway. "Okay. Powder, Captain, an arm apiece. Hernandez, you hold her behind."

"God," said Freah.

"We got to try," said Liu. "I know it's a long shot."

"*Screw* that horseshit," said Powder, hoisting the poor woman up over his shoulder. "We are going to do this! Yo, husband, you get back here with Hernandez. Let's do it."

"You heard him," said Danny.

"Push!" yelled Liu.

The woman groaned.

"Push!" yelled Liu again, moving his hands below her waist, trying to coax the baby's rear end through the tiny birth hole.

"Argh!" said the woman, leaning forward and down so hard she nearly toppled Powder and Danny.

"Push!" yelled Powder and Danny and Liu.

"Push!" yelled the entire Whiplash team, even General Elliott.

"Argggh!" screamed the woman, falling back.

"Oh, God," said Powder.

"Next one, everybody," said Liu.

The woman bolted upright and screamed again.

"*Push!*"

"*Argh!*"

"*Push!*"

"*Wahhhhhh!*" cried a new voice, never before heard in the world.

"Kick ass!" shouted Danny.

"About fuckin' time," said Powder, who made sure no one was looking as he wiped the tear from his cheek.

AS WORD SPREAD ABOUT WHAT WAS HAPPENING ON THE slope, most of the others went down to try and help out. Zen and one of the CCTs ended up manning the surveillance post. Zen sat in his chair, bundled against the cold in a blanket as well as a parka. Cold and fatigue curled around his head, stinging his eyes, twisting the noises of the night. His mind felt as if it had found steps inside his skull and climbed to the top of a rickety stairway, wedging itself into an attic cubbyhole and peering down a long hallway at his eyes. At times he felt the hollowness he associated with leaving Theta during the ANTARES mind experiments; he wanted to avoid that sensation, that memory, at all costs, and when he felt it slipping over him, he grabbed the wheels of his chair, welcoming the shock of cold on his bare fingers.

ANTARES had teased him with the idea that he might walk again, that he might become "normal" once more. It was a false hope, a lie induced by the drugs that made ANTARES work. But it was impossible to completely banish the hope.

The figures on the screen began to jump up and down and cheer—obviously the baby had been born. The CCT turned from the screens and gave Zen a thumbs up. Zen nodded back, trying to smile as well, but he could tell from the airman's reaction that he hadn't quite pulled it off.

"A boy!" said Jennifer Gleason when she returned from the slope a few minutes later. She was the vanguard of the slow-moving caravan bringing mother and child to a heated tent where they would be sheltered for what remained of the night. "A boy!"

Zen tried to sound enthusiastic. "It looked wild."

"It was. She just pushed him right out. *Peshew*."

The scientist made a sound something like a hockey puck whipping into a net.

"Pretty cool," said Zen.

He wheeled himself around to the cement area to watch the group surrounding the mother's stretcher. Breanna, flanked by Danny Freah and one of the Whiplash soldiers, carried the baby. She smiled at Zen as she passed but kept walking, part of an unstoppable flow.

"Quite a show, Jeff, quite a show," said Brad Elliott, stopping. The general looked about as proud as a grandfather. "A hell of a thing—this is why we're here, you know. To save lives," added the general. "This is it—this is what I wish we could communicate to people. This is what it's all about. People don't understand. You know, American SF forces stopped a massacre of Kurds in northern Iraq after the Gulf War, not far from here."

At Dreamland, Brad Elliott had given several pep talks on some of the projects they were working on; never had Zen seen him quite so enthusiastic.

"Things like this happened all the time," continued the general. "Our planes dropped tons of food, our medics saved hundred of lives a week. We saved people from Saddam—why doesn't the media report that? We should have had a film crew here. This is the sort of story people should see."

"I agree," said Zen, not sure what else to say.

Elliott put his hands on his hips. "We'll get a helicopter in here in the morning, help this kid. Maybe we can get him a college fund going. Sergeant Habib says these people are Turkish Kurds. Hard life. This is what we're about. We have to get the story out."

"Yes, sir."

"Make the place safe for that kid. That's what we have to do."

Zen watched Elliott practically bound away.

"A boy!" said Breanna, slipping her arms around him from behind. She snuggled next to his neck and kissed him. "God, you're cold," she said.

"Hey," he said.

They kissed again.

"You should have seen it, Jeff. Sergeant Liu—God, he is awesome."

"I couldn't get down."

She described the birth, the woman pushing, everyone shouting, the tip of the baby's behind appearing, once, twice, and then a rush of baby and fluid.

"You ought to sleep," said Zen when she finally finished.

"I'll sleep," she said.

"You haven't, and you have a mission in just a few hours now."

"I slept on the way over," she told him. "Chris and I traded off. Don't worry about me, Jeff." She bent down and gave him a quick peck on the cheek, then started back toward the tent where they had installed mother and child. "Warm up the bed. I'll be along."

"Yeah," was all he could think to say.

Dreamland
1700

"LET ME JUST BLUE-SKY THIS FOR A MOMENT, BECAUSE THE implications truly are outrageous."

Dog watched as Jack Firenzi danced at the front of the small conference room off the hall from Dreamland Propulsion Research Suite B, one of the subbasement research facilities in what was informally called the Red Building. The frenetic scientist had come to Dreamland as an expert on propulsion but now headed research into the hydrogen-activated wing platform, or "Hydro" as he referred to it. His audience consisted of two NASA officials, a senior member of the House Armed Services Committee, and an undersecretary of Defense, all of whom had started out somewhat bewildered by the sartorially challenged scientist, yet now were focusing not on his Yankee hat, sneakers, or three-piece suit, but his rapid-fire praise of inflatable wings.

"Imagine an aircraft that can travel at Mach 6, yet with

the turning radius of an F/A-18," continued Firenzi. Dog had heard the presentation before, so he knew that Firenzi would now talk about the XB-5 Unmanned Bomber Project, where the Hydro technology could increase the aerodynamics of the large airframe. Today the scientist's optimism knew no bounds—he took off his hat and began using it to describe additional applications, including microsensor craft scheduled to begin testing in the next phase of the project and an improved U/MF on the drawing board. Under other circumstances, Dog might have watched the VIPs to make sure their reactions remained bemused awe at the eccentric scientist who backed up his enthusiasm with a blackboard's worth of equations. But Dog was preoccupied with the Whiplash mission. The news from Iraq was relatively good—twelve hours of air strike sorties that hit about eighty-five percent of their targets, with no new American losses.

Brad Elliott's Razor theory seemed to be gaining adherents—and yet, the very fact that no planes had been shot down in the past few hours weighed against it. The Iraqis were clearly using new tactics, and also seemed to have many more missiles, or at least launchers, than anyone thought. One of the F-15s had been photographed by a U-2, and the damage appeared consistent with missile fire. But that didn't rule out a laser acting on the others. Everyone was scrambling for intelligence.

"You had mentioned commercial applications?" asked one of the congressmen, Garrett Tyler.

"Oh, yes," said Firenzi. "One possibility is to replace or augment variable geometry. The trapezoid wings used on the Dreamland MC-17 demonstrator—see, that's actually a perfect example of the benefits here. Because (a), that technology—basically a folding slat, let's face it—is very expensive and prone to wear and tear, and (b), it's always there, on the wing, in some manner, and while they've done a lot with the airfoil to reduce drag, it does add to drag. The C-17 is always a C-17. It's never going to break the sound barrier. But imagine a cargo aircraft with a wingspan the size of an F-104—you remember those, the Starfighter? Tiny wings. Fast as hell. So imagine a plane with a fuselage the size of a 767 but wings like that. Takes off—all right, we're still coming up with an acceptable propulsion system, but that can be solved, believe me; that's my area of expertise. You have these narrow, small wings and can go incredibly fast, then, when you want to land, you slow down, pop!"

Firenzi yelled and threw his arms out at his sides. All of his audience, even Dog, jumped up in their seats as the scientist mimicked a plane coming in for a landing.

"Zip," said Firenzi triumphantly. "Enough wing surface inside twenty-five seconds to land on a road. A road! Really. It's the future. Imagine the civilian commercial applications—airports could handle two, three times the traffic. We'd reconfigure runways, change approaches— there would be parking and no traffic jams!"

"You know, I think we're probably all in the mood for dinner about now," said Dog, sensing that any further performance from Firenzi would convince the congressman he was crazy. "Unless there are other questions."

There were a few, but Firenzi handled them as they walked to the elevators. There wasn't enough room for the entire party to fit comfortably; Dog stayed behind with Knapp to wait for the second gondola.

"Anything new from Iraq?" Knapp asked as they waited.

"No details of the raids," Dog told him. He couldn't assume that Knapp's clearance entitled him to know that Dreamland had sent the Whiplash team and two Megafortresses to Turkey.

"Should've dealt with the SOB when we had the chance," said Knapp.

"Can't argue with you, sir," said Dog.

"Like to get a look at what's shooting down our planes."

"So would I." Dog folded his arms.

"The President's counting on you," said Knapp.

"We do our best."

"Joint Chiefs wanted to put you under CentCom for this, but he wouldn't let them."

Dog, unsure exactly how to respond, simply shrugged. The elevator arrived. Knapp grabbed his arm as the door opened.

"Colonel, you understand of course that that was said in confidence."

Dog smiled. "Absolutely."

"I happen to agree that Dreamland and Whiplash should be independent. But best be careful. Dreamland's future may well ride on your standing with the Secretary as well as the President."

"I don't get involved with politics if I can help it. Not my job."

"Maybe you should help it," said Knapp.

Dog had to put his hand out to stop the door from closing, since they hadn't entered the car yet.

"General Magnus may not be your boss forever," added Knapp as they stepped inside.

Dog could only shrug again as the elevator started upward.

Aboard *Quicksilver*, on High Top runway
29 May 1997
0650

"POWER TO TEN PERCENT. ENGINE ONE, TEMP, PRESSURES green. Two, green. Three, green. Four, green. Recheck brakes. Holding. I'd recommend new drums at twenty thousand miles," quipped Chris Ferris, deviating from the checklist. "You might get by with turning them down, but then you risk shimmy stopping at highway speeds."

"Thank you, Mr. Midas," answered Bree.

"We're your under-car-care specialists," said the copilot without losing a beat. "Power to fifty. System checks. We're in the green. Augmented list for assisted takeoff. Green, green, green. My, we *are* good. Flighthawks are plugged in and ready to cook."

"Jeff, how we looking down there?"

"Flighthawks are yours," replied Zen.

"You sound a little tired this morning, Flighthawk leader."

"Not at all, *Quicksilver*. I got two hours of sleep."

Breanna knew Zen was in a bad mood and wouldn't be kidded out of it. He'd told Fentress he wasn't needed today, which had obviously disappointed the apprentice pilot. Fentress looked like he wanted to say something, but Zen had simply rolled himself away.

Not that Fentress shouldn't have spoken up. He needed a little more of Mack Smith in him—not too much. Still, Mack had spent the morning pestering everyone with possible missions he could undertake, and while he was more than a bit of a pain, you had to admire his gung-ho attitude.

From afar.

"Takeoff assist module on line," said Chris. "On your verbal command."

"Computer, takeoff assist countdown," said Bree.

The slightly mechanical feminine voice of the computer began talking. "Takeoff in five, four . . ."

"Okay, crew. Let's go kick butt for little Muhammad Liu, Dreamland's newest addition," she told them.

Someone on the circuit laughed, but the roar of the power plants drowned it out as the Megafortress accelerated. Controlled by the flight computer, the Flighthawk engines acted like rocket packs, augmenting the massive thrust of the EB-52's own P&Ws as the plane shot forward on the mesh. Breanna held the stick loosely, little more than a passenger as the plane rolled past the halfway point of the runway. A slight sensation of weightlessness followed as the plane's wheels skipped off the pavement.

"Gear," she prompted, at the same time nudging the stick. The computer stepped away, content to remain only a backseat driver until called on again. Chris, meanwhile, made sure the landing gear was stowed, did another quick check of the instruments, and then worked with Zen to refuel the Flighthawks through the Megafortress's wing plumbing. The mission specialists began the lengthy process of firing up and calibrating their gear.

The Cold War had given rise to a variety of reconnaissance aircraft, most famously the U-2 and SR-71, which were essentially high-altitude observation platforms able to focus cameras over—or in some cases alongside of—enemy territory. Less well-known were a series of collectors that gathered electronic data ranging from radar capabilities to live radio transmissions. B-29s and B-50s, essentially Superfortresses on steroids, were first pressed into this role; RB-47s replaced them. But it wasn't until vast improvements in electronics in the late sixties and early seventies that the type really came into its own. While a number of airframes were used, the workhorse was based on one of the most successful commercial aircraft of all time—the Boeing 707. Known as the C-135 (and later, E-3) and prepared in dozens if not hundreds of variations, the plane provided an unassuming platform for some of the most sensitive missions of the Cold War. Bristling with antennas and radars, a Rivet Joint or Cobra Ball aircraft might spend hours flying a track in international waters near the Soviet Union, monitoring transmissions during a missile test or a military exercise. It might note how the local air defense commanders reacted when American fighter aircraft approached. It might check the radars used, their capabilities and characteristics. It showed the enemy's strengths and weaknesses, helping to compile a considerable library of information.

As valuable as they were, the planes remained 707s— highly vulnerable to attack. Even JSTARS, a real-time flying command post that revolutionized combat intelligence during the Gulf War, had to stand off at some distance from hostile territory.

That was where the EB-52 came in. Bigger than the 707 or even the 757 airframes proposed to replace it, the Megafortress was designed to operate in the heart of the volcano. One aircraft such as *Quicksilver* could perform the functions of several, detecting and jamming radars, snooping and disrupting radio transmissions, all in places and at times previously unthinkable. Along with an AWACS version and their Flighthawks, the Megafortresses promised to revolutionize warfare once again.

Today's mission, simple in outline, tested some of those basic concepts. *Quicksilver* would fly eastward thirty thousand feet, vectoring south at a point exactly equidistant between Kirkuk and the Iranian border. Thirty miles south of Kirkuk it would loop back north. At roughly the time it swung parallel to Kirkuk about four minutes later, two packages of attack planes would strike their targets, 88 Bravo and 44 Alpha. *Quicksilver* would listen to the Iraqi response, compiling intelligence that might locate the laser or whatever it was that was attacking the allied planes.

"Looking good, Zen," Breanna told her husband as the second U/MF rolled off their wing and sped off to the east. The robot planes had to stay within a ten-mile radius of the Megafortress because of their wide-band communications link.

"Hawk leader," acknowledged her husband stiffly.

"Still cranky, huh?" Chris said as they began their run south.

"He's not much of a morning person," said Breanna.

"Have some J bands, gun dish—looks like a ring of Zsu-23s using their radars," said O'Brien, who was monitoring the radar intercepts. The computer system guiding him would have been the envy of any Cobra Ball operator, able to glide between a dozen different sensors, prioritizing intercepts and pointing out suspicious activity without prompting. Then again, they might not have been envious—it did the work of eight crewmen, making all of them eligible for early retirement.

"Dog Ear detected—they're looking for low fliers at Eight-eight Bravo," added O'Brien.

"Let's pass that on," said Breanna. "They're still a good distance away."

"Coyote Bravo leader, this is Dreamland *Quicksilver*," said Chris.

"Coyote Bravo. Go ahead *Quicksilver*."

"We have an active Dog Ear looking for you at Eight-eight Bravo. Indication is they have a Gopher missile battery along with their Zeus guns."

"Coyote Bravo acknowledges. Thanks for the heads-up, *Quicksilver*."

The Gophers—also called SA-13s by NATO—were short- to medium-range SAMs that used infrared radar to lock on their target, similar to the more common SA-9s though somewhat larger and more capable. The Dog Ear radar was used to detect aircraft at a distance. After detection, a range-finding unit would allow the commander to launch the missiles; their all-aspect, filtered IR sensors would then take them to their target. The systems were relatively sophisticated but defeatable if you knew they were there.

"Have an E band radar that's not on my menu," said O'Brien. "Low power, really low power—lost it. Plotting. Wow—never seen anything like this."

**Aboard *Quicksilver*, over northern Iraq
0742**

ZEN WORKED THE FLIGHTHAWKS AHEAD OF *QUICKSILVER*, alternating between *One* and *Two*. He was at twenty thousand feet, considerably lower than the EB-52 but well outside the range of the low-altitude AAA and shoulder-launched weapons that were ubiquitous below. His helmet visor was divided into two sections; the upper two-thirds fed an optical view from one of the Flighthawks, simulating what he would see if he were sitting in the cockpit. A HUD ghosted over altitude, speed, and other essentials. The lower screen was divided into three smaller sections— an instrument summary for both planes at the far left, a long-distance radar plot supplied by *Quicksilver* in the middle, and an optical cockpit view from the other plane. The visor display could be infinitely customized, though Zen tended to stick to this preset, using it about ninety percent of the time when he was flying two robots. The voice commands *"One"* and *"Two"* instantly changed the main view, a phenomenon he thought of as jumping into the cockpit of the plane. He controlled the small planes with the help of two joysticks, one in his right and one in his left hand. Control for the planes jumped with the view, so that his right hand always worked the plane in the main screen.

"O'Brien, you find that E band radar?" asked Zen.

"Negative. Threat library thinks it's a Side Net but it's not clear what it would be connected to. Definitely early warning. I can't even find the source."

"How about approximately?" Zen asked.

They plotted it below 88 Bravo and a bit to the east, which put it fifty miles away and dead on in *Hawk One*'s path near the Iranian border. A Side Net radar was a long-range target acquisition unit, capable of detecting a plane the size of an F-16 at roughly ninety-five miles; with its uncoated nose, the Megafortress was possibly though not definitely visible around the same range. The Flighthawk would be invisible at least to ten miles, and might not even be seen at all.

Of course, with the radar off, it could see nothing at all. Zen's threat radar was clean.

"What do you think it's working with?" Zen asked O'Brien.

"Ordinarily I'd say an SA-2 and SA-3 battalion," answered O'Brien. "But at this point it's anybody's guess. There are no known sites in the area."

"Maybe this is the sucker we're looking for."

"Could be. They're not on the air. Tracking some other stuff," added O'Brien. "Man, there are a *lot* of radars up here—didn't we put these suckers out of business five years ago?"

"I'm going to get a little lower and see if I spot anything," said Jeff. "We'll store the video for the analysts."

"Sounds good, Captain. I'll alert you if I get another read."

"Strike aircraft are zero-three from their IPs," said Chris, indicating that the attackers were just about to start their bombing runs.

Zen concentrated on the image in his screen as he tucked toward the earth, looking for the semicircle of launchers and trailers the Iraqis liked to set their missiles up in. SA-2s were large suckers always accompanied by a variety of support vehicles; they could be obscured by netting and other camouflage but not totally hidden. SA-3s were about half the size, but they too should stick out if they were positioned to fire.

O'Brien's rough plot was centered around a farming area on a relatively flat plain about two miles square. With no indications of any military activity—or any activity at all—Zen nudged the Flighthawk faster and slightly farther east, widening his search pattern.

"*Losing connection,*" warned the computer as he strayed a bit too far.

Zen immediately throttled back, letting *Quicksilver* catch up. As his speed dropped, a row of black boxes appeared in the lower left screen.

"Magnify ground image," he told the computer. A scanner tracking his retinas interpreted exactly which images he meant.

"O'Brien, I have four stationary vehicles, look like they might be radar or telemetry vans. Not set up."

"You see a dish?"

"Negative," said Jeff. "No missiles."

He slid the robot plane closer to the ground. Razor was mobile, roughly the size of a tank.

"*Losing connection,*" warned the computer again.

"Bree, I need you to stay with *Hawk One.*"

"We're at our turn," Breanna told him. Her priority was the attack package, at least until they saddled up and headed home.

The first vehicle was a car, oldish, a nondescript Japanese sedan.

Two pickup trucks.

A flatbed.

Not Razor, not anything.

"Radar—something," said O'Brien.

"*Connection loss in five seconds,*" pleaded the computer. "*Four, three—*"

Zen flicked his wrist back, bringing the Flighthawk west to stay with the Megafortress.

"Vehicles were clean," he told Breanna.

"Acknowledged," she said.

"Got something else," said O'Brien. "Jayhawk—airplanes on A-1."

"Sitrep map," Zen told the computer. "Identify A-1."

A bird's-eye view with *Quicksilver* and the Flighthawks highlighted as green blips materialized in the main screen. A red highlight and circle identified A-1 as a small airfield northeast of Baghdad, about 120 miles away.

"MiG-21 radars," added O'Brien. "They must be getting ready to take off."

"*QUICKSILVER,* BE ADVISED WE HAVE A PAIR OF BOGIES coming off A-1 south of Eight-eight Bravo," said the controller aboard *Coyote,* the AWACS plane. "Stick Flight is being vectored in. Please hold to your flight plan."

"*Quicksilver,*" acknowledged Breanna. "We have radar indications from those planes. Looks like two MiG-21s. Working on radio intercepts," she added.

O'Brien and Habib started talking together behind her.

"One at a time," scolded Ferris.

"Indications are MiG-21 or F-7 Spin Scan-style I band radars. Old soldiers, these boys," said O'Brien.

"Tower has cleared four planes," said Habib. "I have his transmission loud and clear."

"Lost radars."

"You're sure about four planes?" Breanna asked.

"Yes, Captain. No acknowledgments, though. I have some ground transmissions. Computer says it's an HQ code. I can put more resources on the descramble."

"Concentrate on the planes," Breanna told him. "O'Brien—any sign of that laser?"

"Negative."

"*Coyote*, be advised that we believe there are four planes, not two," said Breanna.

"Tower remains silent," said Habib. "No ground control radio that I can pick up. We're doing a full spin," he added, meaning that the snooping gear was now scanning or "spinning" through frequencies looking for hits at low power or wide distances.

"No radars," said O'Brien.

"Thanks for the information, *Quicksilver*," answered the AWACS. "We continue to have only two contacts, MiG-21s, in the bushes. Eagles are being scrambled. Hold to your flight plan."

High Top
0830

"I'VE RIDDEN MOTORCYCLES THAT GO FASTER."

"Major, I'm telling you—two hours with these engines and you have twenty percent more power. Probably thirty. Thieves, hungry for power."

"That's not another stinkin' Dylan song, is it, Garcia?"

"Knockin' on heaven's door, Major," said the techie, beaming as if he'd just hit Powerball.

A Pave Low heading in toward High Top began shaking the air, kicking off a sympathetic rattle in the Bronco's props—and Mack's teeth.

"If we were at Dreamland—five-bladed prop, variable

pitch—reinforce the wings, maybe a rocket pack for that quick boost, sellin' postcards at the hangin'," continued Garcia. "This is a great platform, Major. A fantastic aircraft. See this?" Garcia ducked under the wing and slapped the rear fuselage. "Four guys in here—five if they don't have B.O. This ain't workin' on Maggie's Farm, I'll tell you that."

"So if it's such a great plane, how come the Marines gave it up?" Mack asked.

"They didn't want to," said Garcia. "You ask—they went kicking and screaming. These are boots of Spanish leather."

"You know, Garcia, you ought to lose that speech impediment."

Dust whipped toward them as the helicopter pushed in. Mack turned his back and covered the side of his face. As the rotors died down, he turned back to Garcia. "Let's refuel and get back in the air."

"Uh, Major, didn't you hear what I said?"

"That's another Dylan song?"

"What I've been trying to tell you is that I have to re-tune the engines to work with the Dreamland fuel," said Garcia.

"What?"

"Well, it all started during the first oil scare. See, what the problem is—ten-shutt!"

Garcia snapped to attention so sharply a drill sergeant would have swooned. General Elliott, lugging his overnight and a serious frown, tossed off a salute.

"Mack—when the hell are we taking off?" asked Elliott.

"I don't know, General. There's some sort of fuel thing."

"Few minor adjustments to the engines, General," said

Garcia, who had served under Elliott at Dreamland. "As you recall, sir, it was under your command that JP-12B-2 was developed as a special blend for the Flighthawks, with the Megafortress engines tuned to accept it. The mix is just a little different from your JP-8 or JP-4, and over time or in extreme—"

"That's quite all right, Garcia," said Elliott. "Just make it work."

"I just have to make a few adjustments. Not a big deal. Now, if we were back home—"

"It's okay," said Elliott. He put out his hand as if he were a traffic cop. "Mack, I'm going back on the Pave Low. Get the plane back to Incirlik in one piece, all right?"

Aboard *Quicksilver*
0830

ZEN PUSHED FORWARD, HIS BODY LEANING TO THE RIGHT as he whipped both Flighthawks in that direction, the U/MFs about five miles apart, parallel at a separation of three thousand feet. The radar detector screen in the middle of the lower visual band showed two large yellow clumps peeking upward at him; the transmissions were ID'd as I band and the yellow indicated that, while they were active, they did not yet pose a threat to the small, stealthy Flighthawks.

"Gun Dish," said O'Brien, adding coordinates to his warning that a Zeus radar was looking for him.

The two MiG-21s were old and primitive aircraft, easy fodder for the Americans. Zen suspected that the Iraqis were using them as decoys for the other two planes Habib had heard—which he guessed would be MiG-29s using passive sensors. The planes were approaching from the southeast, roughly eleven o'clock off *Hawk One*'s center line—they didn't have a precise location, but they would have to be very low not to be detected by the AWACS.

If they'd been in *Galatica*, the gear would have them dotted by now.

"Connection loss in five seconds," warned the computer.

"Bree!"

"Zen, you have to stay with me. The attack package isn't clear. Let the Eagles get the MiGs."

"I can nail them myself. There's an RAF flight just south of them; if the MiGs divert, they'll run right into them."

"The AWACS is aware of that. It's not our show. Let the Eagles do their job."

"Connection loss in three, two—"

Zen yanked back on his sticks, pulling the robot planes back closer to the Megafortress. As he did, the radar in *Hawk Two* caught another plane flying from the south low enough to scrape a grasshopper's belly.

"Contact, bearing 180—shit, I lost it," he told Breanna.

"Nothing," said O'Brien quickly.

"Blue Bandits!" shouted one of the Eagle pilots, his voice loud and excited at seeing the enemy MiG-21s. "Nine o'clock."

"Tally," replied the other pilot, as calm as his wingman was excited. The two interceptors had run up from the south behind the two small planes at tremendous speed, closing to visual range to avoid the possibility—slim, but real—of locking onto friendlies in the tangled fray. With their limited radars and no ground controller to warn them, the two Iraqi jets probably didn't even know they were in the crosshairs.

"I have the MiG on the left."

"Two," acknowledged the wingman.

Zen could visualize it perfectly. The pilots would have their heaters—AIM-9 Sidewinders—selected as the enemy planes grew in their HUDs. The missiles would growl, indicating they could sniff the enemy tailpipes. But the Eagle jocks would wait a few seconds more, closing the gap. At the last second the MiG pilots would sense something, catch a reflection, a shadow, a hint—they'd start to maneuver, but it would be too late.

"Fox Two!" said both pilots, nearly in unison, as they launched their heat seekers.

"Connection loss in five seconds," warned the computer.

Zen tucked *Hawk One* back to the east and gave *Two* a little more gas, catching up to *Quicksilver*. He got another contact in the bushes; it seemed to be turning.

MiG-29. Bingo.

"Quicksilver, I have a bogie. I need you to break ninety," Zen told Breanna, asking her to cut hard to the east.

"Negative, Flighthawk commander. Give the contact to Eagle Flight."

Screw that, thought Zen. The MiG turned toward him, and now there was a second contact. The planes were flying so low they could be pickup trucks.

Twenty-five miles away. If the Flighthawks had radar missiles, they'd be dead meat. But the U/MFs were fitted with cannons only.

"Mission on Eight-eight Bravo is complete," said Ferris. "We're cleared."

The MiG-29s continued their turns, heading south now, running away. They'd probably caught his radar.

He'd have to juice it to nail them.

Hit them now before they got within range of the RAF flight.

"Bree! I need you to stay with me. Check the Flighthawk screen."

"Hawk commander, we're following our game plan. The bogies are out of reach."

"Shit! I have them positively ID'd as MiG-29s. There's an RAF attack package just southeast of them."

"Location has been given to Eagle flight and *Coyote*," said Ferris.

"Shit!" Zen fought the urge to rip his helmet off and throw it against the side of the cabin.

"Jeff, they're out of range," said Bree.

"Yeah, now."

"Missiles in the air!" warned O'Brien. "Launch—no wait—no launch, no launch. Slot Back radar, may be looking at an SA-2. Jeez—everything's crazy. What the hell? I'm blank."

"ECMS," BREANNA TOLD CHRIS.

"On it already. We're clean."

She nosed *Quicksilver* ten degrees to the west, following their briefed course.

"Bree—we could have nailed those MiGs," said Zen. His voice frothed with anger.

Her thumb twitched, but she stayed on her course.

"Flighthawk leader, our priority was the attack mission."

"We could have nailed them," Zen told her.

She didn't answer.

"Our fuel's okay," Chris told her.

She nodded instead of saying anything, checked her instruments quickly, then asked O'Brien about the SA-2 contacts he'd reported.

"I'm not sure—I got some sort of indication, a flash from the east. I'm not sure if it was a screw-up or what."

"No missiles?"

"Not that I could find. Maybe they tried a launch and had an explosion, or it could have been something on the ground totally unrelated. Two or three radars flicked on at the same time, including at least one standard airport job. Iran had a long-distance air traffic on as well. I haven't had a chance to go back and sort it out."

"Laser?"

"Well, not that I can tell. No IR reading. I can go back and run Jennifer's filter over the data."

"Wait till we get down. We're fifteen minutes from High Top, maybe a little closer."

"Hey, Bree, you might want to listen in to this," said Chris. "AWACS is reporting they lost contact with an RAF Tornado. The plane disappeared completely from their screens."

IV

Unnecessary Risk

"NEVER EVER TALK TO ME THAT WAY WHEN WE'RE FLYING. Never." Breanna felt her heart pumping as she confronted her husband beneath the plane.

"I could have had those MiGs," Zen said.

"The attack flight was our priority."

"Those MiGs nailed the Tornado."

"No way."

"Listen, Bree—"

"No, you listen, Jeff." Breanna clasped her hands together to keep them from shaking. "Anyone else talked to me that way, I'd have them thrown off the plane."

"Oh, bullshit. I outrank you."

"I'm in charge of the aircraft, not you."

"Those MiGs nailed the Tornado, and I could have gotten them," said Zen. He pushed his wheelchair back slightly on the pavement below the right wing of the Megafortress. "We could have prevented that."

"That's bullshit and you know it."

"Bullshit yourself."

"I have work to do." Breanna turned, furious with him, furious with herself. She *had* done the right thing, she thought, and there was no way the MiGs nailed the Tornado. The F-15s would have been all over them.

Each stride was a grenade as she stomped toward the mess tent. Every glance pulverized the rocks around her. The large tent was nearly empty; only Mack Smith sat in the far corner, nursing a cup of coffee. She took a bottle of water and a sandwich from the serving counter, then walked to the table farthest away from him, even though it was also the farthest from the heaters.

The wrapper claimed the sandwich was ham and cheese, though the meat looked suspiciously like roast beef. She bit into it; it tasted more like pastrami.

"Better than MREs, huh?" said Mack, coming over. "Next Pave Low's bringing steaks."

"Leave me alone," she snapped.

"Uh-oh, somebody's in a bad mood. Tell Uncle Mack all about it."

"One of these days, Major, someone's going to knock that smirk so far down your throat it comes out your ass."

"I only hope it's you," said Smith, taking another swig of his coffee.

ZEN FURLED HIS ARMS IN FRONT OF HIS CHEST. BREANNA was right—he'd been out of line to talk to her that way in the plane.

He was right about everything else, but he still shouldn't have talked to her that way.

But damn—he could have nailed both of those bastards. The Eagles claimed they chased the MiGs away—they said they headed into the bushes and ran back to base—but that was just cover-my-ass bullshit, he thought. If the MiGs didn't get the Tornado, who did?

There were a dozen candidates, starting with a stray Zeus flak dealer and ending with General Elliott's Razor clone. Not to mention plain old mechanical failure or even pilot error; he knew of at least one Tornado that had pancaked into a mountain during the Gulf War because the pilot had lost his situational awareness.

Still, the Eagles should have made sure the MiGs were down. And out. He would've.

But Breanna was right about their priorities; where *Quicksilver* went was her call. His job was to escort, to protect her. Yes, he extended their reach, flushed out threats, and passed along the information to everyone else in the air. But his job, bottom line, was to protect her, not the other way around.

Had he wanted to nail the MiGs for the glory?

Bullshit on that.

But he could have nailed the mothers.

He owed Breanna an apology. Unsure where she'd gone, he wheeled himself toward the mobile Whiplash command post, then decided the mess tent was a better bet.

I'm sorry, he rehearsed. *I was a hothead. I used to be cool but now I'm just a hothead. I've lost a lot of self-control since the accident.*

No. Don't blame it on the accident. That was bush league.

I'm sorry. I was out of line.

Zen was still trying to decide exactly what he would say when he entered the mess tent. Breanna was there, sitting next to Mack Smith.

Zen pushed himself toward the serving tables. A small refrigerator held drinks; there was a pile of sandwiches next to it and a large metal pot of soup, or at least something that smelled like soup. Zen took two of the sandwiches and a Coke and wheeled himself over to the table.

"Hey," he said to Breanna.

"Hey there, robot brain," said Mack. "Have fun this morning?"

"I always have fun, Mack." Zen pushed his chair as close to the end of the table as he could get it, but that still left a decent gap between his chest and the surface. He had to lean forward to put his soda and sandwiches down.

"Those sandwiches are about a week old," said Mack. "Check 'em for mold before you take a bite."

Zen bit into them defiantly. He was halfway through the second when Danny Freah, Chris Ferris, Captain Fentress, and the two mission specialists crewing *Quicksilver* came in. Fentress had a map rolled up under his arm, along with a pair of folded maps in his hand.

"Majors, Captain," said Danny. "Just talked with Major Alou. He's inbound. We want to have a briefing over in the trailer as soon as he's down. CentCom is going to nail that SA-2 site we picked up and they need our help."

"Is that what got the Tornado?" Zen asked.

"No one's sure," said Danny. "At this point it's possible he wasn't even shot down. But CentCom wants to hit something, and it's the biggest target in the area. Even if it didn't get them—and I don't think it did—it should be taken down."

"How close were the MiGs Major Stockard saw?" Breanna asked O'Brien.

"It's possible they could have gotten the RAF flight if they were using very long-range missiles," said Chris Ferris, answering for the radar specialist. "But we didn't sniff anything in the air, and as far as we know, the AWACS didn't have any contacts either. Not even the Eagles could find them."

"Nothing," added O'Brien. "If they fired Alamos, we would have known it. Their guidance systems would have given them away."

"Alamos with heat sensors," suggested Zen. The Alamo missiles—Russian-made AA-10s—came in at least three varieties, including a heat-seeker. But the longest-range version known to the West, the AA-10C, had a range of roughly twenty-two miles and used an active radar, which would have been detected. The infrared or heat-seeking version would have a much shorter range.

"Million-in-one shot," said Ferris.

"Alamos at twenty-five miles?" said Mack. "What the hell are you guys talking about?"

As Ferris explained, Zen looked at Breanna. She was still steaming, he could tell. He tried to send his apology via ESP, but it didn't take.

"Had to be a laser," said Mack when he heard the details. "Only explanation."

"So where is it, then? With the SA-2s?" said Ferris.

"Shit, they'd hide it in a mosque or something," said Mack. "You know these ragheads."

"That might be right," said Danny.

"Maybe it's with one of these radars that flicks on and off," said Zen.

"Possible," said Ferris. "On the other hand, none of the sites seem large enough to house an energy weapon."

"It doesn't have to be that big," said Zen. "Razor's not big at all. It moves a tank chassis."

"I don't think the Iraqis could make it that small," said Ferris.

"I bet it's in a mosque," said Mack.

"Whatever size, they'd try to make themselves as inconspicuous as possible," said Bree.

"There—we look for what's inconspicuous," said Mack.

He meant it as a joke, but nobody laughed.

"Our best lead is the radars," said Zen. "Because even if it were mobile, it would have to be getting a feed from them somehow. Maybe it can go from one unit to another."

"Or they have a dedicated landline, with high speed connections, fiber optics," suggested Bree.

"You really think the Iraqis can do that?" said Ferris.

"They're doing something," said Mack.

"I think I can narrow the area down on where that Slot Back radar was if you give me a half hour," said O'Brien. "It wasn't briefed. There may even be another one down there, though the signal was really weak. I'll tell you one thing," he added, "either the operator is damn good or they've got some sort of new equipment down there, because the computer couldn't lock it down."

JENNIFER GLEASON FOLDED HER HANDS OVER HER MOUTH and nose almost if she were praying. She had only a rudimentary notion of how the coding for the program governing the IR detection modes worked, and without either the documentation or the raw power of Dreamland's code analyzers, she could only guess how to modify it. The secure data-link with Dreamland was still pending; once it was in place, she would be able to speak with the people there who had developed the detector. But the pilots wanted the plane to fly before then, and she thought it shouldn't be that hard to figure out. She replayed the EB-52's recorded inputs from the last mission, watching the coding to see how she might tweak the IR detector to find a momentary burst in the infrared spectrum.

Shorter than a launch, but stronger?

Jennifer reached for her soda on the floor of *Quicksilver*'s flight deck, pulling it up deliberately. She took two sips and then set it down, all the while staring at the blank multipurpose screens at the radar-intercept operator's station. She ran the detection loops over again, watching her laptop screen where the major components of the code were displayed. The interface program took data from different sensors and configured it for the screens; it was monstrously complex because it had to accept data from a number of different sensors, which had been designed without a common bus.

Her laptop flagged a bug in the interface that had to do with an errant integer cache. It was minor—the interface program simply ignored the error.

Odd. It should have been trapped out by the interface. The error handling section was comprehensive, and in any event included an "if all else fails" section where anything unexpected should have gone.

But it hadn't. Jennifer traced the error to an ambient reading from the sensor. The detector had flicked onto something and sent a matrix of information about it on to the interface. The interface didn't understand one of the parameters.

An error in the sensor that hadn't been caught during the rigorous debugging of the interface at Dreamland?

Certainly possible. Happened all the time.

Except . . .

Jennifer reached down for her soda again. It could just be an error—there must have been a million lines of code there, and mistakes were inevitable.

But if it wasn't a mistake, it would be what they were looking for.

Well, no, it could be anything. But anything wasn't what she was interested in. She needed a theory, and this was it.

She could get a base line with some flares, see what happened, try to screw it up. Use those numbers to compare to the error, calculate.

Calculate what, exactly?

Something, anything. She just needed a theory.

If Tecumseh were here, she thought, he would tell her to figure it out. He would fold his arms around her and rub her breasts and tell her to figure it out.

Jennifer jumped up from the station, scooped up her can of soda, and ran to find Garcia.

Incirlik, Turkey
1230

TORBIN FINISHED HIS TAE KWON DO ROUTINE, BOWING TO the blank wall. He was alone in the workout room, still a leper despite the semiofficial admission from General Harding that his gear and the mission tapes checked out; he wasn't at fault in the shoot-downs.

Not at fault, but impotent nonetheless. The Phantom remained grounded until further notice. Its next flight would undoubtedly be to the boneyard.

Torbin folded his arms at his sides, trying to maintain his composure. He belonged back in the rear seat of the Weasel, back over Iraq. They could nail the damn radars one by one, no matter what bullshit tactics they were pulling. Hell, maybe he could jimmy around with the gear somehow and scope out their tactics.

Whatever.

Something heavy roared off the nearby runway.

Ought to be me, he thought, deciding to run through his routine again.

High Top
1300

THE HEAT WAS SO HIGH IN THE TRAILER, DANNY FELT SWEAT rolling down his neck as he studied the map. On the other side of the table Major Alou finished telling the others about CentCom's plans. There was no doubt now that

Iraq had some sort of new weapon or weapons. Six planes had been shot down; four men were still missing. The ratio of sortie to loss was just above twenty to one. Even the most conservative reckoning of the statistics from the Gulf War put the sortie-to-loss ratio well over a hundred to one. Maybe it wasn't a laser, but something big and bad was going down.

"They're bringing in a pair of U-2s from the States to increase surveillance," said Alou, "but they're worried about how vulnerable they'll be, and in any event they won't arrive for another twenty-four hours or so. The game plan in the meantime is to take out every radar and missile site we can find."

"The bastards keep rolling them out," said Chris Ferris. "They've been keeping them in the closet, or what?"

"They've spent the money they got for food the past five years on rebuilding their defenses," said Alou. "Damn country's starving while Saddam's buying new radar dishes and vans. The missiles they've had. They just haven't fired them until now."

"They're not on long enough to hit anything," said O'Brien. "Has to be a laser."

"They might be synthesizing the radar input," said Ferris. "If you had a sophisticated computer, you could compile all of the inputs from a diverse net, then launch. No one radar would ever stay on long enough to seem like the culprit. They could move the radars around, use some and not others—that would explain why they duck the Weasels and the other jammers."

"Pretty sophisticated," said O'Brien.

"Jennifer said it's doable," said Ferris. "And then they barrage launch at the contacts. That's what they're doing."

"We're jamming like hell. Guidance systems ought to be confused."

"Maybe they've improved them," said Ferris.

"If that is what's going on," said Zen, "then what we should do is nail the coordinating site."

"How do we find it?" asked Breanna.

"We follow the communications net," he suggested. "Listen in. See where the center is. That's what *Quicksilver*'s good at."

"I still think it's a laser," said Mack. "Got to be."

"Sure," said Zen. "But we can find that the same way. Instead of looking for the weapon, we look for the guidance system. That's how Weasels work, right? They nail the radar van."

Danny straightened from the map. He felt like the odd man out as they continued to discuss the situation and what to do. He felt like he ought to contribute something, help plan a mission somehow. He and his guys were sitting on the ground playing babysitters—literally, with the Kurd kid Liu had plucked out.

Protecting the planes was an important job. Still, the Marines provided more than enough security, and the Navy Seabee guys they'd brought in with them were going great guns expanding High Top—if they had their way, it would be the size of O'Hare in another forty-eight hours.

So Whiplash was free to do more important things.

Like?

"All right," said Alou. "Let's work up some surveillance tracks to coincide with the missions for CentCom."

"You know it seems to me that if this radar computer gear is that sophisticated, we ought to try to get a look at it," said Danny. "Get pictures, data, that sort of stuff."

"Hey, Captain, why don't we just grab it?" said Mack.

He probably meant it as a put-down—Smith could be a real asshole—but the idea struck Danny as eminently doable.

Or at least more interesting than babysitting.

"If I can get a Chinook or a Pave Low in here, we could take it out, no sweat," said Danny.

The others seemed to ignore him.

"I still think it's a laser," said Mack.

"*That* would be worth taking," said Danny. "Big-time."

Finally, everyone realized he was serious. The conversation stopped; they all turned and looked at him.

"We could," said Danny. "Or at least get intelligence about it."

"You serious?" asked Zen.

"Shit yeah."

"Unnecessary risk," said Alou. "Even if we could find it."

"Risk is our job," said Danny. He knew he was pushing further than reasonable, but what the hell—Whiplash was created exactly for missions like this. Besides, except for the target, it was a straightforward armed reconnaissance mission behind enemy lines. Anyone could do it.

Pretty much.

"We're not even positive where the site is," said Breanna. "We don't have a target for you, Danny."

"So get me one."

AS THE OTHERS FINISHED WORKING OUT THE DETAILS FOR the missions, Zen wheeled himself through the narrow door and down the ramp. A gray CH-46E Sea Knight or "Frog" was just arriving, bringing in more Marines. The two-rotored helicopter looked like a scaled-down version of the more famous Chinook—though in fact the development had been the other way around, with the Frog coming first.

Darkening the sky behind the Marine helo was an Osprey, just tipping its wings and rotors to land. The MV-22 was Whiplash's chariot of choice, twice as fast as most helicopters, with considerably longer range.

Zen wheeled toward *Quicksilver*'s parking area. He'd rejected numerous suggestions that he get a battery-powered chair—definitely a macho thing—but at times like this, skidding through potholes and ducking rocks, even he would have admitted it'd be useful.

He hadn't apologized to Bree. He knew he'd have to, and the sooner the better—stale apologies were even more difficult to make.

Send flowers or something. Blow her away if he could get them up here.

Jennifer Gleason and Louis Garcia were standing beneath *Quicksilver*'s tail, pointing at the large black semisphere and wire guts of the coverless IR sensor above.

"Hey, how's it going?" he shouted, rolling toward them.

"Lousy," Jennifer told him. "I tried to recalibrate the programming and now there's a bad circuit on the sensor. It's going to take at least an hour to get it working."

"An hour? We're supposed to take off then. Forty-five minutes, actually."

"Oh," said Jennifer.

"I can get this back together quicker than a rolling stone," said Garcia. "But then I have to help prep the plane."

"Okay." Jennifer took a strand of her hair and pulled it back behind her ear. "We'll toss flares off the Flighthawk."

"What for?"

"I want to see what the data sequence should be. There's an error I'm trying to make sense of."

"I can launch the flares, no sweat." Zen glanced toward the U/MF already loaded onto the Megafortress's wing.

"Good. I'll grab something to eat and my flight gear."

"Hold on, cowboy." Zen whirled his chair across her path as she started to duck away. "Who says you're coming with us? It's a war zone."

"And Somalia wasn't?" Jennifer put her hands on her hips defiantly. "If there is a laser out there, you need me in the air. Don't worry, Jeff, I can take care of myself."

"I didn't say you couldn't."

"Hmmmph," she said, stomping away.

"I'm having a bad day with women," Zen said softly.

"Honey, give me just one more chance," sang Garcia.

"Huh?"

"Just a song, Major."

"Garcia—is *everything* in life a Dylan song?"

"Pretty much."

Dreamland
0523

"TEST CODE CHECKS, SIR," SAID THE LIEUTENANT AT THE communications desk in the secure situation room triumphantly. "You're good to go."

"Make the connection," said Dog. He stood in the middle of the floor in front of the screen, waiting for the transmission from Turkey. The test pattern on the screen blipped blue. The words CONNECTION PENDING appeared in the middle of the screen.

He wanted to talk to Jennifer in the worst way. But of course that wasn't what this was about.

"Hey, Colonel, good to see you finally," said Danny.

The screen was still blank.

"Well, you can see me but—wait, there we go," said Dog as the video finally snapped in. Danny Freah sat at the table in the Whiplash trailer. His eyes drooped a bit at the corners, but his face and hands were full of energy. Before Dog could say anything, Danny launched into an argument for undertaking a ground recon of the Iraqi Razor clone.

"And hello to you too, Captain," said Dog when he finally paused for a breath.

"It'd be a real intelligence coup," said Danny. "We could use the helmets to beam back video. Then we can take key parts back."

"Do we know where it is?"

"No, sir. But the missions they're on now—they'll find them."

"Assuming, of course, it exists."

"Hell, if we can get some help, we could grab the whole thing."

"Let me get Rubeo and our Razor people down here to talk about this," said Dog. "It may be useful."

"It'll be damn useful."

"Relax, Captain. From what I've heard out of Cent-Com, they're not even one hundred percent sure it's a laser. No one can explain how Saddam would have built it."

"If it's not—let's say it's a radar and missile setup we don't know about—we should take a look at that too," said Danny. "See what they're up to. Jennifer Gleason suggested that they may have some way of taking a lot of different inputs and cobbling them together. Software for that would be worth grabbing too, don't you think?"

"Captain, while I don't want to dampen your enthusiasm," said Dog, "why don't we take this one step at a time. How about an update on your status?"

"Sure," said Danny. He gave him a complete rundown, working backward from the last mission. Then he told him about the baby who'd been born the previous night. It sounded like just the thing the Pentagon PR people would eat up—except, of course, that the mission was code-word classified, and would undoubtedly remain so.

"Kinda makes you a grandpa, huh, Colonel?" said Danny.

"I don't think so," said Dog. "What kind of shape are our people in?"

"Top notch, sir."

Danny's mention of Jennifer gave him the perfect excuse to talk to her—he ought to hear about her theory from her, he thought. Certainly if it were Rubeo or one of the other scientists, he'd ask to talk to him directly.

But Dog hesitated. He didn't want to cross over the line.

Of course he should talk to her.

"Is Dr. Gleason there?" he asked, finally giving in. "I'd like to hear her theory on the radars."

"She's up with the Megafortresses, sir," said Danny. "She's going on a mission."

"Mission?"

"Yes, sir. They're modifying the IR detection gear to search for lasers."

Dog pursed his lips but said nothing.

High Top
1510

MISSION PREPPED, BREANNA GAVE IN TO AN IMPULSE BEfore heading back up to the Megafortress and jogged over to the baby's tent after relieving herself in the Marines' new latrine. She wanted to see the cute little guy before she took off.

For good luck. Just for good luck.

She expected mother and child would be sleeping, but as she neared the tent she heard laughter. The tent was crowded with Whiplash members and Marines, who were taking turns holding and cooing the infant.

"Guarding against a sneak attack?" said Bree, trying to squeeze inside.

"Can't be too careful about colic," said one of the men, deadly serious.

"Well, let me hold him for good luck," she said, sliding near Sergeant "Powder" Talcom, who was holding him. The sergeant gave the baby up very reluctantly.

"You're a cute one," she said, gently cradling the baby.

Little Muhammad Liu looked at her with very big brown eyes. Then he furled his nose and began to cry.

"Aw, Captain, you made him cry," said Powder, immediately reaching for the infant. The other men closed in; Bree suddenly felt very outnumbered.

"There there," she told the infant, rocking him gently. "Aunt Breanna isn't going to hurt you."

The baby sniffed, burped, then stopped crying.

"You got the touch, Captain," said one of the men.

"Well, I'm quitting while I'm ahead," she said, handing the baby off.

Iraq Intercept Missile Station Two, northern Iraq
1510

MUSAH TAHIR ROSE FROM HIS PRAYER MAT AND BOWED once more in the direction of Mecca before starting back to his post in the radar van. For the past three days Allah had been remarkably beneficent, rewarding his poor efforts at improving the Russian radar equipment with fantastic victories over the Americans. Volleys of missiles—a combination of SA-2s, Threes, and Sixes—had brought down several aircraft.

Or at least his commanders told them they had. Tahir was aware only of his own small role in the war as both technician and operator. He had studied engineering at MIT as well as the Emirates, and in some ways this job was a million times below his capability. But fate and Allah had brought him here, and he could not argue with either.

Tahir settled on his narrow metal bench before the two screens he commanded and began his routine. First, he made sure that each line of the Swiss-made system in the console on the left was working, punching the buttons methodically and greeting the man on the other line with a word of peace and a prayer. When he reached the third line, there was nothing—Shahar, the idiot Shiite, no doubt a traitor, once again sleeping at his post. Tahir waited patiently, speaking the man's name at sixty second intervals, until after nearly ten minutes the observer came on the line.

"Planes?" Tahir asked, cutting off Shahar's apology. He knew the answer would be no—he had not received the warning yet from the spies at Incirlik that the infidels' planes had taken off. But the question would serve as a remonstrance.

"No," said the man.

"Remain alert," snapped Tahir, hanging up. He sat back at his console, frowning as one of the guards walked past his doorway. There was only a small security contingent here, a half-dozen men; anything larger might have attracted the Americans' attention. Besides, so far behind the lines, there was no need for troops. Tahir several times had considered the fact that the men had probably been posted here to keep an eye on him.

That was hardly necessary. He went through the other lines quickly. When he had determined that all were operating, he proceeded to the next set of checks. These were more difficult, involving the buried cables that ran from the various collection sites. More than two dozen radars and six microwave stations were connected to Tahir's post via fiber-optic cable that had been buried at great expense, in most cases before the infidel war. If it were laid out end to end it would no doubt reach Satan's capital in Washington.

Only two of his sites had been hit in the morning's bombardments. That was well within acceptable parameters. At this pace, it would take the Americans a full week to eliminate his radars. By then the army would be out of missiles anyway.

Tahir glanced at the television monitor in the corner, then picked up his cell phone and adjusted the headset. When that was on, he carefully placed the second headset—a Soviet-made unit older than he—over it. He had to position it slightly to the side so he could hear from both sets, but the trouble and the pressure against the edge of his ear and temple were worth it; he could talk and monitor his radar at the same time. Prepared, he let his glance sweep across the console before him one last time, then drew his body upward with a great breath, exhaling slowly as he delivered his trust to Allah, waiting for the alert.

**Aboard *Quicksilver*, over Iraq
1602**

ZEN HELD *HAWK ONE* EXACTLY SEVENTY-FIVE METERS BE-hind *Quicksilver*'s tail, waiting for the signal to hit the flares. The Megafortress's airfoil shed air in violent vortices, and holding the position here was actually more difficult than closing in for a refuel.

"I need another few seconds," said Jennifer, fingers violently pounding one of the auxiliary keyboards at the station next to him. "Hang tight, Zen."

"Yup."

"You ready upstairs, O'Brien?" she asked. "I need you to initiate sequence two right now."

"Sequence two initiated," said the electronic warfare officer.

"Zen, on my signal . . ."

"Okay, Professor." Zen nudged his power ever so slightly as the Megafortress tucked forward, riding an eddy in the wind.

"Now."

"Bingo," he said, punching the flares, which were ordinarily used to decoy IR missiles.

He couldn't tell whether the test had worked or not, and neither O'Brien nor Jennifer said anything. Zen held his position, wanting to get on with things. But such was the life of a test pilot—weeks, months, years of routine, spiced by a few seconds worth of terror.

"All right. That worked well. I think we're okay," said Jennifer. "Let's do it at one mile."

"Two minutes to border," said Breanna.

"Acknowledged, *Quicksilver*," said Zen. He tucked his wing, hurling *Hawk One* toward the ground as he started to loop out to the launch point for the flare. Jennifer wanted him to pickle it as close to the ground as possible and had calculated a precise angle, twenty-two degrees from the sensor. Zen tucked down toward a wide rift, his altimeter marking his altitude above the valley at a thousand feet.

"I'm going to put it at fifty feet," he told Jennifer. A large cliff loomed on his right; he nudged the Flighthawk onto its left wing, clearing the rocks by twenty feet. A wide valley opened up in front of him. A river sat near the center of it. His speed had dropped below 200 knots. Sliding his nose forward, he ducked below seven hundred feet, six hundred, burrowing into the valley.

"Almost there," he said as he passed through five hundred feet.

"Transmission!" yelled Habib, breaking in over the interphone circuit.

"You're at the right angle," Jennifer told Zen.

"Five seconds," said Zen, concentrating as the Flighthawk slid down below a hundred feet.

"Transmission—I have an American voice—Guard band!"

"Hawk leader, hold off on the test," said Breanna calmly. "Habib, give us a location."

"Trying!"

"What?" asked Jennifer.

"We have one of the downed pilots," Zen told her. He pulled level, did a quick check of his instruments, then started the preflight checklist on *Hawk Two*, still sitting on *Quicksilver*'s wing.

"He's behind us. I don't have the location—I can't—he said he saw us fly overhead," said Habib, his stutter no doubt matching his heartbeat.

"He saw *Hawk One*," said Breanna, her voice almost quiet. "Zen, tuck back up the valley. We're going to slide back around. Habib, get us a good location. Chris, talk to the AWACS and tell them what we're up to."

"I'd like to launch *Hawk Two*," Zen told Breanna.

"Let's hold that until we have a good location on the flier," she said. "I don't want anyone getting distracted up here."

"Hawk leader." Zen banked *Hawk One* back in the direction it had just come from. He had the radio at full blast but could hear nothing; reception in the Flighthawks was extremely limited. Then again, *Quicksilver*'s standard radio wasn't picking up the signal either. Only the sophisticated gear Habib controlled was capable of finding and magnifying the faint signal, which was undoubtedly being distorted and weakened by the rocky terrain and towering mountains.

"You're headed back toward him," Habib told Zen. "He can't see you, but he hears something."

"Could be bogus," said Breanna.

"Aware of that, *Quicksilver*. RWR is clean."

"I concur," said O'Brien.

"You're overhead—he thinks you're at about fifteen thousand feet."

"Tell him I'm about a fifth of the size of an F-15," said Zen. "I'm a hell of a lot lower than he thinks."

"I can't talk back to him," said Habib. His listening gear was just that—built for listening, not talking. They'd have to wait until they got close enough for *Quicksilver*'s set to make contact.

Zen magnified the visual feed ten times but saw nothing but large rocks. A cliff loomed ahead; he climbed, deciding to circle above the hills where he wouldn't have to worry about running into anything.

"I still don't have him on standard Guard band," said Chris over the interphone. "Can you pipe your input into our radios?"

"Negative," said Habib.

"Are you sure you have his location right?" asked Breanna.

"I don't have it nailed down," said Habib. "But we're very close."

"I have a radar," said O'Brien. "Slot—no, I'm not sure what the hell it is."

Zen's RWR went red, then cleared.

"Clean," said O'Brien.

"Hawk leader copies. I had a blip too. Jen?"

"I can't tell if it was a blurp or the real thing," she said.

"He's lost you," said Habib. "I lost him."

"I'm going to goose a couple of flares over that valley where he must have seen me," said Zen. "Let's see if that wakes him up."

High Top
1620

DANNY FREAH WATCHED AS THE MARINES OFF-LOADED gear from the transport helicopter, ferrying large bundles out the rear to a six-wheeled trolley that looked like something they'd borrowed from a Home Depot outlet. A separate crew of Marines, meanwhile, refueled the CH-46E from one of the barrels of fuel it had brought with it. One of the pilots hopped out of the cockpit, ambling over to say hello.

"Have a cigar?" The Marine, tall but fairly thin, had left his helmet in the chopper. He had at least a two-day-old beard, so rare for a Marine in Danny's experience that he wondered if the pilot was a civilian in disguise.

"Don't smoke," said Danny. "Thanks anyway."

"Hey, not a problem," said the pilot, who took out a pocketknife to saw off the end of the short cigar. "You're Captain Freah, right?"

"Yeah?"

"Name's Merritt." He took out a Colibri lighter and lit the cigar, sending a pair of thick puffs into the air before continuing. "Friend of yours asked me to say hello. Hal Briggs."

"You know Hal?"

"I do some work for him, every so often. A lot of these guys in the MEU do, SF stuff," said the pilot, adding the abbreviation for Special Forces. Danny knew that his old friend Hal Briggs was deeply involved with covert actions for ISA, but operational secrecy meant he was hazy on the details.

The pilot exhaled a thick wad of smoke. There was a decent wind, but Danny still felt his stomach turning with the scent.

"Hal says you're outta your mind if you're predicting

the Yankees make it to the World Series. He wants Cleveland," said the helo pilot.

"Hal doesn't know shinola about baseball," Danny told the pilot. "Cleveland. Where's their pitchin'?"

"Cleveland? Ha!" A laugh loud enough to be heard two or three mountains over announced the arrival of Captain Donny Pressman, the pilot of the MV-22. Pressman was a sincere and at times insufferable Boston Red Sox fan. "Now, if you want to talk about a team—"

"Bill Buckner, Bill Buckner," taunted the Marine, naming the first baseman whose error had cost Boston the World Series against the Mets several years before.

"Old news," said Pressman.

"Yo, Merritt—we got a situation here," yelled the other helicopter pilot from the front window.

Danny and Pressman followed the pilot back to the chopper.

"AWACS says one of the Megafortresses has a line on a downed pilot. He's just over the border. We're the closest asset to him."

"Shit—we're not even refueled."

"We are," said Pressman. "Let's go!" He started to run toward his aircraft. "Get me some guys."

Danny twirled around and saw two of his men, Powder and Liu, pulling guard duty at the edge of the ramp area. "Liu, Powder—grab your gear, get your butts in the helo. Now!"

"What's up, Captain?" asked a short, puglike Marine sergeant a few yards away.

"Pilot down!" yelled the helo pilot. "We got a location."

"We're on it," said the sergeant. Two other Marines ran up.

"Into the Osprey," said Danny. He didn't have his helmet and was only wearing the vest portion of his body armor, but there wasn't time to pick up his gear. Danny,

Liu, Powder, and the three Marines barely got the rear of the Osprey closed before it began moving forward on the short runway.

"We got a location from the Marines!" shouted the copilot, appearing in the doorway to the flightdeck. "Twelve minutes, fifteen tops, once we get the lead out."

Aboard *Quicksilver*, over Iraq
1640

THOUGH DESIGNED PRIMARILY TO DECOY HEAT-SEEKING missiles, the Flighthawks' small flares were fairly conspicuous, even in the strong afternoon light. Zen shot off six, a third of his supply, then circled back.

He had a good feel for the layout now; the valley ran almost directly north-south, bordered on the east and west by steep mountainsides. A river ran in an exaggerated double Z down the middle; a small town sat along the apex of the second Z at the south end. There were two roads that he could see. One cut through the village and headed east into the rocks; it was dirt. The other was a hard-pavement highway that curved about five miles south of the village. It extended into an open plain and, from the altitude that he peered down at it, didn't seem to connect to the town, at least not directly. But while he figured there'd be at least a dirt trail connecting them, he couldn't find it. The rugged terrain gave way in the distance to relatively fertile areas. Zen glimpsed a patchwork of fields before reaching the end of his orbit and doubling back once again.

The pilot was most likely in the foothills at the northern part of the valley; farther south, and the people in the village would have tripped over him by now.

"Anything?" he asked O'Brien.

"Negative."

"I'm going to take it down and ride along the river," said Zen. "See if I can find anything. *Quicksilver?*"

"We copy," said Bree. "Be advised we have a helo en route. Captain Freah is aboard."

Zen rolled the Flighthawk toward the earth, picking up speed as he plummeted. He'd take this pass very quickly, then have Jennifer review the video as he recovered. It was the sort of thing they'd done together plenty of times.

It was also the sort of thing he could have done easily with Fentress on the other mission, though he'd balked.

What did he have against Fentress?

Rival?

Hardly. The guy seemed afraid of his own shadow sometimes.

Zen put the Flighthawk to the firewall, maxing the engines and tipping the airspeed over 500 knots. At about the size of a Miata sports car, the robot plane was not overwhelmingly fast, but she was responsive—he pulled back on the stick and shot upward, tucked his wings around and flashed back southward. The entire turn had been completed in seconds, and took perhaps a twentieth of the space even the ultra-agile F/A-18 would have needed at that speed. Zen galloped through the air with his aircraft, looking for something, anything.

Light glinted near the village. He throttled back and plowed into a turn, trying to give the camera as much of a view to check it out as possible.

"Makeshift airfield there," said Jennifer. "Two very large helicopters—about the size of Pave Lows. Three helos, sorry. Barracks. Uh, big enough for a company of men. Platoon—nothing major. Big helicopters," she added.

"Hinds, I'll bet," Zen told her. "Get the location, we'll have to pass that on—it's a target."

"Flare indicator—hey, I think I have our pilot!" shouted O'Brien.

Zen continued northward along the valley about a mile and a half before spotting the flare's contrail over a foothill on his right.

"Yeah, okay," he said, pushing toward it. "Where's his radio?"

"No radio," said Habib.

"Our Osprey is ten minutes away," reported Breanna. "They're holding for a definite location."

"Those Hinds could be a problem," said Ferris.

Zen cut lower, working the Flighthawk toward the rocks. Even at two thousand feet it was difficult to pick out objects. The river zigged away on the left side; a dirt trail paralleled it. Something was moving on the trail well to the north. The village lay behind him, roughly four miles away.

"I can't see him," said Zen. "I'm going to roll again and try my IR screen."

He selected the IR sensors for his main view as he made another run over the hills. This side of the valley was still in the sun; finding the heat generated by a man's body would not be easy.

"Got a radio—Iraqi," said Habib. "Hey, he's talking to someone, giving coordinates."

"Must be a search party," said O'Brien.

"Just necessary conversation," snapped Breanna.

"Major, he's giving a position five kilometers north of the village, a klick off the road. You see a road?"

Zen flicked back to his optical feed. "I see a dirt trail. I don't have a vehicle."

"He sees you," said Habib. "You're—he's going to fire!"

"Missile in the air!" shouted O'Brien as Zen pulled

up. "Shoulder-launched SAM. They're gunning for you!"

Aboard *Dreamland Osprey*, over Iraq
1650

DANNY FREAH CAUGHT HIS BALANCE AGAINST ONE OF THE Osprey's interior spars as it pitched violently to the right, hurtling southward as low to the ground as possible. The MV-22 had many assets, but it wasn't particularly easy to fly fast at low altitude in high winds—a fact made clear by the grunts and curses emanating from the cockpit.

Not that anyone aboard was going to object.

The aircraft started to slow abruptly, a signal that it was getting ready to change from horizontal to vertical flight.

"Get ready!" yelled Danny.

Powder and Liu were crouched near the door. They had their smart helmets as well as their vests, M-4s, a medical sack, and grenades. The Marines were standing along the side behind them, one private holding an M-16, the sergeant and the other with Squad Automatic Weapons, light machine guns whose bullets could tear through an engine block at close range.

"I miss the Pave Low," said Powder as they began stuttering toward the ground. "Cement mixer smoother than this."

"Pave Lows are for wimps," barked the Marine sergeant. "You need a Marine aircraft."

Powder's curse-laden retort was drowned by a sudden surge from the engines as the Osprey whipped to the side and then shot up. All Danny could see out the window was a sheer cliff.

"We don't have contact with the pilot yet, but we're

only two minutes out!" shouted the copilot from the flight deck. "Area is hot!"

"Just the way I like my pussies," yapped the gunnery sergeant.

Aboard *Quicksilver*, over Iraq
1654

ZEN TOSSED FLARES AND CURLED THE FLIGHTHAWK TO THE right, jinking away from the shoulder-launched SAM. The fact that he was actually sitting nearly 25,000 feet higher than the Flighthawk was of little comfort to him; he flew as if he could feel the missile's breath on his neck. More flares, a roll, hit the gas—the U/MF zipped within inches of a cliff wall before dashing into the clear beyond the row of mountains forming the valley.

"Missile self-detonated," said Ferris, monitoring the situation from the flight deck. "You're clear, Hawk leader."

"Hawk leader. Thanks, guys."

"He's not on the air," said Habib.

"Yeah," said Ferris. "We're still clear on Guard."

"Maybe it was a decoy," suggested Bree. "Trying to ambush."

"Maybe." Zen pushed back in his seat, scanning his instruments as he got his bearings. Fuel was starting to get a bit low. He had only two flares left. Full load of combat mix in the cannon, at least.

"The Iraqi's transmitting again. He's on the move," said Habib.

"Helicopter is ninety seconds away," said Bree.

"Better hold the helo at sixty seconds, if he can," said Zen. "I'm going to try following our friend in the vehicle."

He circled back toward the north end of the valley,

dropping back to three thousand feet. He saw a rift to his right, glanced quickly at the sitrep or bird's-eye view to make sure it led to the valley, then whipped into it. As he came through he pushed downward but nudged back power.

"Iraqi is off the air," said Habib.

"Another flare," said O'Brien.

This time Zen saw it, about a mile on his left, ten yards at most from the dirt road. He still couldn't see the vehicle.

"All right—I got something," he said as he saw movement on the road. "Computer, frame the object moving on the rocks."

Before the computer could acknowledge, he saw a brown bar of soap turn off the road.

"I think I see our guy in the rocks. Nailing this truck first," said Zen. By the time the words were out of his mouth, he'd already squeezed the trigger to fire.

Aboard *Dreamland Osprey*, over Iraq
1700

THE NOSE OF THE OSPREY BUCKED UPWARD AND THE WHAP of the rotors went down an octave as it cleared a rift in the hills. The pilot had just kicked up the throttle, nearly tripling its speed, but to Danny Freah the sudden change in momentum made it feel as if it had slowed down. Powder and Liu clutched their rifles. Danny realized how much he missed the smart helmet—no map, no real-time view of the battlefield. But much more important, he'd jumped aboard with only his personal handguns—a service Beretta in his holster, and a small hideaway Heckler & Koch P7 M13 strapped to his right ankle. That meant no MP-5 with its target scope slaved to his helmet; he didn't even have his HK Mark 23 SOCOM with its laser pointer and thick silencer.

There was something to be said for the good old-fashioned feel of the Beretta in his palm. He took it from his holster as the MV-22 skittered forward, and peered through the window on his right at a narrow furrow of gray and black smoke.

"Flighthawk!" Liu yelled to him over the whine of the GE turboshafts.

Danny saw it too—a small white wedge twisted through the air about fifty yards away, red bursting from its chin as if it were on fire. It figured that Zen and the others would be in the middle of this.

Standard combat air rescue doctrine called for rescue aircraft to remain at forward bases until definitive contact was made with a downed airman. Occasionally, those procedures were relaxed to deal with difficult situations—on several attempted rescues during the Gulf War helicopters had actually waited inside Iraq during searches. But they were really freelancing here—according to what the copilot said, *Quicksilver* had heard the pilot but not seen him. They were listening to Iraqi units search, and had been fired upon.

Definitely could be a trap.

"Downed airman is near the road, near a truck they're smoking!" yelled the copilot. "We got a spot to land right next to it. We're going for it."

"They talk to him?" shouted Danny.

"Negative, sir. They're sure, though. Hang on!"

"Okay, ladies!" yelled the Marine sergeant, moving toward the door. In the next moment, the Osprey pitched sharply, pirouetting around and descending in nearly the same motion, dropping so quickly that for a half second Danny thought they'd been hit. Then there was a loud clunk and he knew they'd been hit. But they were on the ground, it was time to go, go—he fought back a sliver of bile and lurched toward the door behind his men as the door kicked down.

The Osprey settled harshly onto the uneven surface of the scratch road. Danny was the fifth man out. An acrid smell stung his nose; the Flighthawk had smoked a pickup truck, which was burning nearby.

"Yo, Marines—my guys on point! Whiplash on fucking point!" yelled Danny. It wasn't a pride thing—it made much more sense to have the people with the body armor in the lead. The Marines finally caught on, or maybe they just grew winded as Liu and Powder motored past.

So where the hell was their guy?

The Flighthawk whipped overhead and wheeled to the right, then shot straight upward about three hundred yards away. But it wasn't until the plane rolled and dove back down that Danny realized Zen was trying to put them on the downed pilot.

"There! There!" he shouted, pointing. "Powder, your right. Right! Right!"

No way the pilot didn't hear the Osprey. So why wasn't he jumping up to greet them?

They had to clamber over a twenty-foot-wide rock slide before finally reaching their man. As he cleared the rocks, Danny saw the pilot sprawled on the ground, his radio lying smashed on the rocks. Powder was just getting to him; Liu was a few yards behind Danny.

Powder threw back his helmet and put his head down in front of the pilot's face. Danny noticed a black stain on the pilot's right pant leg; congealed blood.

"Breathing. Shit, I thought he'd fucking bought it," said Powder. "Hit by something."

Liu threw his medical kit in front of him as he slid close. He glanced quickly over the pilot's body, then reached into his pack for the quick-inflate stretcher. He pulled a wire loop and held onto the side as compressed air exploded into the honeycombed tubes. Liu took a pair of titanium telescoping rods from the underside of his go-bag, then propped the stretcher on rocks next to the stricken man.

As they moved him to the stretcher, a second radio fell from his hand. His face had been bruised badly during the ejection, and his right hand burned; besides the leg there were no other outward signs of injury. Liu had his enhanced stethoscope out, getting vitals. The stethoscope had a display screen that could be used to show pulse rate and breathing patterns; intended for battle situations where it might be difficult to hear, the display also helped convey important information quickly to a full team. The downed airman's heart beat fifty-six times a minute; his breathing code was yellow—halfway between shallow and normal.

"Leg's busted," said Nurse. "Compound fracture." He checked for a concussion by looking for pupil reaction, then listened to make sure the pilot's lungs were clear. "Cut by something, but if it was a bullet, it just grazed him. Looks like that's the worst of it. Not too much blood lost. Cold, maybe hypothermia. He'll make it."

Powder jumped up and trotted a few feet away, scooping something up from the rocks. "Pencil flares. Musta meant to shoot 'em, then the bad guys came."

"Grab the radio and let's get," Danny told him.

Nurse secured the pilot with a series of balloon restraints, as much for cushioning as a precaution against back and spinal injuries. Danny took the back end of the stretcher and together they began making their way to the Osprey.

The Marine sergeant met them about halfway.

"Let's go, ladies!" he shouted. "Uh, you too, Captain.

Something big's kicking up some dirt up the road. Your pilot's starting to get some twists in his underwear."

Aboard *Quicksilver*, over Iraq
1655

ZEN PITCHED THE FLIGHTHAWK BACK SOUTH WHEN HE NO-ticed the three vehicles leaving the village on the dirt road. He was moving too fast to target them.

"Vehicles on the highway, coming out of the village," Zen told Breanna. "Alert the Osprey. I'm rolling on them."

"You sure they're not civilians?" asked Breanna.

"What do you want me to do, ask for license and regis-tration?"

"I don't want you to splash civilians," said Breanna.

"Hawk leader," he said.

Zen didn't want to kill civilians either, but he wasn't about to take any chances with his people on the ground. The rules of engagement allowed him to attack anything that appeared to be a threat. He tucked *Hawk One* into a shallow dive, angling toward the lead truck. When it came up fat in the crosshairs, he fired.

One of the most difficult things to get used to about fly-ing the robot plane in combat was the fact that the cannon provided no feedback, no shake, no sound. The pipper changed color to indicate the target was centered, and blackened into a small star when the gun was fired—that was it. He couldn't feel the momentum-stealing vibration or the quick shudder as the gun's barrels spun out their lead. But at least he could see the results of his handi-work: the lead vehicle, a four-door pickup truck with three or four men in the back, imploded as the bullets split it neatly in two. He nudged his nose upward and found the second truck, this one a more traditional military troop carrier; a long burst caught the back end but failed to stop it. Zen broke right, regrouping; as he circled west he saw the Osprey on the ground two or three miles away.

It had been hit. Black smoke curled from one of the engines. Zen tore his eyes away, looked for a target.

The third vehicle, another pickup, left the roadway, spitting along the riverbank. Zen swooped in on it from behind, lighting his cannon as the letters on the rear gate of the pickup came into focus. His first shell got the circle on the second O in Toyota; his next two nailed something in the rear bed. After that he couldn't tell what he hit—the truck disappeared into a steaming cloud of black, red, and white. Zen flew through the smoke—he was now down to fifty feet—and had to shove himself hard left to avoid running into the Osprey, which despite the damage was lifting off, albeit slowly. As he came back toward the road, he realized the second truck he'd hit had stopped to let out its passengers. They were spreading out in the sand, taking up firing positions. He double-clutched, then put his nose on the clump closest to the MV-22 and pulled the trigger. His bullets exploded in a thick line across the dirt; he let off the last of his flares as he came over them, hoping to deke any shoulder-launched SAMs.

"Osprey is away," Breanna was saying. "Osprey is away."

"Hawk leader acknowledges. Osprey is away. They okay?"

"Pressman says he lost an engine but he'll get back before Boston wins the Series."

"Yeah, well, that could be a century from now at least."

Zen continued to climb, flying east of the mountains, well out of range of anything on the ground, before easing back on the throttle and looking for *Quicksilver*.

"Fuel on ten minute reserve," warned the computer.

"Hawk leader to *Quicksilver*," said Zen. "Bree, I need to tank."

WHILE ZEN BROUGHT THE FLIGHTHAWK UP TO TWENTY thousand feet for refueling, Breanna polled her crew, making sure they were prepared to resume the search for the SA-2 radar. O'Brien and Habib seemed to be champing at the bit, riding the high from having located the pilot and helping rescue him. Chris Ferris was his usual cautious self, advising her on fuel reserves and shortened flight times, but nonetheless insisting they should carry on with the mission.

Zen was all for continuing. He'd fly the Flighthawks down closer to the ground, using the video input to check on any radio sources, and look for buildings big enough to house a laser. Jennifer Gleason, working on her sensor coding in between monitoring the Flighthawk equipment, as usual was almost oblivious to what was going on, agreeing to keep at it with a distracted, "Shit, yeah."

The normal procedure for the Flighthawk refuel called for the Megafortress to be turned over to the computer, which would fly it in an utterly predictable fashion for the U/MF. Six months ago the refuel had been considered next to impossible; now it was so routine that Breanna took the opportunity to stretch her legs, leaving Chris at the helm. She curled her body sideways, stepping out gingerly from behind the controls, stretching her stiff ligaments as she slipped back toward the hatchway. A small refrigerator unit sat beneath the station for the observer jumpseat at the rear of the EB-52's flight deck; Breanna knelt down and opened it. She took the tall, narrow plastic cup filled with mint ice tea from the door and took a steady pull. Refreshed, she turned back toward the front of the plane and watched over Chris's shoulder as he monitored the refuel.

Zen had blown off her question about the trucks, but it was a real one. They were here to kill soldiers, not civilians.

True, you couldn't ask for IDs in the middle of a fight. And their rules of engagement allowed them to target anyone or anything that seemed to be a threat. But if they didn't draw a distinction, they were no better than Saddam, or terrorists.

Was that a distinction God drew? Did it matter to Him that only soldiers were in the crosshairs?

Did it matter to the dead?

"Refuel complete," said Chris as she slipped back into her seat. "Computer has course to search grids. I've downloaded the course to Zen. He wants to launch the second Flighthawk about five minutes from the grid."

"Thanks."

Breanna flicked her talk button. "How are you doing down there, Zen?"

"Fine. Yourself?"

"I wasn't trying to be testy about the civilian trucks."

"I know that. They were army or militia or whatever."

"The Kurds use a lot of pickups."

"Yup."

"You okay, Jeff? Do we have a problem?"

Breanna realized her heart had jumped into overdrive, pounding much faster than it had during the action. She was worried about their relationship, not their job. A deadly distraction. She couldn't work with him again, not in combat.

"Major Stockard?"

"Not a problem on my end, Captain," answered her husband.

"Thank you much. Computer says we're on course and ten minutes from your drop zone," she said, trying to make her voice sound light.

Iraq Intercept Missile Station Two
1720

MUSAH TAHIR SAT BEFORE THE ENORMOUS, INOPERATIVE screens, waiting. Kakii had called ten minutes ago, but Abass had not; it was possible that the planes had passed him by, but there had been no call from the airport at Baghdad, where the air traffic radar was still in full operation. The Americans might be attacking somewhere north or east of Kirkuk, but if so, it made no sense to turn on his units; they would be out of range.

Tahir envisioned himself as a spider, standing at the edge of a highly sensitive web, waiting for the moment to strike. He had been entrusted with great responsibility by the leader himself—indeed, by Allah. Turning on the radars, even for a moment, was a matter of great delicacy, since the American planes carried missiles that could home in on them; the decision to initiate the search and launch sequence was dictated by his sense of timing as well as his computer program.

Now?

No. He must wait. Perhaps in a few minutes; perhaps not today at all. Allah would tell him when.

Over Iraq
1720

ZEN TOOK *HAWK ONE* TO THE END OF THE SEARCH GRID, pulling up as he neared a cloud of antiaircraft fire from the Zsu-23. A pair of the four-barreled 23mm flak dealers had opened up just as he started his run; optically aimed and effective only to five or six thousand feet, they were more an annoyance than a threat. He came back south, running four miles parallel to *Quicksilver*. He would turn *Hawk*

One over to the computer while he launched *Two*.

"Anything, O'Brien?"

"Negative," said the radar detector's babysitter. "Clean as a whistle."

"I have a cell phone cluster," said Habib. "Several transmissions, coded. Twenty-five miles southeast of your position, *Hawk One*."

"Okay. Mark it and we'll get down there later," said Zen. "Jen? You see anything?"

"Nothing interesting," said the scientist, who was monitoring the video feed from *Hawk Two*, which was being flown by the computer. "No buildings large enough for a radar. There were two trailers parked beneath the overpass we saw, that was it."

"Yeah, okay, let's check those trailers out. They used to hide Scuds under the overpasses during the war," said Zen. He jumped into *Hawk Two*, which was flying approximately eight miles to the north of *One*. He started to descend, approaching a town of about two dozen buildings nestled in an L-shaped valley. The overpass was just south of the settlement.

"Major, we're getting down toward bingo," said Chris Ferris.

"Hawk leader. We have enough to get over to that area where O'Brien had the cell phones?"

"We should," answered Ferris.

"I'm still trying to get a definite fix," said the radio intercept operator. "Roughly thirty miles south of us. Map says there's nothing there."

"That makes it more interesting," said Breanna.

"Roger that," said Jeff, still flying *Hawk Two*. He dropped through two thousand feet, tipping his wing toward the overpass. The two trucks looked long and boxy, standard tractor-trailers.

Undoubtedly up to no good or they wouldn't have been

placed here, but he couldn't just shoot them up—as Breanna would undoubtedly point out.

"Trucks look like they're civilian types," he said. "We can pass on the location to CentCom."

Zen turned *Hawk Two* back toward *Quicksilver* and told the computer to take it into a standard trail position. Then he jumped back into *Hawk One*, streaking ahead of the Megafortress as it angled southward toward the coordinates O'Brien had given. Breanna had pushed the throttle to accelerate, staying close to the U/MF.

"I believe you're ten miles north of the source," said O'Brien.

"Roger that."

The Megafortress flight crew, meanwhile, prepared their missiles for a strike, in case Zen found something worth hitting. The large bomb bay doors in the belly of the plane opened and a JSOW missile—a standoff weapon with a two-thousand-pound warhead that guided itself to a GPS strike point downloaded from the flight deck—trundled into position.

"We'll nail the son of a bitch if we have a positive target," said Bree, talking to Ferris. Between the open bay doors and the uncoated nose, *Quicksilver* was now a fairly visible target to Iraqi radar, though at nearly thirty thousand feet and stuffed with ECMs and warning gear, she'd be tough to hit.

The pilot they'd rescued probably thought the same thing.

"Zen, do you have a target?" asked Bree.

"Negative," he said, eyes pasted on the video feed. A series of low-lying hills gave way to an open plain crisscrossed by shallow ditches or streams. There were no buildings that he could see, not even houses.

"It's exactly five miles dead on your nose," said O'Brien.

"I'm still looking for the building," said Jennifer.

Zen saw a large, whitish rectangle on his right at about three miles. He popped the magnification and began to tell Bree that they had something in sight. But he'd gotten no more than her name from his mouth before *Quicksilver* shuddered and moved sideways in the air. In the next moment it stuttered toward the earth, clearly out of control.

**High Top
1750**

MACK SMITH RESISTED THE URGE—BARELY—TO KICK THE toolbox across the tarmac. "When is the plane going to be ready, Garcia?" he said.

"I'm working on it, sir," said the technician, hunkered over the right engine. "You're lucky I took this apart, Major. Big-time problem with the pump."

"Just—get—it—back—together."

"I shall be released."

"And if I hear one more, just one more line that sounds like a Dylan song, that could be from a Dylan song, or that I *think* is from a Dylan song, I'm going to stick that wrench down your throat."

"That's no way to talk to anybody," said Major Alou, walking over to see what the fuss was about.

"Yeah," said Mack.

"Louis, I need you to look at *Raven*," said Alou. "The pressure in that number three engine—"

"No way!" yelled Mack as Garcia climbed down off his ladder. "No fucking way. He's working on my plane."

"The Megafortresses have priority here," said Alou. "Garcia works for me. You're a guest, Major. I suggest you start acting like one."

"Yeah? A guest, huh? A guest?"

Mack booted the tool case in disgust. A screwdriver flew up and nailed him in the shin.

Aboard *Quicksilver*, over Iraq
1750

BREANNA FELT HERSELF THROWN SIDEWAYS AGAINST HER restraints, the Megafortress plunging out from under her like a bronco machine on high speed. Pitched in her seat, she pushed her stick gently to the left, resisting the urge to jerk back and try to muscle the plane back level.

The plane didn't respond.

She bent forward, right hand on the power bar on the console between the two pilots. The front panels looked like Christmas trees ablaze with caution and problem lights.

The engines were solid, all in the green.

Rudder pedals, stick, she thought. *Stick,* damn it.

"Computer, my control," she chided.

The computer did not respond.

ZEN'S HEAD SPLIT BETWEEN THE FLIGHTHAWKS AND THEIR plummeting mothership. *Hawk Two* had snapped out of trail, aware that the EB-52's actions were not normal. Zen pulled *Hawk One* back toward the stricken plane, setting its course on a gradual intercept. Then he jumped into *Hawk Two*, tucking it down to get a visual on whatever damage had been done to *Quicksilver*. In the meantime, he checked the radar, scanning to see if they were followed or if other missiles were in the air. The threat bar was clean; somehow, that didn't seem reassuring.

Quicksilver was still descending rapidly, her right wing tilting heavily toward the earth. Two streaks of red flared near the front fuselage.

They were on fire.

Hawk Two passed through five thousand feet; *Quicksilver* was about a thousand feet ahead. If they were going to bail, they were going to have to go real soon.

"*Quicksilver?* Bree?" he said.

There was no response.

UNTIL NOW IT HAD FELT LIKE A SESSION IN THE MEGA-fortress simulator in the test bunker. Breanna sniffed something—the metallic tang of an electrical fire—then decided the computer had either gone off line or malfunctioned. She hit the hard-wired cutoff, initiating the backup hydraulic system. The backup control gear had been installed thanks to a malfunction she dealt with some months before. Something clunked beneath her, as if she were driving a very large truck that had been switched on the fly into four-wheel drive. The stick jerked against her hand so hard she nearly lost her grip.

"My control. We're on hydraulics," she told Ferris.

She wrestled the plane for a few seconds, momentum and gravity working against her. The EB-52 began to shudder—the plane was approaching the speed of sound. The rocks below grew exponentially.

Breanna felt herself relax as the pedals jerked against her feet. She ignored the panel of instruments, ignored the warning lights, ignored everything but the immense aircraft. It became part of her body; her face was squashed by gravity, her sides compressed by the buffeting wind. She brought herself to heel, leveling off at a bare two thousand feet, clearing a mountaintop by thirteen feet.

It was only when she came level that she realized they were on fire.

"Chris?" she said calmly. "Chris?"

When he didn't respond, she turned and saw him slumped forward against his restraints. Bree looked over her shoulder—O'Brien was fighting off his restraints. Long, thin ribbons of smoke filtered from one of the panels at the rear of the flight deck.

"Stay where you are," she told O'Brien over the interphone circuit.

Either the circuit wasn't working or he didn't understand. Breanna waved at him emphatically; he saw her finally and settled back down.

The Megafortress was equipped with two fire suppression systems. One injected high-pressure foam into noncrew areas of the aircraft; this worked automatically. The other, a carbon-dioxide system designed to deprive a fire of oxygen, required a positive command from the flight deck, since anyone not on oxygen would be smothered along with the flames. Breanna could see that everyone was okay on the flight deck, but she had no way of checking downstairs. Zen would certainly have on his gear, but the techies who flew with him almost never did. Which meant that fighting the fire might very well kill Jennifer Gleason.

Her father's girlfriend.

"Jen—get on oxygen," she said. "Everyone—now! We have a fire."

There was no acknowledgment. The plane's com system was dead.

Breanna pressed the manual warning switch. The cockpit was supposed to flash red but it didn't.

Smoke was now pouring into the cockpit. She had to put it out.

"Fire suppression!" she shouted as she reached over and thumbed the guard away from the button.

* * *

JEFF HEARD THE METALLIC HUSH OF THE CARBON-DIOXIDE fire suppression system, then felt his teeth sting—the sound was remarkably similar to the sound of a dentist's suction tool, amplified about a hundred times. The sudden change in the pressure as the gas whipped in made the cabin feel like a wind tunnel.

There'd been no warning light or tone.

Jennifer—she never wore the gear. She'd be breathing pure carbon dioxide.

"Trail Two," he told the Flighthawk computer. He pushed up his visor and turned toward her station.

She wasn't there.

Something cold hit him on his right shoulder. He turned and saw her standing there, shaking her head vigorously up and down, a mask on her face.

BREANNA RESTABILIZED THE PRESSURE IN THE CABIN, RE-stored the normal airflow, then began dealing with the caution lights on her panel, assessing the damage. Fuel tanks were intact. Environmental controls—the AC system—was on backup. Oil pressure in the number four engine was now high, but just barely in the yellow. The flight computer was off line, as were the interphone and the radios. All of her backup instruments were operating. The flight controls felt a bit kludgy on hydraulic backup, but otherwise were fine. The interface with the Flighthawks, which forwarded data from the robots' sensors, was out.

Small bits of shrapnel had burst through the cockpit; one had apparently hit Ferris in the helmet, knocking him unconscious. There was some blood on his arm, but judging from his breathing, he was okay. Habib and O'Brien both gave her thumbs up.

When Breanna pulled off her mask to talk to her two

crewmen, her nose tingled with the metallic smell that lingered from the CO_2 system. Power to the radar tracking station had been cut completely; Habib's eavesdropping gear had been knocked off line, but some circuits still had power. Breanna told O'Brien to go downstairs and see about the others while Habib worked to see if he could get something from the radio.

"God, let Jeff be okay," she found herself saying as she ran a quick self-check on the INS. "Don't let him die. Not after everything else."

JENNIFER HELD HER MASK TO THE SIDE TO TELL JEFF WHAT she'd found at the circuit locker at the rear of the Flighthawk deck. The breaker on the lines regulating the com link between the Megafortress and the Flighthawks had blown out and wouldn't reset, but otherwise they had full power. Whatever had hit the Megafortress seemed to have taken out the right underfuselage quadrant of the Flighthawk's wide-band antennas, but his backups should be sufficient.

"We have full power on the monitoring suite, but the interphone system is off line," she told him. "I think they're on backup."

"The fire," he yelled, still facing forward and controlling the U/MFs.

"I think it's out."

"It is if you can breathe." Zen pulled his mask off and looked up at her. "What the hell hit us?"

"No idea. Should I go up and see if they're okay on the flightdeck?"

"Yeah," he told her. "Tell them I'll survey the outside and pipe it up. Something hit the fuselage on the right side—I saw the fire. Jen—" He grabbed her arm as she started for the ladder. "It may be pretty brutal."

"No shit." She pulled free, then bolted for the ladder. Someone was coming down. "Hey!" Jennifer yelled, stepping aside.

"Hey, yourself," said O'Brien. "You guys okay?"

"Yeah—what's going on up there?"

"My gear's out. Captain Stockard's okay. Captain Ferris got hit by something, knocked cold."

"Radio?"

He shook his head.

"Where was the fire?" Jennifer asked.

"Not sure."

"Come on, we have to check the gear in the rear bay."

"I'll go," said O'Brien, spinning around and charging up the ladder to the rear area.

Jennifer clambered after him, reaching the top in time to hear him scream in agony.

"My hand! My hand!" he yelled, rolling on the metal grate of the floor and cursing in agony.

One of the equipment panels was open; Jennifer guessed that a short had juiced the panel. She reached into the small passage between the bay and the flight deck, grabbing the first aid kit off the wall. O'Brien writhed in pain so badly the first thing she did was stab him with the morphine syringe. She rammed it into his leg, right through his uniform. Then she dug into the box for the burn spray—a high-pressure can of antiseptic solution that was so cold as she sprayed, her own hands turned to ice. By the time she had gauze on his hands, O'Brien had calmed down. She helped him back onto the flight deck and got him strapped into his seat as his eyes closed.

"What happened?" asked Breanna.

"One of the panels is hot—there's a short. Maybe if I had a schematic—can you access the on-line manual?"

"Negative—everything associated with the computer is out."

"If you have control of the plane, we shouldn't mess with it," said Jennifer. "I don't want to screw up something else."

"Agreed," said Breanna. "How's Jeff?"

"He's fine," said Jennifer. "He should be giving you a visual."

"I have no feed from him," said Breanna. "The computer's out."

"Oh, yeah. Well, he's fine. He was worried about you," she added. Jennifer thought of Breanna's father, worried about him for a moment, even though he wasn't the one in danger. "I'll find out what it looks like and come back."

"Good luck," said Breanna. "We're about ten minutes out of High Top. If the damage is too bad, we'll have to go on to Incirlik. I don't want to mess with a short-field landing."

IT LOOKED LIKE A GIANT HAD STUCK HIS THUMB ONTO *Quicksilver*'s fuselage just before the wing on the right side. The center of the thumbprint was dark black; streaks of silver extended in an oblong starburst toward the rear where bits of the radar-evading hull had been burned away. There were one or two long lines extending toward the back of the plane, along with a small burn mark on the panel where the rear landing gear carriage folded up. There were some other pockmarks, including a large dent on the cover to the chute they needed to deploy to land on the short field.

"The thing looks bad, but it looks intact," Jeff told Jennifer. "I don't know about the chute, though."

"Okay."

"Tell Bree I think I should land the Flighthawks at High Top and we should go on to Incirlik. I should be able to talk to the AWACS through *Hawk One* in about thirty seconds. I'll have the controller about a minute after that. You'll have to play messenger."

"Not a problem," she said, starting back.

He checked his instruments. The U/MFs themselves were in good shape.

The only thing that could have done this sort of damage was a laser. Maybe they'd believe Brad Elliott now.

High Top
1830

CAPTAIN FENTRESS DIDN'T KNOW WHAT WAS GOING ON UNtil he saw Major Alou hustling toward his plane, followed a good ten yards back by the rest of his crew. He ran after them, shouting for information. Kevin Marg, the copilot, explained that *Quicksilver* had been hit by a SAM.

Zen and Bree and the others—oh God.

Zen.

"The Flighthawks—they'll be in a fail-safe orbit if the control unit was blown out," Fentress told them. "They can help us find them if they go down. Let me come with you?"

Alou yelled something that he took to be a yes. But as he ducked under the plane he heard the soft whine of a Flighthawk in the distance. Fentress trotted back out in time to see the robot tilt her nose up above the far end of the runway, skimming in like a graceful eagle hooking its prey. The second plane came in two seconds later, just as smoothly.

Would he ever be able to land like that?

He had fifty times—on the simulator.

"Hey, *Quicksilver*'s heading over to Incirlik," yelled

the copilot from the ladder. "We're going to fly shotgun—Major Alou wants to know if you're coming aboard or not."

"I better look after the Flighthawks," said Fentress.

"You got it, Curly."

"I'm not Curly," he shouted, starting to trot toward the robot planes.

Aboard *Quicksilver*, on the ground at Incirlik 1905

ZEN WATCHED FROM HIS WHEELCHAIR AT THE BACK OF THE Flighthawk deck as they carried O'Brien and then Ferris out. Jennifer had already gone down to see if Alou was landing or if she could talk to him over the radio; *Raven* had escorted them here but there had been no way to communicate outside of hand signals.

After he landed the Flighthawks, he'd had plenty of time to go back over the video. There was only one site in the area they had flown over that could have possibly held a laser—a dilapidated factory a half mile off a highway, a mile and a half from a fair-size town in northeastern Iraq. Two trailers were parked outside of it. There were no defensive positions that they could see, but there was a long trench running between the trailers into the building. Cables might be buried there.

While the fire had cost them the data needed to coordinate it positively, it was at least roughly where the cell phone calls and radio transmissions had originated from. It had to be where the laser was.

"Hey," said Breanna, coming down the ladder. "You okay?"

"I'm okay."

She glanced back upward, as if she'd forgotten no one else was aboard. "Listen, I'm sorry," she told him.

"What for?"

"We haven't—you and I have been kind of off kilter lately. I don't know why."

Zen shrugged.

"I love you," she said.

"Yeah, I love you too," he said. The words sounded odd to him, too rushed or too quick, not as sincere as he meant. But if she noticed, she didn't say.

High Top
2010

DANNY FREAH GLANCED OVER FROM THE COMMUNICA-tions section in the Whiplash trailer, making sure he was still alone; the HQ had become something like a rec room for the base personnel. Ordinarily he didn't mind, but the conferences with Dreamland Command and *Raven* were to be conducted in total secrecy.

Bison was at the door, enforcing the secure protocol with his M16A3, full-body armor, and a day and a half's worth of unshowered B.O. Danny gave him a quick wave, then turned back to the main com screen, adjusting the volume on his headset. The excitement of the rescue—and the harried ride back on only one engine—had been eclipsed by news of what happened to *Quicksilver.*

"The damage was done by some sort of energy discharge weapon," said Alou, who was en route back to High Top Base in *Raven.* "I saw it myself. Had to be laser."

"We concur," said Dog.

"The radio transmission data points to a small warehouse complex, more like a building and some trailers in Box AB-04," said Alou. "It should be just about big enough for a laser."

"Give me the coordinates and we'll look at it," said

Dog. "The mini-KH is now on line. We can have it maneuvered into place by morning."

"I want to move right away," said Alou. "I say we return to refuel, and go."

"The colonel and I have been discussing another option," said Danny before Dog could answer. "I'd like to get us in there and take a look at it before we blow it."

"Why?" asked Alou.

"Because if we just destroy it, we're not going to settle any of the questions," Danny said. His words raced from his mouth. "I say we get on the complex ASAP, Colonel. From what Jennifer Gleason relayed, it's an easy shot."

"You don't know that the laser itself is there," said Alou. "It's probably mobile."

"It *may* be mobile," said Dr. Rubeo, who was in the secure room with Colonel Bastian. "If it's as advanced as Razor. If—a big question."

"See—we have to get that question answered," said Danny.

"There's no way you'll have the Osprey repaired in time to join us," said Alou.

"We'll find other transportation," said Danny, who already knew it would be several days before they had a new engine to replace the damaged one. "If this map is right, there are no defenses whatsoever. Nearest armed units would be in a town a mile and a half away. We're in and out before they know what hit them. Ten minutes of video on the ground, maybe grab some pieces—that would be invaluable."

"Big risks," said Bastian. "Even just a bombing mission. Granted that *Quicksilver* was more vulnerable to radar, but *Raven* will still have to open its bomb bay to fire. That would make even a B-2 visible, at least in theory."

"I concur," said Rubeo.

"One thing I noticed," cut in Alou. "And maybe it's a coincidence or maybe it has to do with the radars, but the altitude of all the planes hit was at least twenty thousand feet."

"And?" said Dog.

"Maybe it can only hit aircraft at that altitude or higher. Maybe it's optimized for that."

"If this is a laser, it can strike anything from five centimeters to thirty-five meters off the ground," said Rubeo. His face filled the screen as he spoke, the video feed automatically concurring with the active voice feed. "I suggest we wait and plan a full raid," added the scientist. "I agree with Captain Freah about the utility of a close inspection, but the operation should be properly planned. We'll have the mini-KH positioned in six hours."

"They may move it by then," said Alou.

"Unlikely," said Rubeo.

"Razor's mobile."

"Pul-ease. We are dealing with Iraq," answered the scientist. "Even if this is mobile, they can't go scurrying around the countryside with it. They'll hide it in a building."

"I agree with Merce," said Danny. "The sooner the better. They won't be expecting it."

"We're not sure if this is the site, though," said Dog.

"It's got to be, right, Doc?" asked Danny, sensing the scientist would back him.

"Possibly. It's within parameters. Even if they were a full generation behind—and let us say that is more likely—the building needed for the director would not have to be very large," said Rubeo. "I believe anything above two thousand square feet would do, assuming some of the equipment were contained on a second level or even in an auxiliary station. The director itself is not particularly large, and at least a portion of it has to be exposed so it can fire. Razor, of course, can be mounted on a large tank chassis. That greatly increases the possible number of sites."

"What the hell is the director?" asked Danny. "The command post?"

Rubeo gave him one of his best "what a bonehead I'm dealing with" expressions.

"The director focuses the laser or high energy beam," explained Colonel Bastian. "It'll look a little like a very large searchlight. It will have some baffling on it to prevent ambient light from changing the focus during daylight."

"Precisely," said Rubeo. "We will feed you some conceptual drawings that you can use for a target. It's the easiest part to destroy. Now, if the Iraqis are more than a generation behind—"

"Then it wouldn't work at all," said Colonel Bastian.

"Precisely," said Rubeo. "Thank you, sir."

"Good," said Danny.

"The director itself is interesting, but not the highest priority for intelligence," said Rubeo. "The software that controls it would be extremely interesting. We'd want to ID the gas makeup, of course. An exact signature could help us determine who built it and—"

"I'll get you everything you want," said Danny.

"The chemical warfare sniffers you carry can be modified to give us a reading," said Rubeo. "You'll have to find Sergeant Garcia and tell him to follow the directions I send."

"Whoa, not so fast boys," said Dog. "You haven't outlined the risks, and we haven't solved the problem of getting there, or of grabbing intelligence for the strike."

"We can use the Flighthawks for intelligence," said Alou. "They're at High Top."

"Zen isn't."

"Captain Fentress is there. He'll fly them," said Alou.

"The risks are worth it, Colonel," said Rubeo. "If this is a laser, intelligence on it would be overwhelmingly valuable."

"I'll be the judge of that," said Dog. "What are the risks?"

"Well, the risks—we could fail," said Danny, leaving it at that.

"And you get there how?" asked Dog.

"I was hoping to chop one of those Marine transports, but we won't have any inbound until daybreak," said Danny, who'd checked twice. "But I have something else in mind, something much better, that we could use right away."

"YOU'RE OUT OF YOUR FUCKING MIND, FREAH. OUT OF your fucking mind." Mack Smith shook his head, then slapped the side of the OV-10. "You want to ride in the back of this?"

"Plenty of room. Garcia tells me four or five guys can fit, with full gear."

Garcia, who had been hovering nearby, tried to interject. Danny waved at him to be quiet.

"The Marines did this all the time in the Gulf War," he told Mack. "The building isn't ten feet from the highway, which is long and flat, plenty enough for you to land. You come in, zip around, take off. Easy as pie."

"Pie, huh? Apple or peach?"

"You're awful touchy today, Major," said Danny. "You were looking for action—well, here it is."

"Action and suicide are different."

"You don't think you can do this?"

"I can fuckin' do it. There is nothing I can't fly. This—this is a piece of cake."

"Great. How long before we're ready to take off?"

**Dreamland Command Center
1315**

COLONEL BASTIAN WALKED BACK AND FORTH BEHIND THE console, waiting for the connection to go through. He'd decided to give CentCom's commander a heads-up about the Razor strike.

Like all of the U.S. joint service commands, CentCom was headed by a four-star general, in this case Army General Clayton Clearwater. He was an old-line soldier with a reputation both for daring—he'd been with an airborne unit in Vietnam—and stubbornness. Dog had met him exactly once, during a three-day Pentagon seminar on twenty-first century weaponry. Clearwater had given a short address during one of the sessions, talking about force multipliers and asymmetric warfare. While the speech had been aimed at the Joint Services Special Operations Command, his ideas were in line with the Dreamland/Whiplash concept.

Of course, that didn't mean he wouldn't view the Razor mission as interfering with his domain. But his reaction was beside the point. Bastian wasn't calling him to ask for permission—the Whiplash order clearly gave him the authority to proceed.

Still, touching base was politic.

"Nothing?" Dog asked the lieutenant handling the center communications board.

"Just getting through now, sir."

The lieutenant spent a minute haggling with his equivalent at CentCom's communications center before being transferred to the general's line. A tired-sounding Marine Corps major—CentCom didn't have the high-tech secure video gear Dreamland used—finally came on the line.

"Bastian?" he said curtly.

"I need to talk to General Clearwater."

"You'll have to talk to me," said the major. He was an aide to the general's chief of staff—pretty far down the totem pole and undoubtedly lacking code-word clearance to talk about Whiplash, let alone any of Dreamland's weapons.

"I need to talk to the general himself," Dog told him.

"I'm sorry, Colonel, I can't put you through."

Dog folded his arms in front of his chest, trying to martial his patience. "This is a top priority item. It involves a matter of immediate importance," Dog told him.

"Then explain it to me," said the major.

"I can't," said Bastian.

"Then this conversation is over," said the major, who snapped off the connection.

"Asshole," said the lieutenant in a stage whisper.

Dog began pacing again. In fairness to the major, he probably didn't understand why a "mere" lieutenant colonel would need to speak right away to a four-star general, especially since that colonel was ostensibly calling from Edwards Air Force Base, where the duty roster showed he was assigned to support squadron.

Ordinarily a good cover, but in this case perhaps a bit too good.

Magnus could get through to Clearwater, he thought, and would appreciate the heads-up himself. But Dog hadn't been able to hunt him down in D.C. He'd had to use the secure e-mail message system to tell him about the damage to *Quicksilver* and the fact that it had been forced to land at Incirlik, and still didn't have an acknowledgment.

Dog glanced at his watch. Less than fifteen minutes until takeoff for the mission.

No way he was going to delay it.

"Listen, Lieutenant, I'm going to go catch a breather. Page me if General Magnus or General Clearwater calls, and if there's anything from Whiplash or the Megafortresses. Otherwise, I'll be back in twenty minutes."

High Top
2302

"YOU TAKE THAT KNEE OUT OF MY SIDE RIGHT NOW, POWder, or I'm going to twist it back behind your head."

"If you had room to twist it behind my head, Bison, it wouldn't be in your goddamn side."

"That ain't his knee," said Liu.

"Real funny, Nurse," said Powder.

"We taking off today or what?" said Egg, the fourth member of the Whiplash team crammed into the rear of the Bronco. He wagged his flashlight toward the roof, throwing bizarre shadows across the M-4 carbines, grenade launchers, and MP5s they'd lashed there.

The Marine Corps had outfitted several OV-10s for special operations, turning the rear area into a passenger compartment. While no Marine was ever heard to complain—at least not within earshot of his commanding officer—the accommodations hardly fit the definition of spartan, let alone cramped. And that was in a plane specifically designed, or at least modified, to their specifications. This aircraft made the Marine versions seem like 747s. Sitting on their rucksacks, each man had his helmet and backup oxygen in his lap. There was no light, and no communication with the cockpit.

"Which one of you didn't take a shower?" Bison asked.

"Hell with that," said Egg. "Liu had some of that soup."

"Jesus," groaned the others together.

"About time," said Powder as the airplane's engines started up with a roar. The vibration from the engine worked into his spine and skull.

"Man, this is nuts," said Bison. "Powder, take your damn elbow out of my ribs."

"Where do you want me to put it?"

"You want me to tell you?"

"You don't watch yourself, I will."

The plane jerked forward as the engine noise jumped fifty decibels.

"Man, I gotta go to the can," said Egg.

"I think we're taking off!" yelled Bison. He dropped his flashlight as the plane stuttered upward, and the Whiplash assault team was left in temporary darkness.

Just as well, thought Powder. Dinner roiled in his stomach. He'd gone over to the Marine mess and scoffed up a few helpings of roast beef and mashed spuds. He thought now the gravy had been a mistake.

"Whoa—we're up," said Bison.

"I been in trucks smoother than this," said Egg.

"Sixty-seven minutes away," said Powder.

"Hey," said Egg. "Anybody smell roast beef?"

DANNY BRACED HIMSELF AS THE BRONCO PULLED NEARLY four g's, turning around a sharp crag in the mountains en route to their target.

"Captain, are you still with us?" asked Dr. Ray Rubeo over the Whiplash circuit, which was being fed by the tactical communications satellite into his smart helmet.

"Yes, sir."

"As we said before, video of the director unit would be very useful. We want measurement of the focusing apparatus, but you needn't bother with taking parts from it. Simply blow it up."

"Right."

"The chemical samples, the readings—those are higher priorities. The disk array is what we specifically want. Now, if the weapon is Razor size, you can expect the computer gear to be fairly small. On the other hand, if it's stationary, I would imagine you'll be hunting for something about the size of a large cabinet, similar to some of the memory devices we use here with the work stations."

"Gotcha," said Danny. They had already gone over the priority list and the likely layout of the weapon and any facility housing it twice.

"We'll be right here, watching what you do," added the scientist as Mack warned that he was going to take another sharp turn.

"Great," groaned Danny as gravity knocked him sideways.

MACK SMITH CHECKED THE ENGINE GAUGES AGAIN. THE turbos were maxed out, but with all the extra weight, they were barely doing 190 knots. Fortunately, they didn't have to climb; he'd laid out a zigzag course through the passes and then a straight run down to the site. The night was dark, with only a small sliver of moon, but he figured that was in their favor—the darkness would make it tough for anyone on the ground to hit them.

Once past the last peaks ahead, he'd have a clear shot. Landing on the road, though, was going to be a bitch—he figured he'd have to drop a "log" flare on a first approach to see the damn thing, then hustle back in before the light burned out or anyone on the ground nailed him.

At least he wasn't flying completely naked. He'd managed to talk Alou out of a pair of Sidewinders. Garcia had mounted them on the OV-10's launcher.

He almost hoped he had a chance to use them. This sucker turned on a dime. He'd lure a MiG onto his butt, turn quick, then slam the two heat seekers right down his tailpipe.

All in all, he had to admit the Bronco was a lot of fun to drive.

Drive, not fly, he thought. You couldn't really call moving under 200 knots flying.

"We're running behind," said Danny, who was sitting in the copilot-observer's seat behind him.

"Really?" he replied over the Bronco's interphone circuit. "Well hold on while I hit the rocket power."

Aboard *Raven*, over Iraq
2320

FENTRESS FELT HIS CHEST IMPLODE AS MAJOR ALOU counted down the seconds to launch, taking *Raven* through the alpha maneuver to exert maximum separation force on the Flighthawks.

People's lives depended on him doing his job without fucking up. That had never been true before.

Alou thought he could do it. To Alou, there wasn't even a question.

And Zen?

Fentress hadn't asked. As far as he knew, no one had.

Alou was in charge of the mission. He thought he could do it. He would do it.

"Alpha," said Alou.

Fentress's pinkie jerked with some kind of involuntary reaction on the joystick controller, even though he'd turned the launch over to the computer.

"Flighthawk launched," confirmed the computer.

Though it was night, the view from the robot was as clear and defined as if it were day. In fact, he could tell the computer to present it as a cloudless sky at high noon and it would do so. It was best to keep it in the greenish starlight-enhanced mode, however; it helped keep him oriented.

Zen's advice.

"You're looking good, Hawk leader," said Major Alou. *"Wild Bronco* is twelve minutes from target."

He hesitated before acknowledging—it felt odd to be called Hawk leader; that was Zen's title.

"Twelve minutes," he said. He was going to overfly the building, check for last second developments. The Megafortress was five miles from the building, the Flighthawk now a little closer.

"Low and slow like we planned," said Alou.

"Low and slow," he repeated.

"Gun radars two miles ahead of you, just came on," warned the radar operator a second before the warning flashed in the Flighthawk screen. "North of that town."

"Got it."

Incirlik
2320

TORBIN DOLK HAD JUST CLIMBED INTO BED WHEN THE knock came at his hotel room door. He thought about pretending he was already sleeping but figured that wouldn't save him; though nominally a private hotel, the building was reserved for military use, and the only person knocking this late would be here on official business.

"Yup," yelled Torbin, still hesitating to get out of bed.

"Captain Dolk?"

"The same."

"Lieutenant Peterson, sir. General Paston sent me over."

Paston was a two-star Army general, the ranking Cent-

Com officer at Incirlik. Dolk realized he was about to be fried big-time.

Very big-time.

Shit. Harding had told him he was in the clear.

Worse thing was, they didn't even have the decency to hang him in daylight.

"Give me a minute." He slid out of bed and got dressed, fumbling as he pushed both feet through the same pant leg. His eyes were a little fuzzy and he had to tie each shoe twice.

"You awake, Captain?" asked the lieutenant when he finally opened the door.

"Yeah. Uh, maybe we can grab some joe in the lobby."

Two Army MPs stood behind the lieutenant in the hall. Two other soldiers with M-16s were standing a short distance away. They all followed as Torbin and the lieutenant walked to the elevator, where two Air Force sentries were stationed. No one spoke, either in the elevator or in the lobby, where Torbin sniffed out the boiled grinds in the overheated carafe next to the front desk. Then, cup in hand, he followed the lieutenant to a staff car outside.

The soldiers followed in a Humvee as they raced through the security perimeter and then back to the base. Torbin thought several times of telling the driver to slow down; five minutes one way or another wasn't going to make much difference. But at least he managed not to spill his coffee.

Security at Incirlik was ordinarily very strong; even when Iraq was quiet, it probably ranked among the most heavily guarded facilities outside of the U.S. During the past few weeks, the troops guarding it had been doubled, with a number of high-tech snooping and identity-checking devices added to prevent saboteurs and spies from getting in. And now the security had been heightened further. Two companies of heavily armed soldiers stood outside the fence; another platoon of men and a pair of tanks stood along the access road. A short line of vehicles waited at the gate to be searched. The fact that a two-star had summoned him didn't allow them to cut in the line either.

"Wasn't this crazy before," said Torbin when they were ordered out of the vehicle for the security check. "What's up?"

The lieutenant didn't say anything, nor did the MPs looking them over. Finally cleared, the lieutenant didn't wait for their escorts. He took the wheel himself and drove toward a hangar area at the far tip of the base. As they approached, Torbin realized why the security had been tightened—a huge Megafortress sat in the middle of the access ramp. Passing through yet another security cordon, they approached the plane slowly, having been warned that the guards in front of the aircraft had orders to shoot any suspicious vehicle.

Torbin had never seen a Megafortress in person before. The aircraft seemed very different from a B-52, even though it had supposedly been built from one. Its long nose—silver, not black like the rest of the plane—extended toward the car as they approached; the aircraft seemed to be watching them. Perhaps the shadows made the plane seem bigger than it actually was, but the Megafortress definitely stood several feet higher than a stock B-52. Its wings seemed longer, sleeker. Her engines were single rather than double pods; with fins along the underside, they looked more like rockets than turbofans. The plane's V-shaped rear stabilizer or tail rose above the nearby hangar, a pair of shark's fins waiting to strike.

A soldier dressed in camo and wearing a green beret walked to the center of the roadway as the car approached, holding out his hand. The lieutenant immediately stopped and got out. Torbin followed, trailing along as several other Special Forces soldiers appeared. The lieutenant presented credentials; the soldier nodded grimly and stepped back, allowing them to pass toward the tail area of the plane. A figure in a flight suit approached; Torbin was surprised to find it was a woman.

And a very beautiful one at that. Five-six maybe, 120 or so—could be a little less.

Eyes like heat-seekers.

"You're Dolk?" she said.

"Yes, ma'am."

"I'm Captain Stockard. Breanna." She held out her hand. She gripped his more firmly than any hand that smooth had a right to grip. "I understand you're an electronic warfare officer, a pitter. You fly in Weasels?"

"Yes, ma'am."

"We need some help," she told him. "You had an engineering degree too."

"Well, uh, yes ma'am."

"I realize you don't have clearances. We'll backtrack later. If there's any reason you can't help, you tell me now. If you don't—well, if you don't want to get involved right now for any reason, any reason at all, turn around and go back to bed. No questions asked. If you come with us and something comes up—you'll be fried. No one will bail you out. You understand?"

Her eyes held him. What was she talking about?

God, she was beautiful.

"Captain Dolk?" she said. "Staying or going?"

"I, uh—I want to help."

"Good." She smiled. "We're trying to get things put back together, and we need someone to help our technical person. She'll tell you what to do."

Breanna started walking away, then spun back toward him.

"Yo—get your butt in gear, Dolk," she barked. "Onto my plane. We have work to do."

Dolk hadn't been spoken to like that since basic training, perhaps not even then. He snapped to quickly, breaking into a full run but failing to catch her as she disappeared up the ladder of the black Megafortress.

CentCom HQ, Florida
1330

"BARCLAY, WHAT THE HELL ARE YOU DOING OUT IN THE goddamn lobby when I need you in here?"

"General Clearwater, I was—"

"Get your butt in here, Barclay, without back lip."

Jed Barclay had been told to wait in the outer office by Clearwater's chief of staff, who had conveniently melted away before the four-star general appeared. But he'd been dealing with the head of Central Command a great deal over the past few months—he'd been told about not using back lip at least ten times already—and so he took the admonition in stride, following along as the general walked briskly down the hallway of his Florida headquarters.

"You see that report from Elliott?" asked Clearwater. The general was in his early sixties and looked at least ten years older. But he walked fast and was rumored to work around the clock.

"Yes, sir," said Jed.

"Well?"

"Uh, I agree. The damage to the first plane was almost certainly a laser. And since the Iraqis don't have the technology—"

"Who says they don't?"

"Uh, everyone says they don't."

"Everyone's the CIA. Those spooks couldn't read the writing on a billboard at twenty paces. Why in hell would the Iranians be attacking our planes?" continued the general. "We're in Iraq. Why would Iran attack us?"

"I didn't say they did. I said the Iraqis—"

"Brad says they did. *Iranians*, not Iraqis."

"He thinks they may have sold it to them. The Iranians as well as the Chinese have shown interest in Razor, and as a matter of fact—"

"Lasers. Fancy Dan Bullshit." Clearwater practically spit. He was a foot soldier at heart; last week he had lectured Jed for ten minutes on the value of a rifle that never jammed. But while he claimed he didn't go for "fancy Dan bullshit," the record showed that he'd made sure his men and women were equipped with the latest technology, including hand-held GPS devices, satellite phones, and laser-dot rifle scopes.

"If there's a laser, why haven't the satellites seen it?" Clearwater asked, echoing the CIA's main legitimate argument against the laser.

"There's only one launch detection satellite near enough to cover that part of Iraq," said Jed. "And it's not designed to detect laser bursts."

"Fancy Dan bullshit."

Clearwater turned the corner and entered a conference room. Jed followed along. There were six other people inside, none lower than a brigadier general.

"You boys know Jed," said Clearwater. "NSC sent him down to keep our noses clean."

"Well, uh, that's not exactly my, uh, job, sirs," said Jed.

Admiral Radmuth, sitting next to Jed, gave him a wink. The men, who headed different commands organized under CentCom, apparently knew that Clearwater himself had asked to borrow Jed for his technical expertise—not to mention his backdoor access to the White House.

"Gentlemen, let's get this donkey cart in motion." Clearwater slapped his hands on the table. "I want a full update, starting with what we're hitting this axlehead Saddam with, and what we can expect in return. You have ten minutes. Then Boy Wonder and I are on the plane for Incirlik."

"On the plane?" Jed's voice squeaked involuntarily. "I'm going to Turkey?"

Clearwater turned and smiled at him, probably for the first time ever. He clicked his false teeth, then turned back to his lieutenants. "Gentlemen, I believe pride of place belongs to the Air Force. We have nine and a half minutes left."

Aboard *Raven*, over Iraq
2345

CAPTAIN FENTRESS LEANED TO THE RIGHT WITH THE Flighthawk as he came out of the turn, nudging the throttle slide to max. The Flighthawk picked up speed slowly at first, but once it got through 330 knots, it seemed to jump forward, slicing toward the target building. The metal warehouse sat to the left; as he approached, Fentress saw that the sides were missing from one of the two trailers, revealing what looked like a pair of generators. The Flighthawk whipped past, following Fentress's prompts as it slid above the empty roadway parallel to the building. He backed off the thrust and began to turn, misjudging his speed and ending up far wider than he'd planned for the next, lower run over the area.

Piloting a Predator typically took four people, and that

was a slow-moving, low-flying aircraft, relatively forgiving of mistakes. Light-years more complicated, in some ways the Flighthawk was actually easier to fly—its sophisticated flight control computer, C^3, did myriad things for the pilot. But in other ways piloting the U/MF at speeds close to Mach 1 was as demanding as doing a binomial equation in your head while pushing a tractor-trailer through an uphill maze. His thoughts were consistently a half second behind the plane, and his reactions another second or two behind that.

Not bad for a rookie, maybe, but the six men in the Bronco needed him to be a hell of a lot better.

He'd die if he screwed up. Just die.

C^3 noodled him, showing how far off course he'd gone with a dotted red line. Fentress brought it back, kept his speed low, getting a look at things.

"Whiplash team is ninety seconds away," said Alou. "We're patching your feed through."

Fentress felt his heart pound.

"Hawk leader, this is Whiplash," said Danny. "The vehicles on the east side beyond the parking area of that second building—can you take a pass so we can find out what they are?"

Vehicles? He hadn't seen any.

"Roger that." Fentress slammed the Flighthawk into a turn so abruptly that the computer gave him a stall warning. He eased off, took a breath—it wasn't a big deal; Zen got those warnings all the time. The computer was just a big sissy.

He knew that Zen would have fried his ears off for that. But Zen wasn't here.

Concentrate, he told himself.

Fentress told the computer to switch the viewing mode on the main screen from starlight to IR, which would make the vehicles easier to spot. He found his course, following the dotted line drawn up by the computer, and dropped through five thousand feet, nudging his speed back until he was just under 200 knots. Running toward the site from the northeast corner, he saw nothing but a flat field and a torn fence, but as he pulled overhead and began to turn he spotted two tanks dug into the ground about a hundred yards from the building, right near the road the Bronco was supposed to land on.

He'd have to take out the tanks.

"Hawk leader, this is Whiplash."

Fentress could get them both in one pass, but it would be easier, surer, to take them out one at a time. Go for the sure thing.

Zen would agree.

He was already lined up.

"Weapons," he told the computer. The screen changed instantly, adding crosshairs, targeting data, and a bar at the bottom that could automatically indicate whether he should fire or not once he designated the target.

"Hawk leader?"

Something buzzed into the top left of his screen.

Fentress felt the blood drain from his head directly to his legs. He was nailed, dead.

No—it was the Bronco!

"Captain Fentress?" said Alou.

"Tanks, two tanks, on the road, dug in," he said.

Tanks? Or the Razor clone?

Tanks—he could see the lollipops on top.

By the time he had it sorted out, he'd overflown them. He started to bank.

"They're definitely tanks," said Fentress. "Nothing else down there, nothing big enough for Razor, at least outside of the building. I'm going to take the tanks."

"Whiplash copies," said Danny. "We'll hold for your attack."

Fentress banked to the right, sliding toward the warehouse to get it in view of the sensor. As he did, a yellow light erupted from a low hill on the right.

"Flak!" yelled a voice he hadn't heard before. It had to be the Bronco pilot, also plugged into the circuit.

Flak, a Zeus firing 23mm slugs. Not even—something lighter, a machine gun.

Take that out too, after the tanks. People there, another vehicle.

Razor? Razor?

Calm down, damn it. Just a pickup.

Fentress pushed on, scanning the warehouse through his turn before starting for the tanks. He got his nose onto the first one, tried to ignore the pounding of his heart. His target bar flashed red.

Fire, he thought. *Fire.*

His fingers cramped. He couldn't move them.

He was beyond the tank.

"What's going on, Hawk leader?" demanded the Bronco pilot.

"Targeting tanks," said Fentress. He cut southward, came back quickly—too fast. The tanks blurred.

Just fire!

He pressed the trigger and bullets spewed from the front of the Flighthawk. Extended bursts took quite a bit of momentum from the small aircraft, but the computer compensated seamlessly.

Beyond it. He was beyond it. Had he missed?

Get the other one.

"Hawk leader?"

"Keep your damn shirt on," he told the Bronco as he looped back to get the second tank.

Aboard *Wild Bronco*, over Iraq
2350

DANNY GRABBED THE SIDE OF THE COCKPIT AS THE PLANE wheeled away from the gunfire. He tried to ignore Mack's voice over the interphone and concentrate on the view in the smart helmet, which showed bullets flaring and then erupting in a fire.

"Any day now, Fentress," said Mack.

"Relax," Danny told him, watching the screen as the Flighthawk circled back over the road. Both tanks had definitely been hit. There was no one near the building, as far as he could see.

"Let's get down," Danny told Mack.

"About fuckin' time. Hold tight—there'll be a bit of a bump before we stop."

THE ENGINES REVVED, THEN DIED. THE PLANE PITCHED forward and seemed about to flip over backward.

Powder was sure he was going to die. Someone began to scream. Powder opened his mouth to tell him to shut the hell up, then realized it was him.

The aircraft stopped abruptly. There was a loud crack on the fuselage and the rear hatch slammed open. Bison fell out of the plane and Powder followed, slapping down the visor on his smart helmet so he could see.

"Let's go!" yelled Captain Danny Freah. "Let's go— the building's there. Two tanks, road behind us—they're out of commission. Come on, come on—Liu, Egg, Bison— run up the flank like we planned, then hit the door. Powder— you're with me. This ain't a cookout! Go!"

Powder trotted behind the captain, his brain slowly un-scrambling. His helmet gave him an excellent view of the hardscrabble parking area near the building. A small white circle floated just below stomach level, showing where his gun was aimed.

"Okay, flank me while I check the back of the building," said Danny.

Powder trotted wide to the right like a receiver in motion, then turned upfield. The building sat on his left. It looked a bit like the metal pole barn one of his uncles had built for a car shop back home, though a little less faded and without the exhaust sounds. Powder scanned the field behind it, making sure it was empty. He turned to the right, looking down in the direction of the road and the tanks.

"Looks like we've got the place to ourselves, Cap," he said.

"For ten minutes, tops. Watch my back."

Danny began making his way toward one of the two doors they'd spotted on the side of the building. Powder saw something move near the road out of the corner of his eye; he whirled quickly, then realized it was the airplane they had landed in, taxiing for a better takeoff position.

Bastard better not leave them. Then again, considering the ride down, walking home might be a better option.

"Powder?"

"Yes, Cap?" Powder turned back toward the building, spotting the captain near the wall.

"Flash-bangs. Window halfway down," said Danny, who gestured toward it. "I'll take the window. You go in the door on the left there. See it?"

"Yes, sir."

"Don't move until I give the word."

"Wouldn't think of it."

On the ground in Iraq
2355

DANNY TOOK THE TAPE OFF THE GRENADE AS HE LOOKED AT the window. Best bet, he thought, would be to knock the glass out with the stock of his gun, toss, jump in after the explosion.

Not a tight squeeze. Landing would be rough, though.

He could hear Rubeo talking to someone back at Dreamland in the background on his satellite channel. The scientist had warned him that there ought to be at least a dozen technical types running the laser, maybe even more. Danny didn't expect much resistance from them, but you could never tell. Some of the people at Dreamland could be pretty nasty.

"Front team ready," said Bison, who had come out around the corner to liaison.

"Powder?"

"Hey, Cap, this door isn't locked. We might be able to sneak in."

"Bison, what about the front?"

"Hold on."

As he waited, Danny switched to infrared mode and tried to see beyond the window inside. He couldn't make out anything.

Might be a closet. Would there be a window in a closet?

How about a john?

A top-secret facility without much security and an open back door?

No way the laser was here. Danny felt his shoulders sag.

"Front door's locked, Cap. We're going to have to blow it."

"All right, the way we rehearsed it." Danny slid the

window open and readied his grenade. "One, two—go!" he said, breaking the glass. He popped the grenade through, then hit the side of the building as the charge flashed. In the next second he rose and dove inside. A burst of gunfire greeted him. He leveled his MP-5 and nailed two figures about fifty feet away. As they fell, he realized the gunfire had come from the other direction; he whirled, saw he was alone—another automatic weapon went off. He was hearing his own guys, firing up the enemy.

A pair of tractors for semitrailers sat alone in a large, open area. Otherwise this part of the warehouse was empty.

Danny slapped his visor to maximum magnification. The tractors were just tractors.

No laser.

No stinking laser.

Powder was on the floor to his right, working toward him on his hands and knees. They couldn't see the others—there was a wall or something between them.

Empty. Shit.

"Wires all over the floor," said Powder. "Phone wires and shit."

"Cut 'em," said Danny. "Cut the fuckers. Two guards up there, maybe someone else beyond the wall."

THE EXPLOSIONS HAD PIERCED MUSAH TAHIR'S DREAM AS he slept on the cot not far from his equipment, but his mind had turned it into an odd vision of water streaming off the side of a cliff. He saw himself in the middle of a large, empty boat on a bright summer day. A calm lake stretched in all directions one second; the next, the water turned to sand. But the boat continued to sail forward. A large pyramid came into view, then another and another.

It began to rain, the drops suggested to his unconscious mind by the gunfire outside.

Tahir bolted straight up. Gunfire!

His AK-47 was beneath the bench near the computer tubes. He needed to get to it.

There were charges beneath the desk. He could set them off if all else failed.

As Tahir pushed out of bed, something incredibly cold and hard slammed into his chest. As he fell backward onto the cot, he saw two aliens in spacesuits standing before him. They held small, odd-looking weapons in their hands; beams of red light shone from the tops of them. The alien closest to him said something; too frightened to respond, Tahir said nothing. One of the men grabbed his arm and pulled him from the bed, and the next thing he knew he was running barefoot outside, pushed and prodded toward God only knew where.

"GOT AN IRAQI, CAPTAIN," DANNY HEARD LIU SAY. "THREE guards, dead. Doesn't seem to be anyone else. Screens, black boxes, whole nine yards. This must be the computer center."

"Record everything you see, then pull whatever you can for the plane. Computers especially. Look for disk drives, uh, tape things, that sort of stuff. Go!" said Danny.

"What do we do with the Iraqi?" asked Liu.

"Bring him with you. We'll take him back and question him."

"Hey, Cap, no offense but where's he going to sit?"

"On your lap. Go!"

Dreamland Command Center
1600

"WHY TAKE A PRISONER?" SAID RUBEO. "IS HE SUPPOSED to be our consolation prize?"

The others stared at Dog from their consoles. The feed from Danny Freah's smart helmet, relayed through the tactical satellite and the Whiplash communications network, played on the screen at the front of the situation room. It showed him searching the large warehouse behind the scientist.

"He can tell us what they're doing there," Dog said.

"If he's not the janitor," said Rubeo. "It's a parking garage."

"I believe it's a covert communications facility," said one of the scientists. "The trenches outside indicate large cables. The work stations—"

"We have more complicated systems working the lighting," said Rubeo. "Obviously, we made a mistake— this isn't a laser site."

"The section at the left of the bench area included two radar screens. This must be where they're coordinating the missile launches from," insisted the other scientist. "Don't be so dismissive."

"I'm being a realist," hissed Rubeo. "Missiles didn't bring down those planes. They're merely wasting them, just as we are wasting our time here."

"Bull."

"All right, everybody take a breath," Dog said. "We've got a ways to go here. We're not even off the ground."

Aboard *Wild Bronco*, on the ground in Iraq
2400

MACK LEANED DOWN FROM THE PLANE AS DANNY FREAH ran up, the props still turning slowly. He had what looked to be the CPU unit of a personal computer in his arms.

"So?" he yelled to him.

"We got a prisoner and some gear. We're grabbing all the computer stuff we can grab. I'm going to throw this on the floor of my cockpit."

"You have to secure it or it'll shoot around the cockpit when we take off."

"I'll sit on it."

Shit, thought Mack. These Whiplash guys were all out of their minds. "So are we taking the laser or what?"

"There's no laser here. It may be some sort of communications site, maybe not even that. Can you get the plane closer?"

"Yeah, I guess. Wait—what do you mean, a prisoner?" demanded Mack.

Freah ignored him, tossing the computer piece into his end of the cockpit.

Two of the assault team members ran up with pieces of equipment. They looked like looters who'd hit an electronics store during a power blackout.

"Where we going to put this prisoner?" Mack shouted.

"Shove him in the back with the guys," said Danny.

"That's too much weight."

"We're taking him back, Major. One way or the other. I'll strap him to the wing if we have to."

"Shit, Danny—"

"You're telling me you're not a good enough pilot to get this crate off the ground, Major?"

"Hey, fuck yourself," said Mack, but Freah had already

disappeared. He kicked the dirt once, then turned back to the airplane.

This wasn't like driving a truck. Weight was critical, especially if they were going to make it over the mountains. He'd worked it out to the pound before the flight, figuring they'd carry away only two hundred pounds of gear.

No way they were going to hold it to two hundred. Shit. They could start an electronics shop with this stuff.

Grousing to himself, Mack reached into the cockpit for his flight board. An experienced Bronco pilot would know where he could cheat, but he had to rely on the specs.

The Iraqi added how much? Another 150.

Hopefully.

The tanks were another problem. The explosion had pockmarked part of his runway. Stinking idiots did that on purpose, just to make his life difficult.

Mack worked over the numbers, trying to make sure he could make the takeoff on the small runway. The problem was, he had to climb almost right away, and had no face wind to help. He wasn't going to make it. Had he screwed up his calculations before? He was close to 500 pounds too heavy.

There had to be more margin for error. Somewhere.

Drop the Sidewinders. That'd do it.

Shit, fly naked?

Who was he kidding, though? The only thing he could use the heat-seekers for was as booster rockets.

Mack turned back to see two of the Whiplash people hauling a sack forward. They were almost on top of him before he realized the sack was a person.

"Hold," he said, walking to them. "How heavy is he?"

The two troopers were wearing helmets and apparently

couldn't hear him. He grabbed hold of the Iraqi, whose eyes were so wide and white they looked like flashlights. He held him up, shaking him a bit.

A hundred fifty, maybe a little more.

"You're lucky," he told the EPW after dropping him on the ground. "Few more pounds and we woulda had to cut your leg off to get airborne."

Aboard *Raven*, over Iraq
30 May 1997
0012

THE COMPUTER FLEW *HAWK ONE* IN THE ORBIT AROUND the area at eight thousand feet as Fentress took a break. His heart wasn't beating so crazily anymore and he felt good, damn good—the ground team confirmed that he had nailed the tanks.

Actually, they'd turned out to be armored personnel carriers. Same difference.

Zen would be proud of him.

"Bronco is ready to take off," said Alou.

Fentress retook the stick and began to come back north. Smith grumbled something over the open circuit about wanting wind. Fentress banked, watching as the Bronco struggled to get airborne, its nose bobbing up and down violently as it approached a curve in the road. Fentress felt a hole open in his stomach—he'd never seen an airplane crash before, not in real life.

He didn't now. The Bronco kept going straight, apparently airborne, though just barely.

"Bronco is up," he told Alou.

"Good. How's your fuel?"

He checked his instruments, running through a quick

scan before reporting back that they were right on the mark as planned. They traded course headings, double-checking the positions the computers plotted out for them as the Bronco slowly began picking up speed.

"I didn't think he'd make it," Fentress told Alou. "Take off I mean."

"Mack Smith always cuts it right to the bone," said Alou. "That's the way he is."

"A little like Zen."

"In a way.

"Mack helped develop the Flighthawks," Alou continued. "He's never flown them, but I'd guess he knows them as well as anyone, except for Zen. He helped map the tactics sections."

"Why didn't he fly them?"

"Doesn't like robots."

Fentress had *Hawk One* flying above and behind the OV-10, following the slow-moving plane much as he would follow a helicopter. He would arc behind at times to maintain separation, while still keeping close to his escort. At the same time, he had to stay relatively close to *Raven*, which was flying a kind of spiraling oval back toward the base at high altitude.

"Mack was in the air when Jeff had the accident that cost him his legs," said Alou. "Not that they got along too well before that. But, uh, I'd say there's still some bad blood there."

"I didn't know that."

"Yeah. Not the sort of thing you want to bring up in casual conversation with either one of them, I think."

"Yes, sir."

Alou laughed. "Hey, relax, kid. You're one of us now. You kicked ass down there. Zen'll be proud of you."

"Yes, sir. I mean, uh, right."

Alou guffawed.

Fentress tucked the Flighthawk's wing toward the ground, rolling around and back to the south before circling back. He scouted the valley as he flew; at eight thousand feet, he was lower than many of the mountain peaks ahead. The Bronco, weighed down with its passengers and climbing to get through the hills, continued to lag behind. Just as *Hawk One* drew back into its trail position, the RWR blared.

"Zeus ahead," Alou warned Mack. "Can you get higher?"

"Not without divine intervention."

A green and yellow flower blossomed in the darkness before him, then another, then another. An upside-down cloud rose from the ground—there were a half-dozen Zsu-23s down there. Fentress accelerated over the exploding shells. "I'll take out the flak dealer," he told Mack.

"I'm counting on you, Hawk boy," said Mack. "Get 'em quick—I don't want to waste any more gas turning around."

Fentress tucked left, zigging as another emplacement opened up. He was about two thousand feet over the effective range of the guns—though probably close enough for a lucky shot to nail him. The radar operator on the flight deck warned that there were at least two other guns farther up the valley that hadn't started firing yet.

Shells exploded above him—heavier weapons, Zsu-57s maybe. Unguided but nasty, their shells could reach over twelve thousand feet, about twice as high as the Zsu-23s.

Fentress realized he was boxed in by the antiaircraft fire. He started to dive on his first target anyway.

"I'm going to run right past them, real low," said Mack. "Keep their attention and—"

The rest of his sentence was drowned out by the warning tone of the RWR. A new threat screen opened up—the passive receiver had found a helicopter radar ahead.

"Bogey," Alou told Mack. "Low. Closing on you. It just came out of nowhere."

"I'll get it," said Fentress, flicking his stick left as C^3 marked out the contact as a Russian-made Hind helicopter. He began to accelerate, but as he went to arm his cannon, his screens went blank.

Aboard *Wild Bronco*, over Iraq
0042

THE MUSHROOMING ARCS OF GREEN-TINTED ANTIAIRCRAFT fire suddenly flared red. There was a flash of light so bright that Danny Freah thought a star had exploded.

"Jesus, what was that?" he said.

"Something just nailed the Flighthawk," said Mack Smith.

"Shit."

"We got other problems. Hang tight. This is going to be a bitch."

"We're flying through the flak?"

"Close your eyes."

IT WAS A WORTHLESS GESTURE, BUT MACK POUNDED THE throttles for more speed, hoping to somehow convince the lumbering aircraft to get a move on. The air percolated with the explosions of the antiaircraft guns; the wings tipped up and down, and the tail seemed to want to pull to the right for some reason. Cursing, Mack did his best to hold steady, riding right through a wall of flak.

The helicopter was dead ahead, four miles, and coming

at him, fat and red in the Bronco's infrared screen.

Served him right for leaving the damn Sidewinders on the ground, he thought. Son of a bitch.

"Bronco, stand out of the way so we can nail that Hind," said Alou.

"Thanks, Major, but where exactly do you want me to go?"

"Circle."

"Fuck off. I can't afford the gas, and sooner or later these bastards are going to nail me."

The Bronco bucked upward, riding the currents into a clear space beyond the flak. Another ball of tracers puffed about a mile ahead.

"Take out the guns," said Mack.

"Helo's first," said Alou. "They're stopping the flak— they don't want to hit him."

"How sweet," said Mack, tucking his wing to the left as sharply as he dared, then back the other way as the helicopter closed. He could feel the plane's weight change dramatically and tried to compensate with his rudder, but the plane slid away from him. They flopped back and forth, the OV-10 alternately threatening to spin, stall completely, or roll over and stop dead in the air. The helo began firing, barely a mile from his face.

Aboard *Raven*, over Iraq
0050

SOMEWHERE FAR ABOVE HIM THE FLIGHT CREW TRADED snippets of information on the location of the helicopter and the triple A. There was a warning—an AMRAAM flashed from the belly of the Megafortress.

Fentress had only a vague sense of the world beyond

the small area around him. His eyes were focused on the gray screen in front of him, his consciousness defined by the two words in the middle:

CONTACT LOST.

He was dead, nailed by the flak dealer.

Aboard *Wild Bronco*, over Iraq
0050

MACK SMITH SAW THE GAUGE FOR THE OIL PRESSURE IN the right engine peg right and then spin back left. It could have been tracking the weight distribution of his plane—he could feel the assault team rolling back and forth in the rear with his maneuvers.

"Tell your guys to stop screwing around back there," Mack told Danny.

The captain made a garbled sound in reply, either cursing or puking into his mask.

Mack wrestled the stick to try to get back level. The Hind passed off to his right, its gunfire trailing but missing.

The stinker was probably going to fire heat-seekers next.

So where the hell was Alou and his magic missiles? They weren't that stinking close, for cryin' out loud.

Mack pushed the stick forward to throw the Bronco into a dive. He tossed diversionary flares. A second later something whipped past his wings, trailing to the right after a flare. Something else exploded well off to his left.

A fresh volley of tracers kept him from gloating. The helicopter was still on his butt.

Mack slapped the stick and jammed the pedals, pushing the plane almost sideways. The Hind shot past, arcing to the right so close that Mack could have taken out his handgun and shot the bastard through the canopy. Instead he lurched left, figuring the helicopter was spinning for another attack. He tucked his wing and picked up a bit of speed and altitude north before tracers flared on his right once again. He thought he heard something ting the aircraft, but it could have been one of the Whiplash crew kicking against the side.

"Hey, Alou—any fuckin' time you want to nail the raghead is okay with me," he said, slapping the plane back left.

As he did so, a sharp downdraft pitched his nose toward the rocks. An AMRAAM from the Megafortress had found the Hind.

"Hey, there's two more helicopters on the ground down there," said Freah.

"We'll save them for next time," said Mack, pulling the plane level.

Incirlik
0100

JENNIFER TURNED FROM THE EQUIPMENT CONSOLE AND put her head down to the laptop screen, rechecking the sequence she had to enter. She typed it without looking, cursed as she made a mistake, backspaced, then reentered. The others on the flightdeck—Breanna, General Elliott, the handsome but somewhat stuck-up colonel from CentCom, and the RIO they'd borrowed to help work the gear—all stared at her.

"Just a second," she told them.

"We're waiting for you, young lady," said the CentCom colonel.

General Elliott looked like he'd strangle him. She'd always liked him.

Jennifer studied the map again, then entered the last set of coordinates. She hit Enter; the laptop spit back the numbers without hesitation.

"So?" asked Breanna.

"It was definitely a laser flash. The gear got a pretty good read. But it wasn't in that building Whiplash targeted," Jennifer told them.

"Where was it?" asked General Elliott.

"According to the data, fifty miles inside of Iran."

V

Allah's Sword

———

**High Top
30 May 1997
0154**

DANNY FREAH PRIED HIMSELF OUT OF THE BRONCO'S cockpit and walked to the back of the plane, where several Marines were already helping with the prisoner. The Iraqi had to be held upright; while he offered no resistance, the flight had turned his legs to jelly, and even with help he moved across the old asphalt like a toddler taking his first steps. The man kept looking to the sky, obviously unsure of where he was.

Then again, the same might be said of the Whiplash team, shuffling gear back and forth tipsily as they got out of the plane.

"You're green, Powder," Danny said.

"I ain't never flying in an airplane ever again, Cap. Never. No way. Not unless I'm pilot."

"That'll be the day," said Nurse.

"Inventory and tag the gear; we're routing it to the NSA," said Danny, who'd already received the order to do so from Colonel Bastian. "Isolate the prisoner in an empty tent, then find out if the Marines have an Arab speaker. I'd like to see what the hell he does before we hand him over to CentCom."

"As soon as the place stops spinning, I'm on it," said Powder.

High Top Base now looked like a small city, albeit one made almost entirely from tents. Whiplash's two bulldozers, along with a small Marine vehicle, were working on the southern slope, grinding it down into a depot area to accommodate some of the supplies two C-130s had brought in for the Marines. Gators—revved-up golf carts with military insignia—charged to and fro with stacks of gear. Two platoons of Marines were extending the defensive perimeter along the road below; another company was erecting a temporary metal building twice the size of the Whiplash HQ trailer at the far end of the aircraft parking area to be used for maintenance work on the planes. The runway would soon total three thousand feet; Cent-Com was hoping to use it as an emergency strip. In the meantime, air elements of the MEU(SOC)—six Harriers and six Cobra gunships—were due in late tomorrow or the next day to provide support for any Marine ground action in the Iraqi mountains to the south.

That might come soon. The rumble of artillery could be heard in the distance. The Iraqis were moving against their civilian population in the north. Unlike 1991, there had been no exodus of Kurds from the towns—an ominous sign.

Besides the Marines, a dozen technical people from Dreamland were due; they had been rerouted to Incirlik on the MC-17 to look after *Quicksilver.* As Danny understood it, the damage to the plane was much less than it might have been; the laser had managed to catch it with only a short burst, probably at the far edge of its range. The experts believed this confirmed that it was using a barrage pattern to saturate an area based on minimal or primitive radar coverage. They also said it was possible that the laser had been thrown off by the partly stealthy profile of the big plane, or even the presence of the Flighthawks. In any event, *Quicksilver* would be back at High Top and available for action within a few hours.

Danny made his way to the medical tent, blinking at the bright lights inside. The EPW, or enemy prisoner of war, stood before the empty cot, eyes shifting nervously around. He either didn't understand the corpsman's gestures or declined to take off his clothes so he could be examined.

"We're not going to hurt you," Danny told the prisoner. The man gave no indication that he understood anything Danny was saying; it wasn't entirely clear that he could even hear.

"Can you examine him like that?" Danny asked the corpsman.

"I guess. He doesn't seem to be hurt."

"Get him something to eat and drink. Try and be as friendly as possible."

"Yes, sir."

"Do you guys have an Arab speaker?" Danny asked the corpsman.

"Not that I know of, sir."

"All right. Go easy with him." The man looked like he was in his late thirties or forties, but Danny suspected he was somewhat younger; he clearly didn't eat well and probably didn't have much opportunity to take care of himself. Danny had seen in Bosnia how war and malnutrition aged people.

The man held up his shirt gingerly as the corpsman approached with his stethoscope. His ribs were exposed; he had several boils on his back.

"Take pictures," Danny told the Marines. "I don't want anybody accusing us of torture."

"Yes, sir," said the corporal in charge. "What do we call him?"

"Call him 'sir.' Be as nice to him as possible. Nicer. Treat him like your brother."

"I thought I was supposed to be nice."

Danny left the tent, heading toward his headquarters to update CentCom and then Dreamland Command on their arrival back at the base. He had just checked on the arrangements for a Pave Low to evacuate the parts and prisoner when the lieutenant he was talking to was interrupted. Another officer came on the line, identifying himself as a Major Peelor, an aide to CinC CentCom.

"Are my people hearing this right?" said the major. "You have an Iraqi?"

"That's right," said Danny. "We're shipping him to Incirlik so you and the CIA can debrief him. It's all been arranged through—"

"You went into Iraq and kidnapped an Iraqi citizen?"

"I captured a prisoner. We believed he was part of the laser operation. Our guys think his site may have been coordinating the radar operations, but it's too soon to—"

"Did you clear this with the lawyers?"

"Lawyers?"

"Taking the citizen."

"He's a soldier."

"Did you clear it with the lawyers?"

"Why the hell would I do that?" asked Danny. "What lawyers?"

"Who approved this mission?"

"Look, Major, you don't have the clearance for this conversation."

Danny punched out the connection.

Dreamland Command Center
29 May 1997
1622

"DON'T WORRY ABOUT IT," DOG TOLD DANNY. "I'LL HANDLE CentCom. The left hand doesn't know what the right hand's doing over there. Send the prisoner to Incirlik as we said."

"But what's this bullshit about lawyers?"

The colonel stared at Danny Freah's face on the screen at the front of the situation room. It was a tired, drawn face, one barely capable of suppressing the anger he obviously felt. "I haven't heard anything about lawyers," Dog told him honestly.

"Major Heller or Peelor, or whatever his fucking name, is accusing me of kidnapping an Iraqi citizen. Are we fighting a war here or what? What is it with these guys?"

Dog reached down to the console for his coffee. The cold, bitter liquid did nothing to relieve his own fatigue, but the pause let him consider what to tell his captain.

The absurdity of modern warfare—you needed a legal brief before taking prisoners. And all sorts of sign-offs and findings and cover-my-ass BS.

"I don't know what Peelor is talking about," said Dog. "You don't have to worry about it. You work for me, not CentCom. You proceeded on my authority, and you followed a lawful order."

It was the mildest response Dog could give him, but Freah still looked like he'd been punched in the stomach.

"The prisoner goes to Incirlik to be debriefed and processed," said Dog. "*Quicksilver* has been patched up and should be en route shortly. We're pulling together everything we have on the site you hit. We're pretty sure it was networking the radars, but we won't be positive until the NSA analyzes the gear you took. Whether it's related to the laser or not, at this point no one knows. You did a good job, Danny. Go get some sleep."

Dog clicked the remote control in his hand, cutting the connection.

"Better get me General Magnus," Dog told the specialist at the com board.

Over Turkey, en route to Incirlik
0400

JED BARCLAY THUMBED THROUGH THE PAGES OF SATELLITE photos on his right knee, looking for the latest batch from the sector north of Baghdad. Finding what he was looking for, he pulled the sheets to the top, then compared them to radio intercepts culled by *Raven* the previous day and balanced on his left leg. Under his chin were troop reports provided by CentCom, but what he really wanted now was the preconflict CIA assessment listing likely commanders and their call signs; that was somewhere in the briefcase near his feet, unreachable without sending a flurry of papers through the cabin of the C-20H Gulfstream.

"Son, you look like you're cramming for an exam," said General Clearwater, looming over him from the aisle.

"No, sir, just trying to work out some things."

"And?"

"Well, sir—" A sheaf of papers fell from his left knee onto the seat next to him, starting a chain reaction of cascading paper as they knocked several files and an awkward pile of maps onto the floor. Jed looked up from the mess helplessly; the general stared at him as if he didn't notice.

"Well, first of all," Jed began again, "the barrage tactics had to have been carried out with the help of a network of spotters. The radars only come on after the aircraft pass two points in northern Iraq. I would guess that there's at least one source in Incirlik, even though the NSA hasn't filtered the intercept yet. The barrage spread of SAMs includes a Chinese missile based on the S-3, at least if the telemetry is to be believed. But given all that, the damage to the first plane and the Megafortress—at least those two, maybe the others—had to have been caused by a laser. And on the Megafortress, assuming the preliminary information from the AWACS is correct, it seems clear that the laser was operating independently. I'd like to speak to the Dreamland people once we're down, but from everything I have here, there's definitely a laser."

"Where is it?"

"I don't know. Razor works with a dedicated radar, similar to a traditional SAM site. But that's not the only way to do it. From what I understand—and it's not my area of expertise—the laser could fire through a gridded arc after an aircraft is detected by a long-range radar or some other system."

"Run that horse at me again," said Clearwater.

"Think of it this way," said Jed. "You have a one-out-of-five chance to win a poker hand. You play a hundred rounds, you'd expect to win twenty times. Well, if the laser could cycle quickly enough—in other words, reload—it could fire one hundred shots into an area where it expected the plane to be. One shot out of X would hit."

"I've known lucky poker players in my time," said the general. "Played like they stepped in shit."

"Yes, sir. The point is, you could fire through a grid where you thought the plane was and expect to get a hit a certain number of times. Of course, we have no idea how many times they're firing. We don't record the misses, just the hits. They may be really lousy shots."

"We'll keep your point in mind while we peek at the cards," said Clearwater, clicking his false teeth.

"Sir?"

"How's your Arabic?"

"Uh, well, my top tier languages are German and Russian and of course—"

"Do you speak Arabic or not, son?"

"Well, I do, I mean at my last proficiency exam, I had a 4.2 out of five but there are different dialects. See, spoken standard Arabic, that's one thing—"

"Good enough," said the general. "Your friends at Dreamland have found us someone they think may be a radar operator. He's inbound at Incirlik right now. CIA's going to handle the debrief with some of our people, but I'd like you to take a shot at it as well. CIA officers with language skills are all south of the border at the moment."

"We, uh, we're—"

"They'll hold the horse until we get there."

"Uh, I was, uh, thinking I might, uh, sleep, sir. I haven't slept in—"

"You have twenty minutes before we land. Hop to it, son."

"Yes, sir."

On the road near Saqqez, northwestern Iran
0500

IN THEORY, BRIGADIER GENERAL MANSOUR SATTARI commanded the Iranian Air Force and its nearly five hundred aircraft. In theory, the click of his fingers could summon four fully equipped squadrons of MiG-29U Fulcrums and six slightly less capable F-5E Tiger IIs, two dozen MiG-27 fighter-bombers, a handful of F-14As and Phantom F-4D and F-4Es, a host of support aircraft, and nearly forty helicopters.

In reality, Sattari's command came down to a single Fokker F.28 Friendship VIP transport, which was actually listed under a French registry. True, he could count on the loyalty of several squadron commanders if called upon to fight—but only if he could reach the men personally.

Brigadier General Mansour Sattari, a veteran of the revolt against the Shah, a decorated fighter pilot who had personally led attacks against Baghdad during the Martyrs' War, had come to symbolize the demise of the once great Iranian Air Force, and Iran itself. A few short weeks before, his mentor and friend General Herarsak al-Kan Buzhazi, the supreme commander of the Iranian armed forces, had been outmaneuvered in a power struggle with the imams; he had been assassinated just minutes after meeting with the Ayatollah and learning the full depth of his humiliation. Even worse than Buzhazi's ignoble death were the Chinese troops that had entered the country at the Ayatollah's invitation; those troops now effectively controlled the country.

And so as he bent toward Mecca to say his morning prayers, he did so with honest humility, knowing firsthand how the God of all could show his overwhelming power even to the most just of men. Sattari did not presume to know why Allah did what He did, nor would he dare question the path the world took. He knew only that he must act according to his conscience and not his fear. His actions must ultimately be judged not by those on earth or even those who claimed to know God's will, but by God Himself.

Sattari was also a realist. And as he rose at the end of his prayers, still in a contemplative mood, he looked briefly in the direction of Iraq, the lifelong and enduring enemy of the Iranian people. For it was there that hope lay for his people. If the infidel Chinese were to be removed, if the cowards who hid behind their black robes in Tehran were to be taken from the stage, the Iraqi devils must play their role.

Thus far they had done so even better than Sattari had hoped. Seeking a solution to the Kurdish problem once and for all—a problem largely encouraged by Buzhazi before his demise—Saddam Hussein had embarked on a typically reckless plan of simultaneously tweaking the Americans and attacking the Kurdish Peshmarga, or "freedom fighters," in their homeland. Kicking out UN inspectors, aggressively launching surface-to-air missiles—the Iraqi actions were so well-timed that Sattari had considered holding back his own plan to use the stolen laser. Unfortunately, the Iraqi tactics had proved inadequate to provoke a large American response; it was only when Sattari began shooting down the American and British aircraft that the westerners had become sufficiently enraged to launch an all-out attack. Sattari had to carefully coordinate his attacks with the Iraqi radar and SAM launches to make it seem as if they were responsible. This had limited his target possibilities and made his timetable beholden to the Iraqis as much as the Americans. Still, the first phase of his plan had met its objectives. American troops were streaming into the region; more significantly, American diplomats were sounding the Iranian government out about a tentative rapprochement.

The next step involved his few allies in the diplomatic corps, who must strike a deal worth kicking the Chinese out for. Sattari did not feel that would be too difficult; the Chinese were not liked, even by the black robes, and they had already brought the country considerable pain. Nor did the Americans want much from Iran, beyond the assurance that they would not help Saddam—an assurance very easily given. Some small thing might move the talks along—an American air crew downed near the border and recovered, turned over after being treated as honored guests.

With the Chinese gone, Sattari could move on to the third and final phase of his plan—restoring the military, and the air force, to its proper place.

Sattari did not want power in the government. Nor did he necessarily believe that his plans would succeed. Ever the realist, he saw them as fulfilling his duty rather than his ambition. For the alternative—the Chinese, the black robes—meant quasi-servitude, if not death for his country.

And certainly death for himself. The ayatollahs blamed the Americans for Buzhazi's death. It was possible—Sattari had flown with them during the early days, and knew their cunning. They had certainly helped foil General Buzhazi's plans. But it was just as likely that the black robes themselves had killed the general, or at least allowed the Americans to do so.

Sattari did take some satisfaction in the fact that his country's enemies would be used to liberate it. He hated Iraq beyond rational measure. It was not enough that Sattari's younger brother died in the Martyrs' War; the bastard Saddam had killed his mother and father with a Scud missile attack against their city. The day the American President Bush had stopped the so-called Gulf War without killing the dictator even now rated among the saddest of Sattari's adult life.

The general walked back to his Range Rover, nodding at the driver before getting in. Two other SUVs with handpicked bodyguards sat twenty yards back on the road, waiting. Another was traveling about a quarter mile ahead.

"To Anhik," he told the driver, using the name of the village near the laser compound. "As planned."

The driver nodded and silently put the truck in gear. Sattari turned his attention to the countryside over the course of the next hour, studying the mountains as they shrugged off the last of the winter snow. Ice mingled with bursts of green. A small herd of animals—goats, most likely—moved along the side of the road, prodded by a pair of young women dressed in heavy peasant garb, except for their boots. As a child, General Sattari had heard stories that made the Kurds out to be demons. As a young man he had looked down on them as ethnically inferior louts. But his experience with them following the Martyrs' War had shown they were at least as competent and brave as any other Iranian soldier—high praise, in his mind. The fact that his complex at Anhik was staffed primarily by Kurds was in fact something of a comfort; he knew the men could not be corrupted by either the Chinese or the black robes.

The two men at the gate waited until they saw him nod before stepping back to let the Rovers pass. They held stiff salutes despite the wind-strewn dirt.

The site had been built during the Shah's last years, with the intention of constructing a tractor factory; it had in fact been used to construct some mowing equipment but had lain idle for at least two years before Sattari acquired it as one of the air force's top-secret warehouse sites. It had housed a stockpile of Russian air-to-air missiles. These were now long gone, some expended in the futile Persian Gulf action, and more, Sattari suspected, stowed aboard the Chinese vessels that had sailed from the country after the struggle that brought Buzhazi down.

A debt to be paid, along with many others.

They had started building the laser here nearly eighteen months before, when overtures by the Chinese made it clear that the hills kept it shadowed from American spy satellites. It was not completely bereft of coverage, of course—no place on earth seemed to be—but the Chinese intelligence had made development possible.

The laser had been Buzhazi's most closely guarded secret and his prized weapon. It was based largely on plans for the American "Razor," an antiaircraft weapon which, at least according to the specifications Sattari had seen, was considerably more accurate at a much farther range than his device. Razor was also considerably smaller, and mobile. It wasn't just that the Americans had better computer technology; they had found a way to propagate the energy beam much more efficiently and with different gases. And their superior manufacturing abilities undoubtedly played an important role.

But his scientists were doing well, better even than they had expected. The laser was housed in a long shed-like building with roof panels that could be slid open to target an aircraft. The mechanism looked as if it had been pilfered from a planetarium—and a sewage treatment plant. Pipes ran in two large circles and from both sides of the plants. Wires crisscrossed thick cables. Computer displays stood in two banks on steel-reinforced tables; more work stations were said to be networked here than in all the rest of Iran, outside the capital.

Sattari, not a particularly scientific man, had been somewhat disappointed on his first inspection. He'd expected to see something more like the devices in the American *Star Trek* movies. When the inventors described the use of the chemical gases to create a focused beam, they sounded more like cooks than weapons specialists. Nonetheless, he could not be happier with the results.

His caravan passed a small battery of Hawk missiles and headed toward the main building. Hidden under camo netting, the missiles dated from the Shah's era, and the crews manning them had never been able to launch one, even in training; they were too precious. Their best protection was stealth and the Americans' obsession with Iraq. The laser could not be protected against a concentrated air attack, and he had quartered a hundred-odd men here to guard against the Chinese and black robes, not the Americans, who in any event wouldn't attack by ground. Because of the secrecy of the project—and also because some of the scientists who worked here were not as enlightened about Kurds as Sattari—the soldiers were kept from the main compound by a double row of barbed-wire fence.

Sattari's vehicle stopped near the underground tunnel that led to the laser shed as well as a bomb shelter off to the side. He liked to start his inspections here, as it allowed him to get into the very heart of the laser shed almost immediately, in effect taking the scientists there by surprise. But today it was his turn to be surprised, for as he got out of his vehicle, two figures stepped from the underground steps. One was Sattari's commander here, Colonel Kaveh Vali. The other, considerably more ominous though nearly a foot shorter than the colonel, was Shaihin Gazsi, Ayatollah Khamenei's personal representative to the air force.

Sattari felt the blood vessels in his neck pop as Gazsi approached. Khamenei had shown his considerable disdain for Sattari by appointing a woman to represent him.

"General, I see you have finally arrived," said Gazsi. Barely thirty, she seemed to rise above the traditional feminine garb, her veil and headdress fluttering behind her as if struggling to catch up. Her nose might be a half centimeter too long, but otherwise she would be a perfect beauty.

If she weren't such a bitch.

"And you? Why are you here?" he said. He was, of course, surprised to discover that his secret was no longer secret, though this was the best he could do to hide his shock.

"You will address me with respect," said Gazsi. "I am the Ayatollah's representative."

His whore, perhaps, though Sattari doubted the old bastard could get it up.

"Why are you here?" he repeated.

"The Ayatollah wishes to speak with you immediately."

"I am at his service," said Sattari. "I will leave in the evening."

"You will leave now," she said. "My helicopter is prepared for you."

"I will leave this evening," said Sattari. He caught the worried look on Colonel Vali's face. "Or sooner, if my business here is completed before then."

"I suggest you conclude it within twenty minutes. I will wait," said the horrible woman as he descended the stairs, Vali in tow.

**High Top
0600**

ZEN UNHOOKED HIS CHAIR FROM THE ELEVATOR MECHA-nism on *Quicksilver*'s access ladder and began wheeling himself slowly toward the Whiplash HQ trailer. He kept looking for Fentress, dreading seeing him yet knowing he had to talk to him.

But what would he say?

No more time to rehearse—he was standing just outside the Whiplash trailer, nursing a cup of coffee.

"Yo, Fentress, rule number one, don't break my plane." Zen meant it, or wanted to mean it, as a joke, something to break the tension. But Fentress looked down at the ground and seemed nearly ready to cry.

"Hey, don't worry about it," Zen said, wheeling over to him. "I'm busting your chops. It wasn't your fault. Right?"

"Major Alou wanted me to take the mission," mumbled Fentress.

"You did okay. Really." Zen knew his words sounded incredibly phony. But what else could he say?

Well, for starters, that he shouldn't have flown. But like the kid said, that had been Alou's call.

Alou should have checked with him—a point Zen had already made, though Alou had dismissed it. The kid had done damn well under the circumstances, Alou had argued.

Bullshit, Zen said. He'd been shot down.

Alou hadn't answered.

Water over the dam now. Zen knew his job was to encourage the kid, get him going.

Kid—why the hell was he thinking of him as a kid? Guy was pushing thirty, no?

"Come on, Curly," Zen said, wheeling ahead to the ramp. "Let's get back on the horse. These things are flown by remote control for a reason, you know? Could've happened to anyone. You did okay."

Inside, Danny was laying out plans for an operation to hit a laser site in Iran—once they had a good location. Merce Alou and the others, including Breanna, were nodding as he spoke.

"This'll work," Danny said. "I haven't gone to the colonel with it, and we'll need CentCom to come along, but it'll work. Hey, Zen." He leaned over the table, pointing his long black forefinger toward a lake and mountains in northeastern Iran. "According to what Jennifer figured out, the laser has to be somewhere inside this twenty-five-mile square. Mahabad is just to the north, there's a major highway right along this corridor. The Dreamland mini-KH covered most of that area yesterday. The resolution's limited, as you know, but we can ID the major structures."

Zen pulled over the Iranian map while the others looked at the photos. Using a pen and his fingers as a crude compass, he worked an arc from the target square.

"How sure are we of this?" asked Zen. "All of the shoot-downs were within two hundred miles of the edge of your box. Razor's range is close to three hundred." Zen slid the map back so the others could see.

"Rubeo says it's likely this laser isn't as effective," said Danny.

"That's where it was fired from," said Jennifer. "Where in that area, I don't know, but it's there somewhere."

"Radar?" asked Zen.

"There's airport-type radar in the vicinity. The laser would be there, or simply wired into it," said Jennifer. "I've checked with our people—it looks like they're using barrage firing."

"Like the Iraqis with their missiles?" asked Zen.

"Except it works," said Major Alou.

"The way to find out what they're doing is to hit the site," said Danny. "You missed this, Zen. There are five possible targets, X'd out on that map. We draw people from the MEU. Two Cobras or more on each possible site. Assault teams follow. The Megafortresses provide intelligence and fuzz the radar, that sort of thing."

"Air defenses?" asked Zen.

"The Iranians have missiles near all of the sites, though it's not clear what's operational and what isn't. There are three air bases within range to intercept. You know their situation, though—it's anybody's guess what they can get off the ground. The one break I see is that the Chinese aren't this far north, so we don't have to worry about them."

"The Marines up for this?" Zen asked.

"I don't know," said Danny. "I imagine they will be, but I can't talk to them until Colonel Bastian gives the word."

"He has to go to CentCom to get them cleared for the mission," said Alou. "We can't just chop them."

"We have to do a quick hit," said Danny. "Dr. Ray says it's possible the thing is mobile and might be moved."

"So when are we talking to the colonel?" asked Zen.

"Now," said Alou.

Dreamland Command Center
May 29
2100

"THE PENTAGON LEGAL PEOPLE ARE RAISING HOLY HELL about taking the prisoner," said Magnus. "And Cent-Com's furious that they weren't told about the mission."

"We saw an initiative and we took it," said Dog, who decided he didn't want to parse whatever boneheaded argument the lawyers raised. "I stand by both actions."

"That won't affect the political reality," said Magnus. "And going into Iran will only make it worse."

"We have to destroy the laser, no matter where it is."

"Have you been looking at the satellite data?"

"Of course."

"Then you realize that Saddam is launching an all-out assault on the Kurds in the north. There are rumors he's loading Scuds with anthrax to fire at the Kuwaitis as well as the Kurds."

"I don't put much stock in rumors," said Dog.

"That's not the point, Tecumseh. This is becoming an extremely complicated situation—a geopolitical situation. If things escalate, we may need Iranian help."

"You're telling me the Iranians are our allies now?"

"I didn't say that at all."

"There's a laser in Iran shooting down our aircraft," said Dog. "We can get it."

"*If* your data is correct."

"Given the number of aircraft that have been shot down, it's worth the risk."

"Not if it encourages the Iranians to ally themselves with the Iraqis. And not if it pushes the Chinese to declare war in support of the Iranians."

"The Chinese are paper tigers," said Bastian.

"Paper tigers with the world's third largest army. Think of the impact of a nuclear strike on Saudi oil, Tecumseh. Talk to your friend Brad Elliott about them."

"I have the authority under Whiplash to stop whatever is shooting down the planes," said Dog, making his voice as calm as possible. "That means the laser, and that means going into Iran. Are you withdrawing that authority or reversing the order?"

"You know I can't do that," said Magnus.

Only the President could.

"Are you saying that I shouldn't proceed?"

Magnus stared at the screen but said nothing.

"We have a good plan," said Dog softly. "All we need is support from CentCom. My people there have outlined a good plan."

"CentCom doesn't have authority to engage in ground operations in Iraq, let alone Iran."

"We have to attack the laser quickly," said Dog. "My scientists say there's a good chance it's mobile or at least can be made mobile. Even if it stays right where it is, no plane flying over northeastern Iraq is safe. Let alone one flying over Iran."

A thin red streak, so bright it could have been paint, had appeared across Magnus's forehead. "You know, Dog, you sound more and more like Brad Elliott every fucking day."

The screen flashed and went blank.

Dog had never heard Magnus use a four letter word before.

"So what now?" asked Major Cheshire, whom Dog had asked to sit in with him.

"We find a way to go ahead without CentCom," Dog said.

"Magnus seems against it."

Dog thought back to his conversation with Knapp. Not exactly something to hang a career on.

"The Whiplash order hasn't been revoked," he said. "We have to proceed."

"Do we destroy the laser, or try and send Danny in?" said Cheshire.

He hadn't anticipated using her as a sounding board when he'd kept her at the base, and until now she hadn't been. But Cheshire did fill the role of alter ego admirably. Mid-thirties, a career officer with a wide range of experience—a woman with the perspective of someone who'd had to fight her way into what was essentially a closed club, in reality if not in theory.

A good alter ego. A good wife, in a way.

Jennifer was the one he wanted. This would put her in more danger—she'd barely escaped the laser strike on *Quicksilver*.

Not a factor in his decision.

"If we can't use CentCom, we can't send Danny," said Dog finally. "But we have to proceed."

"What about the Chinese?"

"Questions, always questions," he said with a laugh.

"Well? Are we risking World War Three here?"

Dog began to pace in front of the mammoth view screen at the front of the room. At the time the Whiplash order had been issued, the threat was largely thought to be a new radar system or a technique involving radar. The President had probably put Whiplash in motion as insurance for CentCom, intending them to augment the conventional forces. He hadn't foreseen this development.

But the fact that the threat turned out to actually be a directed energy weapon did not change the essential nature of the orders—something was still shooting down American planes, and he was empowered, ordered, to stop it if possible.

The orders were predicated on the threat being in Iraq, not Iran.

It wasn't hard to guess why Magnus hadn't volunteered to take the matter to the President. If things went wrong, and even if things went right, the mission could plausibly and legally be described as a rogue adventure by a misguided underling—Lieutenant Colonel Tecumseh Bastian. His head could be offered up to whomever wanted it: Congress, CentCom, the Iranians.

They had to proceed with the mission. If they didn't, more Americans would die. The laser might be refined and sold to other countries, beginning with the Chinese— who might even already have it. It might be used to threaten commercial air flights or against satellite systems.

But proceeding might very well mean the end of his career.

And the death of his lover, daughter, and friends.

"Colonel?" asked Cheshire.

"Open the channel to High Top," Dog told the lieutenant on the com panel. Then he turned to Cheshire. "We're moving ahead."

Tehran, Iran
1000

FOR ALL HIS EXPERIENCE IN COMBAT, FOR ALL HIS BRAVADO, General Sattari still felt awe as he stepped into the chamber of the Council of Guardians in the capital. He might have no respect for the robed men who sat here, he might think that the Ayatollah Khamenei was essentially a coward and a traitor to his people, but he could not forget that these men, for all their failings, were teachers with a special relationship with God. Perhaps they abused their power, perhaps they made decisions motivated by greed or expedience rather than piety—but they nonetheless contemplated the Creator with a depth of attention that he could only admire.

The marble floors, the large open room, the rich tapestry—all reinforced the humility of his position. His steps faltered; he felt his fingers beginning to tremble and his heart pumping faster, adrenaline mixing, accentuating his nervousness. When he saw Ayatollah Khamenei sitting calmly before him, he felt his tongue grown thick. He had been wrong to proceed without his blessing; he had been wrong to underestimate the religious leader's skill and control.

He considered saying nothing. He considered, even, running from the building.

A glance to the Chinese guards flanking the door steeled his resolve.

"You have caused us great difficulty," said Khamenei in a voice so low Sattari practically had to stop breathing to hear.

"The difficulties are with our enemies," Sattari said. He reminded himself he was not without leverage. Nor was his weapon unguarded—before leaving Anhik he had deployed most of his men on the highways south of the base to guard against any move by the Chinese; spies at the air bases they used would warn if any bombers or transports took off. While Sattari did not believe Khamenei would order such an attack against him—he would have done so already, rather than summoning him here—the Chinese could well choose this time to move unilaterally.

"How does the American attack on the dog Saddam help us?" asked the Ayatollah.

"Because, your excellency, it takes their attention away from us, and at the same time weakens our enemy. Our people in Basra pray for deliverance."

The continued suppression of Shiites in the southern Iraqi city had been the subject of many of Khamenei's edicts, but the Ayatollah showed with a frown that he would not be so easily persuaded. Sattari felt an urge to shout at him that they must take advantage of the American preoccupation and push off the Chinese; they could rearm with American help as long as the Americans were obsessed with Iraq. American weapons were far superior to the Chinese hand-me-downs; this had been proven time and time again. And even if the Americans offered no aid, they could be used to cow the Chinese into a better arrangement.

Surely Allah was against the pagan Communists as well as the demon Christians.

Did it matter that American planes were destroyed? Did it matter that Iraqis were killed? These were good things.

Sattari remained silent.

"We were not informed that the weapon was ready to be used," said the Ayatollah when he spoke again.

"Reports of the tests six months ago were delivered in this very hall," said Sattari. "At that time, readiness was discussed."

And projected as being five years away, if not more. Sattari had helped coach the scientists on what to say, and listened carefully. The laser's actual location had also been carefully left out of the report.

Khamenei stared at him, not bothering to point out the contradiction.

"You wish your power restored," said the black-robed

imam instead. "You feel that by these actions you will restore yourself to a position of eminence."

"My interest is Iran, and the glory of God."

"That does not rule out your own glory, does it?"

He thought to supply a formula from the Koran to the effect that personal glory means nothing except as it contributes to salvation, but the stirring of some of Khamenei's cohorts in the row behind him diverted him.

"My interest is Iran, and the glory of God," he repeated.

"So be it," said the Ayatollah. "But I will be the judge of the success of your action."

Sattari considered the words. Khamenei had conceded nothing—but neither did he order Sattari to stop what he was doing.

He was willing to play the game. Perhaps he detested the Chinese and the Iraqis as much as Sattari. Or perhaps he had his own plans; his face gave nothing away.

It occurred to Sattari that he might be stronger than he realized. He didn't have to angle for power—he had it. If he could arrange for a purge of some of the more religious junior officers in the air force, he might combine them with his Kurd allies and control the northwest provinces on his own.

It was not among Sattari's plans, but the idea did warm his chest against the coldness of the hall as he took his leave.

Incirlik
1100

THE AMERICAN'S ARABIC WAS CLEAR ENOUGH, THOUGH HE seemed an odd bird, limbs and legs constantly in motion as he stumbled for the right phrase. Neither he nor any of the other Americans seemed to realize that Tarik spoke

English, or that he had spent several years in America. He believed that was very much for the good, especially since he had overheard his captors say several times that he must be treated with care. Certainly they had been good to him so far.

They wanted to know how he managed the radar network. They asked of a laser, and missiles, but to every question he feigned ignorance.

He would say nothing. That was his duty.

**High Top
1110**

TORBIN HAD TROUBLE CONCENTRATING ON THE RADAR screen as Jennifer Gleason reviewed the settings for him. If the plane's captain was the most beautiful woman Torbin had ever seen—and she was—Jennifer was number two.

Very different, though. Not military. Long hair, thinner. Cursed like a stinking sailor. Smarter than any ten people he'd ever met.

"So you hit this sequence here, that just tells the computer to screw over its normal programming," she told him. "Then you manually move the cursor to prioritize, or use verbal commands, like this."

The scientist began speaking in a calm, almost quiet voice, using the screen ID codes to identify the targets.

"The thing to remember is that you have to precede instructions with the word 'Computer.'"

"Got it," said Torbin.

"Okay. You run through the simulation program I just set for you. I have to help install the laser detection gear in *Raven*, so I'm going to download some programming while you're practicing. Then you're going to come over to *Raven* with me and help calibrate it."

Jennifer bent down to examine something on the screen of her laptop, exposing a small bit of flesh near her waistband.

"Okay," said Torbin, wrestling his eyes away with great difficulty. "Okay, okay."

High Top
1115

WITHOUT THE MARINES OR OTHER CENTCOM SUPPORT, the best they could do was blow up the laser. Even then, it might be tricky—they had only six JSOWs left, to use against the three likely sites.

"We can get there in the Bronco," insisted Mack, who had suddenly become enamored of the turboprop plane. "In and out."

"Your loaded radius just won't cut it," said Zen. "Especially if it turns out to be that site out near the lake. I'm sorry, Danny. Colonel Bastian's right. This is the way we have to go."

"I'm worried that we don't even have all the possible sites," said Alou. "From what Rubeo says, those four smaller buildings could be it too."

"Once they fire at the Quail, we'll know for sure," said Bree.

"If they fire at the Quail."

"They will." The Quail was a decoy drone, essentially a cruise missile with a profile and "noisemaker" that made it appear to be a B-52 on radar scopes.

"I think they'll go for it," said Zen. "And Rubeo's wrong about it fitting in a small building. Jennifer says it has to be one of those three sites."

"She's not an expert on lasers," said Alou.

"She's an expert on everything," answered Zen.

Danny listened as they continued to discuss the contingencies, pondering how effective the JSOWs would be against a hardened site, even though Rubeo said it would be impossible to place the director or firing mechanism behind one.

In a perfect world, a massive strike by F-15Es would cover any possibility. But if it were a perfect world, Danny thought, he would have CentCom support.

He glanced at the map. If it made sense to survey the laser site when they thought it was in Iraq, it made even more sense now.

Two of the three most likely sites were within the Bronco's radius, albeit just at the edge.

So maybe they should be in the air, just in case.

"What?" Zen asked him.

"Listen, if you're going to use the Quail to try and find the site, then I'll take a team in the Bronco in case it turns out to be one we can hit," Danny told him.

"Now you're talking," said Mack.

"Iraqis'll shoot you down before you get to the border," said Zen. "They're running Zsu-23s up north like ants rushing to a picnic."

"It's an awful long shot," said Bree.

"Granted. But the payoff would be high."

"Not if you're shot down," said Alou.

"Hey, screw that," said Mack. "I'm not getting shot down."

"You almost got shot down by a helicopter," said Alou.

"Not even close. And this time I won't leave my Sidewinders behind."

"Then you'll never make it into Iraq," said Zen. "It's too far, Mack."

"Don't wimp on me, Zen boy."

The back and forth might have been amusing if so much weren't riding on it. Danny wondered if he sounded like Mack—willing to take enormous risks just to get in on the action.

Was that what he was doing?

Dreamland Command Center
0100

THE FACE THAT FLASHED ONTO THE SCREEN SURPRISED Dog so much he found himself momentarily speechless.

"I hear you've been looking to chew my ear," said General Clearwater, CentCom CinC. "Fire away."

"Well, actually, it's academic now," said Dog, who'd just come back to the command center after catching a few hours sleep. "I wanted to inform you of a mission into Iraq."

Clearwater moved his closed mouth, as if shifting his teeth around. "Well, your boys pulled that off very well, Colonel. Congratulations. Were you looking for assistance?"

"Just wanted to keep the lines of communication open, sir. A heads-up."

"Very good." The general seemed ready to sign off.

"General Clearwater, I wonder if we might have your support on another mission."

"What's that?"

"We believe we know where the laser is that's been shooting down our aircraft. We want to hit it right away."

"It should be a target. Have you talked to Jack?"

Jack meant Jack Christian, the Air Force general in charge of target planning for CentCom.

"It's in Iran," said Dog. "What I'm looking for—"

"Iran's out of bounds," said the general. "Are you sure about this?"

"Yes, sir."

Clearwater moved his jaw again. The deep lines on his forehead grew even deeper. "How sure?" he asked.

"Very."

"My orders at the moment are very explicit, and I've gone over similar ground with the Defense secretary twice. I understand your orders may be different," added Clearwater before Dog could say anything else. "But for the moment at least, my hands are tied."

The screen blanked before Dog could say anything else.

High Top
1150

THE IDEA HAD FORMED IN DANNY'S MIND EVEN BEFORE THE Marine Corps major came to see him. It was outrageous and even far-fetched—which made it perfect.

"I know you're busy," said the Marine commander, helping himself to some of the coffee on the trailer counter near the worktable. "I was wondering if I could arrange a briefing on the valley you flew through on your way back from the Iraqi radar site. We have a mission just north of there. We're going to pick up some Kurd leaders and bring them to Turkey for a conference. I'm authorized to take out anything that gets in the way."

"I'll give you the whole rundown," said Danny. "There's a helicopter base down there that you ought to wipe out along the way. They have at least two Mi-24 Hinds on the ground."

"We'll nail them," said the Marine.

"Wait. I'd like one of the helicopters," said Danny.

"What for?" said the major.

"You don't want to know," said Danny.

The Marine, who knew only that Whiplash was not part of the normal chain of command, nodded. A few minutes later Danny and he had worked out a plan to snatch one of the Hinds.

Zen and Alou were considerably more skeptical than the Marine.

"We take the helicopter into Iran. The Iraqis won't shoot at it, because it's theirs," said Danny.

"The Iranians will," said Zen.

"Not before we hit them."

"I don't know, Danny."

"It'll work," he insisted. "It has the range, even without extra fuel. And we'll take plenty. Payload's there. It's low risk."

"Bullshit on low risk," said Alou, and even Zen rolled his eyes.

A small part of him said to back off—he and the team were tired, this was way out there. But another part of him, the much larger part, pushed ahead.

They could do it.

"Who's going to fly the helo?" asked Alou.

"I got a guy," Danny told him.

"Who?"

"Egg Reagan. He has a pilot's license and everything."

"He's flown Hinds?" Zen asked.

"He can fly anything," said Danny. "We can take the chopper, no sweat. As long as the Marines can get us there, we can do this. Egg flew a Pave Low just the other day. He can do this."

"We can't go without Colonel Bastian's approval," said Alou.

"He'll approve it," said Danny.

Dreamland Command Center
0210

"VERY RISKY, DANNY. I DON'T KNOW IF SERGEANT REAGAN can fly the aircraft."

"I know he can, Colonel. He's been sleeping or I'd have him here to tell you himself."

Dog started pacing. He knew as well as Danny what the sergeant would say; the word "No" didn't seem to be in the Whiplash vocabulary.

But could he *really* do it?

"He flies the Pave Lows," added Danny. "They're more complicated, I guarantee."

The payoff was immense. Pull it off, and they'd have a treasure trove of information.

But this was far riskier than the earlier plan.

He played back the conversation he'd had earlier with Clearwater. The general wasn't opposed to hitting the laser. On the contrary, it seemed. But he clearly wouldn't go against his orders, and clearly wouldn't directly support a mission into Iran until the orders were changed.

That could take days. If the laser were mobile, it'd be gone then.

"Colonel?"

"CentCom needs one of the Megafortresses to help suppress antiair on a mission south about the time this is supposed to go off. We're going to have to work that in," said Dog.

"Okay," said Danny.

"I'll talk to CentCom about the action inside of Iraq."

"Hot dog."

"I haven't authorized the ground mission," said Bastian quickly. "Let me think about it."

"But—"

"I'll get back to you," said Dog, punching the End Transmit.

High Top
1225

"KNOCK, KNOCK," SAID EGG, OUTSIDE DANNY'S PERSONAL tent. "Hey, Captain, you wanted to see me?"

"Come," said Danny.

Powder and Bison came in with Egg, filling the tent with an odd odor.

"Enjoy your nap?" Danny asked Egg.

"Yes, sir," said the sergeant.

"What the hell?" said Danny. "You guys smell like baby powder."

"Hey, just checking on the kid, Cap," said Powder. "You know. We're like uncles."

Danny rolled his eyes. "Listen, Egg, we have something a bit hard to tackle and I'm wondering if you'd be up to it."

"Hard's his middle name, Cap," said Powder. "Just before 'on.'"

"Yeah, and Powder would know," said Bison.

Danny ignored them. "Egg, would you be up to flying a helicopter?"

The sergeant shrugged. "Yeah, no problem."

"Good. It's an Mi-24 Hind."

"A what?"

"A Hind. Commie helicopter. Think you can handle it?"

"Jeez, I don't know. I don't know that I've ever flown one of those before."

"A helicopter's a helicopter, right? Jennifer Gleason says there's a database on the controls and performance aspects in the Megafortress database," Danny added. "She's setting it up so you can review it. And I talked to Dr. Ray at Dreamland. He's going to dig around for an expert to talk you through it. We can set up a direct line."

"Jennifer, the babe scientist," said Powder. "Jeez, I'll do it."

"I volunteer," said Bison.

"I don't know, Cap," said Egg. "I mean, I probably could figure it out if I have a little time."

"I'll do it," said Powder.

"Screw yourself," said Egg. "This isn't a bulldozer we're talking about."

"I can learn it, Cap," insisted Powder. "Will she whisper in my ear?"

"All right, guys, back off," said Danny. "Outside the tent."

He watched Egg as they left. The normally self-assured sergeant wore a worried face.

"We can come up with something else," Danny suggested.

"I can do it." Egg flexed his shoulders back. Danny worried that he was pushing too hard—he didn't want Egg to say he could do it just to please him.

On the other hand, a helicopter was a helicopter, commie or not, right?

"Where is it?" asked Egg.

"We passed it on the way home," Danny told him. "The Marines are going to help us steal it."

"Shit, I'll do it, Cap," said Powder outside.

"Fuck off," said Egg.

"Go play with the kid," yelled Danny.

Powder and Bison moved a few feet away from the tent, though he could tell they were still nearby.

"I'll figure it out, Captain," said Egg. "If I get some help. When are we leaving?"

"Half an hour too soon?"

Egg just scratched his head.

Dreamland Command Center
0255

DOG WATCHED THE CNN FEED, HIS MIND DRIFTING BLANK. The connection with High Top was pending; he intended to give Danny the go-ahead to use the Hind, long shot though it was.

He'd double-checked the sergeant's piloting credentials, gone over the sat pictures, reviewed the flight plans. He'd listened to the scientists debate the value of the intelligence. He'd spoken once more to Clearwater, who personally approved the Marine involvement in the helo snatch, but set the limits there. Dog knew he was making the right decision; the odds were against the mission, but it was exactly the sort of long shot they'd put Whiplash together to undertake.

And yet, he was still searching for some signpost, some indication that he was right to put his people at so much risk.

It wasn't there. Even on an easy mission, nothing could guarantee everything would fall in place.

There were no easy missions. On the other hand, if they completely screwed up, if things went totally wrong, the implications were enormous.

Worse than the situation if they did nothing?

No.

The CNN footage showed Iraqi tanks continuing their attacks against the Kurds. Didn't we fight this war already? Dog wondered.

"Captain Freah is on his way," said the lieutenant at the com panel. "He should be on in five minutes, maybe less."

"Okay. Where's Jed Barclay?" Dog asked.

"Incirlik."

"Get him, would you?"

The operator punched his keys. He spoke to someone on the other end of the line in Turkey, then told Dog they wouldn't have video.

"Not a problem."

"Colonel?" Jed's voice boomed so loudly in the room the techie had to squelch the volume.

"Jed, can you get me to General Elliott?"

"He's left to go back to Europe."

"You can get me in touch with him, can't you?"

"Uh, yeah. Take a minute."

Two minutes later the technician said they had an incoming transmission from Class Two—General Elliott aboard a VIP Gulfstream.

"How are you, Colonel?" boomed Elliott.

"Personally, not so good." Dog laughed, facing the blank screen. "Want your old job back?"

Elliott laughed. "I'd take it in a heartbeat." His tone grew serious. "It's a little different being a colonel. You don't have the perks to go with the responsibility."

"I still have to do what I think is right."

"It's not always easy to figure out what that is," said Elliott.

Dog didn't intend on asking him what to do, and he'd known Elliott wouldn't volunteer advice. So why had he contacted him?

Moral support? Word of encouragement?

Not even that. Talking to him, though—it was like making a pilgrimage to a sacred shrine or a battlefield. Looking out over the hills at Gettysburg made you understand something, even though you couldn't put it into words.

Elliott as Gettysburg—he'd roar at that.

"Thanks, General," said Dog. "I have to go."

"That's all you want?"

"That's all I need, sir."

Dog bent to the console and picked up the land-line phone, punching in his office. Ax answered immediately.

"Ax, how are we doing with that expert on Russian helicopters?"

"Should be aboard the Dolphin by now, sir," answered the chief master sergeant.

"Hustle him down here as soon as he clears security."

"Yes, sir."

Dog put down the phone and turned to the lieutenant. "I'd like that connection to High Top today, son."

"The connection's there, sir. It's Captain Freah we're waiting on."

Dog straightened and looked at the screen. When Danny Freah's tired face finally appeared, Colonel Bastian said only one word: "Go."

Aboard *Fork One*, over northeastern Iraq, 1400

DANNY FREAH STOOD NEAR THE DOOR OF THE MARINE HE-licopter, watching as the CH-46 Sea Knight dubbed *Fork One* whipped across the landscape roughly twenty feet over the ground. The Marines liked the old helicopters, claiming they were more dependable than Pave Lows or even Chinooks, their look-alike big brothers. Danny wasn't so sure. If he had to pick a Marine transport, he would have much preferred an Osprey or even a Super Stallion, the Corps' three-engined version of the MH-53 Pave Low, ferociously quick monster choppers with plenty of power to spare.

On the other hand, he didn't think he could do better than the Marines accompanying them. If it went well, the whole operation would last maybe fifteen minutes: Flighthawk hits the two Zsu-23-4s protecting the approach, followed closely by the Cobras, which would strike the two BMPs at the base and a pair of machine guns near the buildings. The troops would then fast-rope into the complex. One group of Marines and the Whiplash team would land near the helicopters; the Marines in the second chopper would hit the buildings. Two of the eighteen men squeezing into the rear of the aircraft with Whiplash carried Shoulder-launched Multi-purpose Assault Weapons—SMAW 83mm rockets—to be used against the fortified position near the Hinds and anything else that came up. The others carried standard M-16s and a variety of grenades. Two of Danny's boys, Powder and Bison, had SAWs, or light machine guns, to lay down support fire at the start; the others carried MP-5s for close work at the finish.

Boom, boom, boom, assuming it went according to plan. Then the real fun would begin.

Egg fingered his gun nervously. The expert who was supposed to help him fly hadn't shown up in the Dreamland command center yet, but Jennifer had downloaded several pages worth of data, and one of the Marine helo pilots had offered plenty of advice. Every so often Egg would look up from his notes toward Danny and nod confidently.

It had the opposite effect from what he intended. Egg looked about as self-assured as a kid coming off the bus for basic training.

It would work, Danny told himself. And if it didn't—

It would work.

Aboard *Raven*, over Iraq
1420

THROUGH THE PREFLIGHT, TAKEOFF, AND LAUNCH OF THE
Flighthawks, Zen tried to think of something to say to
Fentress, who'd come along on *Raven* to act as an assistant. Frankly, he would have preferred to have Jennifer,
but she was too exhausted. And besides, there was no reason not have Fentress there, helping—the kid had proven
he could handle the U/MFs, even if he'd been shot down.

He wasn't a kid, Zen told himself again.

He wasn't out after his job either.

Zen lifted his helmet visor as the Flighthawk settled
onto the course toward the target area. He glanced over at
Fentress, trying to think of what to say. The kid—the
other U/MF pilot—was studying the latest photo relay
from the mini-KH, orienting himself. There was a little
less than five minutes left before fun time.

Zen felt he should say something, but all he could think
of was generic bullshit about how he knew Fentress
would do a good job. Finally he simply slid his visor back
and said they were ready.

"Yup," said Fentress.

Zen cracked his knuckles and rolled his neck on his
head, loosening his muscles. Then he took the robot back
from the computer. "Hawk to Whiplash leader. Danny,
you got me?"

"Loud and clear," replied Danny, who was in one of the
Marine helos.

"We're getting ready to dance," Zen said. "Captain
Fentress will feed you the visuals."

"Ready to rock."

Zen tipped his nose forward, and the Flighthawk
screamed toward the earth, lining up on its first target.

The Iraqi facility looked more like a strip mall than an airport; the two Hinds were located at one side of a short span of hard-packed dirt. Across the way were two buildings, guarded by a pair of Zsu-23-4 antiaircraft weapons mounted on mobile chassis. What appeared to be the entrance to a bunker sat just beyond the weapons at the north end of the field; it looked to be either a bomb shelter or a storage facility. At the other end of the field there were three small buildings that probably garrisoned the troops assigned to work with the helicopter. There were two BMPs, Russian-made armored personnel carriers, parked on a ramp halfway between the buildings and the runway. Zen would nail the antiair; as he finished with the second, the Marine Cobras should be just getting in range to knock out the BMPs and then scald the barracks.

His weapons bar began to blink red as the preprogrammed target grew fat in the crosshairs.

Too soon to fire. He held steady, speed picking up steadily—450 knots, 460 . . . A black plume appeared on the left side of his screen—the other set of guns had already begun to fire.

At two and a half miles to target, Zen pressed the small red button that triggered the 20mm cannon in the chin and belly of the Flighthawk. Adapted from the venerable M61A that had served in every frontline American fighter from the F-15 to the F/A-18, the six-barreled gat spat slugs out at a rate of six thousand a minute. About a second and a half later the shells began grinding through the torrent of the mobile flak dealer, chewing a curlicue into the Russian-made steel. One of the Zsu barrels flew off the top of the chassis into the second emplacement, detonating the fuel tank in its carrier. Before Zen could get his nose on that target, it was enveloped in flames. He fired anyway, then quickly rolled his wings, powering the robot plane into a high-speed turn so hard he could practically hear the carbon wings groan.

"Video feed to Whiplash headset," he told Fentress.

"They're on board already," he replied.

"Cobras are zero-two away, Hawk leader," said Alou.

"Copy that. I'm going to run over the landing area and stand out of the way for the helicopters."

Zen pushed on, riding the Flighthawk across the compound toward the barracks area.

"Two more vehicles than we planned on," said Fentress, watching the ground scan. "Missile launcher on the right, your right, as you come in!"

A squat, pudgy vehicle with two rectangular boxes sat beyond the machine-gun emplacements near the barracks area. Either an SA-8 or SA-9—Zen didn't have time to examine it, much less get off a shot; his momentum carried him beyond it before he could get more than a glimpse.

"Computer, identify antiair missile vehicle," he said as he threw the Flighthawk into a turn.

"Which vehicle?"

Which one? There were more than he'd seen?

"All," he said. "Highlight on the sitrep."

The computer's synthesized acknowledgment was drowned out by a radar warning.

"Yo, Alou—LZ is hot. I'm spiked!" he said. The SA-8 radar had latched onto the Flighthawk. A launch warning followed.

"We're jamming!" said the pilot.

"Jam better. Hold the assault package."

"Too late," answered Alou.

"Hold them!" Zen tucked and rolled, zigging back toward the launcher he'd seen. It was an SA-8B mounted on a six-wheeled amphibious vehicle, capable of launching missiles using either semiactive radar or IR homing devices. Zen lit his cannon as the missile launcher swung its rectangular nose toward him. His first few shots missed high, but he stayed on the launcher; a stream of lead poured through the near box containing a missile.

The SA-8B exploded—but not before a long, thin pipe popped from the box farthest from his cannon.

Aboard *Fork One*, over Iraq
1440

THE FLIGHTHAWK SITREP MAP ON HIS VISOR BLINKED RED, indicating that a missile had been fired from one of the SAM trucks. Danny cursed, and shouted a warning to the helicopter crew. A second later the helo twisted downward, one of the wheels whining as it dashed against the ground. Danny clutched his MP-5 against his carbon-boron vest and hunkered down in his seat, sure that the next thing he'd see would be flames. But instead the helo bolted nearly upright, then whipped forward again. Danny switched from the Whiplash frequency that tied into the Flighthawks to the general radio band used by the attackers; unfortunately, there wasn't a way to use both at the same time.

"Missiles in the air," warned one of the pilots.

"Hold off," said Alou over the circuit somewhere.

"We're committed," answered the pilot blandly. "Relax."

The Marine AH-1W Super Cobras charged their targets at nearly 200 miles an hour. The first ship unleashed a barrage of five-inch Zuni rockets that peppered the emplacement area. Half a tick behind him came a Whiskey Cobra armed with Hellfire laser-guided missiles; despite the heavy smoke, he zeroed out both BMPs in rapid succession, then unleashed the chain gun on the barracks.

Both helicopters wheeled off, spraying decoy flares and smoke bombs as they did.

"*Fork*, come on in, the water's perfect," said the Cobra leader.

"Assault team up!" said Danny. "Fentress—how are those Hinds?"

"Here's the visual," he replied, punching in a replay showing the helicopters.

They were being armed and fueled.

**Aboard *Raven*, over Iraq
1452**

ZEN SAW THE NOSE OF THE MISSILE AS IT FLASHED TOWARD him, a blurred spoon of white. He'd already slammed the U/MF's nose downward, rolling the U/MF into a twist so hard that the plane fluttered uncontrollably for a second, caught between the conflicting forces of momentum and gravity. A hole opened in his stomach; acid rushed in, searing a spot beneath his ribs. But he hadn't lost the plane—the missile streaked away, and by the time it self-detonated, Zen had full control of the Flighthawk and begun to climb. He recovered well south of the target area, restoring his sense of the battlefield as well as speed. The Cobras had started their run despite the warnings; the missiles the Iraqis had launched had all missed, probably because they had been aimed at the U/MF and not the throaty whirlybirds.

Zen climbed in an arc eastward as they'd planned, feeding video from behind the smoke screen the Cobras laid as the two CH-46s came in. His radar warning gear was clean and there seemed to be no more antiaircraft fire, though a smart commander would keep his head and hold back until the ground troops appeared.

"Can you get real-time images of those Hinds?" Fentress asked. "I've been feeding Whiplash the shots you took coming in."

"Yeah," said Zen, changing course. "Almost lost it there," he added.

"Nah."

"Yeah, really, I thought I did," he said. "You did okay."

"We got a long way to go," said Fentress.

Zen laughed, realizing that was something he usually said.

**Aboard *Fork One*, in Iraq
1500**

DANNY THREW HIS BODY AROUND THE ROPE, HANDS PUMP-ing. He worked down six or seven feet, then jumped—a little too soon for his right knee, which gave way as soon as he hit the ground.

Cursing, he pushed himself back upright, moving out of the way of the others as they did a quick exit from the Sea Knights. An acrid scent ate at his nostrils. The two large Russian-made helicopters sat maybe forty yards ahead, just beyond a thick wall of smoke. As he reached to flick his visor viewer into IR mode he felt something ping his right shoulder. The gentle tap felt familiar, an old friend catching him in a crowded street, but it was hardly that—a half-dozen bullets had just bounced off his vest.

Danny spun to his right, bringing his gun up. But he had no target on his screen. The area was thick with smoke and dust, swirled furiously by the helicopter blades.

"Whiplash team, we have small arms fire from the direction of the buildings," he told his men as he dropped to one knee.

The knee screamed in pain, twisted badly or sprained

in the jump. Danny ignored it, pushing his MP-5 left, then right. IR mode was hampered by the smoke; he flicked back to unenhanced visual.

"They're in the buildings," said Liu over the team radio.

"All right. I'm going to get the Cobras on it," said Danny. He hit the radio, piping his voice to the attack ships. "Small arms in the buildings opposite the Hinds."

The lead Cobra pilot acknowledged. A second or two later the ground began to shake; a freight train roared overhead and flames shot from the area where the building had been.

Danny was already running toward the Hinds. He broke through the smoke and saw one of the two Iraqi helicopters sitting about twenty yards ahead. There was a weapons trolley near it, a man lying on the ground. Danny pulled his submachine gun level at his waist and laid two bursts into the figure before it fell away.

"Vehicles!" said Bison. His SAW began stuttering to Danny's left. Danny looked over and saw two of his men throwing themselves down; Bison had already crouched a few feet beyond them, his gun blaring at two pickups tearing out from behind the helicopters.

Red flickered from the trucks. Bison hosed the first. As Danny put his own cursor on the second, it morphed into a massive fireball, axed by a Marine SMAW. Debris rained around them. Danny got up, ignoring the pops against his chest as he ran toward a brown-shirted body a few feet ahead. The Iraqi didn't move, but Danny gave him a burst of gunfire anyway. He leaped nearly chest first into the machine-gun fisted nose of the Russian attack bird, rolling left around the fuselage as he eyed the gunner's station and cockpit, making sure they were empty. As he turned toward the belly of the craft he saw a flicker above the wing; he tried ducking but it was too late—three bullets from an AK-47 hit the top of his helmet and threw him to the ground. Instinctively, the captain shoved his gun in the direction of the gunfire as he fell, pressing the trigger for a brief second before his head smacked the ground.

Bullets flew overhead. The ground vibrated so hard he felt his head jumping upward. Voices screamed in his ears. It was all chaos, unfathomable chaos.

Danny had lost the ability to sort it out, lost the ability to do anything but fight to his knees—his right one screaming again—and fire another few rounds in the direction of the stubby wing strut.

White heat flashed in front of him. Danny gulped air and threw himself down a millisecond before the shock wave as the helicopter exploded. The dirt turned molten. He gulped the hot air, tried to get away, finally saw that he had somehow crawled under the burning chassis. He kept going, enveloped by blackness. A sudden rush of heat stopped him.

"The other Hind," he heard himself say calmly. "Secure it."

"Two guys, crew compartment, side facing the buildings," said Powder.

"All right. Get their attention."

Danny had only the vaguest notion of where he was or where he was going—he wasn't even sure whether he'd gotten out from under the burning helicopter. Nonetheless, he began to crawl. After a few feet he got up and began running in what he thought was the direction of the buildings, intending to make a long flanking maneuver and get at the Hind from the back while his guys kept the defenders busy. As he ran—it was more like a limp, thanks to his knee—he clicked back and forth between the IR and enhanced video views in his visor; the thick smoke defeated both. Finally he pushed the screen upward, preferring his own eyes.

The main building sat off on his right. He assumed the second helicopter would be about ten yards on his left.

"Hey, Cap, how we doin'?" asked Powder.

"I'm getting there. Make sure no one blows this one up."

"They won't," said Powder.

Danny finally saw the helicopter on his left, farther away than he'd expected. He took a few tentative steps and saw the aircraft bob.

Shit. The rotor at the top began to spin.

"Powder—there's someone in the cockpit!" he yelled.

A gun burst followed. Danny ran forward, the rotor still winding.

"The cockpit's armored!" Danny shouted.

"Fucking shit," cursed Powder, even as his bullets bounced off the side.

The helo lurched forward. Danny ran as fast as he could, spitting bullets from his gun at the same time. The tail started to whip around; he threw himself to the ground, just missing the wing stub. He jumped up and ran again, hoping for some sort of opening he could shoot through.

A blank, puzzled face appeared in the window next to him, a ghost transported to earth where she didn't want to be.

His wife.

The Iraqi pilot.

The cockpit handle was a clear white bar. Danny fired a few bursts at it, but the bullets all missed or bounced harmlessly away. His knee flamed with pain. The rotors spun hard and the air became a hurricane. Danny dropped his MP-5 and with a scream threw himself forward, fingers grasping the small metal strip where the windscreen met the edge of the metal on the canopy. He could feel the pilot inches away, felt something pound against the side of the helicopter—maybe the pilot, maybe Powder's bullets, maybe just the vibration of the motor. He reached for his Beretta, lost his grip, found himself rolling on the ground, saw the face again—his wife's face, definitely his wife—then realized he was running. He couldn't get into the cockpit, he was too slow, he was going to fail. A black space appeared alongside him, a dark tunnel opening up—he pitched into it, fell into the helicopter.

What kind of lunatic fate was this, to die in Iraq on an impossible mission?

As he started to push back toward the door to jump out, Danny saw a head bobbing beyond the passage on his left—there were no doors on the Hind between the crew area and cockpit.

A small ax hung on the wall near the passage.

Jump.

He threw himself toward the ax as the aircraft stuttered and turned again, still on the ground. His hand grabbed the handle but the ax stayed on the wall, held by a thick leather strap. Danny pulled, and as he screamed he felt himself rushing through the bulkhead, shoulders brushing hard against the side.

The Iraqi's blood didn't spurt or gush or stream. It seeped from each of the three places Danny struck, like a stream lapping the shore, an eddy probing the sand.

The helo slammed down, the engine stuttering dead.

A moment later strong hands grabbed Danny from behind.

"Hey, way to go, Cap," shouted Powder. "Guy must not've been a pilot, huh, cause he couldn't get off the ground. Uh, can I have the ax if you're done with it?"

Aboard *Quicksilver*, at High Top
1500

"ALL SYSTEMS ARE IN THE GREEN," CHRIS TOLD BREANNA as they finished their preflight checklist.

"You ready?" she asked him.

"This'll be a piece of cake after what we've been through," said Ferris.

Breanna nodded. He was right. *Quicksilver*'s mission was easy, detecting radars and fuzzing them for a group of attack planes flying over the central part of Iraq, well out of range of the Iranian laser. Between the repairs and her uncoated nose, *Quicksilver*'s radar signal was nearly as large as a standard B-52's, but the jamming gear was working fine and they'd be escorted by a pair of F-15Cs. At 35,000 feet they'd be as safe as if they were flying over France. Maybe even safer.

But Zen wasn't with her, watching her back. Nor was she watching his.

"You with us, Captain Dolk?"

"Uh, call me Torbin."

"Torbin. What is that? French?"

"Swedish," said Torbin. "I was born near Uppsala. We came over when I was three."

"Sounds like a nursery rhyme," said Ferris.

"Generations of Swedish kings were crowned there," said Torbin.

"And will be again," said Breanna. "Gentlemen, let's roll."

In Iraq
1512

DANNY LEANED AGAINST THE TAIL BOOM OF THE MAMMOTH helicopter as his men finished topping off the fuel tanks. He could hear Egg talking to himself in the cockpit, obviously going over each of the controls, checking and rechecking them. The helicopter expert had still not arrived in Dreamland Command. Danny's knee had swollen so stiff he almost couldn't move it, despite the fact that he kept trying to.

"Ready, Cap," said Bison, who'd been overseeing the refuel. "Got rockets, machine gun. Wingtip pods are empty."

"Yeah. Good." Danny tried bracing his injured leg against the other. It didn't help, but he was going to have to fake it. "Powder?"

Powder had insisted on taking the weapons operator slot, claiming that he had attended some sort of training session in Apaches. Danny was too beat-up to argue; the controls for the nose gun and rockets were fairly straightforward—select and fire.

God, his knee hurt.

"Okay, saddle up," Danny told his team over the com system. He pushed off the helicopter, right hand tightened around the MP-5 against the pain. "Egg, our expert with you yet?"

"Uh, no, sir."

"Well, whenever you're ready, we're good to go."

THE WEIRD THING—OR THE FIRST WEIRD THING—WAS THE blue panel. The Hind's dash was painted a weird blue turquoise that physically hurt Egg's eyes.

The Pave Low the other day had seemed complicated as hell, even though he'd flown a slightly earlier version before. This just seemed like hell.

He knew where everything was, knew what everything did—the important stuff, anyway. On some basic level, all helicopters were alike.

They were, weren't they?

Egg felt his brain starting to break into pieces.

He grabbed the control yoke, steadied his feet on the rudder pedals.

Come on, Egg, he told himself. Come on come on come on.

No way in the world he could do this. No way.

The collective felt almost comfortable in his hand. His fingers wrapped easily around it, and damn it, this was just another helicopter whirlybird rig, as his instructor would say.

Engine panel on right.

Checklist.

Where the hell was the checklist Jennifer had given him?

"Sergeant Reagan—before you begin, please cinch your belts. The g forces can be considerable during maneuvers."

God was whispering in his ears. With a Polish accent.

"Yes," he said.

"Sergeant, my name is Robbie Pitzarski. I'm going to help you fly the Hind," said the expert, speaking from halfway across the world in the Dreamland Command Center bunker. "Before we begin, let me emphasize that if you get in trouble, stick to the basics. It's a helicopter, first and foremost. The Russians place things in odd places, but the blades are on top and the tail's in the back."

"You sound like my old flight instructor," Egg told him.

"Very good. To the right of your seat, almost behind you, there is an emergency shut-down lever that connects to the fuse panel. It has a red knob and looks rather contorted. Let's make sure that has not been thrown inadvertently. It would make it most difficult to proceed."

POWDER HAD TO SQUIRM TO GET HIS BODY INTO THE GUNner's cabin, slamming half the gear on the way. The hatch stuck for a moment, and he nearly broke the shock-absorber-like strut getting it closed. There were grips and gauges and pipes and all sorts of crap all over the place; it reminded him of the bathroom in his grandmother's basement apartment. Luckily, Jennifer the goddess had given him a very good paper map of the cockpit, pointing out the key shit—her word, not his. The optical sight ocular for the missile system was on the right, the armament panel was in an almost impossible to reach position at his right elbow, the delicious gunsight with its well-rounded wheels sat at his nose, her perfect hand-sized mammaries at full attention.

Jennifer hadn't given him those. But he wouldn't need a map to find them.

Rumor was, she and the colonel had a thing. Rank had its privileges.

But hell, she was here, and he wasn't. Dogs got to run.

Truth was, she was so beautiful—so beautiful—he might not make it out of the kennel for all his slobbering.

With great difficulty the Whiplash trooper turned his attention back to the weapons.

THE ROTORS SLIPPED AROUND FOUR OR FIVE TIMES BEFORE the Isotov turboshafts coughed, but within seconds the engines wound up to near takeoff speed, the helicopter straining to hold herself down. Egg took a breath, then went back over the dashboard, making absolutely sure—absolutely one hundred percent sure—he had the instruments psyched.

He knew the whole damn thing. He knew it, he knew it, he knew it.

Stop worrying, he told himself.

"Very good so far, Sergeant," said Pitzarski. His accent garbled some of his vowels, so the words sounded more like "vrr-ee gd sfar, surg-ent."

"You can call me Egg."

"Egg?"

"Yes, sir."

"And myself, Robbie."

"Cool."

"Hey, we takin' off or what?" demanded Powder, breaking in.

"Excuse me, sir," said Egg. "Shut the fuck up, Powder, or I'm hitting the eject button."

"There ain't no damn eject button."

"Try me."

"Ready?" asked Pitzarski, but Egg had already thrown the Hind forward, stuttering, bouncing on the stubby wheels, bucking, pushing forward too fast without enough juice, gently backing off, revving, going—airborne, he was airborne.

TWO MEN CAME RUSHING AT THE AIRCRAFT'S OPEN BAY AS they started to move. Danny cursed; he'd thought everyone was aboard already. He started to reach to help them but the pain in his leg hurt too much. The helo lurched forward and up and he fell against the floor. He lay there for three or four seconds, not sure if Egg was going to fly or crash. Finally he pulled himself up, struggling into one of the fold-down seats, pushing up his leg.

"Liu, wrap my knee, okay?" he said. "I sprained it or something."

A building passed in the cabin window, replaced by

sky, all sky. Liu took hold of his leg and began poking it, not gently.

"It ain't broke," Danny managed. "Just fucking wrap the knee."

"Yes, sir."

"Ligament torn?" Danny asked.

"At least," said Nurse.

Danny looked up. Two Marines were grinning at him through their face paint. One of the two looked vaguely familiar—the gunnery sergeant who'd come on the rescue mission the other day.

"We thought you girls could use some help," said the Marine.

"What are you doing here?" Danny said.

"I'm sorry, Cap—you looked like you wanted to pull them in," said Bison. "So I helped them in when you fell."

"You." Danny pointed at the gunnery sergeant, a short man with a face like a worn catcher's mitt. "You look damn familiar. Before yesterday."

"Melfi," said the sergeant. "You saved my butt in Libya couple months back. Last year, remember? You didn't recognize me the other day."

Now he did—he was one of the guys they'd rescued when they were looking for Mack.

"You're gonna get in shitloads of trouble," Danny told him. "But I ain't dropping you off."

"Life's a bitch," said the Marine.

"All right," said Danny. "Let me tell your commander not to look for you."

"Not necessary," said the Marine. "Let's just say we showed up here accidentally on purpose. Whole platoon would have come with you if they could, sir. But the major kinda figured they'd be missed. Besides, two Marines are worth a dozen Air Force fags. Hey, no offense."

"Jarhead shits," said Bison.

"Bison, give Sergeant Melfi the rundown," said Danny.

"Call me Gunny," said the Marine. "Just about everybody does."

"No they don't," said the lance corporal behind him. "They call you fuckin' Gunny."

"And they duck when they say that," said the sergeant.

Aboard *Quicksilver*, over Iraq
1530

THE GEAR IN FRONT OF TORBIN HAD EXACTLY ONE THING IN common with the unit he was used to handling in the Phantom Weasel—it dealt with radars.

The computer handled everything; it probably even had a mode to make coffee. The large flat screen on the left projected a map of the area they were flying through; the map had presets to display radiuses of 200, 300, and 500 miles out, but could zoom in on anything from five to five hundred. Radar coverage and sources were projected on the coordinate grid, each type color-coded. The screen on the right contained information on each of the detected radars. The computer could not only show whether they had detected an aircraft, but how likely that would be for any given plane in its library. Highlights of the radar's likely function could be hot-keyed onto the screen, along with the preferred method of confusing it. Targeting data could be automatically uploaded to the air to ground missiles in the Megafortress's belly. Under normal circumstances the plane's copilot handled the jamming and bombing details, but the operator's station was also fully equipped to do so. There were several other capabilities, including a mode that would allow the Megafortress's fuzz busters to pretend to be an enemy ground radar, though he hadn't had time to learn all of the details.

Torbin felt like he had gone from the twentieth to the twenty-third century. Any second Captain Kirk was going to appear behind him and tell him to beam up Mr. Spock.

"You all right back there, Torbin?" asked Captain Breanna Stockard.

The equipment was blow-away, and the pilot was a knockout. Somehow, some way, he was going to make this into a permanent assignment.

"Yes, ma'am," he said. "Thank you, Captain Stockard."

"You can call me Bree," she said.

Thanks.

"All right, crew." Captain Stockard's—Bree's—voice changed slightly, becoming a little deeper, a little more authoritative. "I know everyone's disappointed that we didn't draw the laser assignment. But what we're doing, protecting our guys, is still damn important. I know everybody's going to do their best."

As they flew over Iraq carrying out their mission, the rest of the crew seemed almost bored, punching buttons, checking the progress of the attack groups they were helping. Torbin concentrated so hard on his gear that he didn't even have time to fantasize about the pilot.

Much.

"That Spoon Rest radar—is it up?" Bree asked as they hit the halfway point on their mission chart. It was now 1730.

"No," he said tentatively, eyes jumping from his screens to make sure he had the right radar. The unit had come on briefly but then turned off. It was nearly a hundred miles south from the attack planes' target; *Quicksilver* would splash it at the end of the mission, assuming they didn't find anything of higher priority.

The Phantom wouldn't even have detected it. Nor would the Weasel have given him the option of spoofing the radar with a variety of ECMs, ordinarily the job of a

Spark Vark F-111 or a Compass Call electronic warfare C-130.

This was definitely the future, and he liked it very much.

A warning tone sounded in his ear. A purple blob materialized on the left screen sixty-six miles ahead of their present position; beneath the blob was a legend describing the enemy radar and its associated systems as a point-defense Zsu-23-4 unit mapped on previous missions. A color-coded box opened on the right screen with a list of options for dealing with it. The computer suggested NO ACTION; the radar was too limited to see the Megafortress and the gun too impotent to strike the attack package, which was flying well above its range.

Torbin concurred.

"Gun dish," Torbin told the pilots. "Twelve o'clock, fifty miles out. It's in the index," he added, meaning that it had been spotted and identified previously by CentCom.

"Copy," said Ferris. "Mongoose flight is zero-two from their IP. Watch them closely."

Torbin got another tone. This time a red cluster flared right over Mongoose's target.

"Flat Face," he said, "uh, unknown, shit." He glanced at the right screen, where the option box had opened.

"Location," prompted Ferris.

Torbin went to center the cursor on the target, nail it down with a HARM.

He wasn't in a Weasel, though.

"Jam the radar," said Breanna calmly.

"They're being beamed," reported Ferris.

Torbin moved his finger to the touch screen, then froze. He wasn't sure what the hell he was supposed to do.

He had about ten seconds to figure it out—otherwise he was going to lose one of the planes they were protecting. And this time, it *would* be his fault.

Aboard *Raven*, over Iran
1602

ON ZEN'S MAP THE BORDER BETWEEN TURKEY, IRAQ, AND Iran ran sharp and clear, curling through the mountains that swung down from the Caspian Sea and up from the Persian Gulf. On his view screen as he passed overhead, the border was indistinguishable; even in the few places where there were actual roads, the checkpoints tended to be a kilometer or more away from the border, where they could be better fortified. Unrest among the Kurdish population had struck Iran as well as Iraq, and the Iranian army had bolstered its forces near the borders and in the north in general. But the reinforcements appeared to have included almost no air units beyond a few helicopters; the radar in *Hawk One* located a pair of Bell Jet Rangers flying in a valley about ten miles southeast as it passed over the border ahead of *Raven*.

"Civilian airport radar at Tabriz is active," said the radar operator. "We're clean. No other radars in vicinity. Hamadian, Kemanshah, Ghale Morghi, all quiet," he added, naming the major air bases within striking distance.

The Flighthawk and *Raven* were a hundred miles from the first of the three possible targets; Whiplash and its pilfered Hind were running about five minutes behind them. At their present speed, the ground team could reach the closest target in thirty-five minutes, the farthest in forty-five. Alou would launch the Quail in thirty minutes.

Zen kicked his speed up, tucking the Flighthawk close to a mountain pass. As he shot by, his camera caught a small group of soldiers sitting around a machine gun behind a stack of rocks; he was by them so fast they didn't have time to react, though it would have been next to impossible for them to hit the Flighthawk with their gun.

A helicopter would be a different story.

Zen flew up the pass about a mile and a half, making sure there were no reinforcements. In the meantime, Fentress marked the spot for him, giving him a straight-line course to target when he turned back.

"Whiplash Hind, this is Hawk leader. I have a pimple to blot out."

"Whiplash Hind copies." The roar of the helicopter engines nearly drowned out the pilot's voice. "Should we change course?"

"Negative," said Zen as his targeting screen began to flash. "He'll be in Ayatollah heaven in thirty seconds."

Aboard *Whiplash Hind,* over Iran
1605

DANNY PEERED OUT AT THE NEARBY MOUNTAIN UNEASILY, watching their shadow pass on the brown flank. Bits of snow remained scattered in the hollows; water flowed in the valleys in blue and silver threads, sparkling with the sun.

Under any other circumstances, he'd look at the scenery with admiration; now it filled him with dread. They were big, easy targets flying low in the middle of the day.

He should have insisted on a proper deployment at the very beginning, brought his Osprey here, more men. He wasn't working with a full tool chest.

What was he going to do if he got his butt fried? Go back East and into politics like his wife wanted?

Hell, he'd be dead if this didn't work.

Was that why he'd gone ahead with it? Or was it the opposite—was he thinking he'd be a hero if he grabbed the laser?

Danny looked around the cabin at his men, fidgeting

away the long ride to their target. Was blind ambition the reason he was risking these guys lives?

No. They had to pull this off to save others. That had nothing to do with ambition. That was his duty, his job.

"*Hawk One* to Whiplash. Pimple's gone," said Zen on the Dreamland circuit. "Clear sailing for you."

"*Whiplash Hind,*" acknowledged Egg in the cockpit.

"Thanks, Zen," added Danny.

"Bet you didn't know Clearasil comes in twenty millimeter packages, huh?" joked Zen.

"Well, I must say, your code words are exceedingly clever." Rubeo's sarcastic drone took Danny by surprise, even though he knew the scientist would be in Dreamland Command. "I wish I could be there for the fun and games."

"Yeah, me too," said Danny, too tired at the moment even to be angry.

"We have some new ideas about the laser," said Rubeo. "Our friends at the CIA now believe it is part of a project initiated at least a year ago called Allah's Sword. If they're right, it's largely based on technology nearly a decade old."

"Reassuring."

"My sentiments exactly," said the scientist, the disdain evident. "Nonetheless, the spy masters have given us some things to consider. First of all, we're looking for something larger than a tank chassis. Your pilots have already been briefed. As far as you're concerned, our wish list remains essentially the same. Concentrate on the software and analyzing the chemical composition. A physical piece of the mirror in the director would be useful as well."

"You know what, Doc, let's just take it as it comes."

"Danny—"

"That's *Captain Freah* to you," said Danny, hitting the kill switch at the bottom of his helmet.

Aboard *Raven*, over Iran
1700

FENTRESS WATCHED AS ZEN FLEW THE FLIGHTHAWK JUST above the hillside, barely six or seven feet from the dirt and rocks. The plane moved as smoothly as if it were at thirty thousand feet, and nearly as fast. Zen worked the controls with total concentration, jerking his head back and forth, rocking his body with the plane, mimicking the actions he wanted it to take.

Fentress knew he would never be able to fly as well. Never.

The replay of the shoot-down showed he'd flown right into the antiaircraft fire. He'd been oblivious to it in his rush to help Major Smith.

Stupid. Completely stupid.

He could do better. He wasn't going to give up.

"Two minutes to Quail launch," said the copilot. The assault team was now ten minutes away from the nearest target.

THE SMALL, BLOCKY QUAIL 3/B FLUTTERED AS IT HIT THE slipstream below the Megafortress's bomb bay, its ramjet engines momentarily faltering. But then the scaled-down model of an EB-52 bobbed away, its engines accelerating to propel it above the mothership's flight path.

Changes in doctrine as well as electronics and radars had rendered the original ADM-20/GAM-72 Quail obsolete no later than the 1970s, though there were some circumstances under which the "kill me" drone proved useful. Mechanically, the Quail 3/B was an entirely different bird, though it remained true to the function of its predecessor—it gave the enemy something to look at, and hopefully fire at, other than the bomber itself. Where the original had been a boxy, stub-winged glider, the Quail

3/B looked exactly like a Megafortress from above and below. Powered by small ramjets and carefully proportioned solid rockets augmented by podded flares on the wings, it had the same heat signature as an EB-52. Rather than being coated with radar-absorbing materials to reduce its return, the intricate facets on the Quail 3/B's shiny skin amplified its radar return to make it appear to most radars almost exactly the size of a B-52. Fanlike antennas inside the drone duplicated the signals transmitted by a B-52H's standard ALQ-155 and ALT-28 ECM and noise jammers. The Quail couldn't fly for very long, nor could it be controlled once launched, but the decoy was a perfect clay pigeon.

The question was, would the Iranians go for it?

Zen watched the Quail climb from the Flighthawk cockpit, tagging along as the rockets quickly took it through ten thousand feet. By now it would be clearly visible on the Iranian airport control radars; even if the radars were being operated by civilians—something he doubted—they ought to be on the hot line by now.

"Quail is at twelve thousand feet, climbing steady, on course," reported the copilot.

"Nothing," said the electronic warfare officer. "All clear."

"Laser detection gear is blank too," said the copilot, who had the plot on his screen. Jennifer, Garcia, and some of the other techies had installed the tweaked device in *Raven*'s tail, replacing the Stinger antiair mines.

Zen tucked back down toward the mountains, joining the Megafortress in a valley that rode almost directly into the target area. They were no more than fifteen minutes from the farthest site.

"Quail is topping out at eighteen thousand," said the copilot.

"Nothing," said the radar operator.

"We're clean too," said Fentress. "Are they missing it, or do they know it's a decoy?" he asked Zen.

"Not sure," he replied. "Should be pretty fat on their radar."

"I told you we should have put a kick-me sign on the tail," joked the copilot. No one laughed.

"We have to go to Plan B," said Alou.

Zen pulled up the course he'd worked out earlier and pushed the throttle to the firewall, streaking toward the farthest site. The Flighthawk climbed away from the mountainside toward a patchwork of fields. A small village rose on his right, the center of town marked by the round spire of a mosque.

"Radar tracking Quail," said the operator. "MIM-23 Hawk!"

"Confirmed," said the copilot.

"Hey—this fits with the earlier profiles," said the radar operator. "It shouldn't have been in range—tracking the Quail!"

"That doesn't fit the pattern," said Alou.

"Radar is off the air. I have it marked," said the operator. "Hind probably detected," he added.

"*Whiplash Hind,* take evasive maneuvers!" said Fentress.

"Breaking the radar," said the operator, beginning to explain that he had prodded the ECMs to keep the Hawk radar from locking on the helicopter.

"Laser!" yelled the copilot.

Aboard *Whiplash Hind*
1708

THE HELICOPTER LURCHED OUT FROM UNDER DANNY, twisting and falling at the same time. The helo's 18,000 pounds hurtled sideways in the air, directly toward a sheer cliff. Unable to grip the slippery wind, and propelled by the violent centrifugal forces kicked up by the main rotor, the tail twisted, throwing the helicopter into a rolling dive so severe that about two inches at the tip of one of the blades sheered off. One of the two Isotov TV3-117 turboshafts choked, the severe rush of air overwhelming the poorly maintained power plant. The aircraft curled to the right but began to settle, its tail now drifting back the other way, a bare foot or two from the rocks. Danny clawed himself up the side of the cabin, steeling himself for the inevitable crash. He saw the door a few feet away; he'd go out there after they hit, assuming he could move.

But he didn't have to. Somehow, miraculously, Egg had managed to regain control of the helicopter.

"Sorry," he was saying over and over again. "Shit, sorry. Sorry, sorry."

Danny looked across at the rest of his team, groaning and sorting themselves out.

"It's okay, Egg. Settle down."

"Sorry, Cap. I went to get down and I overdid it. Radar had us spiked."

"It's okay. Were we fired on?"

"I don't know. I, uh, if we were, it doesn't show up on the instruments, at least not what I can read."

"Can we keep going?"

"I think so, sir. But, uh, I don't have anything on my radio, I think."

"Hang on." Danny adjusted his own com set. They had lost communications with Dreamland Command, as well as *Raven*.

Had *Raven* been hit?

Helicopters often lost radio contact when they were flying very low to the ground. Even the Dreamland satellite connection was finicky.

"Probably, we're too low to get a good radio connection," said Danny.

"Should I go up?"

"Let's stay low for a while," said Danny. "When we're closer to the target areas, then we'll pop up."

"Yes, sir."

"Whiplash team, sound off. Give me your status," said Danny.

One by one the team members gave a curse-laden roll call. Liu had a major welt on his arm and Jack "Pretty Boy" Floyd had a bloody nose, but none of the injuries were severe. "Powder" Talcom brought up the rear of the muster.

"I think I puked my fuckin' brains out," he said.

Everyone laughed, even Egg.

"Ought to fill a thimble," said Bison. "If that."

Aboard *Raven*, over Iran
1710

"LASER IS CONFIRMED AT SITE TWO," SAID THE COPILOT. "The rectangular building at the far end of the eastern block. Subgrid two. Near the animal pen. Marked now on GPS displays."

"That's where the Hawk radar is. I have the site marked," said the radar operator. "They're off the air."

"The laser got the Quail," said the copilot. "But I can't find the Hind."

"Scanning," said the radar operator.

"Go to active radar," said Major Alou. "Just a burst, then kill it."

"Nothing," said the copilot.

"I'm dropping back to look for them," said Zen, turning the Flighthawk south.

"Hold on, Zen," said Alou. "The laser is our priority. We have to take it out. Then we'll go back for Whiplash."

"They may be dead by then."

"They may be dead already."

Dreamland Command Center
0815

THE HELICOPTER HAD BEEN OUT OF CONTACT FOR MORE than five minutes now. Dog did nothing, continuing to stare at the sitrep screen showing *Raven* over Iran.

They had a good location on the laser. Alou was almost in position to strike it. Should he tell them to turn back and find his men?

No way. The laser was a potent weapon that had to be erased. His men aboard the Hind were expendable.

So were the ones on *Raven*, for that matter. And his daughter in *Quicksilver*. And his lover on the ground at High Top.

"Contact with Captain Freah is still lost," said the lieutenant at the console. "Major Alou wants to know whether to proceed with the attack or hold off for Whiplash."

"Hold off," said Rubeo. "The information is invaluable."

"You're assuming the helicopter hasn't been destroyed," said Major Cheshire, sitting at the console next to the scientist.

"It hasn't," said Rubeo. "It's out of communication range because of the ground clutter. The laser struck the Quail, that was all. It'll take them a half hour to recycle and fire again. I see the pattern now." The scientist jumped up and went over to the com console. "The Hind is just very low and the signal is distorted by the rotor. Let me see those controls."

"We'll give it five more minutes," Dog said. "Then we're going ahead with the attack."

**Aboard *Whiplash Hind*, over Iraq
1718**

DANNY TRIED CONNECTING AGAIN. "DREAMLAND COM-mand? This is *Whiplash Hind*. Can you hear me?"

"Captain Freah—where are you? Are you okay?"

It was Fentress.

"We're on course," Danny said. "We went into evasive maneuvers. We're very low."

"We thought you were shot down."

"We thought the same thing happened to you."

"No, the laser got the decoy. Listen—there's a battery of Hawk missiles right near the laser. Hold off until we nail it."

"Okay. Where's the laser?"

"Site two. The rectangular building in subgrid two. We're about ninety seconds away—we'll feed you video once we've got it. The air force may scramble jets," Fentress added. "We haven't seen them yet."

"Site two. Got it." Danny punched up the map visual on his combat helmet screen. Two was the northernmost site, a set of agricultural buildings. There were farm animals, a big warehouse or barn. "We're five miles away."

"Okay, good. We're targeting the Hawks now. Stand by."

"You hear all that, Egg?" Danny asked his pilot.

"Pretty much."

"All right," Danny told the others. "Five minutes."

"About time," said Powder. "It's getting dark."

Danny downloaded the diagram of the site into his helmet. "We land at the north end of the building. The barracks are just beyond that, across the double barbed-wire fence. Powder, when Egg gives you the word, hit the barracks with the rockets. Don't hold anything back."

"That's my middle name," said Powder.

"You see anything when we come in, give it everything you got."

"What I'm talkin' about, Captain."

Aboard *Quicksilver*, over Iraq
1735

ANTICIPATING THAT THEIR NEW RADAR OPERATOR WOULD have trouble with the equipment if things got hot, Breanna had preset her configurable display to bring up the duplicate radar interception screen on her voice command. Now that the attack planes they were shepherding were being probed by the Iraqis, she moved quickly, bringing up the screen and preparing to attack.

"Chris, open bay doors. Target radars."

"Bay open."

"Our shot, Torbin," she said, overriding his panel. "Take a breath. Fire at will, Chris. I have the ECMs."

"Tacit has target. Launching," he said.

There was an ever so soft clunk deep within the plane as the AGM-136X pushed off the rotary launcher, tracking toward the Iraqi radar. Unlike the original—and canceled—Tacit Rainbow missiles designed to take the place of HARMs, the Dreamland Tacit Plus had a GPS guidance system augmenting the radar homing head. This allowed it to operate in two distinct modes: it could fly straight to the radar site, switching to GPS mode if the radar went off. Or, like Tacit Rainbow, it could orbit an area, waiting for the radar to come back on. The ramjet made it reasonably quick, and gave it a range somewhere over seventy miles, depending on the mission profile.

"They're jammed," said Breanna.

"Yeah, I'm on it," said Chris. "Tacit has gone to GPS mode. Sixty seconds from target."

"Torbin, go ahead and track for more radars," said Breanna.

"Missiles in the air!" warned Chris. "SA-2, SA-9s, a Six—barrage tactics again. They're firing blind."

"Everybody hang tight," said Breanna. "Torbin, maintain the ECMs. Torbin?"

"I'm on it."

"Shit—we're being tracked. More radars," said Chris. "Tacit is thirty seconds from impact—they're just firing everything they got, in case they get lucky."

"Not today," said Breanna. "Brace yourselves."

She put the Megafortress on its wing, rocking back in the other direction as electronic tinsel and flares spewed from the large plane. One of the missiles the Iraqis had launched sailed about five hundred feet from the nose, its seeker thoroughly confused. It had been launched totally blind and had no idea how close it was to its target.

Neither did the SA-9 that strode in on the Megafortress's tail. But that didn't make much difference—sucking on one of the flares, it veered right, then exploded about twenty yards from the right rear stabilizer.

Aboard *Raven*, over Iran
1745

ZEN RODE THE FLIGHTHAWK SOUTH, AIMING TO MAKE HIS cut north as the first JSOW hit the SAM batteries guarding the base. *Raven*, meanwhile, stayed in the mountain valley, where the clutter would keep the Hawk radars from picking her up if they were turned on again.

The computer kept giving him connection warnings as he maneuvered. He still couldn't see the site on his viewer.

"I need you to come south, *Raven*," he told Alou.

"Can't do it," said Alou.

Zen began climbing back. As he did, the Hawk radars came back on. He tucked left but too late; the RWR screen blinked red as the computerized voice told him he was being tracked.

"Come on! Nail those mothers," he told Alou.

"Ten seconds to launch," said the copilot. "Area at the far end, near the livestock pen. Must be camo'd well."

With ECMs blaring and his disposables disposed, Zen plunged the Flighthawk toward the radars, zigged hard and pulled down, trying to both beam the Doppler radar and line up for his attack run. But this was physically impossible—the Hawk targeting radar spiked him. A half second later, the battery launched a pair of SAMs.

Fuck it, he thought, thumbing the cannon screen up. If he was going out, he was going out in style. The barracks building at the south end was just coming into view at the top of his screen.

It disappeared behind a cloud of white steam.

It took him a second to realize it was antiaircraft artillery, firing from inside a pen of milling animals near the building. A thick hail of lead rose from Zsu-23s or possibly M-163 Vulcans in netted pits below the animals, perhaps tied into the Hawk radar. Zen had to break his attack, and he twisted south. Clear, he turned back in time to see the Hawk battery explode.

"Bull's-eye on the SAMs!" said the copilot. "Kick ass."

"Triple A in the pig pen," Zen told Alou. "Kind of figures. I got it."

"Yours," said Alou. "We have three AGMs left. Fentress, get Whiplash in as soon as the flak's gone."

Bullets spewed from the guns as Zen rocked northward. As the closest torrent began to separate into two distinct streams, Zen pressed the trigger on his own cannon. The Flighthawk spewed shells into the dirt and panic-stricken animals in front of the triple-A pit; he rode the torrent into a low wall in front of it and then through the sloped turret. The cloud of gunfire parted and then cleared; Zen turned to the east beyond the target, trying to sort out the battlefield before making another pass. Flames spewed from the Hawk battery. Men were running from the barracks. Two of the flak guns were continuing to fire, one east, one west. The Hind was about ninety seconds away.

And the building with the laser?

It sat at the north end of the complex. The roof panels on the west side were folding downward. There was movement inside but Zen couldn't tell what was going on.

"I think the laser's getting ready to fire," he warned. "I'm going to grease it."

"We'll get a missile on it," said Alou.

"No time," he said, pushing over.

Aboard *Whiplash Hind,* over Iran
1750

DANNY WENT TO THE DOOR AS THE HIND GLIDED INTO A hover, preparing to launch its missiles. Black smoke curled on the other side of the complex, and he could see men running in different directions, some to take defensive positions, others to save themselves.

"Watch the Flighthawk!" he barked, but the warning was drowned out by a thundering succession of whoops from the rocket launchers. The rockets left the wing pod with a furl of white smoke and a hard shake; Danny felt as if a giant had grabbed hold of the Hind's wings and was systematically trying to empty its stores on the enemy. Zen said something about targeting the laser building, then warned about flak, but in the rush of noise and fire and smoke it was impossible to figure out what he was saying. Danny wanted only one thing—to get down on the ground and complete their mission.

"Let's go, Egg, let's go!" he yelled as the rockets stopped. The Hind whipped right, but then twisted backward, away from the target. "What the hell?" he asked Egg.

"Flighthawk is firing!" warned the pilot. "He wants us to stay back."

"Get us into the complex now!" said Danny. "Just do it!"

"Yes, sir. Hold on."

The helicopter lurched eastward. Danny saw the small robot plane pass almost in slow motion, smoke erupting from its mouth. Steam enveloped the side of the target building.

"Down! Down!" said Danny.

As if in response, the nose of the helicopter pitched hard toward the earth.

Northern Iran
1755

THEY WERE NEARLY TWO HUNDRED MILES FROM ANHIK, more than six or seven hours away by car, when the call came on his satellite phone. The connection was poor, but General Sattari understood immediately what had happened.

"Repulse the attack at all costs," he told Colonel Vali, though the command was completely unnecessary. "Reinforcements will be sent."

The general told the driver to go up the road to a high point. When they reached it, he got out of the car with the telephone and walked off the road to a pile of rocks, more for privacy than to ensure good reception. The driver the black robes had supplied was undoubtedly a spy. The bastards hadn't even let him fly back in the helicopter.

No wonder. Thoughts of treachery ran through his head. Khamenei had tipped off the Americans or the Chinese somehow—it wasn't clear who exactly was attacking.

Sattari emptied his mind and calmly began dialing the squadron commanders he knew would be loyal to him.

Smoke rose between the distant hills.

His imagination? Surely he could not see the attack from here.

"Anhik is under attack," Sattari said into his phone when the connection went through. "Send assistance."

He repeated the words six times; each time the man on the other line said nothing more than "Yes" or "Right away." As he clicked the End Transmit button after speaking to the last commander, Sattari turned toward Anhik, as if perhaps he might at least witness the battle there.

The smoke was gone.

His experts had told him the laser was undetectable. Khamenei must have betrayed him somehow.

He remembered getting the news of his parents' death. The message read only, "Your parents have become martyrs."

Had he not expected his dream to end this way?

Sattari walked back to the Rover. "Anhik," he said. "Go."

Aboard *Raven*, over Iran
1803

ZEN KEPT HIS FINGER ON THE TRIGGER, RIDING THE STREAM of bullets through the laser director, across the building and into the flak dealer nearby. The gun rattled and burst like an overheating steam engine, but he was too busy to admire his handiwork. The last gun turned nearly straight up, unleashing its shells at point-blank range. The Flighthawk stuttered momentarily, then tipped right, one of its control surfaces nicked by a shell. The computer immediately compensated and the plane responded to Zen's push on the throttle slider, galloping south.

He took a breath as he banked back to finish the job. As he looked to his left to try and locate the Hind, the antiaircraft battery began firing again, its shells arcing off to his left. Zen thought it must be trying to nail the chopper. Anger welled inside him; driven by instinct and emotion, he rushed to protect his friends, pushing the throttle to the firewall and mashing his trigger even though he was out of range. The ground and smoke and dust parted, replaced by a red tunnel of flame; he pushed the cannon shells into the antiair gun like a knife into the heart of an enemy.

Clearing, he banked left and began to climb. As he rose, he saw *Raven* two miles away to the northwest. It was a shock to realize he was actually sitting back there in relative safety, not dodging through the bullets and fire at the battlefield.

Aboard *Whiplash Hind*, in Iran
1806

THE HELICOPTER'S FRONT END BUCKED BACK UPWARD AS the tail spun hard left. Then the nose and one of the wings crashed through a fence near the laser building. Danny heard Egg and Powder cursing but there was no time to sort out exactly what was going on. The helicopter bounced twice, the first time gently, the second time hard enough to shake Danny's helmet back on his head. He heard a sound like a load of pebbles shooting down the ramp of a large dump truck. There was no time to figure out what it was—they were down.

"Out! Out!" Danny yelled, pushing toward the door. Something hit his face; it was one of the Marines, losing his balance as he tried to get out. Danny pushed the man to his feet and managed to follow onto the ground, running for the gray aluminum wall of the laser building only five or six yards away. One of the Marines was a few feet ahead. The helicopter revved behind him. A shell or rocket landed well off to the right.

There were no defenders between them and the building. Total and complete surprise.

Hot shit.

Between the satellite pictures of the target and the visuals Zen had fed them, the team had an incredible amount of real-time intelligence. Still, no matter how well-prepared or rehearsed, there was always a moment of hesitation and doubt, a split second when the mind had to storm through the adrenaline and gun smoke to find its balance. Danny struggled through that moment now. His lungs coughed dust and burned dirt as he spotted the small trench they'd mapped near the rear wall of the building. It was their first rendezvous point, the spot they'd launch their final assault from.

The difference between a good commander and a great one wasn't the amount of adrenaline coursing through his veins, but the ability to control it, to use it to sharpen his judgment rather than dull it. The process was unconscious; Danny was no more aware of it than he was aware of what his little toes were doing.

"All right, we're good. Bison, open up the wall for us," Danny said as he ran. "Like we planned. Everyone else, remember the dance card. Liu, you're too far left. Go! Go!"

Bison slid in next to the back of the building while Nurse and Hernandez took the left and right flanks, respectively. Bison put two small charges of plastique explosive on the metal then furled back to the ditch.

"Down!" Danny yelled to the Marines. "Go, Bison."

"Three, two—" Bison pushed the detonator at two; as the shock of rocks and shrapnel passed overhead, he bolted forward to leap through the eight-by-ten-foot hole his charges had made in the wall. Floyd followed; they rolled through the jagged gap, MP-5s blazing. Danny and the Marines followed a few seconds behind, Gunny and the corporal watching the flanks as Danny moved inside.

Then everything slowed down.

The building was dark and quiet. Egg and Floyd were on Danny's right and left, respectively, crouching as they scoped out the layout. Two thick tubes covered in white and looking like large pieces of a city sewer system ran the length of the hangar on the left. Black bands extended around several sections, and in three or four places thick hoses like lines from a massive dry vac hung down to the floor, where they met metal boots. The base of the mirror system stood about twenty feet away, surrounded by metal scaffolding and bracing pieces not unlike a child's Erector set. Beyond it stood a collection of devices stacked on metal tables; from his angle in the unilluminated shed it looked like a collection of table saws and TVs.

"People at the far end," hissed Egg over the com link.

"Scientists or what?" asked Danny.

"Unknown."

Probably just technical people or they'd be shooting, Danny reasoned. "How are we outside?"

"Activity at the barracks," said Liu. "Powder's got them pinned down."

"All right. Marines up. They'll cover us." He waved the Marines in, directing them left and right, where they would take over from his men.

"Are you ready, Captain?" said a high-pitched, tinny voice in his headset.

"Thought you'd never get here, Doc," Danny told Ray Rubeo.

"Remember, please, that I am not where you are."

"Hard to forget."

"Please scan the area with the hand camera," Rubeo told him. "The images captured from your so-called smart helmet are practically worthless."

"Just a minute." Danny had unhooked the small rucksack from his back and opened it on the floor. He picked up the small camera—it shot high-resolution still pictures in rapid succession, transmitting them back to Dreamland—and plugged the thick wire connector into his helmet. Then he held up the camera as he rose tentatively. Egg and Pretty Boy meanwhile had removed their torches and were making their way with the Marines toward the Erector set.

"Humph," growled Rubeo.

"Well?"

"Please hold."

"Hold?"

Rubeo spoke to someone in the background, then came back on the line. "The control area. Can you get some pictures of it? And then the accelerators—the double-tube arrangement seems unique."

"I'm going to have to go forward," said Danny, starting to do so.

"Don't get shot," said Dog.

"Agreed," said Danny.

"There are people in there with you?" Dog asked.

"We believe there are, Colonel. But I haven't seen them."

"Two guys, far corner," said Egg. "They're squatting down like they're hiding. Gunny's got them covered. No weapons we can see."

"Leave 'em for now," said Danny. He had reached the scaffolding. He put one strap of the ruck over his shoulder and then began climbing gingerly. A pair of what looked like long, flexible drain pipes rose from a pair of cylindrical containers on his right. Three small control panels sat beyond them, a monitoring or control station of some sort.

"You want me to plug the sniffer into one of those pipes?" he asked Rubeo.

"Just feed us pictures for now, please," said Rubeo. "Pan as much of the facility as you can. We'll tell you the next move when—Captain, please check the settings. You just changed the resolution."

Danny reset the camera, trying not to let the scientist's tone annoy him.

"Better?"

"Much. Your men are at the chemical bag, not the mirror. Tell them not to touch anything until we've finished photographing it. This isn't a toy store."

"No shit, Doc. You're going to have to lighten up," said Danny. "Bison, Pretty Boy, what's going on?"

"Guy here," said Bison. "Dead. Flighthawk must've nailed him on the way in. Two more bodies over there."

"Come back and get ready to take out part of the mirror, okay? The ragheads aren't going to leave us alone forever."

As if in answer, the ground shook with a heavy explosion.

"All right, Captain. Now, take your chemical sniffer and begin getting samples," said Rubeo. "You'll want to move to the tube monitoring station. The others can dismantle the mirror at the director assembly. We only need a cross section."

"What's the monitoring station?" Danny asked.

"The stations are directly ahead of you with the control panels. Slit open one of the collector tubes and run the sampler."

"Which one?"

"Any one. This is very much a work in progress. We'll look for the disk arrays while you're doing that. Those will be our next target."

The ground rumbled again. Danny had to climb up and over one of the equipment benches. As he did, Rubeo told him to stop and take more pictures. Balancing on a long steel pipe, Danny curled one arm around a flexible tube that ran to the ceiling as he panned with the camera. The tube bounced violently as a pair of fresh explosions shook the ground outside.

"Hey, listen, Doc, things are getting exciting here. You better move us along the priority list."

Rubeo sighed. "Just keep doing what you're doing. Do we have the mirror section from the director yet?"

"This fucker is bolted in about twenty places," said Bison. "It's huge."

"We need only a cross section," replied Rubeo. "Two people should be able to carry a piece away from the building."

"You think it's so fucking easy, you do it," replied Bison.

"Relax, Sergeant," sighed the scientist. "We're all in this together."

"Yeah, well, some of us are more in it than others."

"What's going on outside, Nurse?" Danny asked Liu.

"Two BMPs came up. Flighthawk just popped 'em."

"I see some vehicles starting south now," said Fernandez. "Uh, tank I think."

"Captain?" said Rubeo. "Are you still with us?"

"I'm going to take my samples, then we're blowing the whole thing up."

"It would be useful if you could remove the small computer units at the base of the platform first," said Rubeo. "That Sun workstation especially. There is a disk array near it. Take that as well. The units will slide out."

"If we have time," said Danny.

One of the Marines shouted. Danny threw himself down as a flare shot to the top of the building and the interior lit.

"There's a tunnel," said Bison. "A dozen ragheads! More!"

After that all Danny could hear was machine-gun fire.

POWDER BLASTED AWAY IN THE HIND, SPITTING 12.7 BUL-lets everywhere but at the truck he was aiming at. Part of the problem was Egg, who kept flinging the helicopter left and right.

"We'll be an easy target. Get the pickup in front and the rest will be trapped."

"Well, I would if you'd hold steady for a second. This isn't the easiest gun in the world to aim."

"It's a fucking Ma Deuce."

"It's a Russian Ma Deuce. Big difference," said Powder, once again pressing the trigger and once again missing.

"Tanks," said Egg.

The helicopter bolted forward. Powder put his other hand on the gun handle, still pressing the trigger. The stream of bullets swam over and past the pickup, through the animal pen where the flak dealers had been, and toward the barbed-wire fences on the south perimeter. A pair of medium tanks—possibly T-54s or even American M48s— were rumbling along the roadway parallel to the fences.

"You're wasting ammo and you're going to burn out the barrel," said Egg.

"Yeah, no shit," said Powder, though he kept firing.

"Stand back and let the Flighthawk hit them."

"You're the one flying the damn thing." Powder finally let up on the trigger.

The helicopter continued moving forward. Powder could see one or two people on the ground but they were moving too quickly for him to aim. As they banked and came north, the small robot plane swooped nearly straight down on the lead tank. The U/MF's mouth frothed and the aircraft seemed to stutter in the air, skipping along and disappearing in the billowing cloud. The tank kept going.

"Shit," said Powder. "He hit the motherfucker too."

The U/MF's cannon fired shells nearly twice as large as the ones in the Hind's mouth, but Powder unleashed his weapon anyway. He got about six or seven into the vehicle with no apparent effect before the gun clicked empty.

"We're empty," he told Egg.

"I told you not to waste your fuckin' bullets."

"Maybe we should ram it."

"Just hang on," said Egg, throwing open the throttle.

Aboard *Raven*, over Iran
1820

"YOU'RE GOING TO HAVE TO HIT THE TANK WITH ONE OF the JSOWs," Zen told Alou. "My bullets bounced off the turret."

"We're down to three missiles, Zen. We have to make sure we can take out the laser."

"If we don't stop the tanks, they'll reach Whiplash. They're firing."

Zen poked the nose of the Flighthawk around as the tank recoiled from its shot. The shell from the 105mm gun, which had been retrofitted to the upgraded M48, sailed well over the laser building. As the gun started to lower for another shot, Zen dropped *Hawk One* down for a low-level run, hoping his bullets might find a soft spot at the tank's rear. He gave his trigger two quick squeezes and broke right as the tank fired again. Recovering, he spotted a small cement structure that looked like a tunnel entrance at the edge of the barbed wire. Ducking around to get a better view, he saw several troops running toward it.

"Targeting lead tank," said Alou.

"Hold on, hold on," said Zen. "We got some sort of underground entrance, bunker or something. May lead to the laser. Men inside," he said, unleashing thirty or forty rounds before swooping away. He could see another knot of men coming from the shadow of one of the buildings. He tucked his wing and dove back immediately, but they'd made the tunnel before he could get a shot.

"All right, stand clear," said Alou.

Two JSOWs popped out from the Megafortress's belly and nosed toward the tank and the tunnel entrance. Their rear steering fins made minor mid-course corrections about a third of the way home; two seconds later their warheads detonated precisely on their targets, stopping the Iranian counterattack cold.

"Whiplash, we have one lollipop left," Alou said over the shared circuit. "Time to saddle up."

In Iran
1830

WHEN THE MISSILE HIT THE ENTRANCE TO THE TUNNEL, THE concussion blew into the building with enough force to knock over a good part of the laser gear, including the director assembly. But it also killed or dazed most of the Iranians near the entrance, who, unlike Whiplash, hadn't been forewarned. The Marines took care of the rest, spraying their SAWs from a platform on the left side of the building. The metal walls reverberated with the loud rattle of light machine guns, the roar several times louder than a case of firecrackers going off in a garbage can.

The acrid smell of the flare, still burning on the ground, stung Danny's nostrils as he made his way down from the platform toward Bison and Pretty Boy, who were wedged down behind some equipment on the right side of the building.

"Two more guys, back behind that row of cabinets," said Bison, pointing.

"Flash-bang," said Danny. "You go left, I'll go right."

Bison ducked and began moving. Danny took one of the grenades in his hand, tucking his thumb beneath the tape he'd safed the pin with. As he got ready to toss it, Bison shouted a warning and began firing. Danny pitched the grenade over the barrier, then dove to the floor. The loud pop was almost lost in the roar of gunfire. Crawling, Danny managed to reach the end of the row, then hesitated, not sure exactly where Bison was and not wanting to get caught by his cross fire.

"Bison, where are you?"

"Pinned down," said the sergeant.

"Stay there," said Danny. He pitched another grenade over the top of the cabinet and threw himself around the corner a millisecond after it popped. There were bodies everywhere, at least a dozen of them. Two Iranians with heavy weapons were crouched at the far end of the row; Danny's bullets caught them chest high as they began to turn toward him. He ran through his clip, then jerked back behind the row of metal as someone behind them popped up and returned fire.

"There's a million of these fuckers," said Bison.

"Just seems that way," shouted Gunny, who'd come down and around to cover them. "Advance. I got your ass."

Danny rammed home a new clip. When the Iranians' bullets stopped hitting the wall near his head, he threw himself around the barrier again, once more emptying his weapon before ducking back. But this time as he reloaded there was no answering fire.

"Secure," said Bison.

"Let's grab that shit and get the hell out of here," said Danny, scanning the pile of dead before retreating.

The smoke was so thick in the building that even with his low-light mode on he could see only a few yards ahead. When the Marine corporal rose in front of him, Danny cringed for a second, not sure who it was. Then he recognized him.

"This comes with us," he told the Marine, pointing to the disk array. A stack of drives sat on top of each other in a plastic cabinet about five feet high. "Grab whatever you can. Just tear it out and get it into the helo. Go."

The Marine began prying out the disk units with his knife, sliding them out past the flimsy locks that secured them. Danny climbed back onto the platform and retrieved his gas analyzer. He took out his knife and cut open a hole in one of the plastic tubes.

"Put the sensor right on the interior of the tube," said Rubeo in his headset.

"Hey, Doc, I thought you'd gone for coffee."

"Hardly. This is probably an exhaust manifold, Captain. Not optimum. Move to the last pipe in the second row."

"We're tight on time."

"I understand that."

Danny walked to the edge of the platform. His knife made it through the inside layer of plastic, but there was another plastic pipe inside that the point could reach but not quite cut.

"Shit," he said.

"Very good," said Rubeo. "Open the pipe."

"How?"

Rubeo didn't answer. Danny took his pistol and fired through.

"That was expedient," said the scientist. "Please take your sample now."

Danny pushed the modified sniffer probe into the hole. As he stood there he could see the Marine corporal running toward the hole in the wall with an armload of gear.

"Enough," said Rubeo. "Now we would like a measure on the reaction chambers, the large tube structures directly behind you. Do not fire at those," added the scientist. "While puncturing the inner piping is unlikely, if you did succeed, the concentration of chemicals could be quite sufficient to kill you and the rest of your team."

Danny took the ruler from his pocket—a laser unit not unlike those used on some construction sites. He made his way to the end of the tube and shot the beam down to the other end, then struggled to get a good read as the numbers kept jumping on the screen.

"Close enough," said Rubeo. The handheld ruler didn't have a transmit mode, but Danny realized that Rubeo had read it through his helmet inputs. "Now, one of those junction boxes would be very useful. Do you see it beneath the third band?"

"Why don't I just take the whole damn chamber?"

"That would be infinitely preferable," said Rubeo. "An admirable solution."

Danny had to pick his way over two piles of debris to get to the box; as he climbed off the second he realized there was a boot sticking out. He bent down and saw that the pant leg above the boot was tan.

The boot moved slightly. He heard, or thought he heard, a groan from the pile.

Not one of my guys, he thought. Still, he found himself fighting an urge to stop and help the man.

"Do not damage the circuitry if possible," said Rubeo as Danny pried the cover of the box off with his knife. The last two screws shot away and the metal cover fell away.

"Looks like a bunch of wires."

"Yes," said the scientist.

"You sure you want them?"

"Do you want me to explain how the probable current can be determined from the size and composition of the wires, and what other suppositions could be made—or should I skip to the math involved in determining the propagation of electromagnetic waves?"

"Fuck you, Doc," said Danny, hacking at the thick set of wires.

Dreamland Command Center
0742

"MUCH MORE PRIMITIVE THAN RAZOR," SAID RUBEO, turning away from the console.

"In the matter of size, yes," said Matterhorn, one of the laser experts.

"In everything."

"I disagree," answered Matterhorn. "The size of the mirror array and the lack of mobility in the aiming structure indicates to me that they've found a way to target it by focusing individual frames at the reflective site. They've obviously gone operational too soon, but that undoubtedly was a political decision."

"Piffle," said Rubeo. "Razor is several times more powerful."

Dog took a step away from them, turning his attention back to the image from Dreamland's miniature KH satellite. The high-resolution optics on the satellite could not be sent as video, but in rapid burst mode it updated every twenty seconds. The effect was something like watching dancers move across a strobe-lit stage.

Except, of course, the dancers were his people under fire.

"The mission has been invaluable," Matterhorn said, probably sensing Dog's annoyance.

The colonel ignored the scientist. More vehicles were starting from the barracks area. "Danny. Let's get the hell out of there, okay?" he said, pushing the talk button on his remote.

"I'm with you, Colonel."

Aboard _Quicksilver_, over Iraq
1843

TORBIN FELT HIMSELF STARTING TO RELAX AS THE LAST OF the attack jets checked in, hooking onto the course for home. His fingers hurt and his neck was stiff.

"Crew sound off," said Captain Breanna Stockard. "Torbin, how are we looking?"

"Good," he said. "Thanks for picking me up back there. I appreciate it."

"Not a problem. Chris?"

Torbin tried to stretch away some of his cramps as the others joked. Had he screwed up? Normally the copilot handled the missile shots, but he should have taken the radars down himself.

Nobody else thought he'd messed up, though.

Ironic—on the other missions, he'd been the one convinced he hadn't failed, and everyone else pointed the finger. Now it was the other way around.

So was he a screw-up?

The computer snapped a warning tone at him.

"Radars, airborne," he relayed to the captain. "Three, four—helicopters coming north."

"They're not ours?" asked Breanna.

"Negative, negative. ID'd as Mi-8 Hips," he said, reading the legend on the panel. "Assault ships. I have a bearing."

"Hang tight everyone," said Breanna. "Torbin, give the heading to Eagle Flight. Chris will punch you through."

"They're on a direct line for High Top," said Chris Ferris.

"The fighters will take care of them," replied Breanna.

**In Iran
1855**

THE HIND BUCKED AS THEY THREW THE CAPTURED GEAR inside. The rotors revolved at low RPM, their wash making it difficult to move in a straight line. The part of the mirror assembly they'd cut away proved so heavy that the two Marines had to help Egg and Pretty Boy get it out of the building; even then they dragged it most of the way.

"Something moving beyond the fence," warned Liu. "Can't see through the smoke."

"Okay," said Danny. "Liu, Hernandez, fall back. We're buggin' out."

"Two more of those disk things inside," yelled the Marine corporal.

"All right," said Danny. "I'll get the last array and then we're gone."

He tossed his plundered CPU unit inside the Hind, then ran back to the building, heading toward the arrays. Light filtered through the smoke; a fire flared in fits near the tunnel entrance at the other side of the building. Danny moved through the red and gray shadows like a goblin slithering through a haunted house. As he jumped up onto the raised metal platform of the control area his knee gave way; as he sprawled off the side he managed to snag his arm on a metal railing, but then lost it. He fell face first to the ground without getting his hands out to break his fall. He cringed, expecting to hit hard and on his face; instead his chest and face landed on a large, soft pillow.

Not a pillow, but the stomach of a dead Iranian soldier. Danny turned his head to the side, his helmet's visor magnifying the dead man's green eyes. Wide open in the dim light, they stared at him as if to ask why he had come.

Danny pushed himself upward, ignoring his throbbing knee. The disk array sat on the floor a few yards ahead. He moved toward it, meanwhile scanning the interior. Two large suitcaselike arrays sat next to a small screen; he slung his gun over his shoulder and hoisted them from the floor. They were lighter than he thought but hard to hold in his hands as he began picking his way back outside.

He'd gotten about a third of the way when a fresh explosion rocked the building. He stopped, regaining his balance, then began again. He could hear the helicopter revving outside, felt his own adrenaline surging.

This is why I'm here, he thought. How could he tell

Jemma that? How could he explain it to her friends or politicos, to anyone who wasn't right in the middle of things?

It was more than the rush. Part of it had to do with patriotism, or fulfilling your duty, or something difficult to put exactly into words, even to your wife. Danny pushed forward, sliding against a piece of mangled machinery, ducking to his right. An automatic weapon popped outside.

A hand grabbed him from the side, a hard clamp that whipped him around and threw him down. An AK-47 appeared over him as he fell, the gun barrel flaring.

In that moment Captain Danny Freah knew what heaven would be like. For all his years of protesting that he was not religious, for all his poor churchgoing, his infrequent prayers—in the moment that bullets flew toward his chest, he felt the warmth of unending rest. Something soft and feminine whispered in his ear, a voice not unlike his wife's, telling him he had nothing to fear forever more.

Then hell opened up with a violent thunderclap, lightning shrieking in a violent arc. Debris fell around him, clumps of dirt and sod as he was buried alive.

Hands pulled him up, warm hands, old hands.

"Shittin' fuckin' hell, that raghead almost got you point-blank," shouted Gunny, who'd somehow materialized over him. He had his arm wrapped around Danny's chest—Gunny had pulled him down—and began dragging him outside. "Beat shit hell outta your pizza boxes."

"Yeah," said Danny, still dazed.

"Well come the fuck on," said the Marine sergeant. His machine gun still smoked in his hands.

"Yeah," said Danny. He paused at the wall, then leaped back to grab the mangled disk arrays, pulling them with him outside.

The sun washed everything pure and white—even the three bodies of Iranian soldiers who had tried to cut off their escape.

"Let's go!" yelled Liu, running up to grab one of the boxes from Danny's hands. "The whole Iranian air force is coming for us."

"What's that, a pair of fuckin' crop dusters?" said Gunny.

"Try a dozen MiG-29s and six F-5s for starters," said Liu, physically pushing Danny into the helicopter. "The Megafortress is going to blow up the building—we don't need charges. Let's go!"

Aboard *Raven*, over Iran
1903

ZEN HAD TO CHECK HIS FUEL AS HE ROSE TO CONFRONT the jets scrambling from Tabriz. The two planes, ID'd as F-5Es, were relatively primitive, unlike the MiGs coming off the concrete at Hamadian and Kemanshah. But they were more than a match for the Hind and close enough to intercept them.

"I'm zero-two on the lead plane," he told Alou.

"Copy that. Launching JSOW on laser site," replied the pilot.

Raven was running behind the Flighthawk by seven miles; even if the primitive radars in the F-5E Tigers would have difficulty spotting it, by the time *Hawk One* closed on them the black plane would probably be visible, at least as a disconcerting speck in the distance.

There was a dull clunk from somewhere far behind Zen as the smart bomb popped off the rotary launcher in the rear bay.

"I'm going to head-on the son of a bitch," he said, as

much a note to himself as a piece of intelligence for the *Raven* pilot. "Break north. Stay with me."

"Copy that."

"Impact at three, two . . ." said the copilot, counting down the bomb hit on the laser.

Zen lost track of the conversation on the flight deck as the weapon scored a direct hit on the director assembly. Gray and black smoke furled and then mushroomed from the hole in the center of the building. A concussion shook the building, shattering five of the supports and causing the north wall to implode.

Then things got nasty.

As the explosion vaporized the metal tube and stand at the heart of the director, shrapnel from the smart bomb shot through a four-inch gas pipe near the side of the building. A second or so later the escaping gas was ignited by a fire that had licked its way out from one of the control units. The flames flew back into a large, pressurized reservoir tank. This exploded so brightly it set off the IR warning in the Megafortress's tail, even though by now they were a good distance away. The building's roof vaporized into a skyrocketing fireball, which burned so quickly that it blew itself out—though not before rising nearly a thousand feet and incinerating everyone who had been in the shed when the bomb hit.

Zen turned his attention back to his own targets. The Iranian jets, flying at just over the speed of sound, were at twelve and fourteen thousand feet, respectively, separated by about a half mile. They were traveling much too fast to engage the Hind; belatedly, they began to slow. The computer plotted Zen's attack for him, and diplomatically didn't post the odds of a heads-on attack with a cannon working at such speeds. His goal, however, wasn't to nail them but simply break their approach.

The computer cued him to fire before he could even see the first aircraft. He waited an extra second, squeezed the trigger, then corrected right to get a quick shot on the second aircraft. As he started to bank, something red flew through it; one of his bullets had managed to rip through the fuel lines of the lead aircraft, turning it into a fireball. It was a one in a thousand shot—Zen thought to himself that he should have played the lottery that day.

The second airplane turned hard to the north, accelerating away and taking itself out of the equation. Zen didn't care—he threw the Flighthawk south and began hunting for the MiG-29s.

"Good shooting," said Alou.

"Thanks."

"Bandits are accelerating," reported the copilot. "Positive IDs—Fulcrum Cs. You have two bearing one-niner off your nose."

"Slot Dance radar is active. Velocity-search mode," added the radar operator. "Should we jam?"

"Let's hold that off as long as possible," said Alou. "They may not know we're here. Zen?"

"Yeah, roger that. Working on an intercept," he said. "Fentress?"

"Boss?"

"Keep an eye on my fuel."

"Yes, sir."

Actually, the computer would do so, but Zen suddenly felt he wanted Fentress in the mix.

"Hawk One *is being scanned*," warned the computer as he crossed to within ten miles of the easternmost MiG.

"MiGs are coming for us," warned the copilot. "We're inside Aphid range—they don't seem to have us yet."

"Go to ECMs," said Alou.

"If you go to ECMs you're going to cut down my maneuverability," warned Zen. While the Flighthawk and C³ used uninterruptible bands, its backup circuits were limited by the fuzz, and as a precaution the Flighthawk had to stay within five miles of the mothership. "Wait until they lock."

"Full ECMs," insisted the pilot.

Cursing, Zen pulled his stick to the right, looping back to get closer to *Raven*. Breanna would never have punched the panic button that quickly; *Raven* hadn't even been spiked.

"Still coming. Looking for us," said the copilot.

"Prepare AMRAAMs," said Alou. "Open bay doors."

"That's going to increase the radar profile five hundred percent," said Zen. "They'll see us for sure."

"Hawk leader, fly your own plane."

Zen pushed his stick hard left, rolling his wing around and gunning for the two MiGs. The closest was now within seven miles of *Hawk One*—easy range if he'd had a radar homer. C^3, anticipating him, gave a plot for an attack that featured a deflection shot on the close plane with a quick jink that would put him head-on-wing to the second.

"Fuel is down to ten minutes," warned Fentress.

"Hawk," said Zen, acknowledging.

"Being scanned. Target aircraft are locking on Hawk One," warned the computer.

Good, thought Zen. Get me, not *Raven*.

"Scan broken. Thirty seconds to intercept."

"We're spiked!" warned the copilot. "Shit."

"Fire missiles," said Alou. "Brace for evasive maneuvers."

Zen leaned forward into the attack as his cue flashed red. The Iranian MiG pitched downward as Zen began to fire; he followed through a curving arc, aiming ahead of the enemy's nose, in effect firing his bullets so they and the MiG would arrive at the same point at the same time. The copilot and radar operator were screaming about missiles in the air, Fentress told him the other MiG was trying to get on his tail, and Alou ordered chaff as Zen fought to keep his attention on the glowing pipper in the middle of his head, the bright red triangle that doomed the MiG to destruction. The Iranian squirmed and flailed, now left, now right, up then down. And then its nose fell away and the wings shot upward, the Flighthawk's bullets sawing it in half.

"On your butt!" warned Fentress. "Missiles!"

Zen tucked left. A large shadow zipped past his windscreen cam—a missile. He turned right, couldn't find his prey, kept coming, finally saw the large-nosed bird tilting its wing over in an evasive maneuver. Something seemed to pop from the right wing—one of *Raven*'s AMRAAMs hitting home.

"Yeah," said the copilot.

Alou's congratulations were cut short by a thunderclap and the shudder of a volcano releasing its steam. Zen felt himself weightless and then thrown against his restraints so hard one of the belts sheered from its bolt at the base, leaving him hanging off the side as *Raven* rolled into an invert, then plunged into a fifty-degree dive toward the earth.

Aboard *Quicksilver*, over Iraq
1910

BREANNA HEARD THE AWACS ALERT AND KNEW IMMEDIately what had happened.

"Chris, get us a course to the Iranian border." She didn't bother to wait, turning the plane immediately to the east.

"We're almost twenty-five minutes away," said the copilot.

"Understood." The throttles were already at max, but she tapped them nonetheless.

"*Whiplash Hind* is about zero-two from the border," said Chris, plotting their position. "*Raven* is engaging MiGs and F-5Es."

"Okay."

"They'll make it, Bree."

"I know that. What's our ETA now?"

Aboard *Raven*, over Iran
1910

FENTRESS FELT THE AIR PUNCH OUT OF HIS LUNGS AS THE big plane flipped through an invert. A fist welled in his diaphragm, pounding up into his throat.

They'd been hit by one of the missiles. The pilot and copilot were yelling at each other, trying to pull the big plane level.

His job was to help Zen with the Flighthawk. He put his right arm down on the control panel, pulling himself upright, getting back in the game. The main video panel display had a warning across the top portion of the screen declaring a fuel emergency. The aircraft had under five minutes of gas in the tanks.

"Zen?"

Fentress turned. Zen sagged off the side of his seat against his restraint straps. Fentress reached to undo his own seat belt, then stopped. He had to take care of the Flighthawk first or it would go down. He reached to the manual override; the computer listened as he recited his name and the command codes to take over. The fuel emergency shortened the protocol—he only had to give two different commands to take the helm.

By the time the transfer was complete, the Megafortress had stuttered into level flight. Fentress, flying behind it, could see damage to the right tail surface and some rips and dents in the fuselage; one of the engines seemed to be out.

"Hawk leader to *Raven*. I need to refuel," he said.

"We're still assessing damage," said Alou.

"*Raven*, I need to refuel now," said Fentress.

"You'll have to wait."

"Fuck you," said Fentress. "I'm coming in now."

The computer calculation showed he had exactly three minutes and thirty-two seconds before going dry. He'd never completed the tricky refuel in less than seven, and even the automated routine took five.

"All right. Don't panic," said Alou.

"I'm not panicking," he said, his voice level.

He'd never spoken to a commanding officer—hell, to practically anyone—this way. But the shit was on the line. He needed fuel now. And he'd have to gas manually.

Zen could. He could.

"I'll climb," said Alou.

"Just get the boom out," he said.

"*Raven*."

Fentress pushed in as the straw emerged from the rear of the plane. The director lights flashed red; he was too fast and too far right. He knocked his speed down, felt his diaphragm cramping big-time.

"Zen, come on, come on," he muttered to himself. "Tell me I can do it."

Zen said nothing. The Flighthawk chuttered in the harsh vortices of the Megafortress. The computer struggled to help Fentress hold it steady.

Zen would tell me to relax it all the way home, Fentress told himself. He resisted the urge to push the small plane onto the nozzle.

As the last gallon of fuel slid from the Flighthawk's

tanks through its lines to the engine, the nozzle clicked into the wide mouth of the receptacle at the top of the plane. He was in.

Fuel began flowing.

"Computer, fly. Complete refuel," he said. As C^3 grabbed the plane, he tossed off his belt and went to help Zen.

**Aboard *Whiplash Hind*, over Iran
1912**

DANNY PUSHED HIS LEG FLAT ON THE FLOOR OF THE HELI-copter, looking up at Nurse as the medic worked over his knee. They had just crossed back into Iraqi airspace; another half hour and they'd be home.

Home, home, home.

"You want some morphine?" said Nurse.

Danny shook his head. His sergeant didn't take his eyes off him.

"I've hurt my knee before."

"It's not your knee. Your shin's busted," said Nurse. "Something hard slammed the body armor. Would've sliced right through your leg except for the boron inserts. You didn't feel it?"

"I don't think I did." Danny looked down at his pants leg. Nurse had pulled off the lightweight body armor, but Danny couldn't quite see his leg.

"I really think you should take some painkiller, Cap."

"Yeah, when we're on the ground," said Danny. He leaned back, resting against some of the stolen laser parts. "Sure will feel good to be home."

Incirlik
1915

JED SIPPED FROM HIS COLA, LISTENING WHILE THE TRANS-
lator the Turks had supplied repeated the stock questions
about the prisoner's unit and deployment. The prisoner
glared. His attitude seemed infinitely more hostile toward
the Turk than toward Jed—though the results were exactly the same.

Two CIA agents had seen the man. They thought but
could not confirm that he wasn't a native Iraqi. What sig-
nificance that had, if any, wasn't clear.

Jed watched the Turk's frustration grow. Outside, the
interrogator had assured Jed that he had conducted many
interviews; Jed suspected torture was among his regular
techniques, and he made it clear he would not be permit-
ted to employ them.

After a few more minutes of questions met only by
stares, the Turk slammed his hands on the table. He said
something that sounded like a threat involving the prisoner's mother and sisters—Jed's Arabic still wasn't fast
enough to decipher it all—then made a show of leaving in
a huff, probably thinking he was setting Jed up as the
"good cop" in the old interrogation routine.

Jed took another sip from his soda. The Turk would go
down the hall and watch the surveillance feed from the
wide-angle pinhead video cam in the top corner of the
room. He was as much a spy as a translator, but Clearwater had already made that argument to the State Depart-
ment, which insisted that he be allowed to meet the
prisoner.

"So when you were in America," said Jed after a few
minutes of silence, "where did you go to school?"

"RPI," said the prisoner—in English.

"That's in upstate New York?" said Jed, trying to act as if he'd expected the man to answer his question.

"Troy. An ugly city."

"Never been there," said Jed. He scratched the back of his neck, slid his elbow on the table—he could be talking to a guy sitting next to him in a bar after work, except that he never went to bars after work. "That near Albany?"

"Very close."

"What did you think of New York City?"

"A wondrous place," said the Iraqi. "But a place of temptation."

"I've been in the Empire State Building three times," said Jed.

The Iraqi didn't reply.

"Why did you decide to join the army?" asked Jed, trying to keep the rapport up.

Nothing.

"But you're not from Iraq, right? You come from— Egypt?"

Jed waited for an answer. He was still waiting when an aide came to tell him the general wanted to talk to him.

MUSAH TAHIR WATCHED THE AMERICAN LEAVE THE ROOM. He felt a twinge at being left alone—he suspected the Turk would now return and begin to threaten him.

He told himself he must be strong. He must remember that he was doing his duty. He would persevere. He would be rewarded.

The wealth and power of America seemed overwhelming, but it was corrupt power, the reward of the devil for a man's soul. Millions and millions of souls.

He would not surrender his.

The door to the small room opened. He pulled himself

upright, braced himself for the assault. But it wasn't the Turk; it was Barclay, the American.

"I've got good news for you," he said. "You're going home. The Red Cross has arranged an exchange."

A trick.

"You can stay if you choose, you know. Stay with us," said the American.

Tahir smiled. Protect me, God, he thought.

Aboard *Raven*, over Iran
1918

HE KNEW IT WAS A DREAM, BECAUSE HE COULD FEEL HIS legs.

He was playing football, wide receiver, like high school. Zen ran down the field, looking back toward the quarterback—Kevin Fentress. The kid had faded back under the heavy rush of Zen's cousin Jed Barclay and a few of his other old friends.

Zen was wide open. "Throw me the ball!" he yelled. "Throw me the ball!"

The brown pigskin darted upward just as Fentress was swamped. The ball sailed high, but it wasn't far enough to reach him. Zen began running back toward the line of scrimmage.

Running. It felt so damn good. He knew it was a dream.

What he didn't know was where he was having it. He thought he was in bed, pushed to feel Breanna snuggled beneath the covers next to him.

A cold hiss of air shot into his face. Something wet dropped down the side of his temple. He shook his head, felt pain shooting up the side of his neck.

"Zen! Zen!"

"Fentress?" Zen pushed to the right, felt his arm fly in front of him.

Raven. They were in *Raven.* His helmet was off.

The Flighthawk! She was nearly out of fuel.

"We have to refuel!" said Zen. He went to grab the control stick. His hand seemed to move in slow motion for a second, then caught up so quickly he couldn't keep it from smashing into the bottom of the console. He cursed with the pain then stared at his limp hand.

His hand wasn't what hurt him. It was his legs.

His legs? He hadn't felt them for more than a year and a half.

But they hurt like hell. He must still be dreaming.

Aboard *Quicksilver*, approaching Iran
1925

EVEN THE SOPHISTICATED GEAR IN *QUICKSILVER* HAD TROU-ble sorting everything out. Iraq had launched helicopters and MiGs against Kurdish positions north of Kirkuk; two F-16s had moved to engage them. Farther east two Iraqi helicopters were flying either a supply or an attack mission on a vector almost exactly due north. Beyond that, the Iranians had at least a dozen aircraft in the sky over or at the border with Iraq. *Raven,* struck but not disabled by an Iranian missile, was just coming over the border now. *Whiplash Hind* was flying so low not even *Quicksilver* could see her, but she was somewhere ahead of *Raven.*

"Border in ten minutes," Chris Ferris told Breanna. "What are we doing?"

"We'll escort anyone who needs escorting," she said.

"Hang on," said Ferris. "F-15s are engaging the Iraqi helicopter."

"Which one? Tell them to stop," she said without waiting for an answer. "That's ours. That's ours!"

Aboard *Raven*, over Iran
1930

FENTRESS GAVE UP TRYING TO REVIVE ZEN AND JUMPED back into his seat, taking the Flighthawk from C³ just as it finished refueling. He dropped down and began scouting ahead. The Iranian MiGs began to retreat as a flight of F-15s approached.

They'd lost contact with *Whiplash Hind,* though by now it would be between twenty and thirty miles ahead, undoubtedly skimming the snowcapped mountains. Fentress popped the Flighthawk's nose skyward, accelerating to find the helicopter.

Those guys had kicked ass on this, big-time, he thought. Gonna be a full round of beers and attaboys to last a lifetime, or at least a week and a half.

Some for him too. He'd done okay. He was doing okay.

He hoped Zen was okay. Blood had curled from his ear. One of his straps seemed to have broken; his head had probably slammed against the panel, and Fentress guessed he had a concussion. But he was breathing, at least.

The U/MF picked up the powerful radars of a pair of F-15s, screaming over from Turkey.

"Eagle Flight, this is Dreamland *Hawk One*," he said.

"Hawk, we need radio silence. We are engaging an enemy aircraft," replied one of the planes.

Where?

"No!" he shouted. "No! No! No!"

"Fox One!" said the lead pilot.

**Aboard *Whiplash Hind*, over Iraq
1942**

DANNY PULLED HIS MP-5 NEXT TO HIM ON THE BENCH. HE could see white through the helicopter window across from him—snow from the mountains.

Home, almost home. It'd be warm there now, almost spring.

Egg was flying low enough to stop for traffic signals. Hopefully he didn't kick into a goat or something—the CentCom lawyers would be peeved.

Lawyers. Holy shit. What would Major Pee-liar say about stealing a laser from the Iranians? Give it back.

The Iranians had probably stolen it from the U.S. somehow. He had merely returned the favor, Danny thought.

His guys were sharing some MREs with the Marines. They must be really, really hungry.

He started to laugh. His leg twinged.

Then it pounded.

"Hey, Nurse, maybe I will have that morphine," he said, pushing upright again. He twisted toward Liu, but his view was blocked by a flash of bright red and yellow flames. He felt himself falling backward and realized home was even farther away than he'd thought.

VI

Friendly Fire

———

High Top
30 May 1997
1942

AS MACK PROCEEDED THROUGH HIS INSPECTION OF THE Bronco, Garcia followed along behind him, waxing eloquent about what the addition of five-bladed, infinite-pitch propellers and supercharged turbo engines would do to the aircraft's performance. Mack had mustered genuine admiration for the OV-10, but it paled beside Garcia's lust. The pilot would have liked nothing better than to help the techie try some of his improvements, but he was in something of a hurry to get going. He'd been ordered to return to Brussels posthaste and prepare a brief on the recent air campaign. This meant considerable work, though not necessarily the kind he enjoyed—he'd have to listen to CentCom commanders brag until his ears fell off. On the other hand, it also meant serious career chits. No doubt it would help push his campaign to win assignment as squadron commander back onto the fast track.

"A few tweaks here and there, Major, this becomes the best COIN aircraft in the world," Garcia said as they walked toward the rear. "There's an opportunity here. We stick some of the Flighthawk sensors on it, do a mondo upgrade to the engines, telemetry tie-in with the Whiplash team. Add microrobots to extend real-time viewing. Gonna serve somebody—"

"Another song lyric, huh?" Mack ducked beneath the tail. The worn paint was becoming familiar. "Am I going to make Incirlik?"

Garcia looked at him as if he'd just asked if the world were flat. "Well, yes, sir."

"How about Brussels?"

"Assuming you refuel, not a problem."

Mack gave the crewman a thumbs-up. If no one at Incirlik actually asked for the aircraft, well, it wouldn't be right to just leave it in a hangar there. He was personally responsible for its safety. That meant he'd have to take it with him, all the way to Brussels if necessary.

Maybe that French aerospace consultant would like a ride. He'd personally tuck her in.

Hell, at this point he'd settle for Patti Good Teeth.

Mack pulled himself into the cockpit. Helmet on and straps cinched, he gave Garcia the thumb and cranked the engines. The plane tugged at its brakes as he completed the preflight. He still had no weapons, but Garcia had wrung a few more RPMs out of the engines and, even more important, adjusted their whine so they sounded very much like a pack of vintage Harleys tearing down the highway. There was loud, and then there was *loud*; Mack never minded a few decibels as long as his eardrums got pounded in style.

Cleared by the tower, Mack began trundling toward the far end of the runway. Just as he made his turn and went to gun the throttle, a familiar voice broke over the long-range radio.

"We have a helicopter down by friendly fire," said Breanna Stockard. "Repeat, *Whiplash Hind* is down."

"Shit," said Mack. He whipped the turbos and raced

down the mesh strip. Climbing out swiftly, he banked south, veering off his flight plan.

"*Quicksilver*, this is *Wild Bronco*," he said. "What's going on, Bree?"

"The Hind was hit about twenty miles south southeast of the border. Whiplash team is aboard."

"You have a visual?" he asked.

"Negative. We don't have an exact location. Just commencing a search."

"Copy that. Give me what you've got, beautiful. I'm on my way."

Aboard *Raven*, over Iran
1955

FENTRESS'S HEART POUNDED IN HIS EARS, BUT OTHERWISE he felt almost relaxed, his hand moving the joystick smoothly left as he began the new search pattern. He had the infrared view selected; the sensors should have no trouble locating the warm body of the helicopter in the cold air. The computer had already been instructed to highlight possible wreckage "clusters," as they were referred to by the programming.

Pushing the Flighthawk through the long, jagged valley, Fentress imagined he heard Zen telling him to slow down. The slower he went, the better the odds of seeing something or being seen.

As he neared the end of the search grid, Fentress pushed a bit farther west and made a wide, looping bank onto a new search track. He backed the throttle down, forward airspeed nudging toward 200 miles an hour. Flying the Flighthawks fast wasn't very hard; they were bullets with stubby wings. Flying them slow, however, took patience and grace. You had to concentrate on what you were doing, and yet you couldn't get so caught up in the details that you started to fight the computer as you bucked through the eddies.

Fentress narrowed his eyes on the screen, trying to keep his concentration. He had to find his guys.

BREE PULLED ZEN TO THE FLOOR AND THEY STARTED TO dance. His legs hurt but they kept dancing. He pushed his arms tighter around her, holding himself up, resting, but the music got faster and faster. She broke free and danced wildly. He did the same, though his legs were hurting.

It was good that his legs hurt. They hadn't hurt for so long. He'd known in the hospital that they didn't hurt, knew what that meant, though he'd tried not to face it.

Zen fought to walk. Giving that up—and yet not giving up everything else—that was the impossible thing. Accepting his paralysis without accepting that it doomed him—had he ever really done that?

It was only when he decided he wouldn't walk, that he had to concentrate on getting back any way he could, that he made real progress.

He'd give up everything to walk again. Everything.

Bree? Not Bree. Bree he wouldn't give up.

She danced in front of him. The dream began to fade.

His legs continued to hurt.

Dreamland Command Center
1055

DOG PUT HIS HAND ON THE LIEUTENANT'S SHOULDER, steadying the young man as he worked the com gear and flicked back and forth between the different feeds, trying to locate the helicopter wreckage. There wasn't much more they could do from here.

"Feed pending from General Magnus," the lieutenant told Dog.

"Yes, I see. Keep it there. Don't open it."

"Yes, sir."

The door to the secure room opened and Major Cheshire entered, carrying a tray of coffee and doughnuts. "Hey, Colonel," she said lightly.

"Major." Dog stared at the screen.

"Lost the connection with the general," said the lieutenant.

"What's up?" asked Cheshire.

Dog took the coffee and filled her in. "We're hoping they survived," he said, his voice soft. "Only one missile at long range. It wasn't even certain that it hit."

"Friendly fire," she said, a comment, not a question.

"Definitely." Dog glanced back at the screen at the front of the room, which showed a satellite image of the mountainous terrain. At maximum resolution, the houses on the hillsides looked like small cubes of sugar.

"You okay, Colonel?" asked Cheshire.

"I'm fine," he told her. "General Magnus needs to be filled in. Probably, he's not going to like it."

Cheshire nodded.

"Lieutenant, see if you can get that line open to General Magnus."

"Trying, sir."

Dog looked back at the screen. From the perspective of the mini-KH, it looked almost like a little piece of heaven.

Aboard *Quicksilver*, over Iran
2001

NO LONGER WORRIED ABOUT THE IRANIAN LASER OR IRAQI missiles, Breanna brought *Quicksilver* into an orbit at fifteen thousand feet, just high enough to avoid the mountain peaks. Chris worked the video cam in the nose, scanning for wreckage, while Habib snooped for Iraqi radio transmissions.

The Megafortress's radar was not designed to sweep the ground, and even if it had been, the jagged peaks and cliffs would have made it difficult to sort through the clutter of irregular returns. Nonetheless, Torbin was giving it the old college try, routing the radar through his station and fiddling with the filters designed to find very low-flying planes in look-down mode. He was still somewhat tentative, unsure of himself in a non-Dreamland way, but Breanna saw that he seemed to be willing to try to figure things out; he flipped back and forth between override, manually tweaking the radar sweeps.

"How we looking, troops?" she asked.

"Village two miles off that main road," said Chris. "Otherwise uninhabited for miles. You sure this is the place?"

"These are the coordinates the F-15s gave us."

"Maybe try farther north. *Raven*'s coming up from the south."

"Mack's going to take that."

"East, then," suggested Chris.

"We'll give the track one more run, then we'll try that."

"Iraqi command radio," said Habib.

He paused a second, then punched up a location two miles to the south of them. The coordinates flashed on a grid map in Breanna's left multiuse display area.

"What are they saying?" she asked.

"Coordinating some sort of attack."

"Mention our helicopter?"

"Negative. I'm having a little trouble picking it up and translating on the fly."

"You have anything, Torbin?"

"No, ma'am."

"All right, let's go see if we can put some pictures with Habib's words," said Breanna, changing course.

On the ground in Iraq
2006

FOR THE LONGEST TIME, DANNY PUSHED AGAINST THE metal and got nowhere. He clawed and he fought. He rolled to his stomach and then around to his back, but the Hind had twisted itself into a cocoon around him. He could hear voices nearby and felt, or thought he felt, the others moving, but it was impossible to see anything. He tried pushing his arms under himself and crawling forward; when that didn't work, he began to shimmy sideways and got a foot or so before getting stuck again. Finally, he pushed his arms under his stomach and levered the front part of his body up with his elbows. His helmet pushed against something hard. He pushed back, slipped, tried again, felt something give way. Danny pushed again. Pain flashed through his injured knee and shin; he felt himself being pulled forward into fresh air.

"Jeez, Cap, we thought you got crushed," said Powder.

The Whiplash trooper helped Danny upright. Liu ran over, tugging at Danny's helmet to take it off as the captain began walking. They reached a large rock a few feet away; Danny patted it as he sat, resting and catching his breath. There were two or three inches of snow on the ground, a small, unmelted patch. Danny reached over and took a handful, smearing it on his face.

"Bitch of a landing," said Powder. "Missile blew through the engine, just about, and threw us down like a frog getting its brains bashed in on a rock. Good thing Egg didn't know how to fly too high, huh?"

"Egg's legs are broken," said Liu. "The Marine corpo-ral's got internal bleeding and isn't conscious. Bison has a busted arm, maybe some other problems. Otherwise we're cool. Helicopter isn't going anywhere, though."

"All right." Danny, still dazed, looked over at his in-jured men, huddled near a cluster of rocks about ten feet away from the helicopter, which lay smashed against the hillside a few yards beyond them. It looked as if a large hand had grabbed its fuselage and crumpled the sides. Danny couldn't imagine how he'd made it out—or how no one had been killed.

Bison glanced over, then held up the Marine's M-16 to show he was all right.

Danny realized that his leg didn't hurt that bad any-more. In fact, it felt almost as good as new.

He decided he must be in shock.

"All right," he said. "Survival radios—what's working?"

"We've broadcast on everything we got," said Powder, "including an old Prick-90 Pretty Boy had stuffed in his ruck. Nothin' comin' back at us."

"The spins—five minutes after the hour," said Danny, referring to the broadcasts for searching aircraft.

"Gotcha, Cap."

"Sooner if you hear anything. But remember, those batteries may have to last awhile." Danny shifted his weight, again balancing against the rock. "All right. What do we have in the way of a perimeter here?"

Powder laid it out for him. The hill they were on backed a sheer drop of about two hundred feet; below that was another deep gully. Pretty Boy and Gunny were checking the base of the hill below them; they would re-port back in ten minutes.

"Gunny's idea," added Powder. "For a Marine, he ain't too dumb. We gave him Egg's helmet, but damned if he couldn't fit his head into it."

"Shoulda given him yours," said Nurse.

Danny reset his own helmet and tried tapping into the Dreamland circuit but got nothing. It was impossible to tell whether it had been damaged in the crash or if he was just in a bad position to get the satellite.

The cold bit at his face as he pushed his way up the slope, trying to get a sense of where they'd crashed. A shallow ridge across the way blocked his view south, and he couldn't lean far enough away from the rocks to see much east or west.

Liu and Powder, meanwhile, worked to extricate the stolen equipment from the belly of the helicopter. They began making a pile a few yards below the wreckage.

"Fuckin' commie metal ain't worth shit," said Powder as he bent the Hind's sides back to get more gear. "Where's their quality control? Look at this—fuckin' paper."

"Rig some explosives to blow the gear," Danny told them. "My gun anywhere in there?"

As he tried to duck down to see, he heard the rumble of an aircraft running through the mountains nearby.

Aboard *Raven*, over Iran
2010

FENTRESS SAW THE HELICOPTERS AS HE TURNED WEST-ward. They looked like cockroaches scurrying across a dirty kitchen floor.

He could feel the adrenaline shoot into his stomach. He wanted to nail those suckers badly—too badly, way too badly. If he stayed this excited, he was going to fuck it up.

"Bandits in sight," he said over the interphone. He tried to think of how Zen would say it, the offhand tone he'd use.

No, he wasn't Major Jeff Stockard, war hero, fighter

jock. There was no sense even trying. He had to be himself—
a little too shy, a little too ready to salute. Hesitant at first,
but once he was into it, damn good.

Damn good.

"Four Iraqi helicopters on two-eight-zero heading,
edge of our box, right at the edge there, moving fifty
knots," he told Alou. "I'm positioning to engage." He
cleared his throat, pushed upright in his seat.

The computer gave a warning—five seconds to discon-
nect.

"*Raven,* please hang with me," he said.

"*Raven.* Go for it, Hawk leader. I'm alerting the rest of
the troops."

Aboard *Wild Bronco*
2018

MACK CHOPPED HIS POWER AS CLOSE TO STALL SPEED AS
he could; gliders went faster than the plane was flying.
They flew higher too—he was less than two hundred feet
over the rocks and scrubby bushes that passed for vegeta-
tion. The OV-10 Bronco had been designed for taking a
close look at the ground; it was arguably one of the best
forward air control aircraft ever designed. Still, picking
things out from the air was a difficult art. Not for nothing
were Bronco crewmen in Vietnam considered among the
bravest guys in the service.

And just maybe the craziest.

Maybe he was looking in the wrong place. Mack held
his course about a mile farther, then spun back. He began
tacking west, checking the INS against the paper map he
had spread over his right knee. He'd used a grease pencil
to plot his search area; he double-checked it now against
the coordinates he'd written on the canopy glass. From

what he figured, he was maybe two miles north of the spot where the Eagle pilots had nailed the Hind. He plowed through the imaginary X, banked, and brought his speed up to 160 knots, close to what he figured the helicopter would be traveling.

Helo pilot is lower than this, he thought. Radar has him here, missile coming there, maybe he sees it and freaks.

Mack pushed his nose down, sliding even closer to the jagged rocks.

Missile tracking. Maybe the guy in the helo hasn't seen it yet. Maybe the helo deked it a bit, because, let's face it, the helicopter is what, twenty feet off the ground? Even an AMRAAM is going to have trouble in all this clutter.

So maybe it has to cut back, pilot tries to duck around.

Mack jerked his stick up as he came unexpectedly close to a rising slope. He pulled close to five g's, blood suddenly catching in his throat. Another rift opened to his left, a shallow collection of brown hills topped by splotches of white snow, ice, a runoff stream, roads in the distance.

And a ruined helicopter near the top of a hillside five hundred yards on his left, three miles farther west than anyone thought it would be.

"*Wild Bronco* to *Quicksilver*—check that, to *Coyote* AWACS, to any allied aircraft. I have the wreckage in sight. Stand by for my coordinates."

On the ground in Iraq
2019

DANNY COULD TELL THERE WERE AIRCRAFT NEARBY, HE just couldn't see them. Nor could they raise them on the radios. So when Gunny and Pretty Boy reported back that they had seen two trucks coming up the highway in their direction, he realized he had to find a way to make the team visible to the aircraft real fast.

"Liu, you and Powder go to the top of this hill, fire some pencil flares. Whatever is flying is probably ours, and even if it's Iraqi, it'll bring our guys. Once you can see the plane, the damn radios ought to work, even that Prick-90. Especially that. Gunny, you and Pretty Boy get the others ready to evac. Blow the laser shit if we can't get it out."

"Gotcha, Captain," said Pretty Boy.

"Wait. Where's that bazooka thing? You got any missiles left?"

"The bunker buster? The SMAW?"

"Yeah. I'm going to take the trucks out while you guys get picked up."

"Fuck that," said Gunny. "I'll go."

"They may need you here," said Danny.

"Come on, Captain. Those pussies are wet for us down there," said the sergeant, who scooped up the weapon as well as a Minimi and started downhill.

**Aboard *Wild Bronco*, over Iraq
2020**

MACK HEARD ALOU SAY THEY WERE GOING TO SPLASH THE Iraqi helicopters and cursed. The one thing he could probably—make that definitely—nail, and they were a stinking fifteen miles south. Two Sidewinders—pop, pop. That would make their day. If only he had them.

Stinking wimp Iraqi bastards.

He passed low over the wreckage, circling around the peak and keeping the area on his right wing. He still couldn't tell if those were people near it, but they sure as hell looked like people, and damn, what else could they be? Moving trees?

He fought the Bronco a bit around the peak, the mountain air beating the wings like a driver whipping the backside of a horse. The plane drifted to the left but otherwise hung with him after he kissed the throttle. As he tucked back right, white light flashed in the distance, and for a long, cold second he thought they'd been wrong about where the laser was—he thought he was about to be fried. Distracted, he came through his bank much tighter than he'd intended, and so passed directly over the peak before he could get a good look at the ground. As he turned back he realized the flash had come from glass or a mirror that had caught the sinking sun.

This time he had a good long look at the crash site. Two men were standing on the slope above the helicopter, waving their arms. He dipped his wings, then clicked the radio to tell the others that he definitely had people on the ground. At the same time he changed course to find out what had caught the sun.

**Aboard *Raven*, over Iraq
2021**

THE FACT THAT HE HAD TO KEEP HIS SPEED BACK TO STAY close to *Raven* helped Fentress more than he would have imagined, corralling some of his nervous energy. Four helicopters were flying in an elongated and slightly staggered diamond pattern ten miles off his nose. He had a perfect intercept on the chopper on the east wing, the second in line. The computer had them ID'd as Russian-made Mil Mi-8 Hips, general-purpose troop-carrying birds that could also carriage missiles; his attack should be prudent but not overly cautious. The computer's tactics section had a course plotted that would allow him to machine-gun the two wing helos, accelerating past and then around for a rear-quarter attack on the survivors. That would expose him to possible antiair fire from only one of the aircraft while maximizing the damage on the formation. But Fentress realized that might not accomplish his main objective, which was to protect the ground team—the first helicopter would be within four or five miles of the wreckage at intercept; by the time he recovered and caught up, it would be in a position to disgorge its troops.

So he decided on his own plan. He'd take a few quick shots at the wing helo, but then concentrate on the leader, slashing close enough to the formation to scatter it, at least temporarily. The computer acknowledged, dotting the course for him and then stepping into the background as he closed. Fentress tried to deepen his breathing, pacing himself through the long wait—all of twenty-three seconds, counted down by the computer.

"*Raven*, I'm about to engage." He had the wing helo on visual.

"*Raven*. Kick ass, Hawk leader."

"Nail the mothers, Curly."

Zen's voice caught him by surprise. Before he could turn to see if he had truly heard him, the computer gave him a prompt, claiming it was in range to fire.

OBJECTS FLEW AROUND ZEN'S HEAD WITHOUT ANY LOGICAL sense. He saw Breanna dancing, saw himself walking, saw his wheelchair tumbling as if lost in a zero-gravity orbit around his head. He fought to get away from riddled unconsciousness, swam toward reality, the seat on the Flighthawk deck of *Raven*. Fentress was there somewhere. Fentress needed his help.

Fentress stood with a pair of Colt .45s, taking potshots

on the shooting range. Clay pigeons morphed into real pigeons, which morphed into hawks, which morphed into helicopters.

Helicopters, enemy helicopters.

"Nail the mothers, Curly," he shouted. "Lead helo first. Knock the others off course. Go!"

AS THE FIRING BAR FLASHED RED, FENTRESS REMEMBERED Zen's advice about the computer being slightly optimistic. He started to count off three seconds to himself, but his adrenaline got the better of him; his finger depressed the trigger after one. Just under a hundred 20mm bullets perforated the engine and then the cabin and then the engine of the Hip; the chopper dipped and then fell below his target pipper. Fentress let off on the trigger, pushing right for the lead helicopter. The cannon's recoil had stolen some of his momentum, but he managed to turn tightly, and found his target on his right wing. The bar flashed red and he began firing immediately, the bullets trailing downward as the Hip jinked left. Flares shot from the rear of the helicopter. Fentress managed a quick angle shot but couldn't hope to maneuver behind the helicopter.

He hit the gas and boogied away, gaining speed and altitude for a second run. Turning his wing for a dive back, he saw one of the helicopters streak across his view to the left, and he hesitated a moment, surprised that it had managed to get by him. The hesitation cost him a shot on a second Hip, which came at him from less than half a mile away, chin gun blazing. Reflexes took over; Fentress tucked over and dove for the ground, spinning into a tight turn to put his nose back in the direction the helicopters had taken. At the same time, the AWACS controller warned that the rescue chopper, an MH-60 spec ops craft, was zero-one from pickup.

"Hawk," he said, lining up on a Hip.

On the ground in Iraq
2030

DANNY MANAGED TO SLIDE TO THE GROUND BEHIND THE rocks as Gunny shouted; the tight report of the spotting round was followed by the heavier thump and whiz of the 83mm rocket from the Marine's SMAW. Danny pushed up in time to see the rocket plow through the windshield of the pickup truck, exploding in a hiss of steam. The dozen men packed into the rear were caught as they tried to jump; they burst out of the dust cloud in pieces.

The other truck jerked right but stayed on the wide road, avoiding the wreckage of the first pickup and gunning its engine. Three or four men began firing Kalashnikovs over the cab.

"Well, we got their attention," said Gunny, throwing the now empty SMAW down and pulling up his light machine gun.

As the Iraqi gunfire began pinging into the nearby rocks, Gunny poured 5.56mm slugs into the front end of the truck. The white pickup kept coming for about twenty feet, then rolled over in flames. A second explosion shot debris everywhere; Danny felt something whack against his chest and arm as he ducked. He saw or felt Gunny pushing off to his left, trying to swing his gun up; Danny threw himself around and opened fire in that direction. Something shrieked, then cried in pain. Danny continued to fire, spraying bullets left and right. Iraqis were less than twenty yards away, maybe closer.

"All right, all right, all right," Danny yelled, telling himself to stop firing, to get discipline.

Hunkering down, he reached for a fresh clip and slammed the new bullets home. The Marine sergeant was curled against a rock to his left, no longer firing.

God—did I shoot him?

Danny looked to the left up the slope, saw nothing. A bullet ricocheted off one of the stones behind him. He threw himself flat on his stomach, then crawled back toward the road. There were at least two Iraqi soldiers in a ditch paralleling the highway about twenty feet from his position. The truck smoldered behind them; there might be more men sheltered there, though it was impossible to tell.

He knew they'd have a good line on Gunny. He'd have to drag him to cover.

As he got up, one of the Iraqis in the ditch opened fire. Danny dropped. The bullets just missed.

The Iraqis' line of fire only extended about five or six yards up the slope; Danny knew he could probably make it past them, thanks to his body armor. But carrying Gunny would slow him down considerably. He'd have to take out the bastards first.

"Gunny!" he yelled.

No answer.

Jesus, he thought. *If I killed him, what will I do?*

Aboard *Quicksilver*, over Iraq
2035

AT 25,000 FEET, *QUICKSILVER* WAS WELL ABOVE THE AC-tion, though thanks to the continually updated photos from the Dreamland mini-KH satellite, they had a ring-side seat. The Flighthawk was fencing with the Iraqi heli-copters; two were down but the other two were now within two miles of the pickup zone. The rescue Black-hawk MH-60 raced toward the site, balls-out; he'd get there maybe sixty seconds after the Iraqi helos.

"*Quicksilver* to Hawk leader. Stand off. We'll get the Hips with our AMRAAMs," she said.

Her copilot didn't wait for the command, opening the bay door as he zeroed in on the target.

"Hawk leader?" she repeated. "Stand off. We have to nail those helos now. Zen?"

"Zen's not flying the Flighthawk," Ferris said. "Fentress is."

Aboard *Raven*, over Iraq
2040

THE HELICOPTER GREW FAT IN HIS CUE. AS FENTRESS pressed the trigger, he heard Breanna's hail.

He hesitated a second, just long enough for the helicopter to cut right and drop, avoiding him. He tucked right, began shooting anyway, lost the helicopter. He had to throw the Flighthawk left to avoid a looming cliff face—if the rocks had been covered with moss, he would have scraped it off.

"Shit!" he cursed, flailing right after the helo.

"Stay within yourself," said Zen.

"I can't."

"Yes you can."

"Zen?"

"It's me. Hold on—*Quicksilver* wants you to stand off. They're targeting with AMRAAMs."

He pulled back. "Hawk leader to *Quicksilver*. Acknowledged. They're yours."

"Fox One!" said Chris Ferris, the copilot in *Quicksilver*, announcing the missile shot.

In the next second the AWACS controller broke in.

"*Quicksilver, Raven, Wild Bronco*—break ninety immediately! Bandits off runway at A-3. MiGs! Break! Break!"

Aboard *Wild Bronco*, over Iraq
2045

MACK SMITH SAW THE PICKUP TRUCK BURST INTO FLAMES
as he sailed by. There were a couple of guys at the foot of
the hill near the crash site, maybe four or five hundred
yards down the slope; they had to be Americans. He tried
to radio their position to the AWACS but got overrun by
all the excitement. The Iraqi Hips were now less than
two miles away, and smoke filled the lower left quadrant of the horizon as he turned back toward the site.
The Flighthawk and *Quicksilver* were taking potshots
at the Hips, with what sounded like little success; he
couldn't help thinking he would have nailed every single one of the suckers if he'd just had guns on his damn
plane.

Because it was one serious hellcat, if you had the balls
to stick and rudder it. He put his wing just about straight
down as he turned, getting the American position in view.

"*Thunder One*, this is *Wild Bronco*," he said, trying to
reach the MH-60G rescue helicopter on its own frequency. "I have one maybe two Americans on the slope
near the road. You guys hear me?"

No answer. He could see the helicopter, an angry-
looking Pave Hawk specially modified for Special Forces
work. A man hung out the door over a machine gun as it
came in; someone on the ground moved. The helicopter
skimmed into a hover, then touched down a few yards
from the wreckage of the Hind.

Gunfire ripped from the road. There were half a dozen
Iraqis down there. Something flared—a shoulder-launched
SAM?

Shooting at him?

That did it. Mack pushed his stick in and pirouetted in

the sky, kicking out diversionary flares. He'd run the motherfuckers over if he had to.

On the ground in Iraq
2050

THE ROTORS OF THE MH-60G PAVE HAWK SPEC OP HELO continued to spin as the Whiplash wounded were loaded in. The rotors made an odd whirling sound, a kind of low whistle, as if the Sikorsky herself were telling them to get a move on.

Powder helped Liu shoulder the litter into the helicopter as the door gunner let loose another burst in the general direction of the Iraqi ground troops. Something whizzed behind him, and Powder threw himself to the ground. The mountain shuddered, and the helicopter, hovering less than a foot off the dirt, reared to the side.

"Mortars!" he shouted. "Fucks have mortars!"

He jumped up, saw Liu in front of him and grabbed him.

"Into the helicopter!" he shouted. He scooped up his gun from the ground. "Go! Go!"

Liu started to say something, but Powder just pushed him toward the Blackhawk. He heard another round of incoming and dove forward down the slope.

"Get the helo off," he yelled. "It's a sitting duck!"

Aboard *Wild Bronco*, over Iraq
2055

THE BASTARDS DUCKED AS HE CLOSED IN, BUT AS MACK approached the ground a mortar shell shot up toward the slope.

If he only had a stinking gun.

"*Coyote* AWACS—this is Bronco. Get that helo off the ground! Now! They're going to get roasted. Go. Come on. No time to be a hero. Go! Take off. Jesus," said Mack, still talking as he rolled back north.

"*Bronco*. There are two MiGs headed for you," answered the AWACS controller. "Get out of there!"

"Hey, screw yourself," said Mack, though he didn't press the send button. "Think I'm a wimp or something?"

On the ground in Iraq
2057

DANNY COULD SEE WHERE THEY WERE FIRING THE MORTAR from. He had a fragmentation grenade and thought he might be able to reach the mortar if he could get any sort of weight behind the throw. But that would expose him to the Iraqis in the ditch.

Stand up, toss the grenade as quickly as he could, duck back down, he told himself.

That would leave him with two smoke grenades. Use one to cover his retreat up the hillside. Use the other to deke them, give him a clear toss at the mortar.

A fresh burst of AK-47 bullets kicked through the nearby dirt. As the mortar whizzed again, Danny lobbed a smoke grenade in the direction of the ditch, waiting for it to land, judging—hoping—the Iraqis would see it and duck. He counted two seconds, then rose and wailed the fragmentation grenade at the men with the mortar.

His knee buckled with the throw. The grenade sailed only about twenty yards. As he fell his arms sailed out, spread-eagle, a rush of pain coming over him.

Danny swam back through the dirt, grabbing his gun and steadying his aim on the ditch. His eyes narrowed down to slits, compressed by a fresh wave of pain at the top of his head. He felt as if someone had taken a nail gun and plastered a dozen spikes through the top of his helmetless skull. He heard a sound like a vacuum, thought it must be the mortar, and fired wildly. He saw an Iraqi as the smoke wafted clear. The man turned toward him with a pistol, and Danny leveled his MP-5 and fired. The bullets spun him back, his pistol falling at his feet.

The mortar lay on the ground, beyond another body.

The Pave Hawk roared above somewhere. Other helicopters, other planes, gunfire—the noises jammed together. Danny stopped listening. Dirt tore at his eyes. He needed to rest; the sensation overwhelmed him.

Someone was behind him.

Danny spun so fast he lost his balance. An injured Iraqi had struggled to his feet two yards away. He held his hands out, weaponless.

Danny just barely caught himself from pressing the trigger. He wanted to—he felt no mercy, knew he'd be shown none if the situation was reversed. It was wildly dangerous not to fire, but he couldn't bring himself to kill a man who had his arms up.

As Danny continued to stare at him, the Iraqi lowered his eyes. He kept his hands above his head.

A prisoner was the last thing he needed now. But he couldn't shoot the SOB. Just couldn't.

"Go," Danny told him.

The man didn't move.

"Go!" he shouted. He shot a few rounds into the air, yelling and screaming. "Go! Go! Go!"

The Iraqi, terrified, finally began to move.

"Get the hell away from here!" shouted Danny. "Go!"

The man finally seemed to understand. He began to

run, looking over his shoulder after a few steps, ducking his head a bit as if in thanks. Then he put everything he had into his stride, running into the distance.

Okay, Danny thought. *Okay. Now how the hell do I get out of here?*

POWDER REACHED GUNNY AS GUNFIRE ERUPTED A FEW yards farther away, down near the road. There was too much smoke to see anything, but he figured Captain Freah had just taken out the mortar. He turned the Marine sergeant over as gently as he could, staring at him until he saw that he was definitely breathing.

"Hey," mumbled the sergeant. "Didja get the fucker?"

"Who?" asked Powder.

"One of those bastards tried to flank us."

Powder craned his neck up. There was a body maybe ten yards across the slope.

"Any others?" Powder asked.

"Dunno. What happened to the captain?" Gunny gasped between the words.

"Probably around here somewhere."

"Water?"

Powder gave the injured Marine a drink and looked over his wounds. He had been hit in the side and the arm and lost a lot of blood. How serious the wounds were was hard to tell, but it'd all be academic if they didn't get the hell out of there ASAP.

Aboard *Wild Bronco*, over Iraq
2059

MACK TRIED TO SORT ALL THE COMMOTION OUT OVER THE common radio circuit as he shadowed the highway. The

MiGs had their afterburners lit and were two minutes away. Two F-15s had moved up to intercept but hadn't gotten radar locks yet, the amateurs. The MH-60 had been hit but was still flying; its pilot proceeded to argue with the AWACS controller about what he should and shouldn't do.

"*Wild Bronco*, you have your orders. Break ninety!"

"Bullshit. I'm not leaving guys there."

Mack passed the mortar area, saw that it had been neutralized. One of the Iraqis had even been captured.

Hell, he could put down, pick them up, and get the hell out of there before the Eagles even found the stinking MiGs.

So why not?

Why not indeed.

"*Wild Bronco* to *Coyote*—send the Blackhawk home," said Mack. "I'll pick up the rest of their passengers for them."

On the ground in Iraq
2104

THE STACCATO POUNDING IN HIS SKULL GAVE WAY TO THE steadier drone of jackhammers as Danny edged back toward the road. He saw Powder in the distance, just beyond the edge of smoke, waving and yelling something.

What the hell was he saying?

"Duck, Cap! Duck!"

Danny whirled in time to see the Bronco hop once on the highway then beeline for him. He started to back up, then fell on his rump. Grit flew over his face; the next thing he knew, Powder was helping him up. Mack Smith leaned from the open canopy about twenty yards down the roadway.

Smith yelled something but it was drowned out by the whine of the motors. Danny ran through a cloud of dust to the plane, then realized he'd lost Powder somewhere along the way. As he turned to find him, he remembered Gunny, poor dead Gunny. He put his hands to his face, funneling away the noise and grit, getting his bearings. They had to get the Marine out, give him a decent burial at least. He started back, then heard someone yelling behind him—Mack Smith maybe, telling him to get the hell into the aircraft.

"I can't leave a man, even if he's dead."

"Ain't no one dead, Cap," shouted Powder. Danny spun around and saw the Whiplash team member with a large green sack over his shoulder. "We got to get!"

Gunny—in Powder's arms.

Danny's hands fumbled with the latch to the rear compartment. Finally inside, he pulled Gunny's limp body up toward the primitive bench seat. There was no time to put on restraints as the aircraft began to move; he wrapped one arm around a strap and the other around the Marine, huddled on the floor as the aircraft suddenly became weightless.

"You saved my sorry ass again," said Gunny in the darkness. "You got the son of a bitch."

"Who?"

"The Iraqi that tried to flank us. Now I owe you again, huh? I thought I evened it out."

"It's all even," said Danny.

"SERGEANT, YOU TOUCH ANYTHING ELSE BACK THERE AND I'm hitting the eject button. You got that?"

"You can eject me from up there?"

"Damn straight," lied Mack. "You touch anything, no shit, boom, you're outta here."

"This plane's got an eject button too? I thought only

the Ruskies put them in. There was one in the helicopter I flew."

"The Ruskies got it from us," said Mack. "Keep your hands off the stick and enjoy the ride. And if you decide to puke, don't lean forward."

Aboard *Quicksilver*, over Iraq
2115

CHRIS FERRIS REMINDED BREANNA THAT THEY HAD USED their last AMRAAMs on the helicopters.

"Acknowledged," she told him. They had the two bandits on their nose now at eighteen miles, closing quickly.

"Eagles still can't find them."

"We're going to take them out, Chris," she said.

"How?"

"We'll suck them off and nail them with the Stinger air mines," she said.

"Uh, Bree, we're in *Quicksilver*, remember? We don't have Stingers."

"We'll think of something. Hold on."

Aboard *Raven*, over Iraq
2124

THE TEMPTATION TO GRAB THE CONTROLS FROM FENTRESS was overwhelming, but Zen knew the delay as C^3 cycled through the authentication made it pointless. It was all up to Curly boy.

Curly, God. Like Girly. What a horrible name for the poor kid. Shit.

"*Quicksilver* will take the lead MiG," Zen told him, staring at the main video screen. "Keep on your course.

You nail the second SOB when you close. Hang with it."

"What if the Eagles get a lock?"

"Don't worry about anybody but yourself," Zen told him. "Breathe slower."

Fentress nodded. Zen could smell the sweat pouring from his body. The kid was nervous as hell—but he'd done all right against the helicopters, and he was going to do all right here.

"Three seconds," Zen said, anticipating the computer. "I'll tell you—"

"Yo, I got it, damn it."

Zen felt his anger rile up—who the hell was Fentress talking to?

Then he realized it was the voice he'd been waiting to hear since the kid joined the program.

"Kick butt," he told his pupil.

Aboard *Quicksilver*, over Iraq
2128

THE MAMMOTH PLANE TUMBLED OVER ITS WING, SCREAM-ing toward the ground like a peregrine diving on a kill. At somewhere over 300,000 pounds with her fuel and passengers, she was more than ten times as heavy as the Mikoyan-Gurevich MiG-29 Fulcrum she dove toward. But her sleek, carbon resin wings and long fuselage were as limber as the fighter jet's, and her pilot's skill more than made up for any difference in the sheer performance of the two planes.

"Changing course and coming for us," said Chris. "Now what?"

"Torbin, are you tracking that MiG's radar?"

"Yes, ma'am."

"Bring up the weapon board and lock the Tacit Plus on him," said Bree.

"Um, can I do that?"

"You tell me."

"Bree, that'll never work," said Chris.

"Do it, Torbin," said Breanna.

"It's asking me to override," said the radar weapons officer. "I'm going for it. Yeah, we got it."

"Open bay doors."

"Bay," said Ferris. "He's firing."

"Launch," Breanna told Torbin. "And hang on!"

**Aboard *Raven*, over Iraq
2130**

THE MiG ALTERED COURSE JUST AS HE CAME WITHIN CANNON range, cutting toward him. Fentress pulled the trigger and tried to follow at the same time, pulling softly at first then cutting harder as the enemy plane rolled downward in what looked like the start of a swoop to get into a turn behind him. But it was a sucker move—the MiG flipped flat and twisted back the other way. Fentress was caught flat-footed and pointed away from his target. Struggling to stay in the game, he threw his throttle to the firewall and began turning back toward the MiG.

"Stay within yourself and remember your objective," said Zen. "Keep him off the Bronco. You don't have to shoot him down. You're doing fine."

"Right."

"Think about what he's doing. He's flying away from them—where's he going?"

Fentress felt the sweat rushing from his pores. But Zen was right—he checked his sitrep, found the helicopter ten miles north, hugging the hills.

The Bronco. Where was the Bronco?

"Eleven o'clock," said Zen. "Get there."

He had to be reading his mind. Fentress altered his course slightly, not even looking at the sitrep now, just going there.

The MiG was slightly below, a dot ahead, three miles, fading, four.

"Make it fast," said Zen. "Bronco—flares! Jink, Mack, jink, you asshole!"

Aboard *Wild Bronco*, over Iraq
2132

MACK CURSED HIS DUMB LUCK AND TIPPED HIS RIGHT WING down, sliding across the rough air currents like a kid on a saucer scooting across an icy road. He'd reached reflexively for the flares maybe ten times in the past three minutes, only to remember he had none.

One stinking Sidewinder and the MiG would be dead meat. He'd suck him close, turn inside, goose the SOB before he knew what had hit him.

But he didn't have a Sidewinder. All he could do was wait for Zen and Breanna and Fentress and who-all to wax the Iraqi. And they sure as hell were taking their time about it.

He jammed his rudder and threw his weight into the stick, pushing the plane to pivot as he ran down into a rift between two large hills; a hang-glider couldn't have turned harder or sharper.

"Yeah, no shit," he acknowledged as Zen warned that missiles were in the air. "You going to take this sucker out or am I going to have to pull out my pistol and do it myself?"

Aboard *Raven*, over Iraq
2134

ZEN WATCHED THE BRONCO TUCK AWAY FROM THE LAST heat-seeker. Much as he hated to admit it, Mack was a seriously good pilot—he deked the missile down into the hillside without even the help of a flare. Good and lucky—a tremendous combination.

"The MiG's going to slow down now and go to his cannon. Back off your speed!" Zen told Fentress.

"I have him," said Fentress, pressing the trigger to fire.

"Back off!"

Fentress let go of the trigger and slid his thrust down, but it was too late—the Flighthawk shot over the MiG, which threw up its nose to slow in a modified cobra maneuver. It was a fancier move than Zen had pulled with the Phantom drone in their training exercise, but with the same intent and effect: Fentress lost his shot and was now the target.

"Let him come after you instead of the Bronco," said Zen. "Good."

"I wish I did it on purpose," said Fentress as the MiG began firing at him.

AS THE MIG'S BULLETS STARTED SAILING OVER HIS WINGS, Fentress slammed his nose up as if he were going to do his own cobra, then juiced his throttle instead, turning a tumblesault in the sky. The g forces would have wiped out a pilot, but the only thing Fentress felt was a small bubble of sweat diving around the back of his neck. The MiG sailed by as Fentress pushed the robot toward its tail.

"He's still going for the Bronco," said Zen. "He's suicidal."

"Yeah," said Fentress.

Mack's plane ducked and the MiG sailed off to the left, then turned to come back.

Fentress knew he could try a front-quarter attack.

Low probability. Get him from the side as he came in.

Even harder.

The Bronco popped up near the ridge ahead. The MiG dove down, guns blazing. Fentress pressed his trigger, even though he had absolutely no shot, hoping he might distract the MiG.

It didn't work.

Aboard Quicksilver, over Iraq
2134

BREANNA DROPPED QUICKSILVER STRAIGHT DOWN AS Chris worked the flares and ECMs, desperately trying to avoid the heat-seeking missiles launched by the MiG. They rolled through an invert, feinted right, jagged left, powered back in the direction they'd gone.

The Iraqi had fired two heat-seekers at them; one had a defective seeker and dove directly into the earth a few seconds after launch. The other came at Quicksilver's nose, lost it momentarily, then sniffed one of the engines. As it changed course for the third or fourth time to follow Breanna's jinks, it sensed one of the flares and started after it. A half second later it realized this was a decoy and went back for its original target. But the hesitation had cost it; sensing that its target was accelerating out of range, it self-detonated. Shrapnel nicked the top of the Megafortress's fuselage, but there was simply too much plane there for the small shards of metal to do real damage; Quicksilver shrugged the pain away like a whale ignoring a tiny fishhook.

In the meantime, Quicksilver's radar-homing missile

shot toward the Iranian MiG at about 600 miles an hour. The MiG pilot threw his plane into evasive maneuvers, rolling and plunging away behind a hail of flares and tinsel. The missile followed gamely; while it wasn't nearly as maneuverable as an air-to-air missile, it had extremely long legs—the Iraqi's RWR continued to warn that it was gunning for him, even after he went to the afterburner and galloped back toward his base. As far as he knew, the Americans had launched a superweapon at him, one that refused to be fooled by anything he did.

"We're clear," said Chris finally. "MiG is out of the picture. Tacit's still following him," he added, a chuckle in his voice. "We may nail him yet. Good shot, Torbin."

"Thanks," said their newest crewman. "Uh, that standard operating procedure, firing ground missiles at airplanes?"

"It is now," said Ferris.

"We aim to be creative," said Breanna. "Welcome to the team."

Aboard *Wild Bronco*, over Iraq
2135

A STREAM OF TRACERS SHOT OVER MACK'S CANOPY AS HE plunked his nose down again. He cut his throttle and coasted half a second, making sure the Iraqi would overshoot. Then he gunned it and whipped back onto the other side of the mountain.

Mack laughed as he caught sight of the MiG flying parallel to him. Idiot! One stinking Sidewinder and it'd be fried Iraqi for dinner.

He could do this all day, all day.

Mack's laughter turned to a roar as the MiG turned ahead of him, completely out of the game.

At least for the next fifteen seconds.

**Aboard *Raven*, over Iraq
2136**

ZEN WATCHED FENTRESS AS THE MIG CUT IN FRONT OF the Bronco's path. The kid's hands were steady, even if his voice was jumpy and high-pitched.

But he was nearly out of bullets. And the MiG pilot now had an angle on the Bronco, realizing that his best bet was to fire from the edge of his range rather than closing in where the Bronco could easily throw him off by turning or changing speed.

Mack was doing a hell of a job, but sooner or later he was going to get nailed. His plane was too overmatched.

Fentress had enough bullets for maybe one more try.

Zen knew he could nail it. But by the time he grabbed control it would be too late.

Helpless. Like when he lost his legs.

His legs—he remembered the dream or hallucination or whatever it was, the fleeting memory of feelings that had just rummaged through his brain.

This had nothing to do with that.

He looked at his pupil.

"Get him on this pass, Curly. Nail the motherfucker and let's go have a beer," said Zen.

ZEN'S VOICE DROVE THE FRUSTRATION AWAY. FENTRESS drew a breath, then blew it out his mouth with a long, slow whistle. He'd ride the Flighthawk into the damn MiG if he had to.

That wasn't a horrible idea. He had a straight intercept plotted. If his bullets didn't nail the MiG, he would.

Not a conventional solution, but better than letting the Bronco get waxed.

The OV-10 flailed to the right and the MiG snapped back to follow. Fentress's targeting bar flashed red.

Too soon to fire, he told himself, counting.

Aboard *Wild Bronco*, over Iraq
2137

MACK POUNDED THE PEDAL, TRYING TO THROW ALL HIS weight into his foot, and pushed the Bronco back the other way. He could feel the plane stutter, though whether it was because he'd been hit or because it was getting tired of the acrobatics he couldn't tell. The right engine freaked and now he had trouble holding the plane in the air.

The MiG had him fat in its pipper.

"Suck on this, raghead!" he shouted, pushing the OV-10 into a desperation dive as the left engine gave out and the emergency lights indicated it was on fire.

Aboard *Raven*, over Iraq
2138

THE COMPUTER TRIED TO GET HIM TO STOP, BUT HE WAS balls-out committed now. The cannon clicked empty and the MiG kept coming and Fentress could see the Iraqi pilot hunkering over his stick, so intent on nailing his quarry that he didn't even see the Flighthawk closing in. The screen flashed and C^3 gave him a verbal warning as well as a proximity tone, but all he could hear was Zen's calm voice.

"Nail 'em. Now."

The Iraqi pilot saw something and turned his head toward the side, leaning back in the direction of the Flighthawk.

Then the screen went blank.

ZEN FELL BACK IN THE SEAT, AS EXHAUSTED AS IF HE'D flown the plane himself. He let his head go all the way back, staring at the compartment ceiling.

It wasn't exactly what he would have done—it wasn't, quite frankly, as good as he would have done. But Fentress had saved the Bronco.

"Wild Bronco to Hawk leader."

Zen turned toward Fentress, who sat stone still in his seat.

"Yo, Hawk leader. Nice flying, Zen boy." Mack was laughing, the SOB.

"Hawk," said Zen. "But that was Fentress who nailed the MiG."

"Fentress, no shit. Good shootin', nugget boy."

Fentress said nothing, pulling off his helmet.

"What's your status, Bronco?" Zen asked.

"Lost an engine. Probably got a little wing damage. Nothing we can't live with. We ought to get some of these planes at Dreamland," Mack added. "Best stinking plane I ever flew."

Zen turned Mack over to Alou so they could discuss the course home. In the meantime, Fentress eased his restraints and leaned back in the seat. He looked white, beat as hell.

"Hey, that was a kick-ass move," Zen told him. "You used your head."

"Yeah."

"I mean it," said Zen. "You did good. You saved the Bronco."

"Yeah. I did."

"Listen, we can come up with something besides Curly. How about Hammer or Sleek or something?"

Fentress shrugged, then turned his head toward Zen. He looked tired, and sweat had soaked his curly locks. But he still smiled. "Curly's okay. Kinda fits."

"You did okay, kid," said Zen. "You did okay."

Not only did he mean it, he actually felt a little proud.

VII

The Easy Way

———

DANNY GROANED AS HE PULLED HIS ARMS OVER THE MA-rine corpsmen helping him out of the Bronco. Pain and fatigue had settled over him like a patina on a bronze statue; it was so much a part of him that he had forgotten what it felt like not to hurt. Once out of the aircraft, he made an effort to move his legs and began insisting that he didn't need the stretcher waiting a few feet away.

"Hey, Cap, happy Memorial Day," said Powder, walking over.

"Uh-huh."

"Chinook's comin' to evac the wounded over to Incir-lik. That means you, Cap," added Powder.

"Where?" asked Danny.

"Incirlik."

"The helicopter, I mean. Where is it?"

"Inbound," said Nurse. "You gotta go, Cap. That leg's for shit and I bet you got internal bleeding in your chest there. Head's banged too. You look woozy."

"E-ternal bleeding," said Powder.

"Corporal's lost a lot of blood. I'd give him better than fifty-fifty," added Liu. "Gunny's cursing his butt off over there on the litter—you hear him? Took some hits in the chest and leg."

Danny shook his head. Nurse tried to gently prod him toward the stretcher.

"Hey, don't shove me," Danny said.

"We'll take care of stuff here," said Liu. "Major Alou says we're going home soon—Marines taking over the base."

"What happened to the laser parts?" Danny asked.

"Waiting for FedEx," said Powder. "That or the Marines, whoever gets here first. Bison and the boys got them all aboard the Blackhawk before it took off."

Danny heard a helicopter approaching in the distance. He tried turning in its direction, then gave up. Nurse was right—he ought to take it slow.

"Hey, Captain, next time can I drive the helicopter?" asked Powder.

"Sure thing," said Danny, letting them ease him onto the stretcher.

Dreamland Command Center
1700

THE TIME HAD COME FOR THE SHIT TO HIT THE FAN. DOG stood in the middle of the room, waiting for the connection to snap through. When it did, General Magnus's face was redder than he expected, though his tone was one of sympathy and even sadness.

"Colonel."

"General."

"Your men?"

"As far as I know, they're all okay." Dog held his head erect, shoulders stiff. "The missile that hit the Hind struck the top of the aircraft when they were about ten feet off the ground. It carried through the engine housing before exploding. They crashed, but they were very lucky."

"Any friendly fire incident needs a full investigation," said Magnus.

"Yes, sir, of course."

"I heard a rumor that your people carried this out on their own initiative," said Magnus. "That they were responding to a fluid situation, and reacted. Properly, with justification, but without a full plan in place. That would account for CentCom not getting the proper notification."

Something jumped inside Dog's chest. Was Magnus suggesting he lie to avert what might be a politically embarrassing investigation?

Maybe. It might avoid problems, short-circuit months of hand-wringing that wouldn't benefit anyone—including him, Dog knew.

But it was a lie.

"I ordered that mission, sir. I felt the Whiplash directive was sufficient authorization. I stand by my decision."

Magnus nodded. "Colonel, if I told you that you were relieved of command, would that be an order you were prepared to follow?"

"Of course."

Magnus pushed his lips together. Dog felt his neck muscles stiffen; the room turned cold. "Is that what is happening here?"

"No," said Magnus. "Not at all."

"Sir?"

"It's no secret that I and the administration don't see eye-to-eye," said the general, his tone changing.

"If I've done anything—"

Magnus's stern expression broke for just a moment. "You're about the only thing we agree on," said Magnus. "You're a good man, Colonel. You made the right call and you stood behind it." The general paused, but before Dog could say anything else, he went on, his tone even softer than before. "Dreamland is going to be—excuse me, the command structure involving Dreamland is going to be changed."

"In what way?"

"Good question," said Magnus. "All I know at the moment is that you are no longer my concern. Dreamland is no longer part of my command."

Flustered, Dog tried to think of what to say. "JSOC?" he said finally. "Are we under the Special Forces Command?"

"No," said Magnus. "I'm late for a meeting right now, I'm sorry," he added. "Orders will be cut soon. I'm not privy to them."

"Who do we answer to—I mean, who's our commander?"

"The President," said Magnus.

"Of course," said Dog, "but I mean—"

The screen flashed white, the connection cut, without further elaboration.

In Iraq
31 May 1997
0607

JED BARCLAY SETTLED HIS HANDS ONTO HIS THIGHS, FINgers rapping to the beat of the rotor as the MH-60 Special Forces Blackhawk whipped toward the agreed exchange site near Kirkuk in northern Iraq. The Iraqi radar operator sat next to him on the shallow and uncomfortable jump seat, as much of a mystery to Jed as when they first met. The Iraqis had agreed to exchange the remains of the two American pilots who had died for the live prisoner. Jed had objected—though he hadn't told them anything, the man clearly knew a great deal about the state of Iraqi defenses and their tactics. Having gone to RPI, he might be an engineer or some sort of scientist, not merely a technician. But everyone else had dismissed his objections—Americans, even dead ones, were worth more than any information the Iraqi could possibly give.

They had a point. The barrage tactics hadn't been effective; it was clear now that the Iranian laser had shot down most if not all the aircraft lost in the last few days.

Part of their Greater Islamic Glory campaign? Jed had his doubts. They had made overtures to the U.S., acted as if they wanted to help in the war against Saddam, even made noises about getting rid of the Chinese. Perhaps they'd found the communist yoke a little too much to bear, even in the name of Allah.

Jed hadn't even tried to sort it out yet. The NSA intercepts would make interesting reading once he got home. So would the reports on the laser. It was unlikely that they'd killed everyone associated with the weapon. Would it turn up again? If so, where? Iran? China? Something to ponder back home.

The helicopter began banking for a turn. Jed glanced at the Iraqi. His eyes gave nothing away. Maybe he was thinking of the hero's welcome that awaited him on the ground.

MUSAH TAHIR SAT PATIENTLY UNTIL THE AMERICANS LIFTED him from the bench toward the exit of the helicopter. His hands were unbound at the top of the ramp, then his guards gave him a slight push; they seemed almost anxious to be rid of him.

The light of the Iraqi afternoon blinded him. A row of soldiers stood at attention a few feet away. A pair of pickup trucks sat behind them.

Tahir took a few steps, then turned and watched as the pickup trucks backed toward the helicopter. A metal coffin sat in each. Two Americans from the helicopter nodded grimly at the Iraqis in the back of the trucks; they shouldered the coffins and slid them into the helicopters, arranging them awkwardly in the interior. Tahir seemed to have been forgotten.

He had wanted to say good-bye to Barclay. The American struck him as a decent man. But Barclay signed some papers for an Iraqi Air Force colonel Tahir didn't know, then got on the helicopter without looking back at him.

It lifted with a roar. Tahir looked toward the colonel but he had disappeared. Turning, he nearly fell over General Hadas, the man who had first given him his mission.

"General," he said, snapping a salute. "I told them nothing."

Hadas frowned and raised his hand. There was a pistol in it. By the time Tahir realized what would happen, the gun was level with his forehead. He had time only to close his eyes before it fired.

Anhik Base, Iran
0610

THE RUINS CONTINUED TO SMOLDER. THE STRIKE HAD BEEN quick and precise; they had examined the laser, then destroyed it. At least twenty of Sattari's soldiers were dead, probably many more.

His duty was to go to them now, to comfort them, to rally them for the challenges ahead. Khamenei or the Chinese might choose this moment to mount their own attack. Perhaps some unknown rival or rivals might be encouraged.

A small part of him wanted to flee. Another small part

wanted him to end the struggle completely—to give in to the urge of futility, to no longer fight the tide. Suicide would be so easy, a matter merely of pulling the handgun from his belt and placing it into his mouth.

Sattari felt a shiver run through his body. A prudent commander might find it necessary to retreat or even to surrender. But while he lived, there was hope, there was always hope.

Killing himself was the coward's way.

He had one thing to live for now—revenge. He would get the men who did this. He would destroy the black-robed traitors. He might, if his rage continued unabated, destroy the whole world.

Sattari felt his heart stutter in his chest, overcome by the anger he felt.

But then it calmed. It was a soldier's heart, trained to survive. Anger was meaningless to it.

He had known the risks and calculated them; if things seemed bleak now, they were not as bleak as they could be. He would survive, and he would have his vengeance.

The general began to walk down the road, past the parked vehicles, ignoring his driver's call, ignoring the questions from the bodyguards. He would walk into his post by foot; he would comfort his men; he would rebuild.

Incirlik
0805

FACED WITH THE LONG PLANE RIDE HOME AND NOTHING TO do, Zen had decided to do something he hadn't done on an airplane in a long, long time—read a book.

But High Top didn't have much of a library. In fact, it didn't have any library at all. When they landed at Incirlik, Bree told him he didn't have time to explore—they were only here to refuel. And since when was he reading books, anyway?

Fortunately, his cousin Jed Barclay came by to say hello.

"You have any books handy?" Zen asked his cousin after they exchanged the usual back and forth.

"*Computers and Foreign Policy Decisions During the Twenty-first Century*," Jed suggested. "Hot topic."

"How about something else?" said Zen.

Jed, who was lugging his bags en route to a transport, knelt down and pored through them on the Megafortress's Flighthawk deck. "Coonts thriller?"

"Read 'em all. Most of 'em twice."

"Well, I have volume one of Burns's biography of FDR," said Jed, retrieving the book. "Good book."

"FDR?" Zen looked at the large paperback, which seemed to have been used as a football, door stop, and hammer.

Roosevelt. He'd been paralyzed too, right.

Good book for a gimp.

Zen had started to reach for the book but now stopped. He remembered the hallucination of pain he'd had, the feeling that his legs were still part of him.

They were part of him. They were there. They just weren't *there* anymore.

Was he doomed to think about them forever, at his worst times?

"I've been reading it for a year," Jed was saying, holding it out. "When I was in college, this professor—"

"Okay," said Zen, taking the book to forestall a long dissertation.

Knowing Jed, he didn't even make the connection about Roosevelt being paralyzed. Zen's cousin was the perfect absent-minded professor—an expert on the world, oblivious about what was in front of him.

"Wish I could fly back with you," said Jed.

"You can, cuz," said Breanna, coming up the access ladder at the rear of the Flighthawk control bay. "We have a jump seat upstairs. Let me stow your gear."

"Can't." Jed gave her a peck on the cheek. "I'm supposed to be in D.C. tonight."

"Then you better hustle. Your plane's about to take off." She winked at Zen.

Jed turned white. "Oh, man, I'm in for it now," he said, grabbing his things and rushing down the ladder.

"It's not, is it?"

"I was just talking to them on the radio," said Breanna. "He's got an hour and a half."

"You're cruel," Zen told Breanna.

"He's cute when he's dizzy. Kind of reminds me of a puppy I used to have."

"Hmmmph."

"So?"

"So what?"

"How's the head?" She put her fingers softly on the lump at his forehead where he'd smashed it against the panel when the restraint loosened during their evasive maneuvers. Somebody estimated that the force must have been over seven g's. Still, the restraint should have held.

Zen shrugged. He had a mild concussion, along with assorted bruises and whatnot. After losing his legs, other injuries seemed almost besides the point, not even annoying.

Legs again.

"You did okay with Fentress, huh?" said Bree.

"He did okay."

"It's hard, teaching."

"I wouldn't want to do it for a living."

"You said that. But you did okay with him somehow." She leaned into him and gave him a long, soft kiss.

"No smooching on the job," he said when she finished.

"Try and stop me." She kissed him again. "He said he thinks of you as a father figure," she said as they separated.

"Go to hell."

Laughing, she retreated to the ladder. "Start reading, Major," she said, starting up to the flight deck. "It's a long ride home."

If you enjoyed *Razor's Edge,*
then get ready for the pulse-pounding excitement of
AIR BATTLE FORCE . . .

———

Read on to experience the high-octane action
of Dale Brown's new suspense thriller
Available in hardcover from
William Morrow June 2003

Ghowrmach border crossing, near Andkhvoy
Faryab province, northern Afghanistan
January 2003

CAPTAIN WAKIL MOHAMMAD ZARAZI DEPLOYED TWO OF his youngest, most inexperienced—and therefore most expendable—troops right beside the road for the ambush, promising them promotions and high honors if they survived—and a place at the right hand of God if they were killed. Yes, they still believed they would get both.

The boys hid behind piles of snow and rocks until the lead armored personnel carrier, an old Russian-made BMP, cruised by, then threw RKG-3 anti-tank hand grenades under the chassis. When they were rolled under the BMPs they righted themselves, then fired copper-sheathed, high-explosive, hollow-charge warheads up into the crew compartment. The molten copper blew through the ten-millimeter armor underneath, then spattered molten copper throughout the crew compartment, instantly killing any soldiers inside. The BMP died quickly and messily—and hopefully, Zarazi thought, all on board did, too.

His men, emboldened by the success of this first attack, streamed out of their hiding places and went on the offensive, hitting the other vehicles in the convoy with small arms fire. To Zarazi, the company commander of the guerrilla forces that surprised this small United Nations detachment, the apparent success of the hastily-planned ambush was a surprise. His men had been on the move for months in some of northern Afghanistan's worst weather; they were cold, tired, starving, and low on ammunition, morale, and courage, as well as continually hounded by American and United Nations air forces.

Maybe they had such clear success because starving men made better fighters—if they didn't succeed, they were dead.

Their intelligence said this detachment, moving west from Andkhvoy since just yesterday to set up a communications relay site somewhere along the border, would have better security. Zarazi's unit was well below full company strength, but they hurried to be in position to make this ambush anyway because of the chance to capture some better weapons and vehicles to use in their guerrilla war against the Northern Alliance. Zarazi was disappointed at the small size of the detachment—he was hoping for more weapons and more captives. He might only get fifty captives and a few weeks' worth of food and supplies out of this convoy. Still, it was better than nothing.

Zarazi was suspicious, too—a quality that had kept him alive for most of his thirty-eight years, twenty-two of them as a Taliban freedom fighter. Zarazi was born in northwest Afghanistan near Sheberghan. Originally a member of the Mujahadeen guerrilla fighters that battled the Russians, Zarazi's tribe refused to join the so-called Northern Alliance, composed mostly of ethnic Uzbeks, Tajiks, and Pakistanis, and instead took large numbers of Russian weapons and vehicles and moved back to its historic provinces in the northwest. He became a provincial commander of the *Hizb-i-Allah*, or Army of God, a radical and fundamentalist sect of the Taliban regime that harassed the Northern Alliance forces at every opportunity.

This substantial and apparently important detachment, moving thirty kilometers west of Andkhvoy toward the northeastern edge of the Bedentlik wastelands on the Turkmenistan-Afghanistan border, presented the perfect opportunity to make a major strike against the Northern Alliance and its Western puppetmasters. Still, it was strange they had no heavy armor or helicopter support anywhere nearby. The closest helicopter base camp was twenty minutes away; the closest large military base was over an hour away by helicopter. And some bad weather was closing in—a sandstorm, most likely—so help would take even longer to arrive.

The intelligence data was remarkably detailed and timely, too—maybe too detailed and timely. Although the Northern Alliance forces, aided by the United States, had effectively wiped out the Taliban militias in this area, Zarazi thought it strange that the United Nations would dare send such an important detail so far away from their strongholds without support. The Taliban still had a large and, for the most part, well-equipped and viable guerrilla force, especially near the Tajikistan, Uzbekistan, and Tadjikistan frontiers, where friendly forces were more plentiful and the terrain more hospitable. The Turkmenistan-Afghan frontier was nothing but desert for a thousand kilometers—obviously the United Nations forces never thought they would encounter any resistance out here in the wastelands.

The infidels' overconfidence would be their downfall.

The scout vehicles deployed in front of the column were Russian BTR-40 and larger BTR-60s wheeled reconnaissance trucks—fast, nimble, and very well-armed. They turned and scattered as soon as the first BMP exploded. Zarazi's men started lobbing smoke grenades from all over the area—it took dozens of them to create enough of a screen in the ever-increasing, swirling winds, but within moments visibility had been cut to just a few yards. The gunports were already open, the soldiers inside looking for targets.

That was exactly what Zarazi was waiting for. His men dashed out from their hiding places under cover of the smoke, jumped aboard the BTRs, and stuffed tear gas grenades into the open gunports. Within moments, the drivers were forced to stop their vehicles to evacuate the soldiers inside before they were asphyxiated from the noxious gas. Soon, all of the trucks in the convoy had stopped, billowing with tear gas. The hatches and doors opened, and terrified and nearly suffocating United Nations soldiers and workers dashed out, their eyes swollen and burning. The battle took less than five minutes. Zarazi's men had destroyed one BMP and one BTR and captured one BMP, four BTR scouts, and four five-ton trucks loaded with supplies. No casualties. Perfect.

"We hit the mother lode, Captain," Zarazi's lieutenant, Jalaluddin Turabi, said a few moments later as the crews and workers were being herded together. "Looks like they were going to set up a semi-permanent outpost. They have two weeks' worth of food for about fifty men, plus boxes labeled 'Communications Equipment.' I see power generators, fuel tanks, cold-weather tents and clothing, and fencing material. This stuff will sell for millions on the black market!"

"Stop gawking and start unloading those supply trucks, Jala," Zarazi snapped. "If this detail has any air support nearby, they'll be on us any minute. We need to be out of here as soon as possible."

The United Nations soldiers were lined up, kneeling in the snow, hands on their heads. Captain Zarazi paced back and forth in front of them, carefully studying each man and woman. Many nations were represented, mostly from the northern hemisphere: Canada, Northern Ireland, Norway, South Korea. Zarazi allowed his men to strip off the peacekeepers' gloves, scarves, and parkas—many of his men had perished in the Torkestan and Selseleh'ye Mountains due to exposure, and keeping warm was more important than eating to most of them.

"I am Captain Wakil Mohammad Zarazi, servant of God and commander of the Balkh Armed Resistance Regiment," Zarazi said in Pushtun. He noticed the uncomprehending stares, then said in halting English, "Who is interpreter?" There was no reply. Zarazi continued to examine the captives, finally coming across one soldier in a robin's-egg blue helmet but with a beard who appeared to be Afghan. He dragged him to his feet. "Do you understand me?" The man nodded. "Who is the commanding officer?" He did not respond. Zarazi pulled a long knife from his belt, turned to the interpreter, and raised the blade to his throat.

"Stop," a voice said. Zarazi shifted as one of the officers kneeling right beside the interpreter got to his feet, his bare hands still on top of his helmet. "I am Major Dermot O'Rourke, Republic of Ireland, commander of this detachment. We are on a peaceful mission on behalf of the United Nations Afghan Relief and Rehabilitation Council."

After the interpreter translated, Zarazi said, "You are spies for the Northern Alliance and their wild dogs from the United States of America, invading territory claimed by his holiness, Mullah Mohammad Omar, and his sword of vengeance, General Takhir Yoldashev."

"We are not spies," O'Rourke said. "We are here to set up a cellular phone and radio relay site, that's all."

"You are spies and you will all be executed according to the laws of Islam and under the orders of General Yoldashev," Zarazi said. "You . . ."

Just then, Zarazi's lieutenant came running up to him. "Wakil, there's trouble," Turabi said. He ran past Zarazi, over to O'Rourke, and pulled off his beret and stripped off his jacket, searching him. Moments later, he retrieved a small black box on a wire out of the back of the man's battle dress uniform jacket.

"What is it, Jala?" Zarazi asked.

"Our communications officer picked up some kind of high-frequency transponder that was just activated," Turabi said. "It looks like some kind of radio beacon. He must've set it off when the convoy was attacked."

"A trouble signal?" Zarazi asked. "We've detected no other forces in this area. And a helicopter patrol would take hours to come from Andkhvoy or Mazar-e-Sharif. What good would it do . . . ?"

"An air attack—with a jet already in the area, covering the convoy," Turabi said. "That's why our intelligence was so detailed and why this convoy was so poorly protected—it's being covered from the air. It might even be one of those American Predators, the unmanned little aircraft that can fire Maverick missiles. They could be starting their attack *right now*."

Zarazi looked at the officer in puzzlement—and then his eyes grew wide and his mouth dropped open. "Get the men ready to get out of this area and take cover." He stepped over to O'Rourke. "Who is watching us? What is happening?"

"I'd advise you to just surrender, Captain," O'Rourke said. "Just lay down your weapons, put your hands in the air, and kneel down. They won't attack if you surrender."

"Who are 'they'? What are 'they'?"

"There's no time for questions, Captain. Surrender right now."

"Bastard! Unholy bastard!" Zarazi pulled his sidearm and shot O'Rourke in the forehead, killing him instantly.

Several of his men had started unloading crates and removing tarps from pallets in the back of the supply trucks. "*Run for your lives! Get away from those trucks! Run!*"

FOUR HUNDRED MILES TO THE SOUTH, ORBITING AT TWENTY-eight thousand feet, fifty miles south of the Pakistani coastline over the Arabian Sea, an EB-1C Vampire glided lazily, watching and listening. The EB-1C was a U.S. Air Force B-1B Lancer long-range bomber, built in the mid-'80s, but it had been upgraded and modified so much since then that its designers would probably never recognize it now. But as incredible as the Vampire was, the aircraft it controlled were even more amazing—in fact, they represented Patrick McLanahan's future of aerial combat.

"Oh my God, they killed Major O'Rourke," U.S. Air Force Major-General Patrick McLanahan said. He studied the high-resolution digital video display on a large multi-function "supercockpit" monitor before him. "That bastard! He was unarmed! He surrendered . . ." He closed his eyes for a moment, hoping the image he saw would go away. When it didn't, his hate bubbled up past the boiling point. "I count about a hundred men, about two dozen Toyota pickups up away from the road. Stand by to attack."

His aircraft commander, U.S. Air National Guard Brigadier-General Rebecca Furness, squirmed restlessly in her seat. "It's about time," she complained. "Droning around up here for days on end is not my idea of fun."

"Still want to be screaming in on the bomb run at Mach one with your hair on fire, eh, Rebecca?" Patrick quipped. "I guess you'll never change."

"I'd rather be on a bomb run in my own machine than leaving the fighting to robot planes," Furness said. "Thanks to you, we can't have any fun anymore."

The images Patrick and Rebecca were watching were

coming from a StealthHawk Unmanned Combat Air Vehicle, or UCAV. It had been launched several hours earlier from the EB-1C Vampire's forward bomb bay and had been scanning the area around the United Nations truck convoy with its infrared sensors and high-resolution digital cameras. The StealthHawk resembled a large, wide, fat surfboard, its lifting-body fuselage slightly triangular in profile. There was a large air inlet for the aircraft's single turbofan engine mounted atop the fuselage to lower its radar cross-section. It had no wings—the Stealthhawk had a special flight control system called "mission-adaptive lifting body skin" that actually used computers and tiny microhydraulic actuators to change the outer skin on the fuselage to increase or decrease lift as necessary. The EB-1C could carry three StealthHawks in its bomb bays, one in the forward bomb bay and two in the center bomb bay. Each StealthHawk could carry a payload of five hundred pounds, along with enough fuel for several hours of flight.

Patrick touched a control button and spoke—"StealthHawk, commit attack"—and the fight was underway. Orbiting at ten thousand feet over the truck convoy was a second StealthHawk, launched from the EB-1C's center bomb bay. Instead of sensors, this one carried weapons—six AGM-211 "mini-Mavericks," one-hundred-pound, short-range, precision-guided attack missiles.

"*Commit StealthHawk attack, stop attack*," the computer responded. When Patrick did not countermand the order, the computer added, "*StealthHawk engaging.*"

"Excellent," Patrick said. "StealthHawk reporting code one so far."

"Then that would be a first for one of Masters's gadgets," Furness said dryly. Rebecca Furness was the wing commander of the one and only EB-1 Vampire squadron in the world, the One-Eleventh Bombardment Wing of the Nevada Air National Guard located at Battle Mountain Air National Guard Base. Although the Vampire bomber had been used in several conflicts and skirmishes around the world in recent years—from Korea to Russia to Libya—it was still considered experimental, and therefore the aircraft's designer, Dr. Jon Masters, worked closely with Furness's unit to make improvements to the state-of-the-art weapon system to prepare it for initial operational capability.

But Jon Masters, a Ph.D since the age of thirteen and a world-class aeronautical and space engineer, was also a world-class pain in the ass—he was not exactly a people-friendly person. Rebecca's job was hard enough—standing up a new unit with an experimental high-tech bomber at a newly constructed air base in the middle of nowhere in north-central Nevada—without the nerdy and conceited Dr. Masters disrupting her life.

Although Patrick received the sensor data from the StealthHawk on the supercockpit display in the Vampire bomber, the aircraft had already identified most of the vehicles in the target area and had presented its target priority list to Patrick continuously during its surveillance. "The StealthHawk picked out a twenty-three millimeter anti-aircraft gun on one of the Toyota pickups," Patrick said. "That's the first target."

Even Rebecca had to be impressed with the StealthHawk's systems target detection and classification capabilities—she was accustomed to dropping bombs on a group of vehicles or an entire area, not picking out just one vehicle out of many similar ones for attack.

"I count ten vehicles total in the target area—no, make that twelve, two have already bugged out," said Patrick.

"What's it waiting for? Get it in there and let's make some scrap metal."

"It's already on the job," Patrick said. At that moment,

the StealthHawk released a single mini-Mav missile from its internal bomb bay, which fell away from the Stealth-Hawk, gliding toward its target while adjusting its track with lead-computing cues and wind drift correction infor-mation datalinked from the Vampire's attack computer. When it was about a mile from its quarry, the missile's small rocket motor fired, and the missile covered the last seven thousand feet of its attack run in less than two sec-onds. The mini-Mav's warhead was twenty-eight pounds of thermium-nitrate energized high explosive, which had the power of ten times its weight of TNT. The truck and its six occupants disappeared in a cloud of dust, smoke, and yellow-red explosions.

The StealthHawk's laser radar remained locked onto the target for post-attack analysis, but from the large sec-ondary explosions and size of the smoke and fire clouds surrounding the target, it became clear only seconds later that the truck was toast. "Target appears to be destroyed," Patrick said.

"Damn, I'll say," Rebecca breathed as she watched the last moments of the StealthHawk's bomb damage assess-ment on Patrick's multi-function display. She had a lot of experience with the thermium-nitrate explosives and knew that same mini-Mav missile could take out a main battle tank; "overkill" was a gross understatement when describing a thermium-nitrate warhead hitting a little Toyota pickup. "Pretty awesome weapon."

"StealthHawk engaging the second pickup," Patrick said. "Missile two away . . ."

THE STEALTHHAWK LEVELED OFF TWO THOUSAND FEET above the ground and headed for its second target, a col-umn of two Toyota pickups filled with guerrilla soldiers. This time, the occupants saw it coming.

"*Split up! Split up!*" Zarazi screamed. He raised his

AK-74 rifle and opened fire, and the five other men in the back of the pickup opened fire as well.

It was like looking down the barrel of a gun just before the trigger was pulled—and then, realizing the barrel was removed at the very last moment. Moments after Zarazi's pickup truck veered away, the first pickup disappeared under a tremendous explosion. Zarazi and the guerrillas in the second pickup saw the other vehicle emerge from the cloud of fire and smoke looking like it had been blasted apart by a giant shotgun, set afire, and then tossed across the ground.

"Allah, have mercy," Zarazi muttered. "Allah, get us out of this, and I promise I will avenge myself on the infidels that send these demon robot planes to kill your faithful servants. I swear it . . . !"

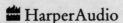